The Bookseller's Gift

Felicity HAYES-McCOY

HACHETTE
BOOKS
IRELAND

First published in Ireland in 2024 by
HACHETTE BOOKS IRELAND

1

Cataloguing in Publication Data is available from the British Library.

ISBN 9781529362107

Typeset in Book Antiqua by Bookends Publishing Services, Dublin
Printed and bound in Great Britain by Clays Ltd, Elcograf S.p.A.

Hachette Books Ireland policy is to use papers that are natural, renewable
and recyclable products and made from wood grown in sustainable forests.
The logging and manufacturing processes are expected to conform to the
environmental regulations of the country of origin.

Hachette Books Ireland
8 Castlecourt Centre
Castleknock
Dublin 15, Ireland

A division of Hachette UK Ltd
Carmelite House, 50 Victoria Embankment, London EC4Y 0DZ

www.hachettebooksireland.ie

LEABHARLANNA FHINE GALL
FINGAL LIBARIES

HA   F

Items should be returned on or before the given return date. Items may be renewed in branch libraries, by phone or online. You will need your PIN to renew online.

Damage to, or loss of items, will be charged to the borrower.

Date Due:	Date Due:	Date Due:

Felicity Hayes-McCoy, author of the best-selling Finfarran series, was born in Dublin, Ireland. She studied literature at UCD before moving to England in the 1970s to train as an actress. Her work as a writer ranges from TV and radio drama and documentary, to screenplays, music theatre, memoir and children's books. Her Finfarran novels are widely read on both sides of the Atlantic, and in Australia, and have been translated into seven languages.

She and her husband, opera director Wilf Judd, live in the West Kerry Gaeltacht and in Bermondsey, London. Her website is felicityhayesmccoy.com and you can follow her on Bluesky @fhayesmccoy@bsky.social, on X @fhayesmccoy, on Instagram @felicityhayesmccoy and on Facebook at Felicity Hayes-McCoy Author.

ALSO BY FELICITY HAYES-MCOY

The Finfarran series
The Library at the Edge of the World
Summer at the Garden Café
The Mistletoe Matchmaker
The Month of Borrowed Dreams
The Transatlantic Book Club
The Heart of Summer
The Year of Lost and Found

Standalone fiction
The Keepsake Quilters

Non-fiction
The House on an Irish Hillside
Enough is Plenty
A Woven Silence

To booksellers and librarians everywhere,
with love, thanks and solidarity

Visitors to the west coast of Ireland won't find Finfarran.
The peninsula and all the characters in this book
exist only in its author's imagination.

CATHERINE

For Catherine, Christmas had always been about wonderful smells. Buttery biscuits just out of the oven. The smell of frost when you took in the milk from the doorstep. Wax candles on Advent wreaths. Gift-wrapped lavender soaps, bought in secret for her mum. Cinnamon, nutmeg and ginger. The scents of citrus and cloves and Demerara sugar. The clean starched smell of linen table napkins that spent the rest of the year folded away.

Better than all of the others was the magical smell of books, a mixture of newness and print and paper, suggestions of glue and resin and, sometimes, the scent of a cloth binding. The slight resistance from a spine when she opened a new book made Catherine shiver. She loved the sharp edges of dust-jacket flaps that had yet to become dog-eared, chapters that began with elaborate curly capital letters, and Christmas books with titles picked out in gold. Raised in a home where there'd been little spare money, her childhood books had mostly been borrowed from the local library. But each year there'd been a train trip to Dublin to spend the book token that came in her gran's

Christmas card. Every card was a little work of art, a pop-up toy theatre that opened to reveal the Babes in the Wood or Aladdin or Harlequin or the characters from *The Nutcracker Suite*. Each would mark the proper start of Christmas and, though Gran lived just a few streets away, they always came in the post.

The day in Dublin always included a matinée at the pantomime, where fairy stories Catherine had first discovered in picture books bought with her gran's tokens appeared on the stage in glorious, scrambled three dimensions: Hansel and Gretel lost alone in the forest, the prince hacking through thorns to waken Sleeping Beauty or Jack climbing the beanstalk to find gold in the giant's castle. Sharing a box of sweets in the back row of the balcony, Catherine would hold her breath for the star-crossed lovers, gasp at explosions and rats transformed to coachmen, and applaud tightrope walkers, comics, chorus numbers, and dancers pirouetting in coloured spotlights.

The smells of Tayto and popcorn and plush velvet theatre seating were as redolent of Christmas as the scents of the books Catherine bought on those annual trips to Dublin, when adulthood had still seemed full of fairytale possibilities. So she'd kept her gran's toy theatre cards in their envelopes for years until, somewhere along the way in a house move, they'd been lost.

WEDNESDAY

18 December

CHAPTER ONE

In summer, during the tourist season, Catherine was used to being run off her feet from the moment she woke till she fell into bed after counting the day's takings. But the off-season could be slack, which was why Christmas week was so important, and why she rushed down this morning to put the finishing touches to her window display. A few years ago, when she and her mum Ann had arrived in Lissbeg, Sheep Street had been a bit scruffy. Since they'd opened their bookshop that had changed. Now, looking out of the window, Catherine could see a little boutique and a hair salon and, further up, there was a smart restaurant. But Lissbeg Books still stood out as the only shop with a bow window, where a deep shelf gave scope for enticing decoration.

Some mornings, waking in the flat above the shop, Catherine could hardly believe her good luck. A bookseller's profit margins were slim and the work could be backbreaking, but how many women in their forties got a chance to live their dream? When she'd left college, she'd worked as a rep for a company that produced office software. At first she'd loved it. She'd travelled the length and breadth of Ireland and, once or twice a year, made business trips to the company's Berlin headquarters. But, after twenty years, the job had grown boring, and she'd simply jogged on for lack of a reason to do anything else. And then, unexpectedly, her mum had made a suggestion that, within only a few months, had changed their lives.

They'd been sitting in Ann's back garden on a sunny June weekend, and Catherine had just returned from a trip up Ireland's western seaboard. Sipping iced mint tea, Ann had asked, 'So, tell me. How was the Wild Atlantic Way?'

'I don't think I even saw it.'

'But why not?'

'Oh, I don't know, Mum. Work. Being exhausted and slumping in front of hotel-room televisions. I suppose the truth is that I'm fed up with all this travelling.'

'Really?'

'I loved it at first. Lately, I've felt as if I'm on a treadmill.'

'Might you change jobs? Is there something else you think you'd like to do?'

Catherine had stretched her legs to the sun. 'Since you ask, I've always dreamed of owning a little bookshop.'

'You have? You never said.'

'Well, other things took over.'

Sitting bolt upright, Ann put down her glass. 'But, Catherine, dreams are for living. They shouldn't be postponed.'

'Mum, I'm doing fine.'

'You're not if you feel you're on a treadmill.'

'That's just because I'm tired. Can we talk about something else?'

That night, unable to sleep, Catherine had lain in the dark, thinking. It had been fun to swan about, footloose and fancy-free. She was good at her job and good with people; she loved the stimulation of new ideas and places, and enjoyed taking responsibility for her own work. The men she'd dated along the way were easy-going and charming and, except once, when she'd found herself falling in love with a married colleague, she was always the one who'd been in control. On that occasion she'd made a clean break, to avoid damaging his marriage or herself, and afterwards she'd worked harder and done less dating. Staring at the grey dawn through her bedroom window, she admitted to herself that, anyway, footloose had begun to feel like footsore, and that unattached men over forty weren't easy to find. Besides, she thought, lately I've been just as happy tucked up in bed at eight thirty, with a mug of cocoa and something gripping to read.

The next day she'd found herself googling *Irish bookshops*. All the cities and large towns had branches of the big chains, but around the country she could see little towns and villages where booksellers who'd set up on their own were, presumably, making a living. What if she did the same? Was it even possible? And, if it was, how would she choose where to go?

The next time Catherine dropped by Ann's house a map of Ireland dotted with little stickers was spread on the table.

'What're you playing at, Mum?'

'Don't pretend you didn't do some research after we talked.'

Catherine laughed. 'I googled a bit, but I didn't create a command centre.'

'I'm just being methodical.'

Humouring her, Catherine sat down, and Ann swivelled the map. 'So, here's the Wild Atlantic Way that you didn't even see.'

'I didn't on that particular trip. I have seen it before.'

'And you know something? I would really like to live there.'

'Have you been drinking?'

'The west coast is stunning and it's full of tourists in summer. You won't want to choose a town that already has a bookshop, but you do want somewhere beautiful with lots of footfall. I've put green dots by all the towns that have bookshops. I used purple for towns that don't.'

In spite of herself, Catherine had been intrigued. 'What about the red dots?'

'Unreliable broadband. You won't want to buy near those.'

'Who says I want to buy anywhere?'

'Can we move on from pretence, please, and engage with practicality?'

'You want practicality? Here's practicality. I can't afford to just go and buy a shop.'

With a gleam in her eye, Ann had taken a deep breath and said, 'You can if you and I join forces. No, don't argue, Catherine. Listen. I sell this house, you sell your apartment, and we find a place on the west coast with beautiful beaches, decent broadband, no bookshop, a tourist trade, and a local population with its own off-season cultural life.'

She paused and, heavily sarcastic, Catherine asked, 'Anything else?'

'Yes. Lots. I've made lists. We'll have to be close to good rail connections. Maybe an airport too. And we'll want to go out to eat sometimes, or take in a concert or something, so we can't be off in the back of beyond where strangers are looked at sideways. We need to pinpoint a small, thriving town that welcomes entrepreneurial outsiders.'

Catherine had found herself nodding. 'There's not many places left in Ireland where strangers are looked at sideways. I do see what you mean, though.' Returning to the map, she said, 'You've focused on the south-west.'

'I didn't at first. But then everything seemed to be pointing to the Finfarran Peninsula. See? More or less between Cork, Kerry and Clare.' Bending over the map, Ann had indicated a town. 'This is Carrick. It's a bit smaller than Athlone or Portlaoise.'

'I know Carrick. There's a place I visit on the Cork side of it.'

'Okay. Well, tourist websites call Carrick the gateway to Finfarran – which, incidentally, they've branded 'The Edge of the World'. There's a good road from Carrick down to the end of the peninsula, where there's a fishing port and a marina. Mountains and a forest in between. Cliffs and beaches. And see here?' Ann's pen had circled a dot on the map, nearly halfway down the narrow peninsula. 'That's Lissbeg. Not far off the main road, served by buses, and close enough to the ocean for evening walks. It was a little market town, and now it's big into tourism.'

Looking thoughtfully at the dot, Catherine had said, 'No bookshop.'

'None. And here's the thing. The town's library is in what used to be its convent school. The school building, the convent itself and the nuns' garden have been developed by the council as a small business hub. It's got offices, studios, hot-desking facilities.'

'Good broadband.'

'Exactly. What's more, the library houses a medieval manuscript. A book of psalms with gorgeous illustrations. It's one of the town's main tourist attractions.' Ann was trying and failing to keep her voice level. 'When I focused my searches, Lissbeg appeared bang, slap in the centre. And that was before I discovered the literary connection.'

There was a pause in which their eyes met and Catherine felt a visceral surge of excitement. 'Big footfall, a literary connection, and no bookshop.'

'I'm telling you, love, it's time to live your dream.'

Standing on tiptoe on the shelf in the shop window, Catherine reached up to the Christmas tree she was building with books. Beginning with a circle of atlases, she'd worked her way up from the bottom, overlapping books of diminishing sizes, and finishing with a little *Collins Gem Dictionary*, which she intended to top with a paper star. Having held her breath until the dictionary was safely in place, she let out a sigh of relief and, stepping down from the window, went outside to see how it looked.

She was standing on the pavement, wondering if she should add some lights, when Hanna Casey, the town's librarian, crossed the street to join her. 'That looks super.'

'Doesn't it? I was certain it would be lopsided, but it's fine.'

The owner of the hair salon was hanging a holly wreath in his window. Catherine waved at him, and called, 'Good morning.'

Turning back to Hanna, she smiled. 'Half the shops in the cities have had Christmas displays for months. I love how Lissbeg holds back until Christmas week.'

'And then we go all-out.' Hanna nodded at the poster displayed on the half-glazed door. 'That's a whopping events programme you've got there.'

'Tell me about it! Friday, Saturday, Sunday *and* Christmas Eve.'

'You and Ann must be exhausted already.'

'Ah, we're fine. It'd be easier if we had a functioning kitchen, though.'

'The work in your flat isn't finished?'

'The guy swore he'd have it done weeks ago. Otherwise I'd never have let him start.'

'How are you coping?'

'Mostly by eating takeaways and boiling kettles in the office. It's a nightmare. He unhooked the kitchen sink yesterday and the whole floor was awash.'

Hanna decided it was kinder not to ask if the kitchen refurbishment would be done in time for Christmas Day. By the sound of things, that might be too much to hope for. Instead she said that at least the weather was fine, which was good for shoppers, and that she probably ought to get on.

'Hang on a minute.' Catherine ducked into the shop and came out with a pile of fliers. 'Would you mind having these in the library? They're takeaway versions of my poster.'

'No problem. I'd say you'll have queues for your book launch anyway.'

'Isn't it amazing? Who'd have imagined the famous Adam Rashid would come to Lissbeg?'

Hanna was tucking the fliers into her bag. 'It's not his first time, you know. He was here before he was famous. Maybe seven or eight years ago. Before you and Ann arrived. He was passing through and volunteered in the Convent Centre garden. He's not been back since, but when he won that English TV thing ...'

'*The Coolest Chef?*'

'That's it. When he won, he started a YouTube channel, got the book deals, and began teaching courses. So, Phil at the Centre decided she should claim him as one of our own.'

Catherine grinned. 'Of course she did.'

Hanna laughed. 'Well, it is her job to promote the Centre. And she does have to justify that kitchen she made the council install. I've heard she promised she'd make it pay within a year, so she had to take action.'

'What did she do?'

'Apparently she called Adam Rashid's London agent and announced it would be perfect for his *Cakes To Come Home To* course.'

'God, that woman's got brass neck! I'm not complaining, though. Not when I've ended up with his Irish book launch. I could hardly believe it when Phil called and said he was up for it.'

Hanna hitched her bag more comfortably onto her shoulder. 'I've seen the book's cover online. It's attractive, isn't it?'

'Gorgeous. Cookbooks always go well at Christmas, and *Cakes To Come Home To* is a lovely title. Plus it never hurts when an author's as handsome as that.' Catherine nodded at the poster, which featured a photo of Adam Rashid receiving his *Coolest Chef* award. Hanna smiled and said she hoped to be there for the launch on Friday. 'I'd say you'll be selling copies hand over fist.'

Back in the shop, Catherine turned the sign to Open. Looking sprightly and well-dressed in a tweed skirt and a gilet, Ann appeared through the door that led to the tiny office, the stockroom and the steep stairs to the flat. She made her way between a display of kids' colouring books and tables of paperbacks, joining Catherine at the till. 'The water's off again. Jason says it won't be for long.'

Catherine groaned. 'That probably means we'll be without it for hours.'

'I wish he'd finish one thing before ambling on to the next. Now there's a half-built cabinet in the living room as well as the half-dismantled ones in the kitchen.'

'I wish he wouldn't keep disappearing. We should never have employed him. Bet you anything he's taken work from several poor eejits at once.'

'We weren't to know.'

'Well, there's no point in dumping him. We'd find no one else at this time of year.'

'Actually, Jason may be the least of our troubles.'

'Oh, God, no! What's happened?'

'You know how Adam Rashid's books were on their way over from England? Well, the pallet they're on has got held up in Customs.'

'What? The event's the day after tomorrow.'

'Let's not panic till we need to. The distributor says they should be released soon.'

Catherine groaned. 'Well, they'd better be. Otherwise we're looking at our first celebrity book launch with a huge celebrity in the shop and no books for him to sign.'

CHAPTER TWO

The Divil slept in the shed behind Fury's house at the edge of the forest, and came into the kitchen each morning for a feed of porridge. Every day at seven a.m., Fury would open the shed door with the question 'Any rat?', and The Divil would proudly show him the night's bag. Lately, it had tended to be no more than a couple of scrawny, grey-whiskered specimens but, as Fury said, you couldn't expect a dog of The Divil's age to go chasing youngsters. 'Mark you, he was a champion ratter in his day. None better.' No one in Finfarran ever doubted Fury O'Shea's pronouncements, at least not to his face. Like The Divil, he was getting old, but in his prime he'd been the peninsula's most sought-after builder, a man with a finger in every pie, who knew all there was to know about his neighbours and felt responsible for their welfare. But by nature he was wily and, even when he was on your side, the bottom line was that Fury would do things his way. Never yours.

The shed door creaked open and The Divil, who was curled on a sack, pretended to be asleep. Next to his bed was a small dead mouse. His eye flicked open and closed again, and he wriggled into a tighter knot of paws, nose and tail. There was silence until Fury had scooped up the mouse on the toe of his boot and flicked it neatly through the shed door. Then he said, 'God, you're a great man for prioritising. Didn't I say to myself only yesterday we'd be overrun with bloody mice if we didn't prioritise?' The furry knot loosened and The Divil pricked up his ears. Without looking back, Fury turned and walked towards the house, a tall, beaky figure in worn cords and an ancient waxed jacket. A grizzled muzzle poked around the open shed door, followed by the rest of the little Jack Russell. At the kitchen door, Fury turned and jerked his head at him. 'Are you coming or not? I've the porridge on and we're freezing our arses out here.'

Ten minutes later, his face saved and confidence restored, The Divil raised his whiskers from his porridge. A couple of envelopes, which had been pushed through the letter flap, had landed on the mat inside the door. Leaving his seat by the fire, Fury went to pick them up. 'Now, would you look at that! *The compliments of the season from Tintawn Terry and Family.* Fair play to that man's wife, she's a real diamond. There's not many these days that send handwritten Christmas cards.' He stood the spangled snow scene on the mantelpiece. Then, opening the other envelope, he took out a letter and read it. For a moment he leaned heavily on the mantelpiece, and The Divil, who had returned to his porridge, turned his head. Fury swung away, thrusting the letter into his trousers pocket. 'Name of God, man, do I have to stand around for ever? Are you going to finish your breakfast or what?' Astonished by his tone, The Divil lowered his head meekly, plunging his nose back into his dish. In the awkward silence that followed, Fury cleared his throat remorsefully. 'I'll get the tools into the van. I might need to put an edge on the axe.' He made for the door and, without looking back, said, 'I can't be doing with business letters at Christmas. It's only an old invoice yoke. I'll deal with it in the new year.'

The sun was high by the time they were bumping down a forest track in Fury's van. The Divil stood on the passenger seat, his front paws braced on the dashboard, his ears pricked and his tongue lapping the wind. Avoiding tree stumps and driving with his elbow out the window, Fury swerved and took corners with a proprietorial swing. His 1960s childhood had been spent among these trees, learning the pathways between them, the shapes of their limbs and leaves, and the nature of their timber: hard or soft, straight or knotted, fit to make furniture, floorboards, joists, or delicate veneer. There wasn't a coppice he hadn't cut, an oak or an elm he didn't know, a burrowing creature, an insect, or a bird nesting high in the canopy that he didn't love and cherish. Generations of his family had cared for this forest and, if stories his father had told were true, they'd owned it for a thousand years. Up ahead, the track forked and a left-hand turn cut through a belt of conifers. A cock pheasant rose between the dark trees and whirred past the windscreen, a flurry of red wattles, green neck, chestnut and golden feathers. The Divil's nails scraped on the scarred dashboard as Fury took the turn and drove on.

Parking the van in a clearing, Fury eased himself down from the cab and went to get tools from the back. The Divil followed, full of anticipation. This was the patch from which the O'Sheas had always cut Christmas trees, gifts for suppliers and shopkeepers in Lissbeg. Armed with an axe and a saw, Fury set out towards the trees he'd chosen. When he reached the first slender conifer he stood and waited while The Divil circled it, barking loudly. Then Fury raised the axe and The Divil stopped barking and sat on his tail in silence till the tree fell. When they moved on, the ritual was repeated, and when six trees had been cut and carried back to the battered van, Fury leaned the axe against it and rolled a cigarette. It was half smoked when he pinched it out and put it behind his ear. A robin that had perched on the axe handle chirped and flew away. The Divil had disappeared back into the forest. Fury whistled. He was answered by distant high-pitched barking and, since The Divil never ignored a summons, he strode anxiously towards the sound. As he approached, the barking became more imperious and, pushing through branches and past holly bushes, he found The Divil circling another tree.

Irritation replaced Fury's anxiety. 'Dear God Almighty, can you not come when you're whistled? We don't need another tree, and we sure as hell don't need that one. Look at the size of it!' It was more or less the same height as the others, but the circumference of the lower branches made it twice as wide. The Divil paused to catch his breath, then doggedly kept going. Fury rolled his eyes. 'Well, if you're going to be like that.' He plunged back through the trees and returned with the axe on his shoulder. 'Stand away, then, and give me room.' With a final bark, The Divil obediently sat on his tail, watching in silent satisfaction as Fury hefted the axe.

Their first drop-off was at Garrybawn House on the main road from Carrick. Recently opened by the council, it offered sheltered accommodation, and a family-size apartment for a manager. The six self-contained residents' flats were said to be the perfect mix of cool design and cosy comfort, the communal spaces easy to run, and the facilities modern, so the manager's job had had dozens of applicants. The successful couple, Theresa and Rory Kavanagh, had worked as nurses in Carrick General Hospital, and now, with a teenage daughter, wanted a less stressful life. When Fury's van pulled up outside, Theresa came to the door. 'Have you brought the tree? You're such a dote, Fury. Thanks.'

'No problem, Mrs K. Is everyone well? How's young Saoirse?'

'Ah, you know what teenagers are. Up one minute, down the next, and never off TikTok. Mind, it hasn't been an easy few years for any child, what with Covid. We've a great family break booked for London soon, so she's wired to the moon about that.'

'Here's your tree.' Fury leaned into the van, apparently choosing at random. 'I trimmed you a decent length of trunk at the bottom for your bucket.' He'd passed a length of rope round each tree, pulling the branches close to the trunks to make them easy to carry. Even so, The Divil's tree, which he pulled out, looked immense. Theresa considered it dubiously. 'You wouldn't have anything thinner, would you? One that'd take up less space.'

Glowering at The Divil, who was watching from the cab, Fury slid out another tree. 'They're much of a muchness.'

'I'm sure they are. This one looks great, anyway. Thanks a million.'

'D'you want a hand in with it?'

'Not at all. It's light as a feather. The perfect size.' Swinging it onto her shoulder, she disappeared into the house. Fury got back into the cab and said to The Divil. 'If we end up stuck with that blasted tree, we'll both know who's to blame.'

The turn for Lissbeg was five minutes down the road from Garrybawn House. They drove into town and Fury swung the van into Broad Street, once a marketplace to which farmers had brought cattle and sheep. Now it had a paved traffic island in the centre, and a one-way system around which the traffic swirled. There were shops and businesses on one side. On the other, a red-brick wall had been removed, opening the street to the newly developed Convent Centre, trees, flowerbeds, a little fountain, and a thriving enterprise known as the Garden Café. Fury drew up at a butcher's shop where customers were queuing to place Christmas orders. Sticking his head around the door, he caught the eye of the man behind the counter. 'I've Mrs Fitz's tree in the van, Des. Will I bring it in?'

Des was cutting rashers with precision. 'Do, Fury. Thanks a million. Stick it there in the corner. Mrs Fitz'll be delighted.'

Fury disappeared and returned with The Divil's tree on his shoulder. He was edging past the queue when Des called, 'Would you have something smaller? No offence, but if you leave her that, there won't be an inch for the goose-fat and sauces display.' With clenched teeth, Fury left and returned with another tree. Twirling a bag into which he'd slid the rashers, Des shouted, 'Good man yerself. Happy Christmas now, if I don't see you again.'

The next stop was the Convent Centre, where Phil pointed out that her corridors got crowded. 'I'd love a tree outside the kitchen where Adam Rashid's doing his course. It'd be a great focus for selfies, and I've photographers coming in. It'll have to be tall and thin, though, Fury. Otherwise, people will always be knocking it.'

Drawing breath sharply, Fury stumped back to the van.

He nearly got away with leaving The Divil's tree with Hanna in the library. 'You could have it behind your desk, up against the glass wall.'

'The wall was designed to draw the eye to the exhibition space.'

'But, sure, the exhibition's closed for the Christmas. You don't want people peering through the wall at your medieval psalm book and feeling let down when they can't get in to see it.'

Hanna wavered, then shook her head. 'Sorry, Fury, I can't have a tree up against that wall. The county council wouldn't allow it.' Fury clenched his teeth and said God forbid that the County Architect would get his arty knickers in a twist. This was a low blow, since Brian, the county architect, was Hanna's partner but, knowing Fury of old and being fond of him, Hanna just repeated that she was sorry.

'Oh, fair dos. I'll take the blasted tree away. Can you fit a smaller one somewhere?'

'You know I can. And I'm awfully grateful, Fury. It'll be really appreciated.'

The Garden Café had installed a chiller cabinet full of chocolate logs sporting robins and sprigs of holly on top. Bríd, the owner-manager, shook her head at The Divil's tree. 'It's too big, Fury. Customers wouldn't see my bûches de Noël.' She gave him a winning smile and added, 'I'd love that other tree, though. The skinny one you've got there. Thanks a million, you're a star.'

By the time they got to Tintawn Terry's Hardware Stores, Fury didn't even bother to take The Divil's tree out of the van. 'There's that one and the other, Terry, and I know which you'll want.'

'Well, it doesn't take a genius. That tree's about eight feet around.'

Terry was a short, burly man in a red woolly hat pushed well up to expose his large ears. Propping himself against a shelf of galvanised buckets, Fury said thanks for the Christmas card and asked after his children.

'They're grand, Fury. In great form altogether. Angela's home for the Christmas. The last few months, she's been up to her ears with plumbing work, and she's just after getting her electrician's cert.'

'Fair play to the girl. There's no holding her.'

'And Declan's signed up for this celebrity cake-making course at the Convent Centre.'

'That'll cost him an arm and a leg.'

'He's been saving up to pay for it from the decorating jobs. I tell you what it is, that lad's got the makings of a fine plasterer.'

Fury said he'd better be getting on.

'Right so. I'll see you round. Thanks for the tree. Sorry I wasn't up for the humungous one.'

By now, Fury and The Divil were barely on speaking terms. As they drove in silence down Sheep Street, Catherine stepped out of her shop. Fury slammed on the brake and opened his window. 'Come here to me, do you want a Christmas tree?' He looked so ferocious that Catherine took a nervous step backwards. The Divil immediately scrambled across and thrust his furry face through the cab window. Charmed by his rusty ears, Catherine relaxed and shook her head. 'I don't need a tree, thanks. I've already got one in my window.' She stood back to give them a view of the book tree, twined in twinkling lights and topped with its paper star. Fury looked at it balefully, said, 'Dear God Almighty,' released the handbrake, and drove away.

He was still muttering under his breath when he turned back into Broad Street and saw Liam Carmody, Lissbeg's estate agent, dodging through the traffic to flag him down. 'Here, lookut, Fury, I'm glad I caught you. Can you come in for a minute?'

'No, I can't.'

'Just for a minute. If you could. It's important.'

Fury got out of the van and slammed the door. Leaning into the cab, he told The Divil to stay put and mind his manners. 'You've been in a strange mood all day. Don't go barking now, and causing a breach of the peace.' Following Carmody down the street to his office, he took a seat and plucked the cigarette from behind his ear. In the heavy silence that followed, Carmody shifted a pile of papers. 'You'll have got my letter?'

Fury lit the cigarette, blew a long plume of smoke, and said nothing.

'Lookit, Fury, I'm sorry. I didn't want to go dumping this on you before Christmas.' Unnerved by Fury's expressionless face, he shifted his papers again. 'Honest, I wouldn't have written only I'm under a lot of pressure. It's a time thing. And I wanted this private word with you because I thought it might help.'

'You reckon I need help, do you?'

'Christ, Fury, how would I know? I always thought the forest was yours. I mean I never knew your brother sold it.' Seeing a dangerous gleam in Fury's eye, Carmody began to stammer. 'It's none of my business, of course.'

'You're right. It isn't.'

Carmody hesitated. 'I've had the instruction to sell. From the owner's solicitor. Well, the owner's widow's solicitor. The man your brother sold it to died. The widow's settling his affairs. And the thing is, Fury, I could let you in on the ground floor. If that's what you wanted. I could say there was hardly any interest in it, and they'd do well to take your best offer. We could wangle it so they don't know who you are.' Fury continued to say nothing. Carmody ran his finger around the inside of his collar. 'I wouldn't say her solicitor would be paying much attention. I mean, he's on the other side of the world, and the deed shows it's just forest.' Glancing over his shoulder, he leaned forward. 'Look, the point is, the land's not worth much with the trees on it, but if it got planning permission for housing ...'

'Now isn't it strange you didn't say that in the letter?'

Carmody sat back hastily. 'I'm saying nothing. All I'm saying is you're a builder, you know the score, Fury. There's a lot of luxury yachts coming into Ballyfin marina. That's the future. The trawlermen hardly scrape a living these days, but there's rich fellas wanting to buy themselves holiday homes here in Finfarran. I'll say no more.'

Pinching out the cigarette, Fury stood up and replaced it behind his ear. He was through the door when Carmody called after him, 'I thought you'd want to know. I mean, everyone thinks you own the land. They think you inherited it when your brother drank himself into the grave. You've been acting like it's yours for fifty years, Fury. This way no one will know it was someone else's.'

Fury returned to the room and closed the door behind him. Placing his two gnarled hands on the desk, he leaned across it.

Carmody hastily scooted his chair back. 'Okay, point taken, no need for anyone to get heated.'

Dropping the words like stones, one by one, Fury said, 'It's Christmas. I've got trees to deliver.'

'Sure. Absolutely. Don't let me delay you. I was keeping it friendly and local. Trying to do you a favour.'

Fury didn't dignify this with an answer. When the door closed, Carmody scooted his chair back to the desk and passed his hand over his sweating forehead. Straightening his tie resentfully, he lowered his voice to a vicious mutter, 'Well, if you're too old and thick to grab a chance to make easy money, I know plenty of smart builders who aren't.'

CHAPTER THREE

That morning, Adam Rashid woke up in a hotel room in Carrick. The previous night, he'd flown from London after a day of meetings, picked up a hire car, driven from Dublin, and got to Finfarran after midnight. The Royal Victoria was Carrick's biggest hotel and, under new ownership, had been given a facelift, new staff and a new manager. Adam had checked that carefully when Phil offered to book him in.

Realising he'd been woken by the sound of his phone, he groped for it and heard his agent's voice: 'Adam! So you made it to the arse-end of the universe?'

'Well, good morning to you too.'

'Don't get smart with me, son. Not when I'm up at the crack of dawn, breaking my bollocks on your behalf.'

'Sorry, Dom. I'm half asleep. What's the story?'

'Nothing locked in yet. Things are looking good, though.'

'I have no idea what that means.'

'You'll know what it means when I tell you. I'm still in negotiation.'

Adam gave up. It was Dom who'd propelled him to celebrity status, scooping him up when he won the *Coolest Chef* title and convincing the production company of his potential for future projects. The agency was one of the biggest in the industry, and Dom was known as a genius for sniffing out talent. At their first meeting, he'd sat Adam down and fixed him with his famous Rottweiler glare. 'So here's the position. I can make you big. Properly big. All I need from you is focus. Give me a hundred per cent and I'll do the rest. You've got looks, you're bright, you're hardworking and the camera's in love with you. You turn up on time, do what you're told, and never lose your nerve under pressure. You've got the ambition to put yourself out there and fight. And you're young, which, from my point of view, means you've got a decent shelf-life.' All this was true, though in fact Adam had entered the competition simply because the chef in whose restaurant he'd been working at the time had suggested it.

Dom had got him guest appearances on every TV programme that mattered, and bullied the *Coolest Chef* company into a road show and a huge internet presence. Then, having established him as a bona-fide celebrity, he'd brokered a book deal, organised and promoted his *Coolest Chef* courses, and assured Adam that within a year he'd have his own TV series. 'And I'm not settling for national coverage, I'm aiming for global syndication.'

Staggered by the fees, the prediction and the workload, Adam had gone along with it all with no sense of where he was going. At an early stage, he'd discovered that Dom didn't take kindly to questions and, anyway, mostly he didn't know what to ask. So, remembering a time in his life when success like this would have been unimaginable, he'd decided that his role was to work and Dom's to do the thinking.

The voice in his ear sharpened. 'I'm looking at serious numbers over here. Don't undercut my position. I don't want anyone knowing your fee for this dumb Lissbeg gig.'

Adam controlled a spurt of irritation at the description. 'Of course not. Anyway, Lissbeg's a one-off.'

'It's an embarrassment, that's what it is. And you'd better not make it a precedent. Hold it. I need to take a call. Talk later.'

Propped up against his pillows, Adam looked around him. It felt weird to be lying in a bed in the Royal Victoria, especially since his being here was a chance in about a million. Normally, small fry like Phil wouldn't have got past Dom's assistant. But, by chance, Adam had been there when the call came through. Overhearing the assistant's derisive snort, and 'Lissbeg', Adam had butted in, talked directly to Phil, and told Dom later that he wanted to make this happen.

'She can't afford you, Adam.'

'I know, but we'll cut back on costs. Pare things to the bone. Don't make a thing of it, though. I don't want her to feel it's a favour.'

'A favour? It's bloody charity.'

'It's three days in Christmas week, Dom, and I really want to do it. Don't I deserve a break at Christmas?'

He'd never stood up to Dom before but, in the end, he'd swung it, and, on the crest of the wave of her success, Phil hadn't noticed she'd been given a whopping bargain. When the contract was drafted, it halved Adam's normal fee, subsistence and travel expenses, and omitted his usual requirement for two trained kitchen assistants. He'd also had to scale back the course, rework the information packs, and lower the cost to participants.

Outraged, Dom had made a last effort. 'If you're so eager to pare things back, why not drop the giveaways? Your merchandise doesn't come cheap.'

'Anybody who's seen my vids will know my courses come with giveaways.'

'They do when people are paying full whack.'

'Giveaways are product placement. They sell books.'

'And that's another thing. If you're going to have an Irish book launch, why not do it in Dublin? What's the point of turning up in some titchy indie bookshop in the sticks?'

'I'm not going to insult Lissbeg by treating it as insignificant.'

'And you reckon the *Coolest Chef* team are going to be cool with this, do you?'

'They're fine. I've talked to them.'

It had taken a lot of talking to convince *The Coolest Chef*'s producers that launching *Cakes To Come Home To* at an indie bookshop in the sticks was a good idea. Eventually, someone had said it could be quirky. 'Edgy, you know? Unique.'

Remembering a useful fact, Adam had said, 'Edgy's the area's buzzword.'

'Why?'

'The tourist board puts it in their metadata. They market the place as 'The Edge of the World Peninsula'.'

'That's pretty edgy.'

'So edgy. Very cool. Plus, it has gorgeous scenery.'

'Photo ops?'

'Masses. And the woman who runs this Lissbeg Kitchen place has great contacts.' He hadn't been sure about that bit, but felt Phil had such brass neck that, given a chance, she'd probably charter a press plane. Eventually, the company had agreed to pay for food and wine at the book launch, and to send along a social-media person. Emerging from their Soho office, Adam had breathed a deep sigh of relief. Provided they got their percentage, and the *Coolest Chef* brand wasn't tarnished, they'd no particular interest in the deals Dom did for his courses. But they did have a big financial interest in his cookbooks and, for this launch to go smoothly, he'd needed to have them onside.

Showered, shaved and dressed, Adam went down to breakfast. Under the new management, the bedrooms' decor had been modernised but downstairs the hotel retained its mid-Victorian vibe. It was an imposing building, faced in granite, set in a quiet terrace off Carrick's main street. A broad flight of curved steps led to mahogany double doors with shining brass fittings and etched-glass panels. Everything was well-polished, from the massive, carved furniture in the reception area to the gleaming rows of glasses that hung above the bar in the lounge. There was a coffee room with writing tables and brass inkstands, loos with real flowers, and a grill room much frequented by bank officials and accountants. The front-of-house staff wore tailored suits with crisp cotton shirts and gilt name-badges, and Adam felt sure that, instead of whites, the team in the kitchen now wore trendy black jackets.

He'd almost opted for a room-service breakfast, but decided the dining room wouldn't be crowded so early. When the waiter seated him, he saw he'd been right. Winter sunlight was falling on yards of starched linen and silverware, but the only other occupied table was over by the window, where a girl of about his age, with dark, curly hair, was eating a poached egg. She glanced up and their eyes met for a moment. Accustomed to people recognising him, Adam looked away, aware as he did so that, this time, he'd have preferred to go on looking. Opening his phone, he ordered coffee and a full Irish, and began to work through emails. There were several from Phil, eager to know if he'd arrived, had settled in, was comfortable, needed anything, and was still okay to come by the Convent Centre, as arranged. He pinged off a line, saying, *All good. See you 9.30.* A reply came at once. *I've booked a little girl called Saoirse Kavanagh to give you a hand with the washing up. She's due in at 10 for a briefing. I'll bring her along to meet you.* So this was what he was going to have instead of two trained assistants. He grinned at the thought of what his guys in Soho would say if they knew, took a forkful of breakfast and told himself appreciatively that the trip would be worth it just for the Royal Victoria's black pudding. But, of course, there was more to it than that. He owed Finfarran a debt that he'd never revealed to anyone, and the next few days were about payback.

Having had no chance to stretch his legs after the long drive from Dublin, Adam decided to walk a mile or so, and catch the bus to Lissbeg at the first stop beyond Carrick. It was a chilly morning and he walked briskly, thinking about the first time he'd travelled this road, on a borrowed bicycle, with only a couple of hours of a summer's day to call his own.

He could still recall his heady sense of disbelief and elation, the sun beating down on his shoulders and the tiredness in his legs. Just beyond the bus stop he was now making for, he'd turned the bike down a side road and begun the climb towards the mountains between earth-and-stone dykes and ditches blazing with fuchsia bushes. With an effort, he'd risen from the saddle and stood on the pedals, to glimpse fields beyond the waving flowers. Accustomed to the streets and pavements of crowded towns and cities, he'd been dazzled by the emptiness of the countryside, where the land rose for miles into the distance with only clusters of farm buildings in sight. As he'd passed a gate, a border collie had barked at him ferociously, eyes bright and body close to the ground.

Startled, Adam had let the bike swerve and, out of control, it had careered into a deep ditch beyond the gate. He'd fallen softly on grass and mud and lain there winded, hearing his front wheel spinning beside his ear. Then he'd turned his head, opened his eyes and seen a broken stem of wild carrot hanging directly in front of his face. Dangling from its pale-green stem, the cluster of flowers looked like a lace umbrella. It was creamy-white but for a single rosette in the centre, which was deep purple. As Adam struggled to focus, the foliage had rustled and the unexpected scent of carrot had become the smell of dog. Two inquisitive eyes met his and a wet nose touched him as the collie that had defended its farm gate so ferociously had pawed him gently to check he hadn't been hurt.

Still possessed by the memory, Adam was jerked back to the present when he boarded the bus and found that the only other passenger on it was the curly-haired girl he'd seen at breakfast.

He sat on the opposite side of the aisle and, after a moment, she leaned across to speak to him.

Instinctively, Adam's muscles tensed. This was something he loathed about his celebrity. The excited recognition. The stammered requests for autographs and selfies. The embarrassing, enforced conversations with strangers, who frequently didn't know his name or what he actually did, but told him enthusiastically that they'd seen him on the telly. More often than not, the autographs would go straight to eBay, and the snatched photos were frequently sold to appear under headlines like *Rashid Looking Rough*. The first few times that had happened he'd told Dom how he felt, but instead of sympathy he'd been given a lecture. Apparently he wasn't supposed to let people get that close. It struck him now that Dom would probably blow his top if he knew he'd been dumb enough to take a bus. But he had, and there was nothing to do but deal with it. He turned his head, braced to meet gushing enthusiasm, but the girl just said, 'Do you know how long this bus takes to reach Lissbeg?'

Feeling foolish, he stammered, 'About fifteen minutes. Unless it gets stuck behind a tractor.'

'Cheers.' She had a snub nose, wide grey eyes, and her dark, springy hair grew in little spirals. Taking a bar of chocolate from her bag, she broke it in two. 'Want a piece?'

'No, thanks. I've just had breakfast.'

'I know. Full Irish. That was impressive.'

So she had recognised him. But only as the guy she'd seen in the hotel dining room. Overwhelmed by relief, he grinned. 'More filling than a poached egg.'

She chuckled. 'Fair comment. I'm Lia, by the way.'

'I'm Adam.'

'So, Adam, what're you doing in Finfarran?'

Instantly, Adam's relief drained away. Whatever he said now would open his stupid celebrity can of worms. Playing for time, he said, 'Just visiting.'

'Well, you're obviously not local. That's a Dublin accent.'

'I'm guessing yours is Australian.'

'Yeah. I've been working up in Dublin since the beginning of the year.'

'How come you're down here now?' As soon as he'd spoken he panicked. He'd wanted to divert the conversation from himself. But what if he'd just sounded nosy? What if, like him, she feared and hated intrusive questions from strangers?

Lia shrugged her shoulders cheerfully. 'I won a competition. A three-day course, plus B-and-B in our fancy hotel. It was one of those TV things you enter on your phone. Me and my mates from the bar up in Dublin were having a few beers after a shift. It was just for a laugh. Actually, I'd forgotten about it till I heard I'd won. So now I'm booked into a cake-making course. It begins tomorrow.'

Completely thrown, Adam heard himself ask what the call had cost.

'A couple of euros, plus standard network charges.'

'So, a pretty good return on your investment.'

Lia broke off another square of chocolate. 'Well, the hotel's fab and the countryside's fantastic. I've always wanted to see the Wild Atlantic Way.'

'Aren't you excited about the course?'

'Meh. Not so much.' She glanced at him sideways. 'Don't get me wrong. I mean what's not to like about cake, right? But it's run by some celebrity chef, and I bet he'll be an eejit.'

With a Herculean effort, Adam produced a convincing laugh. 'You've certainly picked up the language while you've been here.'

'One side of my family was Irish. Transported convicts.'

'Really?'

'No, not really, that's just a line I use.' She licked her fingers. 'It was generations ago. They were Irish, but God knows where they came from and what they did.'

The longer this went on, the more embarrassing it would become, so Adam opened his mouth to admit who he was. Before he could speak, the bus crested a hill and Lia exclaimed, 'Wow, there's the ocean!'

Reprieved, he said, 'The turn for Lissbeg is coming up. When you get off the bus, it's not far to walk to a beach.'

Lia was looking longingly out the window. 'God, I've really missed waves big enough for surfing.'

'I wouldn't try surfing Irish waters in Christmas week. You'd freeze.'

'You know what, though? I could skip the course and just spend my time communing with the Atlantic.' She wrinkled her nose thoughtfully. 'On the other hand, I've never yet been known to turn down a freebie. Oh, what the hell, I'll see how I feel tomorrow. I'll go with the flow.' Adam half hoped this was his way out. If she skipped the course, he wouldn't have to explain himself. He could eat breakfast in his room and avoid her in the hotel. They'd get off the bus, say goodbye, and he wouldn't see her again. No embarrassment. No explanations. Hands down, the best-case scenario. Except for the fact that, despite having spent only ten minutes in her company, he really, really wanted to see her again.

The bus turned down a country road between fields edged with stone walls and ditches. Away to the right, the fields ran down to cliffs and, below them, little beaches. The riot of summer wildflowers Adam remembered had died back, but golden furze still bloomed among prickly stems by the roadside. Lia was still staring out of the window. 'I wish Seán could see this.'

'Seán?'

'We're spending Christmas together. But he's a control freak who can't cope unless he's in charge of everything, so he doesn't want me or anyone else around for the next few days.' Still focused on the view, Lia gave an affectionate chuckle. 'There's the choice of wine, and the chocolates and, I don't know, probably fireworks. I've already had about fifty texts about my present, and I keep having to point out it's supposed to be a surprise.'

Adam's heart sank. She was dating. Of course she was. She was beautiful, relaxed and witty, and had had the sense to order poached eggs and go for 75 per cent, organic, Fairtrade chocolate. Of course someone like that would be attached.

'Oh, wow! Look at that! Talk about wild Atlantic breakers!' As the bus took another sharp bend she scrambled across to his side, and knelt on a seat so close to Adam that he could smell her perfume. Her dark hair was tinged with red and her skin was freckled and creamy. 'Seriously, Adam, look! Have you ever seen anything more gorgeous?'

With a tight feeling in his chest, Adam said he hadn't, and reminded himself that he was in Lissbeg to work.

CHAPTER FOUR

It was only ten days since Saoirse Kavanagh's mum had come home from a knit-and-natter session at Lissbeg Library saying that Phil at the Convent Centre wanted someone to do washing up. 'For a baking course. She knows you've given a hand here in the kitchen, so she wondered if you'd fancy it. It's three and a half days' work in Christmas week.'

Fifteen-year-old Saoirse had been unenthusiastic. 'Washing up's not a job. It's a form of torture.'

'If you don't want to, I dare say Phil can find someone else for this Rashid guy.'

'Wait. What? Adam Rashid?' Saoirse's jaw had almost hit the floor.

'I think that was the name.'

'But, Mum, he's the Coolest Chef.'

'Is he?'

'I mean he literally won *The Coolest Chef* competition. He's huge on TikTok. I've seen all his vids. He's amazing.'

Amused, Theresa had said, 'Well, he's giving a course for Phil. It starts next Thursday.'

'Oh, my God! Get on the phone. Tell her I'm totally up for it.'

'Good. You'll be glad of a bit of spending money when we get over to London.'

Until then, the prospect of a family trip in the new year had been the biggest thing on Saoirse's horizon. But not even London and a West End show could compare to the thought of meeting Adam Rashid. Her heart had been in her mouth until a text came from Phil telling her to come to the Convent Centre for a briefing. She was due there at ten and, though it was only six thirty, she got up, showered, washed her hair, and spent several hours trying on things to wear. Then, suddenly scared she'd miss the bus, she grabbed her bag, bolted downstairs, and charged out of the house.

Other than on school visits to the library, Saoirse had never been inside the Convent Centre. Getting out at the bus stop in Broad Street, she crossed to the traffic island, where a stone horse trough was planted with purple and yellow winter pansies. Across the street was the open space that Lissbeg locals still called the nuns' garden. In summer, foliage and flowering herbs softened its formal lines, but at this time of year you could see the bare bones of it. Herb beds edged by low walls and box hedges were laid out in concentric circles between gravelled walks. In the centre, on a plinth in a wide granite basin, water gushed from carved flowers at the feet of a statue of St Francis.

It struck Saoirse that everything radiated from the statue. It faced a row of stained-glass windows in a grey building where her mum had told her the nuns used to live. At right angles to the building was the old school, with modern signs above the arched doors. The text had said to go through a door marked STUDIOS/WORKSHOPS/LISSBEG KITCHEN and follow a corridor till she came to Phil's office. Having dodged through the traffic, Saoirse crossed the garden and found the right entrance, but it was too early to go in, so she went for a coffee in the Garden Café.

At a table just inside, a guy was threading popcorn and cranberries onto a length of string. People were buying chocolate logs and mince pies, and Bríd was behind the counter, making up sandwich boxes, in a checked apron with a matching scarf over her dark hair. Saoirse ordered a latte and sat at a table with her phone, scrolling through links about Adam Rashid. Lots of them just produced images of amazing cakes. Others linked to magazine pieces and clips from his TV programme. The same bio, which she knew by heart, appeared everywhere. *Adam Rashid: Age 26: Irish/Egyptian: Winner of TV's* The Coolest Chef: *Sustainable food: Ecology: Local Produce*. Searching more widely, she found a link she hadn't seen before, and read that he'd donated money to a charity for homeless people in Dublin. Other links led to press releases about his cookery courses and photos of him with people like Nigel Slater, the Princess of Wales, and some politician beaming at the camera trying to look cool.

She was deep in a rabbit hole of clicks when, suddenly, it was nearly ten and she had to sprint across the garden. For the first few minutes she was so freaked by the thought that she'd nearly been late that she heard practically nothing of the briefing. Then, to her astonishment, Phil stood up and said, 'I'd better take you to Adam. He's in the kitchen.'

Breathlessly, Saoirse followed her past a room where people were singing Christmas carols, and down corridors to a pair of doors over which a sign said *LISSBEG KITCHEN*, and underneath, in smaller letters *Eat at the Edge of the World*. Phil, who'd never stopped talking, said, 'He's expecting you. I told him I'd bring you along when you arrived.' Her phone rang and, grabbing it, she disappeared down the corridor, leaving Saoirse to push open the heavy double doors and go in.

Her first impression was of a big, empty space full of stainless-steel benches, ovens, fridge freezers and massive sinks. Then she realised that, at the far side of the room, Adam Rashid was sitting on a windowsill checking his phone. He looked up when he heard the doors open.

'I'm Saoirse.'

He gave her the smile she recognised from his videos. 'I'm Adam. Coffee?'

Saoirse began to say she'd just had a latte, then stopped, wondering if he'd meant she should make one for him. But apparently not, because he said, 'I've a pot on the go. Milk and sugar?' Saoirse blinked. He was taller than she'd expected. His Dublin accent sounded stronger in real life. He looked even better in jeans and a sweatshirt than he did onscreen wearing his chef's whites. There was a big, scrubbed table at the far end of the room, and an old-fashioned dresser with jugs and plates on it. Saoirse sat down. He poured her a mug of coffee and handed her a folder with *Cakes To Come Home To Cookery Course* printed on the front. 'That's the information pack the participants are sent. Give it a read.'

'I thought I was just going to be doing the washing up.' Saoirse heard her voice sounding squeaky. It felt totally weird to be talking across a table to Adam Rashid, drinking a coffee he'd casually poured for her as if they were mates. His phone buzzed and he glanced at it before looking back at her. His smile was just as gorgeous in real life as it was onscreen. 'You are, but you won't be locked in a scullery. Think of yourself as part of the team. Actually, it'll just be you and me. Are you okay with that?'

Saoirse said, 'Okay. Fine. I'm good.'

'You'll need to keep a sharp eye on the benches. Grab a cloth and dodge in if you need to. There's always some eejit that can't get two eggs in a bowl without dropping them.'

'Okay.'

'It's meant to be fun and relaxed, but things have to be kept disciplined.'

His eyes strayed to his phone again. 'Look, I'm sorry. I've an email that has to be dealt with. Do you want to take your coffee and have a wander? You'll find the sinks and dishwashers down at the end. Watch out, the water's scalding.' As Saoirse stood up, he added, 'Phil says you've washed pots in a professional kitchen before.'

'I've helped out. My mum and dad manage Garrybawn House. It's sheltered accommodation. Most of the residents do their own cooking, but there's breakfast and dinner available if they want them. Like Phil said, I've helped when we're short-staffed.'

'Great. You're an expert, so.'

He'd been so nice that Saoirse found herself gabbling, 'We've got a chef – well, a cook. Mum and Dad don't do the catering. They're registered nurses. They worked in the hospital in Carrick before they took the management job. Back then, they were always on different shifts. I like it better now, because we get more time at home together. Though I didn't like Garrybawn at first. We used to live in Carrick and my friends were there, and my school, and as soon as we moved there was Covid and it was crap. I go to school in Lissbeg now, though, and I've made new friends.'

A voice in her head said, For feck's sake! He's busy, he doesn't want your life story, but he nodded and said, 'My parents worked in a hospital too.'

'Really?'

'Dad was a pharmacist. Mum was a nurse.'

'Gosh.'

His phone buzzed again and he said, 'Look, I'm sorry ...'

'No. Really. I'll just ... I'll go look around. Don't mind me.'

'This won't take long. If you've any questions, don't be afraid to ask them. That's why you're here. I want you clued up for tomorrow.'

Having checked out the benches, Saoirse moved on to the sinks and the big cupboards with sliding doors that held tins and dishes and bowls. Phil had said platters of food would be brought in for lunch. 'On most of these courses, lunch is what the participants make in the mornings. But they can't survive on cake, so I've ordered sharing platters from Bríd at the Garden Café.' Leaning on a bench, Saoirse read random lines from the folder: *Gorgeous Genoise Sponge, Spiced Apple and Hazelnut Surprise Cake, Professional Piping for Christmas Cookies and Biscuits.* Ten people were enrolled on the course, so if the lunches were catered, washing up wouldn't be overwhelming. The participants' day ended at three thirty, and Phil had told her she ought to be done by five. 'But you'll stay till Adam's happy with the set-up for the next morning. He's a stickler for getting things absolutely right.'

From the other end of the room Adam called, 'Any chance of a top-up?' so she carried the coffee pot to the table and filled his mug. He was frowning at his phone and, without looking up, said, 'Take a seat. I'll be with you in a minute. What's my favourite novel, would you say?'

Confused by the question, Saoirse panicked. If she gave the wrong answer would he decide she wasn't up to the job? Then Adam slid his phone across the table and, looking at the screen, she saw a numbered list of questions. It was a Q&A laid out in boxes, some of which were filled in. The first was *Welcome to Finfarran! Tell us a bit about why you love our lovely peninsula.* That had been given a single-line response. The next, which said, *What's your favourite novel?* was empty. The third read *Ballybunion or the Bahamas? Give us the low-down on your favourite holiday hideaway.*

Adam pushed his hand through his hair. 'I hate these things. I never do them. My London guys fill them in and shoot them off into the ether. I would've said no to this one but it's for the *Finfarran Inquirer*. Phil set it up with the journalist and he needs it back today.'

Saoirse picked up the phone and continued scrolling through the questions. There were ten. 'How many words do they want in all?'

'What? Eight hundred, I think. Do you know about this kind of thing?'

'A bit.' She didn't tell him she'd absorbed every word his London guys shot into the ether. 'If I were you, I'd say you don't have time to read novels. Then mention your new cookbook and say you've been totally focused on that.'

'Really?'

'All the celebrities do.'

'Do they? I never read these things either.'

'They're all about promoting your latest merch.' Saoirse returned to question three. 'So. Ballybunion or the Bahamas?'

'I don't have time for holidays.'

'You could just put *That'd be telling!*'

'You reckon?'

'Sure. And, look, this one's easy. *Tea or coffee, and where do you like to drink it?* Put Bubble Tea.'

'I hate that too.'

'Your Insta says you love it. You discovered it in Taiwan.'

Adam grinned. 'Okay. Bubble Tea. In Taiwan. I think I was there on a stopover.'

She scrolled past numbers four and five, which he'd already filled in. 'What's your earliest memory?'

He sat for a moment, then said, 'Fishing with my father.'

'That's good. Where was it?'

'The Royal Canal in Dublin. I don't think we caught many fish.'

'It's nice, though. You could say it was a big thing in your childhood.'

'I could. And it really was.'

His mind seemed to have wandered again, so Saoirse asked, 'D'you want me to fill these in for you?'

'No, it's okay. Thanks for the help, though, Saoirse. I'll see you tomorrow. We'll make a good team.'

The main entrance to Lissbeg Library was from Broad Street, through what had been the convent school's gates. An arched gateway in the side wall of the nuns' garden led to a courtyard outside the library door. Having touched base with Phil, Adam dropped in to see Hanna, who smiled when he put his head round the door. 'Oh, good. I hoped you'd have time to drop in while you're in town.' She was at her desk, dealing with a pile of returned books. Sitting around a low table, children were making paper chains, while Fury's Christmas tree was being hung with pipe-cleaner fairies and woolly robins.

'The library hasn't changed a bit.'

'I'm surprised you can see it under all the decorations. By this stage of the month we've had about six Christmas craft sessions. Between the kids, the art group and the knit-and-natter crowd, I run out of places to hang the results.'

'Phil showed me around the centre earlier. That's a good kitchen she's got there.'

'She's like a cat with two tails about it. I hope you'll enjoy your course. I see it's booked up.'

For a moment, Adam nearly told her about meeting Lia on the bus and how he'd failed to explain who he was. But to admit the potential mess he'd got himself into would be embarrassing and, anyway, he couldn't find the words. Instead, he said he'd just been introduced to Saoirse Kavanagh. 'Phil's booked her to give me a hand. She seems like a nice kid.'

'She's a pet, and I'd say she'll be great. My mother lives in one of the flats in Garrybawn House, these days. It's beautifully run. Saoirse comes from a hardworking family.'

'That's good to know.'

'Actually, my mother's signed up for your course. Mary Casey. She can be difficult to handle so I hope she won't drive you mad.'

He grinned. 'Chefs get used to handling difficult personalities.'

'It seems to be doing you good. You're looking well.'

'Chefs also get to eat a lot.'

Hanna laughed. 'And now you're an author. I'm looking forward to the bookshop launch.'

'I'm not sure compiling recipes counts as being a proper author.'

'Don't put yourself down. It's a huge accomplishment.'

Adam produced a library card. He'd searched for it before leaving London, and found it in an old wallet. 'Would it be okay to borrow a book? The one about the nuns' garden. I'd like to talk about it at the course.'

'No problem. I don't keep it on the open shelves, but it's there in the glass case.'

She went and got him the book, which was about pot herbs and flowers. Adam turned the pages. 'This is where everything started for me. With the nuns' garden and the importance of locally grown produce.'

'It's nice to hear you say that.'

'I'll take care of this.'

'I know you will.'

As Adam turned to go, the door opened and a man came in, sketching a wave at Hanna. She called him over. 'Adam, this is Stephen Gallagher. He lives in Bridge House, up beyond Sheep Street. Stephen, this is Adam Rashid who used to volunteer in the garden.' Stephen, who looked like he was in his fifties, gave Adam a firm handshake. 'Nice to meet a fellow volunteer. I do one-to-one sessions with adult learners. Reading practice. Actually, I've a guy due in a minute so, if you'll excuse me, I'll go through and set up.'

He disappeared in the direction of the reading room and, tucking the book under his arm, Adam said goodbye to Hanna. 'I'll come in again before I leave town.'

'Do. And I'll be at the bookshop for your launch.'

At the door, he was stopped by a couple of women who twittered in excitement, saying they loved seeing him on the telly. Hanna watched the professional charm with which he smiled and moved on, and wondered if they'd have been so ready to stop and talk to him if they'd met him the last time he'd been in Finfarran.

CHAPTER FIVE

That morning Stephen had dawdled over breakfast because in Christmas week his library sessions tailed off. Beyond the conservatory window, a bright-eyed robin hopped about expectantly. Tightening the belt of his dressing-gown, he went out to crumble toast on the bird table, and back indoors to consider the rest of the long day that loomed ahead. The house, a pleasant stone-built home that Fury had renovated, was spick and span and needed no attention, which wasn't surprising since, living alone, Stephen hardly used half of the rooms. In fact, in winter, with little to do in his garden, he sometimes wondered if he'd been right to abandon his city roots and settle in Lissbeg. It had been a hard decision and, thinking about it, he told himself he wouldn't have made it if Fury hadn't meddled.

The work on Bridge House had been intended to turn it into a dream home in which he and his wife Sophie would take early retirement. Fury had got on with it while they sold up in Dublin and talked excitedly about their future. Washing his breakfast dishes, Stephen remembered the shock of the day he'd lost Sophie to a stroke, five years ago and only months before their planned move.

He'd still felt numb when he'd driven down to Finfarran after the funeral, intending to sign off the finished work and put the house back on the market. But when he'd turned the corner from Sheep Street Fury was there to meet him, leaning on the gate with The Divil beside him. The square stone Georgian house with its fanlight door and sash windows had seemed knee-deep in the grass and flowers that crowded its front garden. The door was painted exactly the shade of blue Sophie had chosen, and the rooms were decorated just as she'd planned. When Stephen followed The Divil down the hall to the new conservatory, he could see daisies dotting the lawn that sloped down to the river behind the house. Everything was serene and perfect and, seeing it, he'd struggled with a wave of conflicting emotions. Then Fury, his bony shoulders propped against a doorframe, had lit a roll-up and cocked a knowing eye. 'You can't decide what you ought to do next, can you?'

'It all looks fine. If you'll invoice, I'll send a cheque.'

'Don't be daft, man, that's not what I meant at all. You're in two minds because this is the house you and your wife planned together, and you don't know whether to stay or sell. Well, the choice is yours, and you can tell me to mind my own damn business. But, what I say is, where else do you have to go?'

The truth of this had struck Stephen like a blow. Frozen in the sunlit hallway, he'd realised that the thought of selling the house felt like betrayal. Yet how could he bear to live in it alone? In the end, it was Fury's blunt pragmatism that swayed him. He couldn't outrun the pain of losing Sophie, so he might as well try to live their dream without her.

Hanging up the tea-towel, Stephen stared out at his wintry garden thinking of everything he'd accomplished since that decision. Steeling himself to go out alone, he'd joined a book club at the library. Later, at Hanna's suggestion, he'd done a course about adult literacy and became a volunteer mentor. Recalling plans made with Sophie, he'd spent long summer days working in the garden, hearing the river flow past beyond the wall. Over time, he'd built a relationship with a blackbird that had learned to tap at his window, and with the finches that nested in a sycamore outside his kitchen door. But without Sophie there to share the pleasure of planting and growing, and of fluttering wings when he came down to make breakfast, it didn't feel much like living a dream. He was lonely. Occasionally, people he'd known in Dublin visited at weekends but, as most were still working, he didn't want to impose on time they could have spent with their families. Equally wary of making demands on his new neighbours, he took elaborate care not to seem needy. And few people knew – though he was sure Hanna suspected – that there were times when he turned down invitations simply because he hated coming home to an empty house.

As he went upstairs to dress, the thought of Hanna reminded him of the first time he'd met Catherine. He'd been sitting at the desk when she came into the library, a tall, fair woman with an air of quiet authority, much like his own. 'Are you the librarian?'

'No, I'm just a volunteer. Hanna's down among the shelves, she should be back here in a minute.'

She'd smiled. 'Sorry. I'm new in Lissbeg and I don't know many people yet.'

'No need to apologise. I'm a blow-in too.'

'My mum and I have opened the bookshop on Sheep Street. You could say I'm living my dream.'

This unexpected echo of conversations he'd had with Sophie had raised memories that made Stephen flinch. He'd turned away to hide his reaction, saying, 'Here's Hanna now. You'll have to excuse me. I ought to be in the reading room.' She didn't seem fazed by his abruptness, and as he left, he heard her introducing herself to Hanna.

'What a lovely space you have here!'

'It was extended to house the psalter. We've become a proper community hub, which is just what a library should be, and the exhibition's done wonders for local tourism.'

'I know. It's partly why my mother and I chose to come here.'

'Well, I'm glad you did. Lissbeg needed a bookshop.'

He and Catherine met once again at dinner at Hanna and Brian's. Over coffee, Hanna had explained to Catherine that, for years after a bad divorce, she'd had to live with her mother. 'In the back room of her bungalow. It was hell! You're lucky you and Ann are such good friends.'

'You don't get along with your mum?'

'She's what's known as a difficult woman! And she always hated my husband, so when he turned out to have cheated on me she never stopped rubbing it in.'

'Tricky.'

Hanna laughed. 'Still, she did take me in when I turned up with my daughter and nowhere to live. Jazz was only a teenager then, and I was riddled with guilt.'

'Why?'

'Oh, because I'd uprooted her and dragged her here without warning. I was so desperate to get away from my husband I'd just cut and run. Actually, Jazz loved it here, and she's always got on like a house on fire with my mother. But I worried for years that she'd suffered for lack of a father figure. Things can be buried deep, can't they? She and I were able to talk about it, though, and I guess that's what matters.'

Stephen had noticed with amusement that, though Catherine nodded, she seemed unconvinced that talking things through solved every problem. Given his own sensitivities, he'd found that rather attractive. He'd hardly seen her afterwards, though, except on the few occasions when he'd dropped into her shop to buy a book. They'd chatted a bit then, but mostly about the library.

'I enjoy volunteering, and I think I'm useful. Adults often find it hard to admit they have trouble reading, and finding someone empathetic and skilled enough to help them isn't easy.'

'I haven't really found time to build much of a social life. I keep meaning to join one of Hanna's library clubs but, after a long day in the shop, it's easier just to flop in front of the telly.'

He didn't say that his volunteering was more a way of passing the time than of building a social life. And after that there'd been Covid and isolation, and when things had opened up again and he'd gone in to order a book, he'd wondered if she'd even recognised him. Not that she'd blanked him or anything, but she hadn't seemed particularly pleased to see him. Realising where his thoughts had led him, Stephen frowned and told himself briskly not to be mawkish. Why should a busy bookseller remember who he was? A few brief meetings over the years didn't amount to a friendship. The fact was that, if he wanted to get to know Catherine better, he would have to take action instead of sitting around moping.

CHAPTER SIX

The van was parked in a side street. The Divil was stretched full-length on the passenger seat, his ears flattened and his head on Fury's thigh. The cab was full of smoke, and Fury was on his third roll-up. Everything that had been said in Carmody's office had dug up a past he'd buried. His feckless brother's drinking. Their father, who'd known Paudie wouldn't look after the forest but had left it to him because he was the elder. Their mother had been dead by then, and as soon as his father was buried, Fury, who'd inherited nothing but the family home he'd been raised in, had upped sticks and taken the boat to England. He was sixteen years old and couldn't bear to watch a steady process of dereliction, so he'd sworn he'd never go home while Paudie lived.

Working on sites from Camden Town to Cricklewood, he'd listened to stories of how his brother was selling off parcels of woodland for beer money. Then came the day when he heard that the remainder of the forest had been sold to some maudlin tourist who'd wept into his pint and told Paudie he wanted a piece of the auld sod to leave to his grandkids. That had been fifty years ago, and neither the buyer nor his family had appeared in Finfarran again. So, having come home and restored his house, Fury had simply behaved as if the forest was his as well. Establishing himself as the go-to local builder, he'd cared for the trees he'd always loved, coppicing, clearing paths, and selling timber when it suited him. No one had ever questioned this and, as time passed, it had become known as 'Fury's forest'. He'd banked on being dead and gone before anyone realised he hadn't owned it. But now, when he felt too old and tired to fight, his luck had run out.

'There's no call to do your Greyfriars Bobby impersonation.'

The Divil looked offended and retreated beyond the gearstick. Unable to meet his eyes, Fury glowered at the windscreen. 'You know yourself what Carmody's like. A great man for doing favours, so long as he ends up richer for it himself. Our forest's up for sale, and what Carmody wants is a bidding war. He'll be on a percentage of what it sells for and, mark my words, he's had his ear to the ground. There'll be someone already pulling strings to get planning permission for those feckin' high-rise flats. Don't tell me there haven't been brown envelopes sliding across bars up in Dublin, and cases of whiskey flying around in taxis.' Picking a shred of tobacco from his lower lip, Fury shrugged. 'The bottom line is that you and me are banjaxed.'

The Divil growled.

Fury shook his head at him. 'Don't bother getting your hackles up. I've told you how it is. And I know. I know. We're talking about the last of Finfarran's ancient woodland. Native species. Ecological damage. Well, I guarantee Carmody's on the phone right now to some shyster up in Dublin. Talking infrastructure. Tourism. Local economy. Ticking every bloody box on the planning officer's sheet. And don't you start coming up with objections. There's no point. We all know the shysters don't give a monkey's about the local economy. They don't care about people here, working their socks off building businesses. Putting something back whenever they take something out. You know it. I know it. The boys with the brown envelopes in their back pockets know it. But this is about the kind of money you and I don't have and can't raise. So we'd better get used to the thought that they're going to kill every tree in the forest and throw up luxury boxes that'll stand empty most of the year.'

Still glaring through the windscreen, Fury scratched The Divil's furry ears. 'That's how it is and we're going to have to face it. I'm not going to be raising petitions, and waving placards, and chaining myself to railings above at the Dáil. I haven't the strength to be starting a war at this stage.' Taking a last, deep drag, he flicked his cigarette into the gutter. 'You and I are too old to be taking on rats.'

They drove to the outskirts of the town, where a light industrial centre reached into the countryside. The entry spanned a little river that flowed serenely beneath a concrete bridge. At Shamie Doyle's Builder's Merchants, the man came out of the office and said, 'Christ, Fury, are y'all right? Have you had a go of the flu?' There was a drop at the end of Fury's beaky nose. Disregarding the question, he opened the back of the van and took out the last skinny tree. 'Tell the boss-man I wish him and his family a happy Christmas.'

'I will, of course. The same to yourself.' Looking at him sideways, the man added, 'We've a place doing teas has opened up at the other side of the yard. You could trot a mouse on the brew they make. Great cakes too. You and The Divil would get a warm there, if you're feeling chilly.'

Having rubbed the back of his hand across the end of his nose, Fury clicked his fingers at The Divil. 'We might as well. It's chilly enough. Come on, so. I'll see if they'll do you a doughnut.'

Back in the office, the man pulled a face at a lad who was working on the computer. 'God, you'd hate to see a legend like Fury O'Shea getting old.'

Without looking up, the lad hit a key that totted up the previous week's takings. 'Who? Oh, the oul fella with the terrier. What did he come by for? A Christmas handout, was it?'

Dusk was falling. They drove back into town via Sheep Street, in traffic reduced to a crawl by people's attempts to beat the rush-hour. Shop windows sparkled with decorations. The streetlights were on, and the pavements were slick and shiny from thin rainfall. Fury and The Divil sat side by side, oblivious to Christmas, with the weight of the world bearing down on their shoulders. Having slowed almost to a standstill, Fury glanced over at Lissbeg Books and saw Catherine, outside the shop, apparently arguing with a shock-headed guy in his twenties. As he watched, she put her hands over her face and, with a violent gesture, the guy walked away and disappeared down a lane between the shop fronts.

Catherine lowered her hands, her shoulders heaved, and Fury saw that she was crying. Immediately, his own shoulders squared and, swinging the wheel, he pulled out of the traffic and into the kerb. Saying, 'You stay there,' to The Divil, he got out of the van. Catherine's hands were shaking and her face was deathly white. Behind her, the lights on the book tree in the window flashed cheerfully. Fury said, 'Take it easy, Mam. You've had a shock. What's happened?' She seemed unable to speak, but she turned and gesticulated at the shop. Grasping her by the elbow, Fury pushed the door and went in. Ann was standing by the till, looking equally shaken. At the front end of the shop, bestseller displays were edged with garlands. But the back half of the shop floor was a scene of devastation.

Fury propelled Catherine to the seat behind the till where, looking sick, she laid her head on the counter. Ann stammered, 'It came down. The whole ceiling. There was this dreadful noise, and it came down.'

Striding to the point where Christmas ended and chaos began, Fury peered upward and pointed at an overhead beam. 'Well, that's what saved your front half.'

Catherine still had her head on the counter but Ann said, 'How?'

Treading carefully, Fury inspected the chaos. 'You can see there used to be two rooms here, one in front and a smaller one behind it. It's the ceiling in the back one that's come down.'

Most of what had fallen had landed on a display table with metal legs that had buckled beneath the weight. Dirt, Christmas cards, books, broken laths and large, jagged chunks of plaster were scattered knee-deep across the floor. Above them, there was a gaping hole in the ceiling, through which Fury could see the joists under the floorboards in the room above. He squinted upwards again. Then he approached the mess on the floor and stirred it with his boot. 'And there's the reason for your collapse. This lot's sodden. There's been water running along your joists and pooling above the plaster.' Ann came to look and he snapped, 'Stand back, Mam, there's more to come down yet. That's old-fashioned plaster up there. A chunk on your head could kill you.' Ann backed away and, returning to the counter, Fury spoke to Catherine. 'I take it the little toerag I saw on the pavement has been doing something upstairs in your flat?'

Catherine had sat up and dried her eyes. 'He was refurbishing the kitchen. Actually, at first, he was just supposed to be tiling a splashback.'

'He was, of course.'

'But then there was something the matter with the worktop.'

'There would be.'

'It was old anyway, so I said to go ahead and replace it. But the old cabinets and the new worktop wouldn't marry up.'

'So when did he start messing with your plumbing?'

'A few days ago. He flooded the kitchen floor. But he mopped up. He did it really quickly.'

'I bet he did. And, somewhere along the line, he'd had your vinyl flooring up?'

'A seam went when he shifted the cabinets. He said he could replace the vinyl. He said a mate of his has a shop that sells cut-price flooring, and he could get us a good price.'

Fury swore under his breath. 'The thieving little fecker. Has he had any money off you?'

Ann put her arm around Catherine. 'He wanted an advance. But at that stage we were just talking about doing the tiling, so we said we'd pay him when the work was done.' She looked bleakly at Fury. 'This week's sales were supposed to tide us over until summer, when the tourist trade starts up again. But we can't stay open in this state.'

Catherine's hand flew to her mouth. 'What about Adam Rashid's book launch? There's a massive press list. It's been on social media. There are posters all over town. Mum, what're we going to *do*?'

Fury returned to his inspection of the chaos. Loops of torn wood-chip paper hung from the plaster that remained around the six-foot hole. The fall had largely missed the shelving. The collapsed section was off-centre, leaving a dirty but undamaged way to the door that led to the office and stockroom and, beyond them, to the yard behind the shop. He stood for a moment, then marched back to the till. 'The rest of that plaster has to come down before we start the clean-up. We'll get no skip hire in Christmas week. I'll barrow the whole lot through and we'll have a temporary dump in the yard.'

The two women gazed at him blankly, and Catherine said, 'What are you talking about?'

'I'm telling you no little shyster claiming to be a builder is going to do you out of your Christmas trade.' With the air of a general preparing for battle, Fury went and turned the sign on the shop door to Closed. 'So, first things first, have you a mobile there to hand?'

'A what?'

'A phone. A mobile phone with a camera on it. You'll want the damage videoed for whoever you're insured with. Otherwise they'll question every euro you put in for. I'll do the video now in a minute. I know what the feckers want.' He glanced with magnificent carelessness at the phone Ann held out to him.

'Android. Fair enough. Not what I'd go for, mind. The Divil and I have always been iPhone men.'

Certain at this stage that she must be hallucinating, Catherine heard herself say, 'Each to his own.'

Fury disappeared with the phone and spent the next twenty minutes recording every aspect of the damage, upstairs and down. Catherine and Ann sat slumped on chairs until Catherine stood up and, going to the window, turned off the twinkling Christmas lights on the book tree. They sat possessed by gloom until Fury reappeared and strode through the chaos and back to the counter. 'Right. When's this book launch? Time and date?'

Startled by his energy, which seemed to fill the shop, Ann said 'Five thirty, the day after tomorrow.'

'That's tight, right enough. No point hanging about, then. We'd best get a move on. I'll see you first thing in the morning. Six sharp.'

Three hours later, Ann and Catherine were upstairs in the flat. Ann had gone to bed and Catherine was in the living room, talking to Hanna on the phone. 'We don't even know him. He just turned up, and now he's taken over.'

'Honestly, Catherine, don't worry. Things would be much worse if he hadn't. Anyway, you mightn't know him but Fury knows everyone in Finfarran.'

'I don't see how things could be worse. And look what happened the last time I trusted a builder.'

'Yes, but that wasn't a proper builder. Not by the sound of things.'

Catherine looked at the half-made cabinet jammed against the end of her sofa, and the piles of things that ought to be in her kitchen but were randomly stacked around her living room. 'Actually, that's what Fury said. He called him the kind of lowlife that gives proper builders a bad name.'

'Well, Fury's the real deal. You couldn't do better. Look, have you eaten? You said your kitchen's off-limits.'

'We're not supposed to go in there again till Fury says it's safe. But it doesn't matter. I couldn't eat. I think I'd be sick if I tried. We've got Adam Rashid's launch on Friday, late-night shopping on Saturday, a kids' event on Sunday, and carol-singing on Christmas Eve. The posters are all over the town. The publishers are sending someone from London for the book launch.'

'I know. You told me. Calm down. What does Fury say?'

'He says he'll be here at six tomorrow morning. He'll tosh things up by degrees and no one will notice. He's out of his mind, Hanna. The back of the shop's like a bomb-site.'

'The front part's functional, though?'

'Yes. It's bizarre. You'd look at it and think everything's perfectly fine.'

'So, maybe he can screen off the back while he's working.'

'That's what he said, but I don't see how.' Catherine moved her phone from one ear to the other. 'What does tosh it up mean, anyway?'

'I haven't a clue. But if Fury says it's what you need, it'll work.'

'That's another thing. What kind of weird name is Fury?'

Hanna laughed. 'As far as I know, he was christened Alphonsus. He's called Fury because he goes at things like a whirlwind.'

'How come you know all this?'

'Well, Brian's the county architect, and Fury was once the biggest builder on the peninsula.'

'He was? He looks like a scarecrow.'

'Don't judge a book by its cover.'

Catherine responded with a feeble giggle and, glad to hear her relax, Hanna said, 'He's old and eccentric but I promise you're lucky to have him. You should see the job he did on Bridge House at the top of your street.'

'The old stone house above the river? The one that's owned by the guy who volunteers for you at the library?'

'That's it. Fury did the renovation. Look, you need to eat and you've no kitchen. Why don't I whip round with a flask of soup?'

'No, really, we're grand. Fury set up the toaster on a box at the top of the stairs. There's a kettle too, and a box of food. But thanks a million, Hanna. I wouldn't have slept if we hadn't talked.'

'Well, if Fury's due at six, you'd best get your head down.'

'I will. At least I know now that he's not out to rook me.'

'No, I'd say he's decided to take you on.'

'Dear God, that sounds ominous.'

'He saw you needed help so he's being neighbourly. That's what he does.'

'Okay, that sounds better.'

Hanna laughed reassuringly. 'I'm warning you, though, it'll be a rollercoaster. When Fury takes someone on, he takes over. And, on top of that, he's never been a man to mince his words.'

THURSDAY

19 December

CHAPTER SEVEN

Five a.m. Seated at the kitchen table, The Divil was looking at
Fury over a tin bowl of porridge. Fury bit into a vast sausage
sandwich. 'Don't be giving me grief this hour of the morning.
I couldn't leave those poor bookshop women in the lurch. Not
in Christmas week. Chances are they'd have tried to get that
lowlife back to fix the damage.' The Divil's hackles rose and
he growled ferociously. Reaching for a knife, Fury lavished
mustard on his sausage. 'Exactly. And since there's nothing to
be done about our disaster, we might as well go over and deal
with theirs.' Catching The Divil's eye, Fury threw him a piece of
sausage. 'Look, it beats sitting here waiting for our own world
to come crashing down.'

They parked in the lane behind Lissbeg Books just after five
to six. Catherine opened the back door and took them upstairs
to where Ann was making tea on the landing. Neither woman
looked as if she'd slept. Fury wasted no time making comments
on their appearance. He refused toast, accepted tea, and led the
way to the living room. 'So, one thing at a time and first things

first. Last night, I made a couple of phone calls. We should have Tintawn Terry and Angela here in the next few minutes.' The Divil yelped and, going to the window, Fury said, 'He's right. That's them now, coming into your yard.' Ignoring Catherine and Ann's bewildered looks, he threw up the sash. 'The key's in my van. Bring the sheets in, will you, Terry? I stuck them through a boil-wash last night and they've come out grand. Get my steps too. You can carry them through to the shop.'

Catherine decided she needed to be assertive. 'This is all very kind, but I don't understand. Who's Tintawn Terry?'

'A man who actually does sell flooring and can give you a deal.' Fury took a swig of tea. 'Angela's his daughter. She's a plumber. Terry's got a carpet-tile warehouse out the back of his hardware shop. He'll give a hand generally over the next few days. Angela's going to take a look at your kitchen. God knows what kind of damage that fecker's done to your pipework.'

'But—'

'Lookit, I'm not going to break my back getting your downstairs sorted and leave another leak pending up here.'

'How—'

'You know, we'd get things done a helluva a lot faster, if you two would just speak when you're spoken to.' Cheerfully, Fury handed his empty mug to Catherine. 'You open at ten, right?'

'You can't think we'll open today?'

'You won't if you keep asking stupid questions.'

Catherine looked helplessly at Ann. The Divil was turning his head back and forth, as if watching a tennis match. Angela, who was short and cheerful, appeared on the landing. 'Morning, ladies. Will I have a gander at the kitchen, Fury?'

'Do, girl. Come here to me, did Terry bring the bucket?'

'He did. He's gone out for the steps. We parked our van behind yours in the lane.' Turning to Catherine, Angela asked, 'Is that all right? We don't want the guards complaining.'

'It's fine. This is very good of you all. I – I don't know what to say.'

Fury spoke with a great assumption of patience. 'That'll be why I told you to say nothing. The best thing you two can do is nip out and have a hot breakfast. You want to smarten yourselves up too. No offence, but you both look like you've been dragged through a hedge backwards.'

He disappeared, leaving Catherine looking at the empty tea mug. 'How can we open the shop today? Think of the state it's in.' Before Ann could reply, Angela stuck her head round the door. 'Fury says you'll be wanting to shower before I turn off the water. Ten minutes max, he says, and make it eight if you can.'

Half an hour later, showered and still shell-shocked, Catherine and Ann were drinking coffee and eating fried-egg baps. It wasn't a café they'd been to before. Streams of customers came and went between the Formica-topped tables. Tradespeople on their way to work, early-morning cleaners coming off shift, workers on their way to shops and offices, all stopping in to grab breakfasts, takeaway teas or coffees, heads down and concentrated on where they were going next. Catherine looked around. 'I haven't been in a place like this since I was on the road. Not much communication, but a sense of camaraderie, and everyone topping up on caffeine to keep them functioning.'

'Do you miss those days on the road?'

Catherine gave a reluctant grin. 'On days like this I do!' She put her bap on her plate. 'Look, Mum, I'm sorry. It was me got you into this, and if we go belly-up you'll have lost your savings.'

'I'm not complaining.'

'You do know that if we lose this week's sales we may not survive till the summer?'

Ann stirred her coffee thoughtfully. 'You know what? If everything does fall apart, I won't regret living the dream. I'm just going to feel sorry we haven't lived it to the full.'

'I know. We've been here such a short time.'

Ann shook her head. 'That's not what I mean. Think about it, Catherine. Hanna says Fury O'Shea is a legend hereabouts. He knew who we are, but you and I had never heard of him before yesterday. The people in this café are our neighbours. We haven't spoken two words to any of them.'

'Actually, there's a guy over there who comes into the shop all the time to buy thrillers.'

'Then he's the exception that proves the rule.'

Hunching her shoulders, Catherine sipped her coffee. 'Fury drives around town each year with Christmas trees from his forest. He stopped outside the shop yesterday and offered one to me. I'd no idea it was a gift. I thought he was looking for money.'

'I'd never heard of Tintawn Terry's hardware shop. Had you?'

'I think it's in Bridge Street.' Catherine frowned. 'When we were fitting out the flat and the office, I used to drive to the DIY superstore in Carrick.'

'While Bridge Street was just a walk away.'

Sighing, Catherine said, 'I suppose we've both had our heads down, trying to keep going and pay the bills.'

'So we ended up with a builder we got from a flashy site on the internet, when there's people like Fury and Terry right here in Lissbeg.'

'Maniacs, you mean?' Biting her lip, Catherine said, 'I do see what you're getting at, though. We haven't really engaged with Finfarran.'

'You could say we haven't really been living the dream at all.'

They sat for a moment before Catherine asked, 'Do you think Fury's going to get us through this? I mean, the eccentricity's off the wall.'

'Hanna says we can trust him.'

'I just can't imagine what on earth he's doing back there. Still, I suppose that, if Angela really is a plumber, at least we'll have a working kitchen sink.'

They walked back through the bustling town, where shopkeepers were opening doors and pulling down awnings. It felt weird to knock at their own shop door and, when it opened, to see The Divil's furry face at knee-level and Fury's beaky nose poking out higher up. He flung the door wide to let them in and, beyond the two unlikely figures, Catherine and Ann saw the front part of the shop looking unchanged. But, tacked to the beam that separated the front from the devastation, there now hung what appeared to be two heavy cream-coloured curtains vividly patterned with abstract splashes of colour. At either end, where these met the side walls, there was an eight-foot scarlet banner with 'LISSBEG BOOKS' printed on it in gold.

Dazed, Catherine told herself Fury must have found the storeroom where her pull-down banners and stacking chairs were kept between bookshop events.

At the central point where the curtains met there was a large galvanised bucket and, beside it, a container full of sand. As they gaped, Fury heaved The Divil's tree into the bucket, its branches still tightly bound to its trunk. Steadying it, he said, 'Bed her in there, Terry.'

'She might take another few bricks in the bucket.'

'She will not. She weighs a ton. Jam them bricks that's in there around her, and tip the sand on top.'

Having followed instructions, Terry stood back. 'Right, she's sound as a bell. Go for the rope.'

In one flamboyant slash, Fury cut the rope that confined the branches. They sprang out, reminding Catherine of a Christmas pop-up book. Angled on either side, the banners framed the huge bushy tree, which tapered to precisely their height at the top. The Divil gave an ecstatic yelp and, coiling the rope, Fury announced, 'There you have it. Christmas with a Jackson Pollock vibe.'

Catherine clasped her hands in delight. The splashes of colour on the heavy cream fabric made a vibrant background, and the bucket at the base of the tree produced a gleam of silver below the dark branches. There certainly was a funky suggestion of Jackson Pollock, but the overwhelming effect was of the painted pantomime settings in the toy theatre Christmas cards she used to get from her granny. Mesmerised, she said so to Ann, who nodded. 'It's magical. It really is, Fury.'

With a series of wiggles, The Divil indicated total agreement. Fury snorted. 'It'll do for now, but I'm warning you, it's going to be logistical hell between now and Christmas Eve.'

'I don't understand.'

'I'm going to have to keep making quick changes out here in front while we're working like demons behind the curtains. We need to whip up anticipation. Excitement. Conjure up a bit of theatre. Otherwise people will spot that it's just a Christmas tree and couple of paint-spattered dust sheets.'

'But it's the perfect tree. I don't know how to thank you.'

The Divil gave an outraged howl, and Fury grinned at Catherine. 'All right, fair dos, I'm not going to deny it. It was himself selected it specially for you.'

CHAPTER EIGHT

Mary Casey liked what she called a proper bowl of cornflakes, and couldn't be doing with cheery chatter while she was eating it. She'd said this loudly when Hanna first took her to view Garrybawn House. 'I like a bit of decent privacy when I'm eating my breakfast. And I don't want people turning up at my elbow uninvited. If I shut a door it stays shut till I open it.'

'I know. That's why we thought Garrybawn might be perfect for you. You'd have your own flat with your own front door, and could cater for yourself if you preferred to. Or if you chose to eat some of your meals in the dining room, the other residents would be great company.'

Mary replied that she'd be the judge of that.

Theresa showed them the dining room, the lounge, the charming conservatory with its armchairs, books and magazines, and a flat that had a garden view. Beyond the garden were fields and the foothills of mountains. Mary inspected the flat's bedroom and cosy living room, and the cupboards in the kitchenette. Opening the bathroom door, Hanna said, 'See, Mam? There are grab rails. And everything's a good height. This is what Brian was telling you last night.'

'And as I told Brian, I can still rise from the lavatory unassisted.'

'I know. But a rail is great for helping you to get out of the bath. I've got one.'

'You shouldn't need grab rails at your time of life. You've no core strength, that's your problem.'

Having dismissed Hanna, Mary turned on Theresa. 'Why would I want to sit here at the back of the house, watching grass grow?'

'The flats at the back are the most popular, Mrs Casey.'

'Well, this wouldn't do me at all. I'd want to be at the front with a view of the bus stop, to see who was on their way into town.'

This had been said with the air of one who had dealt her trump card, but Theresa replied that, as it happened, a front flat was vacant. 'They're all the same size. Would you like to see it?'

Grudgingly, Mary said yes. After looking, she'd pursed her lips belligerently. 'I don't know why you're all trying to stick me in a Home.'

'Oh, Mam! That's nonsense. This is sheltered living. You've said yourself that the bungalow's getting too big for you, and the truth is, we worry about you being there alone.'

'I told you when I agreed to look that I won't be railroaded, Hanna. If I make up my mind to move here, it'll be for a good reason. And I'm telling you straight that I haven't seen one yet.'

Hanna had backed off at once, but that evening Jazz, whom Mary adored, had waded in. 'You do know, Gran, that you're sitting on serious equity there in the bungalow? I bet an accountant would say that if you liquidated your assets you'd be making a shrewd move you wouldn't regret.' The accountant she found for Mary backed her up. 'Of course, Mrs Casey, you may wish to leave your property to someone in your will. But were you to sell up, you'd release considerable capital, which you could spend in your lifetime however you liked.'

'Those Garrybawn flats don't come free, you know.'

'It's a council-run facility. Residents make a contribution. The government pays the rest.'

The meeting with the accountant was the clincher. Hanna and Jazz, who both worked, were happily settled in their own homes, while Mary's only income was her state pension. Before going to look at Garrybawn House, Hanna and Brian had sat her down and told her she mustn't trouble herself about money. 'If your savings get low, we'll cover your costs, wherever you choose to live. From our point of view what matters is that you're happy.'

It was kind of them, and Mary knew they meant it, but she hated the thought of losing her financial independence. She also knew they'd been genuinely worried about her lately. Truth be told, she'd been a bit worried herself. Johnny next door had had a break-in that had unsettled her and, lately, she'd found herself forgetting the simplest things, like where she'd left her slippers, why she'd walked into a room, or if she'd remembered to turn off the gas. That kind of thing could only get worse, and when it did, she could lose her independence altogether. So, lying in bed in the bungalow, she'd come to her decision, and having moved to Garrybawn House, she'd never regretted it. Now and then, especially if she had something to boast about, she even took breakfast in the dining room.

Today, wearing a Pringle jumper and matching cardigan, she chose a table, adjusted a strand of pearls on her massive bosom, and looked round for somebody to talk to. It was too early for most of the other residents to appear, so she settled for Saoirse, who'd come to take her order. 'Fried mushrooms with grilled tomatoes on toast, and I don't want basil lurking among the mushrooms.'

'No problem. They're fried to order.'

'Go on, so, I'll have them. And I need to get a move on. I'm into Lissbeg this morning on the nine-thirty bus.'

Saoirse's face lit up. 'So am I.'

Mary frowned at this diversion from the subject of her own plans but, undeterred, she pressed on. 'My granddaughter's booked me a treat, as an early Christmas present. I've been liquidated, so I could have paid for it myself, but Jazz has always been very good to me.'

'That's nice.'

'She's a marketing executive. Very high-powered. She's over in London for Christmas, so she arranged this in advance.'

'Well, I hope you'll have a good time.'

'Isn't London where you and your parents are going in the new year? I'd say you'd get great bargains in the January sales.'

Saoirse said her dad had booked seats for a fabulous show, and that they'd be staying at a West End hotel. Ignoring this, Mary shook out her napkin. 'It's a celebrity baking course in the Convent Centre. Mark you, I was beating meringue to stiff peaks long before you were born. But I wouldn't want my granddaughter to think I'm ungrateful. And sure, who knows, I might give this celebrity boyo a few tips on baking.'

Back in the kitchen, Saoirse relayed this to her mum. 'The idea of Mary Casey giving tips to the Coolest Chef! And she's sure to announce that she knows me. I'll die of embarrassment.'

'That's enough of that. Mind your manners. And, for heaven's sake, use your head, Saoirse. Half the people who do celebrity courses are retirees. Who else is going to be free, or has that kind of money?'

It was a point that hadn't occurred to Saoirse. She'd vaguely imagined the course would be full of glamorous people like Adam. Now she saw that was silly. The participants wouldn't be exciting. They'd be ordinary people from Finfarran, and, as her mum said, the chances were that they wouldn't be all that young. This was slightly disappointing but, handing over Mary's breakfast order, she told herself nothing could change the fact that the Coolest Chef had poured her coffee, and let her advise him on his Q&A.

Adam had spent most of the night lying awake, thinking. Winning the Coolest Chef title had been a huge step forward in his career. He'd worked twenty-four/seven to attain it, knowing the doors it would open would change his life. What he hadn't known was how completely it would remove his privacy. He'd learned to deal with the hangers-on, the internet trolls and the paparazzi, but the look in ordinary people's eyes when they recognised him still freaked him out. That was where his head had been when he'd seen Lia across the Royal Vic's dining room and had looked away as soon as their eyes had met. And then, miraculously, when he'd met her on the bus, it had turned out that she hadn't recognised him. They'd just been two people who'd seen each other across a hotel dining room. It had mattered so much that he'd panicked when he heard she was booked on his course.

Rolling over in bed, Adam winced at the memory. He should have told her who he was, and he had intended to but, somehow, he hadn't been able to find the words. The truth was he'd been afraid. He'd imagined a confused look turning to anger. Friendliness becoming wariness. Interest replaced by embarrassment. It had all happened so fast – and then there'd been the hope of reprieve, when she'd said that perhaps she'd give the course a miss. He clutched at the thought that, if that happened, he could find her in the hotel and talk with nobody looking on. By the time his alarm call buzzed, he'd decided the talk had to happen at breakfast.

But when he went down to breakfast, Lia wasn't there. He considered asking the waiter if she'd already eaten, but knew that if he did it was likely to cause gossip in the kitchen. So, having ordered, he began to scroll through his morning messages. The first was a one-liner from Dom. *You speak French, right?* Baffled, Adam responded *No. Why?* Immediately the phone rang and Dom's voice rasped in his ear. 'For Christ's sake, Adam, all chefs speak French. What's the matter with you?'

'No, they don't.'

'What about all this "Oui, Chef" stuff that goes on in kitchens?'

'It's a convention. I don't speak French. What gave you that idea?'

'I've heard you rabbit on about cuisson and Cordon Bleu and pommes frites.'

'You've also heard me talk about pasta being al dente. That doesn't mean I speak Italian.'

'Okay. Fine. Forget it. Moving on.'

'But why did you want to know?'

'Just an idea being kicked around for your series.' Dom's voice became emollient. 'It probably wouldn't have worked anyway. I said forget it.'

Adam frowned. 'You told me it was early days. I didn't know you were talking format.'

'It is. We're not. It was just a chat in a lift, Adam.'

'But why?'

'Oh, for God's sake, I don't spend my whole life talking money, you know. There's got to be some flim-flam to grease the wheels and keep things moving. Every little executive out there wants to be a creative. You know that. Oh – hang on – incoming call I need to take. Talk later.'

The waiter arrived with toast and Adam buttered a slice, feeling worried. It was weird to think of people kicking ideas around about his future with no suggestion that he might be part of the discussion. He supposed it was just another thing that came with being a celebrity and, increasingly, he wasn't sure he liked it.

An hour later, he put his head round the door to Phil's office. She leaped to her feet. 'I've everything ready. Your ingredients have arrived and they're down in the kitchen. A courier came with the giveaways. I unpacked them. Quality stuff. I've put the aprons out on the work benches – the laundry will pick them up each day and deliver them back in the mornings, so that's arranged. Your lunches are sorted, Saoirse's here already, and I'll pop in and out when I can. And, of course, I'll be there to do this morning's introductions.'

'Great. You're obviously on top of everything.'

'I'm a details person. Focus is my keyword.'

'I don't suppose there's been any cancellations?'

Phil looked puzzled. 'Cancellations?'

Adam had spent the drive to Lissbeg focused entirely on Lia. Blushing, he said, 'I just wondered if any of the participants had cancelled. It happens sometimes.'

'Not here it won't. People can't believe you've come all the way to Lissbeg. If they've broken their legs, they'll be staggering in on crutches.'

'Oh? Okay. Good. I'll go along and set up.'

Saoirse arrived an hour before the participants, as instructed, and was thrilled to be given a *Coolest Chef* apron. It was green linen with cream lettering, and had proper long cheffy strings that went several times round her waist. On each of the benches was an identical apron, a balloon whisk, and the ingredients for a Genoise sponge. Saoirse had studied the information pack till she knew it by heart. A header on each page said *Cakes To Come Home To*, and each day's recipe was on a laminated sheet illustrated with a photo. Adam explained that today, after the participants had made a basic version of the cake, he'd be demonstrating a chocolate Swiss roll with crystallised ginger and Swiss meringue buttercream filling. 'It's a really simple sponge mix. They'll probably all have made it before. The point is to show that it can be elevated, if ...'

Breathlessly, Saoirse said, '"... if you give it some love."'

Adam laughed. 'I was going to say "if you use your

imagination". Anyway, that's our theme. New Twists on Old Favourites. We'll build on it with the other recipes over the next few days.'

Saoirse wished she'd kept her mouth shut. The tagline she'd come out with was one she'd heard him use on TikTok, but quoting it like that had probably sounded totally crass. Retreating to the end of the room where the sinks were, she sat down and read through the information pack again.

The first participant to arrive was Darina Kelly, a tall woman with insecurely anchored hair. She was followed by a retired schoolteacher called Mr Maguire, and two ladies from Cork carrying Orla Kiely tote bags. Starstruck by Adam's celebrity, the ladies from Cork held back, but his easy charm relaxed them and soon they were chatting and sharing jokes with him, like old friends. Saoirse wondered if she ought to offer to take people's coats. Deciding she might as well, since she wasn't doing anything else, she went and held out her hand for Darina Kelly's furry jacket. Adam said, 'Cheers, Saoirse. Everyone, this is Saoirse Kavanagh, my right hand for the next few days.' Everyone looked impressed and, loaded down with hats, coats and scarves, Saoirse wondered what she ought to do next. Luckily, Phil arrived and swept her across the room to a coat rack, where Saoirse hung things randomly, hoping she'd remember which belonged to whom.

More people came in. Mary Casey made an entrance, bowing to Phil and shaking Adam's hand graciously. Saoirse recognised Declan from Tintawn Terry's Hardware, who'd been ahead of her at school and now worked for his dad. Behind him was a square-shaped woman with a friendly face, and, behind the square woman, a quiet couple who looked about the same age as Saoirse's parents.

They had coffee around the scrubbed wooden table. Saoirse sat next to Phil. People were introduced to each other and Adam, in his chef's whites, talked them through the shape of the course. He'd seemed jumpy earlier on, and kept glancing at the door, but once Phil had made her opening speech and declared the course open, he'd relaxed. Coming to the day's recipe, he held up one of the giveaway balloon whisks printed with the *Coolest Chef* logo. 'So, a Genoise is a classic sponge enriched with butter and egg yolk. It's light and moist and fluffy, and the rise depends on how well you whip your eggs. If you use an electric beater, it'll take at least eight to ten minutes over a bowl of hot water. And I warn you, if you use a balloon whisk, you'll end up respecting the chef who came up with the recipe!' Glancing around the table, he flashed a charming, professional smile. 'This morning, along with your complimentary *Coolest Chef* aprons, you'll find one of these whisks on your workbench. It's up to you whether you use it as a challenge, or a reminder. Either way, with this recipe, whisking will be the secret of success.'

There was a buzz of anticipation, interrupted by a sniff from Mary Casey. 'You won't find me using one of them things, nor do I need anyone giving me out a free apron. I've my own crossover bib that's done me for years there in my bag, and I've spent far too many years of my life beating hell out of eggs.'

Crimson to the ears, Saoirse stared down at her coffee. When first they'd sat down at the table, Mary had nudged the woman beside her and said, 'Of course, little Saoirse and I share a house.' The way she'd talked, you'd think they were flatmates or something, so now, presumably, everyone was wondering what kind of weirdo hung around with somebody so terminally embarrassing.

Phil called out, 'I'll have your apron, Mary, if you don't want it.'

'You will not. If it comes with the course, my granddaughter's paid through the nose for it. I'm taking it home and wrapping it up for her, as a Christmas present.'

This produced a gale of good-humoured laughter. Saoirse looked at Adam under her lashes, but it seemed he wasn't bothered. In fact it looked like he hadn't heard a word. Standing rigidly at the end of the table, still holding the whisk, he was staring over everybody's heads. Turning, Saoirse saw that the double doors had opened, and a girl with a snub nose, grey eyes and dark, curly hair had come in.

CHAPTER NINE

'I can't believe you didn't know I was joking.' Lia had clicked her electric beater to Turbo, and Adam was straining to hear her over the whirring sound it made. 'For heaven's sakes, Adam, I won the prize off the telly. It was wall-to-wall clips of your show and shots of you looking rugged ...'

'Rugged?'

'Okay, not rugged. Inviting. Inviting Ireland to put five euros on an outside chance.' Lia lifted the beater. 'Is this what you called the ribbon stage?'

'I said eight to ten minutes, minimum. It needs to triple in volume.'

'Okay. Don't be snirpy.' Lia lowered the beater back into the batter that stood above a bowl of steaming water. 'Of course I recognised you. How could I not? Admittedly, I was slightly pissed when I entered the competition, but the huge mug shot on the information pack would've been a clue.'

Adam didn't feel snirpy. Out of the corner of his eye, he could see Mary Casey edging along her bench trying to hear what was going on. He had no idea and was now more embarrassed than before. Why hadn't he known Lia was joking? How could he have thought that somebody booked into his course wouldn't have recognised him from his photo? Was it possible that you actually did lose your mind when you fell in love? Because, apparently, that was what had happened. Lia had held out a bar of 75 per cent, organic Fairtrade chocolate, and he'd lost the power of rational thought. She lifted the beater again and raised her eyebrows at him. 'Light, fluffy and ribbon-like, yes?'

Adam said, 'You can't rush things at this stage. You'll know it's right by the way it feels.'

He'd moved away and was dealing with Mr Maguire when he realised he'd just told himself he was in love. This was bad. He didn't need it. He didn't want it. He knew exactly what Dom would say, and he shuddered to think about it. And, dammit, there was Seán, the boyfriend, up in Dublin, organising Christmas Day and sending endless texts. Stammering, he lost track of what he was saying to Mr Maguire but, fortunately, Mr Maguire had launched into a speech. 'I heat my sugar in advance, and take the classic Cordon Bleu approach to my bain marie. Two minutes over the heat, no more, and continue *off* it. And I don't believe in trying to aerate with an electric beater. I've never found it satisfactory.'

At the next bench, the square woman winked at a lady from Cork. 'In my house, we just chuck things in and pray.'

Pulling himself together, Adam raised his voice. 'Those of you whisking by hand, like Mr Maguire, will be at it longer, but everybody should end up with a bowl of pale yellow batter. You need to keep at it, but you have to go gently. The same goes for incorporating the other ingredients. And when your cake's ready to go in the oven, don't forget to set your timer. Nothing's drier than dried-out Genoise.' There was a crash at the far side of the room, and a yelp and a stream of apology from Darina. 'Oh, my God, I'm so sorry. The bowl just skidded out of my hand.'

Saoirse was on it at once, unfussed and quietly efficient. Which is more than you can say for me, thought Adam, catching sight of Lia's eyelashes and feeling his heart skid and turn upside down.

With the cakes in the oven, they took a tea-break, during which Adam held up the book he'd borrowed from the library. 'Those of you who live locally know the nuns' garden. Those who don't will have seen it when you arrived. They grew herbs and plants which they used in cooking.' He opened the book and flipped the pages to show a plan of the garden, and recipes illustrated by delicate drawings. 'You can see how cookery skills get handed down through generations, and how, until very recently, gardening and cooking went hand in hand.' Saoirse, who'd been clearing up, came to join them, and Adam gave her the book to pass around. 'It was all about ingredients grown a few steps from the kitchen. People forget how flowers and herbs were used in cakes in the past. For colouring. For flavour. For decoration and texture. Think of seed cake, which uses caraway. Well, caraway leaves are edible too, and the root has a sweet, nutty texture. Those are the kind of ideas you can bring to filling a simple layered sponge.'

Mr Maguire tutted and said, 'Not exactly Cordon Bleu.'

Mary announced she intended to layer her cakes with jam and squirty cream. 'There's nothing to beat it. Mind, you have to give it a shake if you buy it in Cassidy's shop. There's no propulsion at all in that woman's aerosols.' One of the ladies from Cork asked her what kind of jam she made. Mary sniffed. 'Oh, I wouldn't be bothered picking over fruit and boiling sugar. You get blobs on your ceiling. No, I picked up a jar there in Cassidy's while I was getting the cream. Half her stock comes from foreign now, and the prices can't be bet.'

Taking the book, Declan turned the pages. 'My nan used to make sugared rose petals for wedding cakes. She sold them to a bakery in Carrick.'

Lia said, 'Mine made a glaze with lemon myrtle leaves.'

Adam said, 'And lots of herbs we think of as ingredients for savoury dishes work really well in cakes and biscuits. Basil's delicious.'

Mary looked darkly at Saoirse. 'Weren't you trying to hide basil under my mushrooms only this morning?'

'No, I wasn't.'

'Well, you would've if I hadn't put a stop to your gallop. You won't find me putting basil in a biscuit. Nor caraway either. At my age, seeds get in under your plate.'

As the morning went on, Adam got the measure of his group. The ladies from Cork were competent home bakers who'd come to learn as well as for something to talk about afterwards. He'd already been told what to expect from Mary, and Mr Maguire was a type he'd met before. Kevin and Karen, the quiet couple, who'd bought themselves the course as an anniversary present, seemed to have no particular interest in baking, but Declan, who'd explained that he worked as a painter and decorator, had fizzed with enthusiasm from the get-go. Darina was going to spend her time smashing things, apologising, and taking up far too much of Saoirse's time. The square-shaped woman evidently had a sense of humour. And though dealing with Phil was like handling an over-excited spaniel, he'd had the measure of her from the start and knew she meant well.

Only Lia remained an enigma. Her bake had risen perfectly and she'd filled the cooled sponge with a chocolate crème mousseline. When he'd asked where she'd learned the recipe, she'd said, 'From a magazine in the dentist's waiting room. I've a photographic memory. It's a curse.' She didn't fit any of the stereotypes he was used to meeting on courses, which he supposed wasn't surprising since she was there by happenstance. A computer had selected her from hundreds of competition entrants; had it been differently programmed, someone else would have won. The thought of the odds against their meeting made Adam feel giddy. Surely, he thought, it was a sign that Fate was on his side? Maybe Seán in Dublin would fall under a bus or something. Or, better still, fall for someone else while she was away.

With the group's creations complete, he moved on to his demonstration. 'It's a chocolate Swiss roll filled with Swiss meringue buttercream and crystallised ginger. Pretty much the basic recipe you've just used, but with melted chocolate instead of butter. Rolling it up is easy, once you've learned how to do it, and you end up with something that looks impressive as a party centrepiece.' He made his sponge mix and poured it into an oblong tin, knocking it on the work surface to remove any air bubbles. 'When I make the buttercream, I'll chop in the ginger. Whipped cream flavoured with a dash of espresso also works well. It's a sophisticated choice if you enjoy mocha.'

Mary remarked acidly that, as far as she could remember, the nuns had never stepped out of their kitchen to harvest cocoa or coffee. 'Or ginger either, for the matter of that.'

One of the ladies from Cork said she grew ginger in a pot.

Adam gave Mary a smile. 'I'm big on seasonality and locally grown ingredients, but I'm not a fanatic, I promise you. Other things are allowed.'

Succumbing to his charm, she grudgingly returned the smile. 'Well, I'm telling you, Mother Aloysius didn't go in for sophistication. 'Tis far from shots of espresso we were reared.'

Looking up from the recipe, Declan asked Adam, 'Isn't a sophisticated Swiss roll called a roulade?'

'All Swiss rolls are roulades. But not all roulades are Swiss rolls.'

'Like all novels are books, but not all books are novels?'

'Exactly. A roulade is anything rolled up around a sweet or savoury filling. There's a super one that's just spinach leaves wrapped around mushrooms and herbs.' Seeing the look in Mary's eye at the mention of herby mushrooms, Adam went on hastily, 'So, this bake will take twelve to fifteen minutes. Less than your cakes took, because it's a thinner layer in a shallow tin.'

They spent the baking time gathered around the table, looking over each other's shoulders at the nuns' book. Darina was still at her workbench, attempting to cut the single cake she'd achieved into two layers. Coming to look, Adam found her struggling with a long length of thread. 'Oh dear, I swung it about for impetus, and it's wound itself round the clip that holds up my hair.' Clutching both ends of the thread, she looked at him helplessly. 'I'm sure to make matters worse if I let these go. Do you think you could help?' This was the kind of thing normally dealt with by an assistant. Out of his depth, he stared at the cat's cradle on Darina's head, sure that, if he tried to unravel it, things would get even worse.

Then Lia's voice asked, 'Anything up?' and she appeared beside him.

Darina gasped, 'I don't mean to be a bother. I've just got myself in a tangle. It's a method for cutting a Genoise sponge. I read it in *Good Housekeeping*.'

Poker-faced, Lia asked, 'In the dentist's waiting room?'

'Actually, yes. How on earth did you know? You use a knife first to make a shallow incision. Then you twist the thread around the cake, and it cuts right through.'

'Ingenious. So here's a plan. You sit down. Head forward. Perfect. Now Adam holds the ends of the thread, and I untangle them.' Having immobilised them both, she removed the clip in one efficient movement, unwound the thread and grinned at Adam. 'Problem solved.'

Darina was attempting to pull her wispy hair back into a bun. 'I don't know how I managed to make such a terrible mess of things. It seemed so simple.'

'No worries. D'you want a hand with your hair?'

'Oh, would you? I seem to have cheese on my hands. Mascarpone. It's for the filling.'

Lia pulled the hair into a knot and secured it with the claw clip. 'How's that?'

Darina shook her head. 'Good heavens, it's firm.'

'Back to the grindstone, then.' Lia flashed a dazzling smile at Adam. 'Didn't you say that sponge of yours would need twelve to fifteen minutes? Maybe you should take a look? I heard somewhere that there's nothing drier than dried-out Genoise.'

CHAPTER TEN

At the bookshop, Ann was upstairs, helping Angela shift the last of the old kitchen cabinets. Out in the yard, with his red woolly hat pulled down to keep his ears warm, Tintawn Terry was clearing space to use as a temporary dump. Catherine had opened the shop on the dot of ten a.m. and was explaining to a customer that she planned a specially exciting Christmas week. 'It's going to be really theatrical, with magical changes every day to support our festive events.'

'How d'you mean, exactly?'

With no idea how to answer, Catherine looked at him blankly. To her horror, she heard herself say archly, 'Ah, that's for me to know and you to find out.' Damn and blast Fury, she thought, I sound like an idiot. If he's cast me in a pantomime, he could at least have given me lines.

A woman with her hands on her hips was considering The Divil's tree, which seemed to quiver with canine energy. 'It's all very colourful, isn't it, with the curtains and the banners? Would you not decorate your Christmas tree, though?' Instantly, Fury emerged from behind the dust sheets. 'Mrs Sullivan! I haven't seen you for ages. How's the family?'

The woman beamed. 'We're grand, Fury. It's been a while, all right. You'll have to drop in for a drink over the Christmas. I was just saying to Catherine here that her tree's like a big fat fella with no clothes on.'

'Ah, that's because her Christmas events programme is linked in to a wider community project. The pensioners' group at the library is making decorations for it. The art crowd too. You'll have to come back for a look when they're up. They'll be massive.'

'Begod, I might.'

'There's fliers there with all the events listed. Would you take a few and give them around to your neighbours?'

'I will, of course.' Picking up a flier, Mrs Sullivan beamed at Fury. 'Ah, would you look at that! Carol singing on Christmas Eve! Would there be any mince pies getting gev out?'

'You can be sure of it.'

'I'll be back so. There's always a few things to pick up in town on a Christmas Eve, isn't there?'

'And no better thing than a book, Mrs Sullivan. We'll see you then.'

As the woman left with an armful of fliers, Catherine folded her arms and looked at Fury. 'Since when have my events been part of a wider community project?'

'Since I gave Hanna a call last night. The library's hopping with hand-made decorations. She has half of them stuck in the back with nowhere to hang them.'

'I can afford to buy a few baubles and chains, you know.'

'Why would you? It's pure waste. And this way they'll all come in to see their handiwork on display. If you can't sell them a book while they're here, you're not much of a shopkeeper. But look here to me, do you have e'er a plastic bath-cap in the house?'

'Mine's in the bathroom. Mum has one too. Wait, what do you want them for?'

'Prioritisation. The stuff back there landed mainly in the centre. Everything on the table underneath it has gone for its tea. So has the table itself, and the wire display yoke for your Christmas cards. You've got wet stuff in the middle and filth around the edges and, when we knock the rest of the ceiling, the dust will be massive. So we'll hoover the shelves back there first, and get plastic over them. If they're clean and sealed before we start bringing more crap down, the books that's on them can stay put.'

'You mean we've lost all the stock that was on the table?'

'That and all the cards you had on the yoke.'

This was a blow. The table, which was close to the children's corner, had displayed colouring books and jigsaws. The shelves in the rear part of the shop held all her classic titles and second-hand stock. Catherine thanked her lucky stars that at least her latest publications and Christmas bestsellers were unaffected. Then she blinked. 'Hang on a minute. You're going to cover the books in the back with *bath-caps*?'

'Don't be an eejit, woman. We're covering the shelving with plastic sheeting. Me and Terry are going in there masked-up and with industrial goggles. We'll need a couple of bath-caps on our heads.'

While Fury went in search of the bath-caps, Catherine called her distributor, chasing the order that had been held up in Customs.

'I don't want to pressure you, but I've a launch with the author of *Cakes To Come Home To* here tomorrow.'

'It looks like the pallet will be released today or tomorrow morning.'

'As late as tomorrow morning? My event's in the afternoon.'

'As soon as they're in with us, they'll be out with the courier.'

Knowing there was no more to be said, Catherine said thanks and rang off. She was teetering between hope and despair when a head appeared round the door.

'Hi. Hanna asked me to drop off some decorations.'

'Oh, hi. Yes, we've met before. You're Stephen Gallagher.'

Looking pleased, he came in, saying, 'I thought you might not remember me.'

'No, I do. Nice to see you again.'

'I suppose it's been a while. I used your website a lot during lockdowns. You're certainly making a great success here.'

'Yes, well, we struggle on.' Conscious of the soggy chaos only a few feet away, Catherine hastily changed the subject. 'It's kind of you to bring the decorations.'

'Not a problem. I pass your door on my way home.'

'I know. I mean, Hanna said. I mean she mentioned you live in Bridge House.' Catherine peered into the bin bag he'd set down by the counter. 'These are lovely. God knows when I'll get time to put them up, though. Business is booming today.'

'I imagine your music helps. I could hear it out on the street.'

An old CD player brought down from the flat was playing Christmas hits to drown the sound of the vacuum cleaners.

Catherine had already nudged the volume down, fearing a visit from her neighbours or even the guards, but Fury had popped out reprovingly, turned it back up and disappeared again behind the sheets. She smiled apologetically at Stephen. 'Is it too much?'

'Not at all. It's festive.' There was a pause in which he seemed to come to a decision. 'Look, I'm free for the rest of the day. I could do the tree for you.'

'That's awfully kind but I couldn't ask you to.'

'You didn't. I offered. Go on. Why not? I've a passable eye for symmetry, and I'm a sucker for woolly angels and glittery bells.' Standing back, he looked at the tree. 'It's a whopper, isn't it?'

Catherine nodded. 'It was a gift from Fury O'Shea. Do you know him? Oh, but of course you do. Hanna said he worked on your house.' For a moment Stephen's face seemed to close, and Catherine recalled that Hanna had also told her he'd lost his wife and was sensitive about gossip. But if that was the trouble, an apology was likely to make matters worse, so she smiled and added, 'I've never properly got to know my neighbours. Hanna had to explain to me who Fury is. I only met him the other day, when he offered me the tree.'

To her relief, Stephen relaxed and nodded. 'Yes, he worked on my house. So, look, what about it? Will I stick up the decorations?'

'Well, if you're sure.'

Instead of replying, he tipped out the bag's contents and began sorting them. The little angels, made of wisps of sheep's wool and white feathers, were girded with gold thread and crowned with halos. The bells were crimson felt dotted with green sequins, and the art group had used oat straw to make three-dimensional stars.

'Do you have a step-stool?'

'In the stock room. If you'll start with the bottom branches, I'll nip through and get it for you.'

'No problem. I'll get it myself. This way, is it?'

To Catherine's dismay, he lifted the edge of a dust sheet, then staggered away as The Divil came hurtling through from the back of the shop, barking ferociously and planting himself among the angels. He was followed by Fury, wearing Ann's bath-cap, with a mask dangling from one ear and goggles in his hand. Catherine had stepped forwards just as Stephen stepped backwards, and he'd landed heavily on her foot. She winced in pain and he grabbed her by the elbows. 'Are you okay?'

Fury roared at The Divil who abruptly stopped barking and slunk back between the dust sheets. 'Sorry about that. He's used to guarding sites. I tell him a quiet word would suffice but he pays no attention.'

Freeing herself from Stephen's grasp, Catherine rubbed her instep. 'I'm fine.'

'Right so.' Resuming his goggles, Fury announced he'd get back to his plastic sheeting. Left alone with Stephen again, Catherine pulled a face. 'As you've probably gathered, we've had a major disaster.'

'Yes, I spotted that when I moved the ingenious camouflage.'

'It's a nightmare.'

'You could try seeing it as an exciting challenge.'

Flexing her bruised foot, Catherine snapped, 'No I couldn't,' and immediately felt churlish. After all, he had offered to help, and might have been bitten for his trouble. He might also have taken offence at her reply, but he didn't seem to. Instead, he hunkered down and began to gather the scattered decorations.

In an hour or so, the hoovers' whine was replaced by the screeching of tape used to secure sheets of plastic. Terry had carried the step-stool through to the front of the shop for Stephen and, starting by positioning the glittering bells, Stephen was working his way upwards. The angels made sparkling white and gold accents among the dark branches, and the stars hung suspended by loops of crimson ribbon. Catherine watched the progress from behind the till, and several people who'd been in and gone off round the town to do shopping returned to see how he was getting on. Members of the art group began to appear, saying they happened to be passing and, seizing her opportunity, she sold them a couple of sci-fi books and the latest murder-mystery. Two hung around discussing the tree's paint-spattered backdrop, their voices clearly audible over 'Santa Baby' crooned by Eartha Kitt.

'It's so Jackson Pollock, isn't it?'

'But the colours are pure Mondrian.'

'Without the black.'

'Without the black, obviously. But this is a different approach.'

'Anyway, Mondrian's all about straight lines and sharp edges. Look at these fluid shapes, and the gorgeous contemporary swagger. I'm sure I know the artist's name. It's on the tip of my tongue. I think he's Swedish.'

Hastily, Catherine turned away to conceal a grin. Fury had told her the spattering came from fifty years of slapping paint on Finfarran's walls and ceilings. 'And isn't it grand the way the boil-wash got rid of the dirt and kept the colours? I'll tell you another thing. The brightest colours are the oldest. Begod, there's a philosophical thesis in that.'

At noon, Ann came to ask if Catherine would go out for sandwiches. 'Fury says double cheese and ham with pickle and mustard for him and Terry. Angela wants a salad box. I wouldn't mind a tuna and sweetcorn roll.' Looking up from the list in her hand, she gasped and exclaimed at the sight of the tree, which Stephen had just completed. Catherine introduced them. 'Mum, this is Stephen Gallagher. Hanna had spare decorations down at the library. Stephen was kind enough to bring them up and hang them for us.'

'That's amazing. Look, Angela says the Garden Café does the best salad boxes. If Stephen's free, why don't you take him there and buy him lunch, to say thank you?'

'Well – are you free, Stephen? Would you like to come?'

'I really don't need thanking. It was easy enough to drop by.'

'Yes, but look at the time you've spent making the tree look splendid.'

Ann held out the list. 'If it makes you feel better, since you'll be passing the shop on your way back, you can help Catherine carry this lot.'

Laughing, Stephen said, 'Yes, why not? I've worked up an appetite on those steps.'

They walked down Sheep Street and crossed to the traffic island on Broad Street, where a crib had been set up to collect for a charity that housed rough sleepers. As they waited for a gap in the traffic to cross the street to the nuns' garden, Catherine admired the unpainted wooden figures. St Joseph was a young man sitting by the manger, his arms clasped around his raised knees, his forehead resting on them, and at his feet a half-eaten loaf and his bag of carpenter's tools. The Virgin lay on her side with a blanket drawn over her body, one elbow bent and her head propped on her hand. Her hair, which fell over her face, was as delicately carved as the straw on which the swaddled Infant lay. Catherine looked at the tension in the young man's hands, and the exhausted droop of the girl's head. Only a couple of weeks later, she thought, they were asylum-seekers, running for Egypt ahead of Herod's pursuing soldiers. Feeling Stephen's eyes on her, she said, 'I haven't seen a crib like it, have you? It's touching. And I don't suppose they'd actually have been kneeling in adoration.'

'Not if she'd just given birth.'

'Do you have children?'

He shook his head. 'No. Never happened. I was a bit of a hot-shot in film distribution. Travelled a lot. My wife ran a boutique in Dublin with a friend. We had this idea that we'd work flat-out, take early retirement, and come here to live our dream.'

Catherine said, 'I'm sorry. When did she die?'

'A few years back. She had a stroke. There one minute, gone the next.'

A gap appeared in the traffic and they crossed to the nuns' garden, where crimson leaves made pools of colour along the perimeter walls. As they approached the café, Bríd emerged with a stack of platters topped with Perspex covers, and smiled as she passed. Though Catherine wasn't accustomed to putting personal questions to strangers, she paused on the steps, and asked Stephen, 'What was the dream? The one you and your wife had?'

His reply was so long in coming that she feared she'd been intrusive. Then he smiled. 'Oh, just being here. Settling in. Growing things. The garden behind Bridge House runs down to the river. Sophie, my wife, had plans to fill it with trees to attract the birds.' He opened the door and they went into the café. To her astonishment, Catherine found her eyes full of tears.

CHAPTER ELEVEN

When she arrived back at the shop a sign on the door read *Closed for Lunch,* so, hurrying down the side lane and into the yard, Catherine opened the back door and went up to the flat. The old kitchen cabinets had disappeared, the flatpacks of new ones were stacked in an orderly manner along the landing. In the living room, Ann and Angela were drinking tea.

'We've closed for lunch?'

'Health and safety.' Angela put down her mug, which said *Tintawn Terry's Tiles Take the Biscuit!* in red letters round the rim. 'Dad and Fury are just about to bring down the rest of the ceiling. There, you can hear them now.'

A series of crashes and bangs seemed to rock the building. Catherine froze. 'Dear God, what on earth are they doing?'

'Bashing it with a broomstick. It's the preferred method. When you give one loose bit a proper thump, the rest tends to follow.' Another crash produced what sounded like a landslide. 'And that'll be the hundred years' worth of dust that's been under your kitchen floorboards.' Angela looked at the carrier bag in Catherine's hand. 'Did you manage to get me a salad box? They sell out awfully quick.'

'What? Yes. Chickpea, coleslaw and beetroot leaves.'

'Fab.' Angela settled down with her salad, and Catherine handed Ann a tuna roll. 'They didn't have tuna with sweetcorn. I got it with scallions.'

'Perfect. Did you and Stephen have a nice lunch at the café?'

Sitting beside her, Catherine hissed, 'You *know* we never close the shop at lunchtime.'

'Love, there's no point in fighting it. Fury's right. We couldn't risk a customer getting hurt.'

Feet pattered on the landing and The Divil's whiskered face appeared round the door. Angela shook her head at him. 'Mine's a salad box. You wouldn't like it.' He came into the room and, having sneezed at Ann's scallions, curled up in a patch of wintry sunlight and fell asleep.

Ann smiled at Catherine. 'It's a good thing Angela brought her own mug. By this stage, most of ours are lined up, wanting washing. I've reserved all the water we've got for drinking. It's had to be turned off again. Apparently most of the joints in the kitchen were faulty.' Holding up the teapot, she asked, 'Will you have tea? It's still hot.'

'I suppose I might as well, if I can't get back to being a bookseller.'

'You can as soon as the ceiling's down. And don't panic. We've done brilliant business this morning, and lots of people have asked for fliers about the events.'

'I don't suppose Adam Rashid's books have come?'

Ann gave her a gentle push. 'Not yet, and fretting won't get them here any faster. Tell me about this Stephen Gallagher. He seems nice.'

Downstairs, Fury and Terry were covered in plaster dust. Their goggles had left dark circles on their chalk-white faces, and trickles of sweat were running down from their bath-caps to their masks. They were leaning on brooms, ankle-deep in debris, when the door opened and Angela said, 'God, you look like a couple of melting snowmen!' She peered upwards. 'Fair play, though, you got that down in jig-time.'

Terry said, 'It'll take a helluva lot longer to barrow it through to the yard. And longer still if people keep interrupting us.'

Fury removed his mask and looked at Angela. 'A courier knocked with boxes from some distributor up in Dublin. They're by the till.'

'Well, that'll cheer up Catherine. She's come back with the food.'

'Good timing.' Wiping the sweat from his face, Fury squared his shoulders. 'Now. Sandwiches. Then shovels. And tell the women above they can open their door and be selling books.'

Catherine was almost weak with relief when she cut open the box. The cookbook's smart cream cover featured a photo of a luscious chocolate cake topped with blackberries, and a black and white shot of Adam on the back. Ann took a copy from the plastic sleeve. 'Just imagine if these had arrived on time but we'd had to cancel the launch.'

'I don't want to imagine it. This is all too close for comfort.'

Ann put an arm around her. 'So far so good, though. And isn't the tree even better now that it's decorated?'

'Okay, it is. I love how it echoes the book-tree idea. Full marks to Fury.'

'And to Stephen.'

As Catherine began to unpack the books, she remembered the conversation in the café. They'd sat at a corner table with a view over the garden, and ordered the homemade soup of the day with brown bread. The soup was hot and the bread delicious and, to her own surprise, she'd relaxed. Stephen was easy company, quietly witty and well-read. When they chatted, she'd found that, like her, he'd spent time in Berlin for work.

'I used to go each year for the film festival. The first time I saw the Potsdamer Platz, I felt I'd really made it in the business.'

'Our head office was just around the corner, in one of those glass skyscrapers by some trendy architect. To begin with, visiting felt like the pinnacle of sophistication.'

'Then the gloss wears off and it's just a matter of packing and unpacking cases.'

'You just get tired of constantly travelling, don't you? Not that bookselling's a cushy number. If you own your own business, you're always stretched to breaking point.' Catherine had crumbled the bread on her plate. 'Which is why I snapped at you back there. I'm sorry.'

'Forget it. I made a stupid joke.'

'It's just a fallen ceiling. I don't know why I've let myself get so wound up.'

'Because the shop is your livelihood and, besides, someone could have got badly hurt.'

'We've a huge slate of events this week, so we're trying to press on without people knowing what's happened. Well, Hanna knows, but that's different.'

'When it comes to other people's business, Hanna's the soul of discretion. And I won't say a word.'

She'd summoned a smile and tried to change the subject. 'Sorry. I'm being boring. Tell me more about your work.'

'Not while you're sitting there looking freaked. Tell me what you're thinking about.'

She'd heard her voice wobble. 'Oh, God. I don't know where to start. Well, actually, I do. We've a huge celebrity book launch tomorrow. The press are coming. The publishers are sending someone from London. I've no idea what madness Fury's going to come up with next. And the bloody books for the launch haven't arrived.'

'What's the hold-up?'

'They're stuck on a pallet at Customs.'

'ETA?'

'They can't tell me. I'm waiting for a call.' Having been jerked back to the present, Catherine had reached for her bag. 'And I really ought to get back to the shop. Lunch is a busy time.'

'Your mum's holding the fort, isn't she?'

'Yes, but – oh, I don't know – I just need to be there. And don't tell me it won't make a damn bit of difference. I do know that.'

'If you ask me, that's the real trouble.'

'What is?'

'Your whole life suddenly seems out of your control.'

Normally, this analysis would have brought out the worst in Catherine. It was far too intimate from a comparative stranger, and much too close to the mark for comfort. Yet something about the quiet way Stephen said it had made her bite back an instinctive put-down. But the relaxed mood had been broken and her tension had returned. Remembering he was her guest, she'd offered coffee, but Stephen had shaken his head and said, 'Not for me. Let's get back.' When they'd left the café, he'd taken the bag containing the takeaway order, and carried it as they walked to the shop. It was the sort of gesture she'd always rejected from men she'd worked with or dated, feeling it put her at a disadvantage. Yet she hadn't argued and, looking back on it now, she couldn't think why.

Having unpacked the books, Catherine broke down the box and propped it where customers couldn't trip over it. Ann turned the sign on the door and, at the precise moment she did so, loud bursts of thumping and scraping began at the back of the shop. With a resigned groan, Catherine went to the CD player and turned the volume on Bing Crosby's 'Christmas Medley' to max. Plagued by the contradictory thoughts that were banging about in her head, she would have preferred to work in silence. But it was beginning to dawn on her that, for the sake of her sanity, she'd better get used to being out of her comfort zones.

When Stephen left Catherine at her door, he walked on up Sheep Street. Having reached the top, he went and stood on the bridge over the river, from where he could see a glimpse of his own back garden. Birches, with their silver bark and golden catkins, had delighted Sophie so, when they'd bought the house, he'd asked Fury to plant a sapling at the end of the garden as a surprise for her. On the day he'd driven from Dublin intending to put the house back on the market, a pair of finches had fluttered up from the sapling and flown to chirp on the boundary wall. Dry-eyed, he'd closed his hand around the tree's slender trunk, imagining Sophie's reaction if she'd lived to see it. It had hardly seemed possible then to stay and watch it grow without her.

Now, staring down at his garden, he remembered his reaction to Fury's uninvited intervention. As he'd driven back to Dublin with his mind in a whirl and his future in the balance, he'd felt half liberated and half enraged, emotions he now recognised in Catherine. It was no wonder she was edgy. Having erupted into her life without introduction, Fury had simply taken over. It was evidently what was needed, and she was lucky he'd been passing, but having had a shock, she was now coping with an invasion. Stephen wondered if his own effort to be friendly had made matters worse. Because, looked at objectively, hadn't he behaved exactly like Fury? To begin with he'd just walked in and taken over her Christmas tree, and then, in the café, he'd talked to her like an amateur agony aunt. Which was odd because, being prickly about his own privacy, he was always so careful not to encroach on other people's lives.

Still trying to make sense of his uncharacteristic behaviour, he walked home and let himself into his empty house. An envelope sealed with a Christmas sticker lay squarely on the mat, and he recognised the writing as Sophie's sister's. Taking the card from the envelope, Stephen read the note tucked inside, knowing before he opened it what it would say. Sophie hadn't been close to her family, and he had last seen them at the funeral, but since her death, they'd dutifully invited him for Christmas. Do think of coming up to Dublin to join us this year! You know we always cook far too much food, and you'd be more than welcome! Wincing, he screwed up the note and went to stand the card on the mantelpiece. The idea of being the ghost at their feast embarrassed him, and common sense suggested that they probably felt the same. Yet he couldn't find a way to end the annual awkwardness. There were friends to whom he could have dashed off a scrawled thanks-but-no-thanks, but this was Sophie's sister. So, each year, he struggled to word a polite refusal, when what he really wanted was to beg her to stop inviting him.

Alongside the cheerful snowman card there was another, from his godson, which also contained an invitation. *A skiing trip. What d'you reckon? Come and be one of the lads for Christmas.* The idea of being 'one of the lads' in his fifties had seemed grotesque to Stephen, so he'd written a sizeable cheque, and a card saying, *Have a drink on me,* and posted it thinking that snail-mail and cheque-writing dated him too. Standing back, he looked up at the cards, both so kind and so dreaded. The truth was, despite what he'd said to Catherine in the bookshop, he'd far sooner close his door on glittery bells and woolly angels, and hunker down until Christmas had gone away.

CHAPTER TWELVE

As lunchtime approached in the Lissbeg kitchen, Adam sprinkled a tea-towel with caster sugar and turned out his cake. Taking a sharp knife, he trimmed the sponge neatly and scored a line across one end. 'You fold it over the scored line to give yourself a start, then roll it up, using the tea-towel to help to push it along. Then, after you've set it aside to cool, you open it out to fill it.'

One of the ladies from Cork asked if it cracked when you rolled it up. 'I've seen that on a roulade. It makes a nice finish.'

Mary leaned over and poked her sharply in the ribs. 'If you think cracks make a nice finish, you must be cracked yourself. Anyway, that's with a flourless batter, not a Genoise.' Triumphantly, she turned to Adam. 'Am I right or am I wrong?'

'Cracks can be part of the charm, Mary.'

'God, you're as bad as she is. It'll look like a mess you wouldn't offer the cat.'

For a moment peace hung in the balance. Then Bríd arrived with her stack of platters and everyone jostled their way to the table for lunch.

The quality and freshness of the food she'd brought was remarkable, and Adam congratulated her when she returned to collect the platters. 'That was great. Phil tells me your suppliers are almost all local.'

Balancing the platters against her chest, Bríd nodded. 'My cousin Aideen and her husband grow for us on their farm. Some of their land is certified as organic. Lots of gardeners and farmers round here are going organic now.'

Adam looked at the pile of platters. 'Are you okay with that lot? Saoirse could help to carry them back to the café if you like.'

'Not at all. I'd better get back, though. I've left Aideen serving.'

'Well, thanks again. I'm really impressed.'

The afternoon session began with reminiscences about childhood Christmas cakes.

'I remember little plastic snowmen on rock-hard royal icing.'

'Oh, my God, royal icing. My mum used to fork it up into peaks to make snow.'

'It *was* rock-hard. By New Year's Day, you could hardly get a knife through it.'

'D'you remember the silver-paper holly that shops used to put on Swiss rolls? Like something you'd get stuck on the front of a cracker?'

'And the fringed frills people bought to go round Christmas cakes? Your mother would roll them up to use next year.'

'Did your mam make jars of mincemeat go further by adding chopped apples?'

'And nuts. We used to sit round the table chopping them.'

'D'you remember how fondant icing would never stick to marzipan? What was that about?'

Adam said, 'It's because you need to keep marzipan tacky while the fondant settles.'

The quiet couple laughed, and Kevin said, 'Karen's granny always used to brush marzipan with poitín. She told the kids it was holy water, to bless the Christmas cake.'

After the reminiscences, Adam finished his chocolate Swiss roll. 'I enjoy the drama of cutting through the plain, sugared sponge and finding a luscious filling inside. You can decorate the top, though. It's up to yourselves. And remember, Christmas baking is all about the subliminals.'

Saoirse said, 'How d'you mean?'

He reached again for the library book. 'The nuns kept bees for wax to make altar candles, and you'll find honey in lots of their recipes. That's the kind of subliminal you can tap into – honey suggests the scent of beeswax, and beeswax suggests candlelight. Even the golden colour of honey is festive, plus it's a really versatile sweetener.'

He could tell from the ripple of comments that he'd caught their imagination. With a sense of relief, he said, 'Okay, we'll finish up with tea and a slice of Swiss roll. If any of you want to share your own cakes, feel free to. There are boxes on your benches if you'd rather take them home.'

When the session was over, the group scattered, like kids let out of school. Accustomed to coping with larger and far more complicated courses, Adam's sense of relief had surprised him.

Still, this course felt unlike any other he'd given. There was a cheerful anarchy about the group that made every moment a challenge, and Lia's distracting presence didn't help. He could see her at her bench, packing things away neatly, and she left with a thumbs-up to Saoirse and a cheerful wave to the others. He'd half hoped she might want a lift back to Carrick but, apparently, she had plans of her own.

The weather had warmed up since the morning, so Lia strolled across the nuns' garden, wondering how to get to the nearest beach. Seeing Bríd sitting by the fountain with a takeaway coffee, she walked across intending to ask the way. 'Hi. You're Bríd, aren't you? That was a brilliant lunch you brought us.'

'What? Oh, thanks. Are you on the course?'

'Yep. I'm Lia. Do you know how far it is to a beach? I fancy a breath of fresh air.'

Bríd grinned. 'Me too. That's why I'm taking a break. Standing behind a counter is hell on the feet.'

'Tell me about it!'

'Are you in catering?'

Lia sat on the rim of the fountain. 'Nah, I'm just an amateur. I've been travelling round Europe doing bar work.'

'Cool. How long do you plan to stay in Ireland?'

'Till the new year. I'm spending Christmas in Dublin with a gang of mates from the pub.' Wrinkling her nose, Lia squinted upwards. 'Maybe the beach is a dumb idea. It'll be dark soon.'

'It's a good half-hour's walk from here. You'd be coming back by starlight.'

'I like stars. But, yeah, it's a dumb idea. Better to get up early some morning and find it before the course starts.'

'You've a few days of that to go, anyway.'

'Yeah, till Sunday. And then I'll be in Finfarran till Christmas Eve.'

Stretching her legs, Bríd drained the last of her coffee. 'So your mates are organising the Christmas dinner?'

Lia laughed. 'The organisation's down to Seán. He's a spreadsheet guy who likes things done his way, so the rest of us just stand back and give him his head.'

'He sounds gullible.'

'Well, he does get to lounge around on the day while we do the cooking and cleaning. So it's a fair deal.'

Bríd tipped her coffee grounds onto the gravel and said she'd better get back. 'Where are you staying while you're here?'

'In Carrick. Actually, if I run, I can probably get a lift there. Thanks for your help.'

'No problem. Enjoy the course.'

Having stuck his head into the office to tell Phil he was leaving, Adam had decided to return the book to Hanna. Hearing footsteps behind him on the path, he turned and saw Lia running after him.

'If you've brought your car today, could I blag a seat back to Carrick?'

Hardly able to believe his luck, he said, 'Sure. If you like. I'm just dropping this back to the library.'

'Okay. I'll tag along. It's an amazing book. I'm glad I've seen it.'

Inside, he introduced her to Hanna. Looking around, Lia said, 'I'm loving the glass wall.'

'Through there is our exhibition space and a gift shop. They're closed till the new year.'

Beyond the glass wall, low-lit in a darkened room, an open book stood on a lectern in a display case. Hanna said, 'It's a psalter. A medieval book of psalms, made in an abbey only a few miles from here.'

'Damn, I'll be gone in the new year. I'd love to have seen it.'

'Well, I don't see why you shouldn't. Come, and I'll give you a sneak peek.'

The psalter was about the size of a novel you'd buy in an airport. Hand-written, and bound in gilded leather, it lay in its case like an open jewel-box. Almost every inch of the double-page spread was crowded with trees painted with so much energy that they seemed to ripple and move across the vellum. Running between them like a stream was a single line of text. Lia bent to look, then glanced up at Hanna. 'It's in Latin. What does it mean?'

'"Then all the trees of the forest will sing for joy." It's from Psalm Ninety-six.'

Adam said, 'Look at the birds.'

They both leaned over the case and she saw that, within the green foliage, there were multicoloured birds touched with gold. Some had extended wings. Others had flowers spilling from their open beaks. Here and there the leaves, too, had been gilded. Nuts hung from hazels. Oaks spread canopies fringed with acorns. Slender birch trees grew among hollies, where blackbirds, almost invisible except for their bright eyes, perched among the spiky leaves. Hanna said, 'When those pages were painted, much of the peninsula would have been covered in dense forest. The psalmist was probably thinking about date palms and olive trees. The monks were just painting what they saw.'

Lia's nearness was distracting Adam but, to his relief, all her attention appeared to be on the book. At the top of one of the pages, a wren perched on an ash tree, its barred wings painted with precise brown and black brush strokes, and its beak open in song. Behind its head was a gilded halo outlined by concentric circles in rainbow colours, laid on in verdigris, ochre, azurite and vermilion. Lia's hair brushed Adam's cheek as she turned to look up at Hanna. 'Wow. Just wow. Thanks for showing us.'

'You're welcome.'

'Is all the woodland gone now?'

'There's still a few acres left.'

'And the trees there are direct descendants of the ones the monks painted?'

'Many of them. It's mind-blowing when you think of it, isn't it, Adam?' But Adam hadn't heard a word they were saying. The look on his face reminded Hanna of the first day she'd met him, a skinny, wary teenager uncertain of his welcome. Totally focused on Lia, whose gaze had returned to the book, he didn't notice that Hanna had caught his unguarded expression or see the fondness in her eyes when she said, 'You know what, Lia? You ought to ask Adam to take you for a walk in Fury's forest.'

In the car, Lia said, 'You really didn't know I was joking, did you? You thought I had no idea who you are.'

Adam, who had pulled himself together, grinned across at her. 'Yep. I'm an official celebrity eejit.'

'No, you're not. You're modest. I like that.'

'So, genuinely, where did you learn to make chocolate crème mousseline?'

'Genuinely in my dentist's waiting room. I'm assuming he leaves the magazines around to encourage high sugar consumption.' Returning his grin, she said, 'Today was a good day. I learned a lot.'

'So you'll stick with us instead of communing with the wild Atlantic?'

'I might get the wild Atlantic in too. And now I've got this forest on my bucket list as well.'

'You can always come back for another visit.'

'They say you should never retrace your steps. You have, though, haven't you? I mean, you've been here before. And you know Hanna.'

'I passed through once.'

'Sorry. I didn't mean to be nosy.'

'No. You're not. You weren't.'

But he'd sounded embarrassed so she said lightly, 'You're like me. A wanderer.'

'You just wander? No direction?'

'The world's a big place. Wherever you go, there's something.'

'Finfarran's special, though.'

'So special that you passed through and moved on?'

'You don't build a career like mine in Ireland.'

Looking at him shrewdly, Lia said, 'Okay. None of my business,' and, seeing the relief in his face, decided to change the subject. Rummaging in her bag, she produced a bar of chocolate.

'Fairly traded, sustainably grown, and 80 per cent this time, so guaranteed to blow your head off. Want a bit?'

'Haven't you had enough chocolate today?'

'Enough chocolate? Doesn't compute. Anyway, I didn't even taste my gorgeous cake.'

'What have you done with it?'

'Gave it to Saoirse. Apparently chocolate crème mousseline is her mum's favourite thing.' Licking her fingers, Lia cocked an eyebrow at him. 'I bet you don't know the origin of the word 'mousseline'.'

'I do, as it happens. It comes from the French for 'muslin'.'

'Damn, you're good.'

'Of course I am. I'm the Coolest Chef. I also know that the French word comes from the Italian for Mosul, a city in northern Iraq. I even know that monks in Mosul made manuscripts like the one in Hanna's library.'

'Show-off.'

'Actually, I picked up that last bit on Twitter.'

'I'm surprised you do your own tweeting. I thought all celebrities had People.'

'We do, but we're allowed to have lives as well.'

FRIDAY

20 DECEMBER

CHAPTER THIRTEEN

Saoirse had got home from her first day at Adam's course, dying to chat with her mum. But when she'd burst into the flat, Theresa had had her coat on. 'I'm sorry, pet, I'm off to a knit-and-natter.' Her dad had sat down and listened, and made all the right noises, but Saoirse had felt a bit deflated. Later, thinking they'd both looked tired, she'd set her alarm to wake early so she could give a hand at home before catching the bus to Lissbeg.

When she came down to breakfast, Theresa was eating toast at the kitchen table. Taking a piece, Saoirse asked how her evening had gone.

'What? Oh, the knit-and-natter. Fine.' Theresa spoke without looking up from her laptop. 'Actually, we've committee stuff to deal with, so I'll be out at another meeting tonight. Can you make an omelette for yourself and your dad this evening?'

'Sure. Is there anything I can help with before I go into Lissbeg?'

'Not a thing. You've enough to do with this job.'

Saoirse's face lit up. 'It's brilliant, Mum. I brought you a cake. It's a Genoise sponge. One of the people on the course made it. She heard me saying chocolate filling's your favourite, so she offered it to me when they were all going home. She's staying at a hotel in Carrick, so I suppose she didn't need it. I had some with Dad last night. Did he tell you we left the rest in a tin for you? Adam says they dry out if you put them in the fridge.'

Frowning at the screen, Theresa shook her head. 'Dad was asleep when I got in. That's lovely, though. I'll have a bit after lunch with a cup of coffee.'

'It's a chocolate crème mousseline filling.'

'Sounds gorgeous.'

It struck Saoirse that her dad must have gone to bed very early, if he'd been asleep when her mum had come in. When she'd gone to her own bedroom to post photos of cakes on Instagram, she'd left him in the living room, watching TV. But he hadn't seemed to be paying much attention. Maybe he'd been flaked out after a heavy day.

Since she was due at the course an hour before the participants, she hadn't expected to travel to Lissbeg with Mary. But as she was waiting at the bus stop, Mary bustled towards her. 'I'm off to the butcher's, Pat Fitz's in Broad Street. You know it yourself. It's opposite the horse trough. I'm in for an hour at the carols with her before I'm on to the cakes.' None of this made sense to Saoirse but, since Mary seldom stopped for breath, that didn't appear to matter.

'As soon as I knew I was booked on the course, I told the pensioners' group I'd be NA for carol rehearsals this week.'

'Not available?'

'That's it. You have all the jargon. I suppose you get it off the ethernet.' Mary patted the back of her hair. 'Of course, I've trodden the boards in Gilbert and Sullivan. Mind you, my voice has matured since Yum Yum. I'd call myself a contralto profundo now.'

Still baffled, Saoirse tried to look interested.

'Come here to me now, tell me, do you enjoy a Mikado yourself?'

'The biscuit?'

'No! Dear God, is there no music taught in the schools these days? The nuns had me in Pinafores when I was half your age.' The bus appeared in the distance and Mary waved her umbrella at it. Once on board, she followed Saoirse to the back seat, plumping herself down and talking all the way. 'The point is that the pensioners' group inside in the Convent Centre has been rehearsing carols since September. Pat Fitz and I have a solo verse in 'The Holly and the Ivy', and here am I messing about with balloon whisks when, by rights, I should be ironing out her vibrato. So I said to the group I'd nip into Lissbeg an hour early, and Pat and I would go at it steady above the butcher's shop.'

Adam was in the car, on his way to Lissbeg, when Dom called.

'Okay we need to beef up your bio.'

'Do we? Why?'

'Because what I've got here amounts to name, rank and serial number. What I need is something I can sell.'

'I thought you were selling the fact that I won the Coolest Chef title.'

'Means diddly-squat to guys in California, Adam. I need a story. Let's start with your childhood on the wrong side of the tracks.'

'I had a perfectly ordinary childhood on an estate in north Dublin.'

'But your dad was an immigrant, right? Tell me about his struggles.'

'Dad had a perfectly ordinary job as a hospital pharmacist.'

'You're not helping me, Adam. I'm looking for jeopardy. Drama. Talented kid with a burning ambition makes it alone, against all the odds.'

Adam felt a chill in the pit of his stomach. 'Sorry. It's just— Look, Dom, I'm driving. And I've got this book launch today.'

'In a titchy bookshop at the arse-end of nowhere. Oh, yeah, that's where your focus should be.'

Stung, Adam said, 'The *Coolest Chef* guys rate it. They're sending a social-media bod.'

'Yeah, I know. Gaby, the dippy intern. Six months out of college, and impossible to shake off.'

Adam knew this description wasn't too far from the truth. Gaby's dream was to get into film and her strategy was to hang on the arm of anyone who had.

The voice in his ear sharpened. 'There's nothing else going on over there that I ought to know about, is there?'

'What? No. What kind of thing?'

'You tell me.'

'Of course not.'

'Then send me something sexy and upbeat that I can pitch to the coast. And, Adam ...'

'Yes?'

'I want you psyched-up and focused by the time you get back to London. A deal like this needs a hundred per cent, and you'd better be ready to give it. Otherwise I'm wasting my time. And that's not something I do.'

The unmistakable edge to his voice made Adam feel sick. Swerving to get past a tractor that was dawdling on the road, he put his foot down hard and the car leaped ahead. You're an idiot, he told himself. You've come so far from nothing, less than nothing. Dom took you on because you had potential, but lots of people have that, and he could drop you in a heartbeat. You've got to stop thinking about Lia, who isn't available anyway. You've got to concentrate on your career.

When Saoirse arrived, Phil was in the office. 'Oh, good, you're here. We've a press call today and I'm run ragged. Will you be okay to set up on your own?'

'I'll be fine.'

'I have twelve photographers pinned down already, and I'm pretty sure we're going to get *Nationwide*.'

'Wow. National telly. Will they be filming in the kitchen?'

'They will if I have any say in the matter.' Phil tapped the desk. 'Don't go talking about any of this, do you hear me? It's all under wraps until I make the announcement.'

'Okay.'

Saoirse went round the benches, setting out ingredients for the spiced apple and hazelnut cake, along with a steel nutcracker etched with the *Coolest Chef* logo. The quiet couple arrived and admired it. 'It's exciting to be given a little present every day.

Though Mary's right and we've paid for them, really, haven't we?'

'Actually, the giveaways are limited edition. You can't buy them anywhere. You have to go on a course to get them.'

Lia had strolled in and was putting her coat on the rack. '*The Coolest Chef* ought to have you on the payroll, Saoirse.'

Embarrassed, Saoirse said, 'It's just that I happen to be a fan. I mean I follow Adam – well, the *Coolest Chef* thing – on socials.'

'Don't get me wrong. I think they'd be lucky to get you. How did your mum like the cake?'

'Mum was out last night. I had some with my dad. She's going to have a piece today. Dad and I loved it. Mum wasn't in. I told her this morning. I'd say she's going to love it.' Realising she was gabbling, Saoirse wondered why. It was something that happened when she was stressed or nervous, but why should she feel stressed now? Maybe, she thought, I'm nervous about photographers turning up. I'm part of the team: what if I have to say something for the telly? What if I look all shiny-faced and shite?

Excusing herself, she went to the loo to check her mascara, and decided she'd better put on some more. Scrabbling in her bag for her make-up purse, she had a moment of panic when she couldn't find it. Then her fingers touched the drawstring pouch that contained her worry dolls. Make-up forgotten, she pulled out the pouch and stood holding it tightly, feeling the panic that had gripped her subside. Then, afraid someone might come in and find her, she backed into a cubicle, locked the door, sat on the lid of a loo, and tipped the knitted dolls onto her lap.

There were two of them, made years ago by her mum for her Christmas stocking, and for ages they'd just hung about in a drawer. Saoirse had found them again when packing to move to Garrybawn House and, stressed out by that, and then by the weirdness of the pandemic, had begun to toss them from hand to hand whenever she felt bad. It had bothered her mum but her dad had said, 'Leave her at it. It'll do her no harm, and these are strange times.' Then everything had got better and felt ordinary again so, for more than a year, she'd forgotten them. But, apparently, they still had the power to ward off panic. Tucking them into the little pouch her mum had made for them, Saoirse pushed it deep into her bag, and returned to the kitchen feeling glad they were there.

Most of the group had arrived by the time Adam joined them. It felt less like the first day at school, and they'd got to know each other, so everyone was cheerful and relaxed. Mary was the last to appear, sweeping through the double doors and saying she hoped she hadn't kept them waiting. Adam called, 'We're just about to have coffee. Come and sit down and catch your breath.'

'There's nothing wrong with my breath-control. You should have heard me up in the butcher's doing extended Glorias.' Catching sight of the nutcrackers, Mary planted her hands on her hips. 'I sincerely hope you're not expecting me to use of one them things. "Thirty grams of skin-on hazelnuts, halved", it says in the recipe, and a hundred and twenty more, chopped, for the batter. There's nothing about having to crack them ourselves.'

Mr Maguire said thirty grams was about twenty-five nuts.

'That's what I mean. It's a hell of a lot of cracking, and some of us haven't the wrist-action we had.'

Adam gave her his professional smile. 'Don't worry. You'll find the hazelnuts on your benches are shelled. The nutcrackers are just a memento of today's recipe.'

Sniffing, Mary muttered, 'Neither use nor ornament.'

Adam decided it was time to move on. 'Okay, everyone, let's sit down and talk it through. What we're looking at is a sticky, delicious upside-down cake, and the recipe isn't precise because, unlike yesterday's Genoise, it gives scope to the instinctive baker.'

Mr Maguire pursed his lips. 'Not very Cordon Bleu.'

'No. But fun to make. Today's the day you get a chance to express your personalities.'

Edging past Adam with a coffee, Lia murmured, 'And that's *so* important. Especially for an introvert like Mary.'

In the library, Hanna looked up as Phil came in. 'You're not really supposed to use mobile phones in here.'

Phil ended a call. 'Sorry, that was Joe from the *Inquirer*. Honestly, he's more demanding than the nationals. He's had an exclusive Q&A, and now he's wanting photos.'

'Sounds like you've got a big day ahead.'

'I've the whole waterfront covered, girl. You name it. Come here to me, would you be free for a quick photo-op yourself?'

'Me?'

'Say, you and Adam in the garden holding the nuns' recipe book. *Get Gardening and Get That Festive Flab Off.* That sort of thing.'

'I'm not sure I'm dressed for a photo.'

'Ah, no one's going to look at you when they can be looking at Adam.'

As Phil left, Stephen emerged from the reading room. Hanna grinned at him and said, 'I don't suppose you'd like to take my place in a photo-op.'

'Certainly not. You're the librarian, I'm just a lowly volunteer.' Coming to the desk, he picked up one of Catherine's fliers. 'Are you going to the book launch this evening?'

'My mother is, and I'll be there to give her a lift home. I imagine she'll be hoping for a photo-op herself.'

'I thought I'd go along. I'd like to support Catherine.' Catching Hanna's eye, he blushed. 'It's just that it's a big thing for the bookshop. I doubt if she'll even notice me in the crowd.'

At Lissbeg Books, Catherine positioned a copy of *Cakes To Come Home To* at the foot of the book tree in the window. Ann gave a thumbs-up from the pavement, and came back into the shop. Catherine turned to Fury. 'You're sure we're going to be okay for the book launch?'

'I've got the perfect scenario in mind.'

'At this stage, I'd settle for a pen and a table.'

'Ah, have sense. There's a press call up at the course today. There'll be telly, as well as papers, and Phil says she'll shunt them down here later. And what about this social-media person coming from London? We'll need something to knock the sight out of their eyes.' Producing a piece of paper, he said, 'So. Time management. I'm telling you up front that it's going to be brutal.' Taking a stance with his back to the tree, he stabbed his finger at Catherine. 'You'll be out here in front, building tension.'

'How, exactly?'

'Give them a countdown. Make a big thing about exclusivity. Tell them they can't have Rashid's book till he's here to sign them himself.'

'Okay. We can do that.'

'I'll be out in the yard, being creative. Phil has a folding platform she'll lend us, so Terry's got to whip out to collect it. The rest of the time he'll be here, shovelling shit like a blue-arsed fly.' Fury removed his glasses. 'So that's it. Everything looking calm and serene, with normal trade going on, until four thirty. Then we close the shop, black out the window and lash into the transformation. Which is going to take every one of us working like an oiled machine.'

As he spoke, Catherine's phone buzzed on the counter. She went to read the text, then looked at him apprehensively.

'For feck's sake, what's happened now?'

'The girl over from London has just checked in at the Royal Victoria. She wants me and Mum there for a briefing meeting.'

For a moment there was silent consternation. Then Fury shouted, 'It's like trying to get sheep through a bloody gap!'

CHAPTER FOURTEEN

Adam smiled at his expectant bakers. 'First up, you're going to prepare your apples. Dessert apples, okay? Not cookers. Everyone know why?'

The square woman, whose name was Janice, ventured, 'Cookers don't hold their shape?'

'Spot on. The fruit in an upside-down cake needs to stay firm.'

They got started with only a brief disaster, when Darina knocked over a bowl of water. She hovered while Saoirse mopped up. 'I'm so sorry. I think I must have jogged my own elbow. Thank goodness the recipe sheet is laminated.' Saoirse refilled the bowl and Darina eyed it nervously. 'Oh dear. But I do need it, don't I? To stop the sliced apples getting discoloured while I'm faffing about.'

'You ought to be okay. I haven't filled it to the top.'

'I suppose I over-filled it the first time. I've always gone at things like a bull at a gate.'

Phil came in when they were greasing cake tins. 'We're having a press call after lunch. If any of you objects to appearing on TV or in the papers, please say so. I've release forms here for the rest of you to sign.'

Seeing unrest, Adam intervened: 'I'm autographing copies of my new cookbook in Lissbeg today, and that sort of thing always produces a bit of publicity. But I'll be the one who has to pose for photographs, not you, so don't worry.'

Mary snorted. 'I hope you won't be taking your eye off my Upside-down Surprise Cake while you're running around pushing your book.'

Phil said, 'Honestly, Mary! That's offensive.'

'I speak as I find. And, incidentally, I've never found myself surprised by an apple.'

Mr Maguire said that if he was expected to sign a release form, there really ought to be an appearance fee. 'I don't mean to suggest I'd want payment, but nor do I want my methods on show for all to see.'

Declan asked, 'What *are* you suggesting, then?'

'It's not for me to make a suggestion.'

'You did make a suggestion. You said there should be a fee. That's bonkers. It's Adam's methods we're learning, not yours. Anyway, yours are woeful. You've no flair.'

'At least I don't apply buttercream as if plastering a wall.'

Adam caught Lia's eye and she struggled to keep a straight face. As Phil disappeared, he clapped his hands for attention. 'Okay. Ovens preheated. Cake tins greased and lined. Next, combine your sugar and cornflour in your small bowl, and scatter the mixture over the base of your tin.'

Darina looked apprehensively at her food processor. 'And we whizz our nuts?'

'Not yet. You'll whizz the hundred and twenty grams when it comes to making your batter. What you're making now is the topping.'

'Gosh, yes, sorry. I'm useless at concepts.'

'Just take it gently, and you'll be fine. Layer up your apples and halved hazelnuts on top of your sugar and cornflour. Remember, your bottom layer will end up as the top of your cake, so make the effect as attractive as you can.'

Ultimately, Darina's cake became a group effort. Janice helped to arrange her apple slices, and Declan took over her food processor, which she'd somehow managed to stall. Adam watched from the far side of the kitchen as Lia, who'd opened the oven door, guided the tin onto the right rack. He remembered the touch of her hair as it brushed his cheek in the library and the sidelong look she'd given him earlier, when she'd slipped by with her coffee. On the drive back to Carrick the previous night, he'd planned to ask if she'd like to have dinner with him, telling himself it made sense as they were staying at the same hotel. But when they got in, she'd said, 'Got to rush, I've a WhatsApp call. See you.' So sure she was upstairs WhatsApping with her boyfriend, he'd eaten alone and gone to bed feeling depressed.

Now, though the sight of her still made his heart turn over, his mind was wrestling with the conversation he'd had with Dom. When he'd gained the *Coolest Chef* title, he'd been elated, and the fact that he'd won on a public vote had made him feel his philosophy as a chef had been endorsed. So Dom's dismissive tone on the call had shocked him. He'd accepted that celebrity would bring levels of intrusion, but this morning's conversation had taken things way off the scale. He hadn't expected to find his life treated as a commodity, although, looking back, he could see there'd been signs he'd failed to read at the start. And the stupid thing was it was so unlike him to have made the basic mistake of not watching his back.

While the cakes were baking and they were having coffee, Declan asked about Adam's book. 'What gave you the idea for it?'

Usually, Adam replied to this by quoting the blurb on the cover, which oozed nostalgia and had been written by the *Coolest Chef* team. Now he found himself trying to give his own explanation. 'It's sort of a call to arms. Rediscovery can be empowering. It leads to re-evaluation. The thing is that, in a world based on consumerism, we're told that what we've already got is worthless. We're primed to buy into the struggle to gain something bigger and better. But looking at new ways of approaching old favourites can demonstrate that we don't need to build our lives on that struggle. We can love, cherish and take immense pleasure in what we've got.'

For a moment no one spoke, and he wished he'd stuck to the blurb and not taken the risk of sounding foolish. Then there was a ripple of animated conversation, and new energy seemed to fill the room. Feeling it, Adam looked round and realised he'd just articulated what he'd never been able to say to Dom. With a course to teach, he had no time to examine this realisation but, to his surprise, he found that he, too, felt weirdly re-energised, and even empowered.

After lunch, when the press arrived, Darina was in despair about her apron. 'It was so beautifully laundered when I got here this morning. Why can I never remember to use a tea-towel to wipe my hands?' Chivvying her hastily into the background, Phil took hold of Adam. He was posed in the kitchen, outside the kitchen, in the garden with Hanna, at a bench with the group, and alone beside the Christmas tree, which Phil had set up by the kitchen door.

To everyone's delight he was interviewed for *Nationwide*, which involved lights, a camera on a tripod, and someone darting in to dab his brow and fix his hair. Then silence was demanded by the local radio station's afternoon programme *Craic with Caitríona*, and they all held their breath while the host asked, 'So Ballybunion or the Bahamas, Adam? Scared to commit?'

In the yard behind the bookshop, Fury had knocked up a huge frame out of lengths of 3x1 timber. When Ann arrived with tea, he was using a glue gun to make a collage of the posters that had come with Adam's books. 'Gosh, don't those look good, all fanned out round the single one in the centre.'

Fury laid the collage face down on the back of his finished frame. 'Perfect fit. I'll glue it down and slap gilding on the timber.'

'What's it for?'

'Name of God, will you stop standing round asking questions? The afternoon's half gone. Get back in and see if Bríd's here yet.'

Bríd had arrived on foot with a large box of cupcakes, each decorated with the book's cover image. She was fending off The Divil with one hand as Ann came in. 'My car's conked out and there's another four trays of these.'

From behind the dust sheets, Angela shouted, 'Dad's taken his van to pick up the folding platform from Phil. Fury's is in the lane, though. You could drive them up in that.'

'I don't have a licence.'

'But, I do.'

They all swung round and saw Lia in the doorway, wearing an apologetic grin. 'Sorry, I don't mean to stick my nose in. I can drive a van if you're in a bind.' Bending down, she scratched the fur behind The Divil's ears. 'I'm just killing time before your event this evening. Happy to help if you need a hand.'

Fury rolled his eyes when Bríd introduced him to Lia. 'Christ, if it's not one thing it's another. Right, I'll give my broker a call and get you on my insurance for the day. Chuck me your details, girl, and get a move on. I've got ten posts to knock up yet, and yards of rope to paint.'

The van's cab smelt of linseed oil, sawdust and Silvermints. Fastening her seatbelt, Bríd asked, 'Are you sure you can drive this?'

'Course I can. It's titchy compared to what I've driven in Oz.' Lia put the van into gear and it bucked like a horse. 'O-*kay*. This old lady seems to have personality. Any chance of avoiding main roads?'

'You'll have to get round Broad Street.'

'Oh, well. Fortune favours the brave.'

At the café, she helped Bríd load the trays into the van. 'So you own the café?'

'Me and my cousin Aideen began with a deli on Broad Street. After a while, we started doing sandwiches for the café. Then we took it over. The timing wasn't great. I'd sooner have waited before expanding. But it was on the market and, sure, you have to go with the flow.'

'See, that's my philosophy too.'

'Makes for a helluva lot of hard work.'

'And excitement.'

Bríd checked to make sure the trays wouldn't move if the van started kicking. 'There's times I could do without the excitement. I'm catering another thing at the weekend. Plus I've promised mince pies for Catherine's carol concert on Tuesday.'

'That's some schedule.'

'I know. I'm a fool to myself, but we need the income. Mind you, the carols in the bookshop on Christmas Eve are a charity thing.' Bríd's phone suddenly gave a call like a cockerel. 'Shit, sorry, I keep meaning to change that ringtone.' She leaned against the cab to take the call. 'Give us a chance, Fury, we've only been gone ten minutes. We've just got the trays loaded. We're on our way.'

In the background, she could hear The Divil yelping. Fury's voice in her ear shouted, 'No! Hold your horses!'

'What?'

'I need you to stay where you are.'

'I thought we were working to a schedule.'

'Get off the phone. Ring Phil. Tell her to call Adam Rashid.'

'What?'

'Tell Phil to tell Adam to come and find you at the café.'

'Why?'

'I need to measure his seated height for me set-up, and there's people outside the shop door already.'

'Can't he go in the back?'

'He can't be seen arriving, people would probably stampede. Get him to meet you at the café. Throw a blanket over his head, stick him into the back of the van and drive like the clappers.'

'Throw a blanket over his head?'

'There's one in the cab. The Divil likes it when he fancies a picnic.'

'You want me to bundle Adam Rashid into your van with a load of cupcakes?'

'Actually, forget the blanket at your end. Just chuck it over his head when you're running him into the shop from the back lane.'

The phone went dead and Bríd looked at Lia. 'Did you get that?'

'Sounds like a plan.'

'Seriously?'

With a wicked grin, Lia said, 'Absolutely. Adam Rashid's the kind of guy who loves to go with the flow.'

CHAPTER FIFTEEN

Customers were buying books to the sound of 'Joy To The World'. Behind the dust sheets, Angela and Terry trundled barrows at speed along wobbling duckboards. The wine had arrived and Ann was in the office, polishing glasses. The Divil and Fury were out in the yard doing something complicated. Gift-wrapping the book she'd just sold, Catherine handed it across the counter. 'I hope you'll join us later and raise a glass at Adam Rashid's book launch. We're going to be closing shortly to get it set up.'

The woman she'd handed it to beamed. 'I will, of course. I heard him talking earlier on the radio. He wasn't giving much away about Ballybunion, was he? Would you say he has a secret bolthole there?'

Several people in the queue had come to the same conclusion, though one was convinced it was a double bluff. 'That's what my sister says. It's an old celebrity trick.'

'So you reckon he's going to be spending Christmas out in the Bahamas?'

'I wouldn't waste me time on speculation. That's a grand book he's written, though, fair play to him. I love the big cake on the cover.'

'I hear the news is coming to the book launch, and we'll all see ourselves on telly before the night's out.'

'No!'

'That's what everyone's saying.'

When Catherine was free Stephen, who'd been browsing the bookshelves, came to the till. 'So, I hear the news is coming to the book launch?'

'Oh, don't! I've no idea who'll be here or what Fury's doing out the back. According to Mum, he's made a huge gilded frame. Have you come in for a book? Can I help you to find something?'

'Actually, I just thought I'd drop in and see how you're doing. I can go if I'm in the way.'

'No, don't. it's nice to see you.'

For a moment he looked awkward. 'I thought maybe I'd been a bit pushy at the café.'

'Of course not.' To Catherine's surprise, she felt herself blushing. 'Actually, we're doing okay at the moment. Bit of a panic this morning when this social-media person from London demanded a meeting in Carrick. Fury dealt with her, though.'

'How?'

'Grabbed my phone and told her she ought to be at the Convent Centre press call, not calling her own meetings in Carrick. She wilted and said she'd come here for the set-up. I just hope to God that when she arrives she doesn't get under his feet.'

Gaby turned up at four thirty and immediately dashed Catherine's hopes. 'Is this where we're having the book launch?

Because I'm supposed to be live-streaming zhuzh and glamour and, sorry, this place is definitely blah.'

There was a low growl as The Divil's hackles rose slowly, and Catherine saw Fury was looking fit to be tied. She was trying to decide which to restrain, when Stephen appeared at her side. Catherine, who'd thought he'd gone, was surprised when he gripped Gaby's hand and shook it warmly. 'Stephen Gallagher. I have to congratulate you. Your marketing strategy's right on point.'

His air of assurance clearly made Gaby feel she ought to know who he was. At a loss, she said, 'Er, thanks, but it's not *my* strategy, really.'

'Ah, but you implement it, don't you? It's the doers that make the difference, as George Lucas used to say.'

Gaby's eyes widened. 'You know George Lucas?'

'Our paths have crossed.'

The Divil's growling had risen several octaves so, inspired by Stephen's diversion, Catherine took charge. 'I'm taking Mr Gallagher out for tea. Will you join us?'

Gaby wavered. 'Well, I ought to be here to make sure the settings are what I'll need.'

Seeing the look on Fury's face, Catherine took her by the arm. 'Don't worry. My technical director has it covered. Come and let Stephen tell us about his experience of *Star Wars*. Did you know that one of its scenes was nearly shot here in Finfarran?'

Adam had just got out of the shower when a text came through from Phil. *Need to talk. Urgent. Pls respond.* He called her number. 'I'm getting ready for the launch. What's the problem?'

'Fury says you've got to go in undercover.'

'Go in where?'

'To the bookshop.'

'Why on earth? Wait, who's Fury?'

'Bríd says Lia says you're not to argue.'

'What's this got to do with Lia?'

'You're to meet them ASAP at the Garden Café.'

When he got to the café, Bríd and Lia were sitting in the van. Lia rolled down the window. 'Hi. You took your time.'

'What *is* this?'

'Proper celebrity stuff. We're your handlers.'

Bríd scooted round to the back of the van. 'People are gathering outside the shop. Fury says we need to take you in around the rear.'

'Who the hell is Fury?'

Opening the van door, Bríd said, 'Can you hang on to the cupcakes? This is all taking longer than Fury scheduled, so Lia's going to have to step on the gas.'

There was no one in the lane behind the bookshop, so Adam was spared the blanket over his head. As Lia and Bríd led him through the back and towards the dust sheets, Terry and Angela were still trundling barrows. At the front of the shop, with the door locked, Fury was erecting the folding platform, a dais about six inches high. Lia introduced Adam. 'Adam Rashid, meet Fury O'Shea. And this is The Divil who, I gather, is his business associate.'

The Divil gave a cordial yelp and Fury glared at Lia. 'I haven't gathered who you are, and I hope, for your sake, you haven't fecked up my van.'

'She's better than when you gave her to me. I tightened the battery cover while we were hanging round at the café.'

Adam looked back at the chaos behind them and asked, 'Shit, was that a leak?'

Shooting him an appraising look, Fury said, 'Well, you're not blind or stupid.'

In the tense moment that followed, The Divil looked from one to the other, uncertain of what was going to happen next. Then, giving Fury a level stare, Adam said, 'Well-spotted. I'm neither blind nor stupid and, if you tell me what's going on, you might even find I can be helpful.'

Five minutes later, assisted by Adam, Fury had moved The Divil's tree aside, to where one of the banners had stood. He gave the banner to Ann, with instructions to place it on the pavement to mark the top of the queue that was forming outside. 'When that's done, you and Bríd can start on the food and drinks table. The posts for my walkway are still outside drying. Angela's painting the last of the ropes. She'll bring them through ASAP.' As Ann disappeared, he swung round to the others. 'Lia, feck out to the yard and get my hammer. Adam, give me a hand with this frame.'

Adam had shed his parka and rolled up the sleeves of his sweater. 'I'll need ten minutes to change and brush up before you let in the crowd.'

'I'll want you up a ladder first. It's a good thing you had the sense not to arrive in your party frock.'

'I didn't have time to put it on when I got your summons. I just stuffed my things in a carrier bag. They'll probably need an iron.'

'No problem, boy. The women above will have an iron, and Terry's off the barrow in twenty minutes. He'll run over your things like a shot.'

It was almost dark when Catherine, Stephen and Gaby left the teashop. The scarlet banner stood outside the bookshop, its gold lettering caught by the light of a streetlight. A queue of people stretched halfway down the pavement. The black-out had been removed and, between the line of excited figures, Catherine could see the star on her book tree gleaming in the window. As they approached the shop, she sent a text to Fury and, at the moment they reached the door, it opened to let them in. Catherine heard the queue groan cheerfully as the door shut behind her. Then she gasped in astonishment at the transformation.

Dead centre, in front of the dust-sheet backdrop, a table and chair for Adam stood on the borrowed dais. Glasses gleamed on the drinks table, and tealights twinkled along the shelving. Lit by a couple of angled desk lamps, the dais was flanked on one side by the second Lissbeg Books banner. On the other side was The Divil's tree, which had acquired new decorations: little painted ceramic cakes with sprigs of holly on top. The counter was piled with copies of Cakes To Come Home To, and a series of golden waist-high posts linked by scarlet rope created a walkway past the till, round to the dais and, eventually, to the food and drink. The collage of posters hung directly behind the dais, its gilded frame backed by the vibrant colours on the dust sheets, looking like a million dollars. Cool and unruffled in a suit and impeccably pressed shirt, Adam appeared from behind the dust sheets and sat down on the chair. Fury, who looked dishevelled as ever, chortled. 'Begod, we got it spot on, boy. Your head comes to just below the big cake in the centre of the collage.' Turning to Gaby, he asked, 'Right. Is this enough zhuzh for you? Or would you like him wearing a happening hat?'

Gaby was open-mouthed. 'Oh. My. God. It's like the set for a Hollywood premiere.'

Catherine said gravely, 'That's down to our technical director.'

'Can I meet him? Could we talk on my livestream?'

Fury looked at her blandly. 'Now, isn't that a shame? You've missed him. He's on a plane to New York as we speak.'

'No!'

'He just squeezed us in as a bit of a favour. He'll be flying on to LA in a few hours' time.'

'Can you tell me his name?'

'God, no. He wouldn't want it streamed around the gigaverse. There's a lot of stuff happens hereabouts that we like to keep under wraps.'

Gaby's eyes were round as saucers. 'I know. I heard. Catherine says it's a well-kept industry secret that George Lucas uses Finfarran as a location all the time. I mean, that's, like, unbelievably cool.'

'Unbelievable's the word for it. And don't go round spreading the story. If you do, it won't be hard to trace the leak.'

The queue surged in, preceded by Phil and the press. Before joining Ann at the till, Catherine stood on the dais, introduced

Adam, and said how excited they were to be hosting the Irish launch of his book. Adam gave a brief, charming speech and smiled for a barrage of cameras while Stephen made urbane conversation with the journalists. Saoirse poured wine and Bríd handed out cupcakes on gold paper plates. Clutching copies of *Cakes To Come Home To*, a line of people began to move past the till and along the walkway towards Adam. The room buzzed with excitement as he smiled and wrote dedications, personalising Christmas gifts or signing for fans, who gasped in delight when he cheerfully posed for selfies or listened to their descriptions of baking triumphs and disasters.

Though Fury's set-up had been designed to showcase Adam's cookbook, the walkway led past shelves of new bestsellers and Christmas classics, tempting most people to pick up books they hadn't come in for but found they couldn't resist. Beaming with relief and rushed off their feet, Catherine and Ann watched their takings soar beyond their wildest expectations. The excitement rose, journalists thrust microphones under people's noses and over by the tree Gaby, whose eyes were still like saucers, was livestreaming an interview with The Divil. 'So I'm here with the Coolest Chef in the coolest venue in Ireland, secret hideout of the stars, and home to this great little guy who's called The Divil. I mean, that is really cool, right? Say hi to the world, Divil.' The Divil barked obligingly and sat down on his tail. 'Isn't he the cutest? As you can see, the place is jumping and, as you'd expect for the Coolest Chef, we've got a fantastic mix of cool people. There's Fury O'Shea, who's a big local celebrity. I don't know what he's into, and he's told me I mustn't ask! I can see Stephen Gallagher, the mover and shaker in Hollywood films. And here's a lady who's just bought a book, on her way to have it signed. Hi there! Would you call yourself an Adam Rashid fangirl?'

Mary Casey looked her up and down and said, 'I would not.'

'Oh. Okay. Have you bought your book as a Christmas gift for your daughter?'

'My daughter's a senior librarian. She'd have no use for books.'

'I bet you bake great cakes, though.'

'I was liquidated lately. I don't be in my kitchen much.'

Having done with Gaby, Mary stepped sideways and surged ahead with her elbows out. A man said, 'Hey, take your turn,' and she glared at him majestically. 'I've no interest in queue-jumping, if that's what you're implying. Nor would I be part of this queue at all if I hadn't been funnelled into it unbeknownst.'

'Well, can't you hold your hour? We'll be through soon enough.'

'I can not.' Mary elbowed her way through to the drinks table, where a small woman had just accepted a glass of wine from Saoirse. Snatching it from her, she said, 'Dear God, Pat Fitz, are you out of your mind? D'you not know what cheap German wine can do to your vocal folds?'

Incensed, Saoirse said, 'It isn't German. It's Italian. And I bet it's not cheap.'

'I don't care where it's from. She shouldn't be drinking before she sings.'

Pat said mildly that she wouldn't be singing till Christmas Eve.

'Isn't that what I'm saying? If you're singing on Tuesday, you shouldn't be drinking on Friday. You want a full week's detox before attempting them Glorias.'

Winking at Saoirse, Pat said, 'Isn't that unfortunate? Because only last night I had a grand hot whiskey for my chest.'

'I've made no dint at all in your vibrato. Would you not try a bit of self-help and give yourself a fighting chance?'

Approaching the till, Stephen picked up three copies of *Cakes To Come Home To*. As Ann rang them up, she said, 'My goodness! You must know lots of home bakers.'

With no sign of the urbane manner he'd used with the journalists, Stephen stammered, 'Not really. Well, yes, I do. These are Christmas presents. Signed books always go down well, don't you think?'

'Of course they do.'

The queue behind Stephen was pushing, which gave him an excuse to move on. But, watching him leave the counter, Ann saw a shy look pass between him and Catherine and, turning to attend to her next customer, bent her head to conceal a delighted smile.

CHAPTER SIXTEEN

The stars were out by the time Adam left the bookshop, and he walked down Sheep Street feeling frost on the wind. He was bone tired. Reaching the car park, he dumped the bag containing his sweater and jeans on the back seat. Then, pulling out onto Broad Street, he saw Lia standing at the bus stop, intent on her phone. Sure she was texting with Seán, Adam nearly drove by. But it seemed mean to leave her there in the cold, so he lowered the window. 'Fancy a lift?'

'You bet.' Sliding into the passenger seat, she pushed her phone into her pocket. 'You're topping the trends across the socials. No. Correction. The Divil's beating you by a nose.'

'Let's hope my agent isn't checking. He might dump me and sign up the dog.'

Adam was surprised to hear this come out so bitterly but, luckily, Lia didn't seem to notice. Instead she snuggled down in the seat and said, 'It's nice and warm in here.'

After a long day like this one had been, Adam would normally have driven home alone. Exhausted by the demands of his job, but still pumping with adrenaline, his mind would be in overdrive. He felt that way now but, somehow, her presence made a difference. She had closed her eyes but, when he glanced across at her, they opened. 'I liked what you said about your book.'

'At the bookshop?'

'No, at the course, when Declan asked you about your inspiration. How come that isn't on the book's cover?'

'It wasn't down to me. Apparently, nostalgia sells better than a call to arms.'

'Well, if they're using your name and your face to make money, they shouldn't put words in your mouth.' Stretching luxuriously, Lia said, 'I don't know how you do it.'

'Do what?'

'Stay cool under all the pressure.'

Shrugging, he said, 'I'm the Coolest Chef.'

The hotel dining room was full of office Christmas parties wearing paper hats and raising toasts. Defeated by the noise level, Adam turned away to go to the lift. Looking at him shrewdly, Lia said, 'When did you last eat?'

'I seem to remember a surprising slice of Mary's upside-down cake.'

'Well, you've got to have something now, or you won't sleep.'

He knew from experience that he was unlikely to sleep till the hamster wheel in his head stopped turning, and that wasn't likely to be till the small hours. 'I'll be fine.'

'What you need is a square meal, preferably loaded with carbs. They do pizzas and stuff in the bar. Come on. My shout.'

Too tired to argue, Adam followed her into the hotel bar, which was less crowded than the dining room. Lia steered him towards an oak-panelled booth. 'No one will notice us here. Have a seat. I'll order. I know how to catch a barman's eye.' She disappeared and came back with two glasses of beer. 'So. Pasta carbonara. I told him to ask the chef to chuck plenty of parsley on top.'

Taking a long pull of beer, Adam said, 'Sounds perfect.'

'Not very cheffy.'

'Extremely cheffy, believe me. You've never been in a restaurant kitchen after a heavy service.'

Lia sat at the opposite side of the table. 'So is restaurant work what you did before you were cool?'

'Yep. Hotels to begin with. Restaurants later. You've got to be good, but to make it, you've got to get lucky. And you need to know when to stay and when to move on.'

'How can you tell?'

'You can't. You just keep your eyes open. I got lucky in Dublin. The restaurant where I was working opened a London branch in Belgravia.'

'Smart area.'

'The point was the chef there was really good. I learned a helluva lot. Then I moved on and kept moving. Eventually, one of the guys I worked for suggested I go in for the competition.' Taking another mouthful of beer, Adam sat back against the booth's scarlet cushions. 'And the rest is history.'

A girl from behind the bar arrived with two steaming plates and, pushing the pepper mill towards Adam, Lia said, 'Let's eat while it's hot.' Wondering if he'd been boring her, Adam dug a fork into his pasta. It was creamy, eggy, flecked with green parsley, and the ham had obviously been cut from the bone. He'd thought he was too tired to eat, but each forkful revived him. There was a long interval of companionable silence, then Lia sighed and said, 'You can't beat carbs.'

'It's not just the carbs. It's the quality. I bet everything on this plate was sourced locally.'

'Really? Spaghetti trees in Fury's forest?'

'Okay. Maybe not the pasta.' Draining his glass, Adam leaned back again, still tired but more relaxed. 'So Fury the book-launch guy is the guy who owns the forest?'

'According to Bríd. She says he's a force of nature.'

Adam grinned. 'Yeah, I could see that.'

'I liked him, though. Did you?'

'He reminded me of the chef in my first job in London. The kind of guy who pulls no punches, but really appreciates what you've got to offer.'

Lia, who'd finished her own pasta, reached out and twirled her fork round a string of spaghetti on Adam's plate. 'He certainly put you to work. How come you're so handy up a ladder?'

He batted away her question with another. 'How come you know how to tighten a battery cover?'

'Picked it up from my grandma.'

'The one who glazes cakes with lemon myrtle leaves?'

'That's the one. She and my granddad lived in the middle of nowhere. I used to visit them when I was a kid.' Lia tipped the pasta into her mouth. 'I'm going to miss that place. Granddad died a few months ago, so Grandma's selling up and moving to live near my mum and dad.' Reaching out with her fork again, she asked, 'Do you still have grandparents?'

'No, they're dead.'

'That's tough.'

Adam shifted restlessly. 'Not really. Here, d'you want to finish this pasta? I've had enough.'

'Oh, sorry. Do you hate it when people pick food off your plate?'

'No, it's fine. I'm just tired. Look, would you mind if we called it a night?'

His abrupt change of manner had confused her, but she downed her drink and said, 'Sure. I'll get the bill.'

'Let me.'

'It was my shout, remember?' She went to the bar, paid, and came back to find Adam staring at the table. Looking up, he summoned what she'd come to think of as his professional smile. 'Sorry to be a bore.'

'No worries. Anyway, I've got a WhatsApp call. See you tomorrow, Chef.'

Upstairs, Adam checked his phone and found a message from Dom. *Congrats on the socials. I see your bogtrotting booksellers are trending.* Chucking the phone onto the bed, Adam went and took his third shower of the day. Though the needles of hot water relaxed his tense muscles, his brain had flipped back into overdrive. After a few minutes, he went through to the bedroom again, pulled on a dressing-gown and glared at the phone.

When they'd taken him in through the yard he'd seen the state of the back of the bookshop, and pitching in to help had been instinctive. It hadn't been hard to work out that those people were screwed to breaking-point, doing whatever it took to hide what had happened. He'd admired Ann's resolute calm during the breakneck set-up, and recognised Catherine's hastily concealed relief when she'd come in and seen the transformation. Upstairs, changing out of his jeans and T-shirt, he'd taken in the state of the dismantled kitchen, where floorboards were up and joists lay open to the room below. Later, as he'd sat signing books, aware of damp rubble in the room behind him, he'd been full of respect for how Catherine and Ann had handled the press and the public. So, although it wasn't fair to blame Dom for not seeing what had been hidden, the dismissive wording of the text grated.

Not trusting himself to respond, Adam turned off his phone and went to look out of the window. His sixth-floor room overlooked the Royal Victoria's car park, and a wide cobbled yard outside its kitchen entrance. Craning his neck, Adam could see a row of bins in the yard. Their domed tops were edged with frost and, squinting up at the stars, he saw that snow was beginning to fall. Turning back to the room, he looked at the king-sized bed with its piled-up pillows and, with no hope of sleep, lay down under the duvet.

When sleep came it brought a familiar nightmare. Trudging through streets in falling rain, he was desperately searching for something he couldn't remember. The gritty pavements were slick with grease, and jostling crowds surging past kept pushing him in the wrong direction. Then he was alone, standing in huge emptiness with a blanket round his shoulders. He could feel its edges, stiff with dirt. A big dog was dragging at a rope. Someone was shaking seeds out of a folded piece of paper. Then, suddenly, he was in a cell and the bars were closing in on him. The blanket was gone, and so was his phone, and he knew that if he screamed no one would hear him. Beyond the bars the crowds moved on, and he realised that he'd become invisible. The cell was shrinking, his phone wasn't there, and somewhere the hands of a clock were spinning madly. Then a door opened and he was deluged by a flood of icy water. Gasping for breath, he woke to find himself trapped by the folds of his duvet, wide-eyed with fear and drenched in cold sweat.

SATURDAY

21 DECEMBER

CHAPTER SEVENTEEN

At Garrybawn House, Fury's tree was in the lounge, where the residents had decorated it. Upstairs, the family's tree, made of tinsel-covered wire, stood on a round table by the TV. As they'd done each year since Saoirse was small, she and her dad had set it up together, spreading the silver branches and hanging them with little glass birds that spent the rest of the year in a box in the attic.

When Saoirse came into the kitchen on Saturday morning, her dad was at the stove, frying rashers. 'Hi. Where's Mum?'

'Just out of bed and desperate for a black coffee.' Raising his voice to reach the bathroom, he called, 'Fancy a rasher sandwich, love?'

Mum came in, yawning. 'Are you deaf? I said I just wanted coffee.' Sitting down, she asked if Saoirse had enjoyed the book launch.

'It was amazing. So cool. There was a marketing person there from London who said it was like a Hollywood premiere.'

Flipping a rasher, Dad said, 'Saoirse was livestreaming to the world.'

'No, I wasn't. But the social-media person came and talked to me. Like, just for a nanosecond, but it was brilliant. I'd been sort of freaked by the thought of the press, but she wasn't that much older than me, and it wasn't telly so it was cool. And Adam took a selfie with me, right in front of everyone. And the bookshop's amazing.'

'Sounds like you had a great time.'

'You should see the Christmas tree in the shop. It's massive. And Adam was sitting up on a platform in front of a huge gold frame. And there was this funky backdrop that was all splashes of colour.'

'Did you get home in time to make your dad his omelette?'

'Yes, because I didn't have to stay to clean up. Mum, there's another event there this evening. Late-night shopping. They're doing a whole new set-up for it. Could we go?' Saoirse saw Mum and Dad exchange glances. Rory said, 'I think your mum's out again tonight. Isn't that right, Theresa?'

'Yes. Sorry, pet.'

'But you like the bookshop. Dad said so.'

'I do, but – don't fuss, Saoirse. We'll go another time.'

'But it's now that it's all decorated. We could bring Dad and show him the shop. There's a tree in the window made up of books, and the real one inside is massive.'

'You've said that already.'

Saoirse had been about to tell them the tree had been covered in cupcakes and she'd posted photos of it to Insta and got a gazillion likes. Looking down at her plate, she decided this wasn't the time to. She looked at Dad who, seeming harassed, glanced from her to Mum. He came to the table with a couple of rasher sandwiches. 'Here, pet, get one of these down you. You've a busy day ahead.' Taking a sandwich, Saoirse said, 'It's a late-night thing this evening. They'll be open till nine. Maybe you and Mum could drop in at the end, when her meeting's over.'

Mum frowned. 'Leave it, Saoirse, your dad's right. You're doing long days at this job. I don't want you out late, or taken advantage of either. I hope you were paid if you served drinks at this fellow's launch.'

Deflated and confused, Saoirse bit into her sandwich. It felt like something was going on that they didn't want her to know about and, whatever it was, it was making Mum cross, and Dad worried and weird.

The Saturday giveaway was a *Coolest Chef* piping set and star-shaped cookie cutters in different sizes. As the group assembled, the ladies from Cork were enthusiastically describing the book launch. 'And the Christmas cookies we're doing today are actually in the book. They look only gorgeous in the photos. And you wouldn't believe the piping! It's out of this world.'

Darina said she'd spent the night thinking of all the things that could go wrong with a piping bag. 'Even if I don't mess up the bake, my icing is sure to end up nowhere near my cookies.'

Mary was tying herself into a wraparound floral apron. She tossed her head. 'God help poor little Saoirse, with all the work you're making for her. And I'll tell you something you won't find written in Adam's book. There were no cookies in Ireland before we all went off to the States.'

This was just background noise to Saoirse who was still thinking about the look she'd seen her mum and dad exchange at breakfast. She watched Adam assemble the group around the table. 'The point of today is to practise piping skills, okay? So the bakes are quick and simple. I've given you three recipes, a plain spicy biscuit, a honey cookie, and stained-glass gingerbread. You can choose to use one or all of them but, if I were you, I wouldn't miss out on the gingerbread.'

Darina said she could never remember the difference between a biscuit and a cookie. 'I don't suppose it matters, but I always get confused.'

'Basically, a biscuit snaps when you break it. A cookie won't.' He grinned at Mary. 'And in the States what we call a scone is called a biscuit, which can be very confusing if you've just arrived from Ireland.'

Kevin was peering at the illustration on his recipe. 'So, you cut a hole in the gingerbread and bung in a bashed-up boiled sweet, and the sweet melts in the oven and ends up looking like coloured glass?'

'That's it. And, if you put a skewer through the top of each biscuit before you bake them, you've got yourself Christmas-tree decorations.' Seeing Darina looking lost, Adam gave her a smile. 'Don't worry. I'll show you how, and this isn't about perfection. It's the kind of baking the family can do together, to get everyone in the mood for Christmas.'

Saoirse wondered if this might be something she and her mum and dad could do together. Perhaps if she bought the ingredients and took the recipe home they could hang out in the kitchen making gingerbread stars and snowflakes, and the weirdness she'd felt this morning would evaporate, and everything would be ordinary again. Perched on a stool, she decided to concentrate on what Adam was saying, and hoped Darina wasn't going to require too much attention.

Declan turned out to be brilliant with a piping bag. By the time Adam came to check on his progress, he was bent over a sheet of greaseproof paper, creating intricate loops and swirls in royal icing.

'That's impressive.'

'Years of working with flexible filler. If I can do nothing else, I can handle a nozzle.' Sitting back, Declan considered his practice designs. 'I reckon I'll use these for my cookies, and put water icing on my gingerbread.'

When he took his first batch of gingerbread from his oven, Saoirse edged over to look. He'd chosen to make six-pointed stars with a smaller cut-out star shape in the centre, and had used a drinking straw to pierce a little hole at the top of each. Saoirse admired the translucent effect of the melted sweets. 'It really is like stained-glass, isn't it? Like those windows in the old convent.'

'It's amazingly effective for something so easy. I'm going to pipe a white lattice on this batch, and stud it with little silver balls.'

'Mr Maguire says the balls are properly called dragées.'

'Of course he does.' Lifting his biscuits onto a rack, Declan asked if she did much baking herself.

'Not really.'

'You could have a go at these. Adam's right, they'll make great tree decorations.'

'How do you hang them up?'

'Stick ribbon through these holes at the top. I'll need to enlarge the holes, though. They've closed up a bit in the oven.'

Saoirse imagined herself and her mum and dad at the kitchen table, melting golden syrup and butter, tipping ground ginger into flour, and kneading the dark brown dough before cutting it into shapes. They could have carols playing in the background, and mess about making silly jokes. All her favourite Christmas memories were about that kind of closeness with her parents. Waking in the dark when she was little, and feeling the shapes of the gifts in her stocking, and pulling them out one by one. Her bare feet on the cold floor when she ran to her mum and dad's bedroom. Cuddles and kisses, and the warmth of their duvet when she snuggled between them with a half-eaten chocolate Santa.

Her dad would always pretend to be cross about being woken so early. He'd roll out of bed, come back with a tray of coffee, and steal the last of Saoirse's chocolate. Then, propped up in bed with their coffee mugs, they'd chat across her head as she showed them the contents of her Christmas stocking. Now she was older, the contents had changed and, instead of sweets and toys, it contained bath gel, make-up and, last year, transfer tattoos. Though now it was she who made the coffee and brought three mugs on a tray to her parents' bedroom, they'd still sit together, propped against the pillows, sharing a chocolate Santa, and joking about whatever daft little present her mum had knitted to put into her stocking that year.

Bigger gifts came later, under the silver Christmas tree. Among them there was always a nightgown sent from the States by her aunt. For the rest of the year, Saoirse slept in outsize T-shirts, so she used to feel the nightgowns' flounces and ribbons brought glamour to her ordinary life. But since the pandemic ordinary things were what she valued most. The silly gifts her mum knitted were now her favourites, and Christmas brought a sense of continuity that made her feel safe in a changing world.

Now her fingers itched to have a go at piping. It had looked easy in Adam's demonstration, though disastrously complicated in Darina's hands, and most people seemed to be getting the hang of it. Even Mary was doing creative things with fondant, while Mr Maguire had dropped his usual air of lofty disdain and was bashing a bag of boiled sweets with a rolling pin.

At the other side of the room, Lia was watching Adam. With less than half of her mind on the ball of dough she was kneading, Lia remembered hustling him through the back of the bookshop the previous afternoon. After introducing him to Ann and Fury, she and Bríd had returned to the van to bring in the cupcakes. When they'd come back with the first tray, Adam had rolled up the sleeves of his sweater and, balanced on a ladder, was hanging Fury's gilded frame from the beam above his head. Working together without exchanging more than a couple of words, he and Fury had completed the job neatly and stood back to observe the effect. Later, she'd watched him hunker down to help position the folding platform, and then come through from the office with a case of wine on his shoulder. She wondered how many other TV celebrity authors would roll up their sleeves and get stuck in to the set-up for their own book launch, and then appear looking as if they'd spent hours sipping cocktails while being fussed over by a professional hair and wardrobe team.

It was as if each change of clothes revealed a new aspect of his personality. With a hammer in his hand, he looked nothing like he did in his publicity photos and now, in his crisp white jacket and apron, he bore no resemblance to the exhausted figure who'd sat across the table from her in the hotel bar. Stamping out honey cookies with a *Coolest Chef* cutter, she recalled how weirdly the previous evening had ended. One minute they'd been chatting like friends, and the next he'd stiffened and frozen her out politely, as if she was a pushy stranger who'd gone too far. What was that about? And how did the other Adam Rashid fit into the picture, someone so lacking in confidence that he hadn't known she was joking when she'd wound him up that day they'd met in the bus?

Over lunch the group chatted about Christmas preparations, and one of the ladies from Cork said she loved all the secrets at this time of year. 'When I was small, you'd go into a room and people were always whispering in corners or bundling something away.'

The others laughed, and Karen said, 'Oh, I know! I still love that. It's kind of cosy, isn't it? And it adds to the excitement.'

Saoirse had the strangest feeling of isolation, as if she'd been cut off from the laughing group around her and was looking at them from a distance. She could see Mary thumping the table with the flat of her hand to make some emphatic point. Declan was holding one of his gingerbread biscuits to catch the sunlight falling through the window. From the other end of the table, Adam was watching the dancing spots of coloured light falling across Lia's hand. Janice was making Darina laugh about the state of her apron, and Mr Maguire, who was eating a ham sandwich, was deep in conversation with the second lady from Cork.

The chat, the smells of nutmeg, cinnamon, brown sugar and honey, even the shining racks of utensils, seemed to Saoirse to exist in a world of certainty where she didn't belong. She thought of her mum and dad at the breakfast table that morning. They'd exchanged a secret look, but it hadn't felt exciting. They'd just seemed edgy and irritable. So the scene she'd imagined couldn't happen. Not with Mum out all the time, and being snappish when offered a rasher sandwich, and Dad going off to bed early, and looking cagey and anxious. Staring at Adam, Saoirse wished she had someone to talk to. Because, now that she came to think about it, her mum and dad had been acting strangely for weeks. Where was Mum actually going? Surely not just to knit-and-natter sessions? Could there be something massively wrong they were trying to keep from her?

Suddenly her stomach lurched and, hardly knowing what she was doing, she slid her hand down to her bag, which was on the floor beside her, and groped till her fingers touched the pouch that contained her worry dolls. Taking it out and keeping it under the table, she undid the drawstring and inched the two dolls onto her lap. One was taller than the other. Her mum had said they were portraits. 'You and me, Saoirse. I'm the one with hair that looks like I never get time to comb it.'

'And I'm the shortass?'

'Dead right. I'd have done your dad as well, but I hadn't time.'

The touch of the little knitted figures was reassuring. Holding them between her cupped palms, Saoirse told herself firmly that life at home had always been rushed. Dad was always busy, and Mum was always on the go. Nothing had changed, really, so it was silly to start inventing disaster scenarios. And the fact that the room seemed to be coming back into focus had nothing at all to do with the worry dolls. It was just that she liked the feel of them when she turned them over and over, hidden from everyone else and safe in the shelter of her hands.

CHAPTER EIGHTEEN

With the bookshelves still under heavy plastic sheeting, and the underside of floorboards visible overhead, the back of the bookshop looked like a building site. Catherine watched Terry heave her broken display table onto a barrow that already contained stools and benches from what had been the children's corner. Most of the debris was gone and the state of the floor was horribly apparent. Compacted by the weight of fallen plaster, a layer of soggy dust had been ground into the carpet. Christmas cards from the carousel that had stood next to the table were scattered about, torn and spattered with dirt. Jigsaw puzzles had been crushed, toys broken, and pulverised boxes of crayons ripped from the children's colouring books added waxy flecks of colour to the mess. Seeing Catherine's stricken look, Terry said, 'Don't panic. Once your new ceiling's up, we'll sort the floor. I've carpet tiles back in my warehouse that'll be a good colour match and, as soon as they're laid, you can put all this behind you.'

The kindness in his voice brought a lump to Catherine's throat. 'I'm really grateful, Terry. I'm sure you and Angela had other things planned for this weekend.'

'It's no bother. We'll plasterboard tomorrow, and do the ceiling skim and the new tiles on Monday. Angela's going to get onto your wiring today.'

'She said she can install downlighters, like we have in the front of the shop.'

'It'll look champion. The chances are you'd have had this ceiling taken down yourselves, at some point, to match up your lighting.'

'I'd rather have chosen when to do it, though.'

'Ah, but life's not about choices, is it? You cope with what's thrown at you, and count your blessings.'

Back at the till, Catherine relayed the updates to Ann, who said, 'In other news, we've nearly sold out of *Cakes To Come Home To*.'

'But we've late-night shopping tonight, and there are still three days to Christmas.'

'Relax. We're sorted. Gaby got on to the *Coolest Chef* crowd in London. They were so impressed by what they saw of last night's event that they've pulled strings to get stock rushed to us. And, in even better news, Adam pre-signed stock over there. So, when the books arrive, we can slap our Signed by the Author stickers on the lot.'

Relieved, Catherine went behind the counter. 'As Fury would say, if it's not one damn thing it's another.'

The previous evening, with Stephen and Hanna who'd stayed on to help, they'd returned the front of the shop to what Fury called default mode. The Divil's tree once again stood dead-centre against the backdrop, with the scarlet and gold banners on either side of it. Now Fury emerged from behind it and strode purposefully to the counter. 'The tension-building worked like a dream yesterday, so we'll do it again for your late-night shopping. Close for an hour before the event, blackout the window, and open up on a transformation.'

'What'll it be this time?'

'Well, the theme's obvious, given the day that's in it.' Seeing their blank looks, Fury rolled his eyes. 'Dear God Almighty, can you not even follow a calendar? It's the twenty-first of December. The winter solstice.'

Catherine said, 'I know what the winter solstice is. It's the shortest day of the year. I didn't know it was today, though.'

Fury chuckled. 'And you surrounded by books! You should be ashamed of yourself.'

'I'm not sure too many people do know. Will they recognise the theme, d'you think?'

With an unexpectedly bleak look, Fury said, 'Oh, don't worry. It'll be shiny.'

'I didn't mean to suggest …'

'Ah, it's all right, girl. You meant no harm. Look, Terry's giving Angela a hand back there with the wiring. The Divil and I are off out for a few hours now. We'll be back this afternoon in time for the set-up.'

Ten minutes later, Fury appeared in the library with The Divil under his arm. Hanna, who'd been chatting with Stephen, said, 'What can I do for you, Fury?'

'What makes you think we're after something?'

'The look in your eye.'

'Begod, I must be losing my poker face.' With a shameless grin, he cocked his head at Hanna. 'And, as it happens, we are here for a favour. You know those greeting cards you have inside in your gift shop?'

'What about them?'

'The thing is, when the ceiling came down, the women up at the bookshop lost their entire stock of Christmas cards. The twirly display yoke's banjaxed too. And normally there'd be a fierce run on cards at their late-night shopping.'

'Oh, poor Catherine!'

'Well, she can't replace them by nipping out for a bumper pack of robins.' Looking from Stephen to Hanna, Fury added meaningfully, 'Because, obviously, what you want in a bookshop is book-related Christmas cards.' For a moment Hanna didn't see what he was getting at. Then it dawned on her. 'The cards sold in our gift shop are all images from the psalter.'

'Spot on! And there's a rake of pictures in that psalter would make convincing Christmas cards.'

In the storeroom, Stephen helped Fury to lift down a carton of cards. Spreading them out to see the designs, Hanna said, 'There's a suitable one, for starters.' Taken from one of the psalter's marginal illustrations, the card showed a deer running through a forest. The slender, leaping body was framed by oak trees, its feet were picked out in gold, and acorns hung from its antlers.

Rummaging through a second carton, Stephen found a card on which woodland creatures danced around a pool that reflected a starry sky. 'Here's another. There must be half a dozen different designs that would do the job.'

Hanna looked at Fury. 'There's plenty of time to replace these before our exhibition reopens. The bookshop can have as many as they need, and we'll sort the money out afterwards.'

'You're a good woman, Hanna Casey.'

'And, Fury, there's a card carousel in the gift shop. They can have that too. Catherine can return it after Christmas.'

When Fury and The Divil left, Stephen turned to Hanna. 'I could drop the cards and the carousel into the bookshop. My car's outside and the shop's on my way home.'

'If you don't mind.'

'It's no trouble.'

His carefully casual tone spoke volumes but Hanna seemed not to notice. Nodding, she replied, 'I'm awfully sorry for poor Ann and Catherine. Still, at least this drama has given them a chance to know their neighbours better.'

Stephen turned away and began to stack the cards they'd chosen. 'These images are incredibly vibrant. Is it true that the psalter depicts features of the local landscape?'

Accepting the change of subject without comment, Hanna said, 'Some pages do. One has a picture of the mountain range that runs down the peninsula. It's a tiny, perfectly accurate image within a decorated capital letter. Actually, it was Fury who pointed it out to me.'

'Really?'

'He noticed it before any of the scholars who worked on the exhibition. I doubt if there's a rock, a tree or a building on this peninsula Fury doesn't know like the back of his hand. His dad taught him forestry. It's a shame he has no children to take it on.'

'There's no family at all? It's just him and The Divil?'

'There was a brother who died childless, so Fury's the last of his line. He's a great reader too, you know. Apparently, he spent hours in a local library in London, on wet-weather days when work on the sites was suspended. Mind you, when he came home and set up as a builder, he used to tell clients he was illiterate. Brian says it was a smart move to avoid putting things in writing.'

'Sounds like the Fury we know and love.'

'It's sad to think that, when he goes, a lifetime's knowledge and centuries of experience will go with him.'

Bumping along a forest track, Fury looked at The Divil. 'I'm listening for a rattle. Can you hear a rattle? I can't.'

The Divil looked over his shoulder into the back of the shuddering van.

'Not back there, you eejit. There's tools back there, of course they're going to rattle. It's the feckin' battery case. That little one Lia went and screwed it down yesterday, didn't she? And now there's sepulchral silence under the bonnet.'

Unsure of how to respond, The Divil scratched himself vigorously.

'Don't pretend you've a flea, when we both know you haven't. And don't think I didn't see you go all bashful when she kissed you at the book launch. What with that, and posing with fan girls and stealing cupcakes, you came away yesterday evening without a shred of dignity.'

They'd reached a part of the forest where ash trees and rare wych elms created a canopy so broad that, in summer, the earth below seldom saw sunlight. Now, on the shortest day of the year when already the thin winter light was fading, the bare branches made a black lattice against a pearl-grey sky.

Had anyone been there to see him, it would have been abundantly clear that, whoever might hold the title to it, this was Fury's forest: leaving the van by the track, and taking three sacks and long-handled cutters, he and The Divil moved steadily through the trees in single file. Striding and trotting, they passed through beech mast that crunched under foot and paw. A crow called and was answered from a distance. The Divil's nose twitched as a squirrel leaped across their path. Fury stopped occasionally to curve his hand around a sapling, feeling the bark and sensing the pith within.

In a clearing fringed by gnarled oaks they came upon hollies, where leaves and berries grew at the end of long, trailing stems. Whistling as he reached up, Fury selected which to cut, looped each fallen stem and slid it into one of his sacks. The Divil ran in circles, avoiding the bright, prickly leaves as the stems fell. A vixen pacing stealthily through the undergrowth paused and watched as Fury moved on to an ash tree cloaked in ivy. Selecting equally long tendrils, he filled his second sack. Then, at another holly tree, where polished clusters of berries and leaves grew on short, woody stems, he cut enough to fill the third.

By now, the sun had set, dusk had overtaken the forest, and wreaths of grey mist had begun to creep between the trees. At the centre of the stand of hollies a rock reared out of the earth, higher than the height of a tall man. Fury went and sat with his back against it, feeling its hardness through the weight of the woollen jersey he wore, and the heavy waxed cotton of his jacket.

Taking a half-smoked roll-up from behind his ear, he lit it, inhaled deeply and buried the spent match in the earth by his boot. Then he considered the sky, where a single star was glowing. Except for the years he'd spent in England, not a solstice had passed when he hadn't gone into the forest like this, with a dog at his heels and the knowledge that, when the gathering darkness had passed, the new day would bring a sense of the certain return of light. Sure of his own place in a cycle that never faltered, he'd watched the seasons come and go, and seen how a web of roots, trunks and branches fed, sheltered and controlled a shrunken but resilient ecosystem. Now he no longer felt certain of anything. Not his own place in the world, not his forest's future. Not even of goodness in the return of light. The tilted earth's relationship with the fiery sun was changing, Nature's control had steadily been diminished, and his own strength was ebbing so fast that it seemed he could do nothing to make a difference.

Turning to The Divil, he said, 'Did you see one of them cards there in the library? The stag with his antlers laced into the forest, and golden dew on his hooves where they touched the earth?' The Divil whined and came to lay his furry chin on Fury's boot. Fury tipped ash from his cigarette and scratched him. 'There's a picture of that deer on another page, where he's standing beside this rock. A hart with ten tines on his antlers. The antlers are flowers that grow from his head, with insects and butterflies on them, and a stream of water full of fish flows down from the rock.' Pulling The Divil's ear, he asked, 'I suppose you don't read Latin? No, you wouldn't, you haven't the education. I bet half the monks that painted the pictures in that psalter didn't either. They wouldn't need to. I bet there were some that could handle a brush and cut-in a decent straight line, and they'd be let in on the strength of that, and being able to mix paints and draw things. There'd have been women too. Country girls that went into the abbeys because they were orphaned, or hungry, or just wanted pens and ink, and pigments to crush to make colours. Those were the ones who recorded what they saw all around them. They mightn't know what the writing meant, but they knew what they were looking at. They knew its worth, and that's why they were able to paint that picture.'

The Divil shook his head violently and pointed his nose to the sky. Fury looked up at the evening star and said, 'I know. You're right. We'd better get back to the bookshop.' Pinching out his cigarette and burying it alongside the spent match, he took his three sacks and led the way back to the van. It was almost dark beneath the trees. The Divil moved with his nose to fallen pine needles and beech mast. Dust-coloured moths and bats with scythe-shaped wings darted past. Creatures with eyes like jewels stirred in the undergrowth by the path, and beyond a yew tree, where berries gleamed in the half-light, something that might have had antlers turned its head.

CHAPTER NINETEEN

Saturday was a half-day in the library, so Hanna was free to give Mary a lift after Adam's afternoon session. When she opened the door on the passenger side, she was handed a box of biscuits. 'Hold that there now till I'm settled, and don't be shaking or knocking it. There's blood, sweat and tears gone into my honey cookies.'

'Was that what you made today?'

'And the rest, girl. Three recipes he gave us, and "Take your choice," says he. Well, I wasn't going to be left in the ha'penny place with Darina Kelly. Plain spiced rounds were all that woman could rise to and, I'm telling you, her piping skills were embarrassing. No, I went for the honey cookies and a batch of gingerbread stars. And I took the sight out of all their eyes when I did my stained-glass with a bag of bullseyes.'

At Garrybawn House, she invited Hanna in for a cup of tea. 'Go into the kitchen there, and get them to find you a plate for my biscuits.' Knowing Mary was desperate to show off what she'd made that day on the course, Hanna went and put her head around the kitchen door. Theresa, who was checking a fridge, looked up with a smile and said it was nice to see her. 'Have you brought your mum home to us?'

'Along with about a million biscuits.'

'Ah. Okay. Will I bring tea?'

Mary had drawn two armchairs to a table by the Christmas tree and was looking askance at the decorations. 'Dear God, the bits and pieces people have thrown on that!' Sitting down with a plate, and opening the cardboard box of biscuits, Hanna said, 'I think it's nice. They're obviously all well-loved, and they bring personality to it.'

'You call it personality. I'd call it a pig's ear.'

Theresa arrived with a tray, bent to look at the stained-glass stars, recoiled and said, 'Woah! Mary! Serious smell of mint!'

'That'll be the bullseyes.'

'Lovely glassy centres. Kind of dark, though.'

Mary drew herself up, preparing for battle. 'The black stripes ran into the white ones, giving a powerful, dramatic effect. That's what Adam Rashid said when he came round to taste them. "The powerful appearance matches the punch of flavour." Those were his very words.'

'The icing on the honey cookies is lovely.'

'My beehives? Thank you. They don't look like hills.'

'Not at all.'

'And they don't look like bras either, whatever that sniggering Declan from Tintawn Terry's might say.'

Hanna choked on a bite of cookie, and said, truthfully, that it was delicious.

'Thank you. Several people intend to use the stained-glass stars as Christmas tree decorations. They've got holes in the tops of them for a bit of ribbon.'

Seizing the teapot, Mary looked pointedly at Theresa, who took the hint. 'Would you consider letting us hang some of yours on our Christmas tree here?'

Mary inclined her head. 'I wouldn't object.'

'We'll find some ribbon and tie them on.'

'They'll be good as an air-freshener too. You've got twenty-four there, so you'll get the full powerful effect.' Seeing the effect of this on Theresa, Hanna said diplomatically that Mary might want to keep some of the biscuits for herself. 'You could have one with a cup of tea in your own flat some afternoon.'

'One of them things? You're joking. I might be liquidated but I've still got respect for my teeth.'

They were sitting eating the honey cookies – which Hanna now couldn't look at without seeing D cups – when Saoirse came in and stopped to say hello. Theresa gave her a one-armed hug. 'How's my girl?'

'Good.'

'Good day?'

Saoirse stood on one leg, her hands deep in her pockets. 'Fine, thanks.'

She looked the picture of an embarrassed teenager who'd unwittingly walked into an adults' gathering so, to help her out, Hanna said, 'The course sounds super, Saoirse. Are you enjoying your job?'

'It's good.'

Theresa smiled. 'It's great holiday money, Hanna. She'll be buying treats for the three of us in London.'

'You're going over to see a show, aren't you?'

'One of those big musical things transferred from Broadway. It was Rory's choice. I would've gone for a bit more sophistication.' Theresa laughed. 'But that's your dad, isn't it, Saoirse? Nothing sophisticated about Rory.'

Mary asked if the show was by Gilbert and Sullivan. 'It's a common mistake, you know, to call light opera unsophisticated.'

'I don't think it's by them, no.'

'Because some of the notes you'd have to hit as Yum Yum would surprise you.'

'I think the show they'll be going to is more modern than Gilbert and Sullivan.'

Mary sniffed. 'My point is that, if you're properly trained, you can take a run at any kind of music. The nuns used to have us all lined up on the stage belting out Alleluias. It stood to me when I was Yum Yum, I can tell you.'

Certain they were heading for a lecture on vibrato, Hanna cast about for a new subject and hit on the bookshop's late-night-shopping event. 'Are any of the residents here planning to go to Lissbeg for it? How about yourself, Theresa?'

To her surprise, Theresa seemed flustered by the question. It was Saoirse who answered: 'Mum's not going. She's out somewhere tonight.'

Mary said that, whatever about the late-night shopping, she hoped they'd all turn out for the bookshop's Christmas Eve carol concert. Having successfully returned the conversation to herself, she said, 'It's for charity, you know, and we've been rehearsing since September.'

Theresa asked, 'Is that for the halfway house for the homeless in Carrick?'

'It is, and we're pulling the stops out. Glorias to beat the band, and Pat Fitz and I have a solo verse in 'The Holly and the Ivy'.'

'That's nice.'

'If I were you, I'd reserve that comment until I'd heard her vibrato.'

Hanna was about to make a second attempt to divert them from Pat's vibrato, when Saoirse interrupted: 'I'm going upstairs, Mum.'

'Okay, but don't be rude. Say goodbye to Mary and Hanna.'

Shrugging, Saoirse said, 'Sorry. I'm sticky. I need a shower.'

Mary said briskly, 'Well, of course you do, child. With the weight of what you mopped up around Darina Kelly's work bench, I'd say you're practically coated in icing sugar.'

Relieved to have escaped scrutiny, Saoirse went up to the flat. Hanna Casey was nice enough, but Mary was just nosy. If I'd had any sense, she thought crossly, I'd have gone in the back way. Coming through the lounge was asking for trouble, and Mum's like a different person downstairs than she is when we're up here doing family stuff.

In her bedroom, as she got ready to shower, she recalled a family conversation in Carrick before the move to Garrybawn House. Dad had told her that he and Mum wanted a different life. 'With the two of us working hospital shifts, we don't see enough of each other – or of you. The truth is, we're not far from breaking-point.'

Shocked, she'd asked, 'Are you telling me that you're going to break up?' and Mum had said, 'For God's sake, Rory, engage your brain before opening your mouth! That's not what he meant at all, pet. Tell her, Rory.'

Dad had laughed and said that of course he and Mum weren't going to break up. 'I mean we need to break out of this way of life we've got ourselves stuck in, where we're never together long enough to enjoy being a family.'

At the time, that had made sense to Saoirse and she'd accepted it. Now she wondered if she might have been naive. Frowning, she sat on the bed to think about it. If your workload meant that you didn't get to spend enough time together, it must be awfully easy to drift apart. Obviously they wouldn't have told her, since she'd been only twelve at the time, but had they been going through a rough patch in their marriage and decided to make a fresh start? And with Mum out so much these days, and Dad looking anxious and secretive, could it be that leaving their hospital jobs and coming to Garrybawn hadn't fixed things?

Passing the living-room door on her way to the bathroom, Saoirse looked in and saw her mum's knitting bag on a chair. Glancing over her shoulder, she went quietly into the room, knelt by the chair and unzipped the bag. The last time she'd seen the jumper her mum was knitting was on the evening Mum had come in from a knit-and-natter session and told her that Phil was looking for someone to help out at Adam's course. Looking at it now, Saoirse saw that it hadn't progressed at all, though twice since then she'd been told Mum was out for a knit-and-natter.

Staring at it, Saoirse felt her heart sink. Then she heard footsteps. Pushing the knitting back into the bag, she struggled to close it, caught the zip on the needles, and turned to see Dad standing in the doorway. As she stumbled to her feet, probably looking as guilty as she felt, his expression changed from surprise to concern. 'What're you doing in here, rooting around in your mum's knitting?'

'Nothing. I was just checking. I mean I was checking to see how it's getting on.'

'Saoirse, that's not on, love. You can't be going through other people's possessions. Did Mum say you could?'

'No. But she's always taking it out and showing it to us.'

'That's different, and you well know it.' Coming into the room, Dad said gently, 'Respect for people's private lives and spaces is important, pet. We've always taught you that.'

'I know.'

'Were you looking for your Christmas present? You're way too old to be doing that.'

'I wasn't. I was just curious. I was on my way to the shower.'

'Go on, then, so. Have your shower, and leave your mother's things alone. I won't say a word to her, but you're not to be at it again. Do you hear me?'

At the bookshop, Ann was restoring order upstairs. Hearing the sound of Angela's wiring going on beneath the kitchen floorboards, she remembered how tense she'd felt whenever Jason, their useless builder, had been in the flat. The atmosphere was different now. Out on the landing, the empty cardboard flatpacks were neatly stacked against the wall, ready to be taken down to the yard. In the kitchen, the tiling above the work surface had been expertly finished, and the new cabinets slotted into place. Each door opened smoothly on well-fitted hinges, and Ann had seen with her own eyes that the plumbing under the sink was immaculate.

Sitting back on her heels, she let out a deep sigh of relief. There was painting to do, and vinyl flooring yet to come from Terry's, but Christmas meals could now be cooked and eaten in comfort, and the rest would wait for the new year.

When the last plate had been set on a shelf, and cutlery filled the new drawers, she switched on the kettle and set up a tray for a tea-break. The previous night, exhausted after the book launch, she'd found that Stephen had washed mugs left by the workers behind the backdrop. He'd shaken hands and gone away without mentioning what he'd done, and coming upon the mugs upturned in a tidy row on a duckboard, Ann had wanted to rush after him and give him a huge, grateful hug. Now, on her way downstairs with the tea, she met Angela on her way up. 'Dad's nipped out to get me a couple more junction boxes.'

'Fine. So, d'you want to have your tea up here in comfort? I'll join you when I've taken this to the others.'

When Ann came back, Angela was admiring the decluttered living room. 'It's a great place you've got here. Miles bigger than it looked.'

'When we were looking for a place to buy, Sheep Street wasn't the best location but, like you say, the flat's great, and we loved the shop's window, so we just went for it.'

'"If you build it, they will come."'

'That was the dream and, overall, it's working for the business. I think the best part has been the stuff we never dreamed of, though. Meeting so much kindness this week has been amazing. It feels like we've suddenly put down roots and we're home.'

Angela dunked a Rich Tea biscuit. 'You'll always get neighbours stepping in here, if you find yourself down on your luck. When I was a kid, it was Mum had the shop. Dad was a builder. Then the finance for a job went wrong and the bank came down on him heavy. He couldn't get back on his feet, and he got depression. God knows what would've happened if Fury hadn't stepped in. And, you know, he wasn't even close to the family. He just saw what had happened. I don't know exactly what he did, but he helped Mum, and coaxed Dad into expanding the shop. It was slow but, in the end, they turned things around.'

'I can imagine Fury stepping in, but coaxing doesn't sound like his style.'

Angela grinned. 'He does what's needful. And if he doesn't drive you mad, he'll bring out the best in you. That's what Mum says. She calls him the grit in Finfarran's oyster.'

At Garrybawn House, Theresa had left Hanna and Mary to their tea. Hanna was putting the stained-glass gingerbread back into the box when Mary said, 'There's something the matter with that little girl upstairs, you know. She's troubled.'

'Saoirse?'

'She's been in an odd state since lunchtime.'

'Maybe she's tired. Theresa says she's been up at the crack of dawn since your course started. Or it could be over-excitement. She was blown away at the launch when Adam took that selfie with her. I'd say there's a major crush going on there.'

'Ah, give her credit for a bit of sense. She's excited to meet him, but she's not the type to fall for a celebrity. The kids these days are way more savvy than that. Not like you with your George Michael posters.'

'I never fell for George Michael.'

'Just as well. By all accounts, you wouldn't have got very far with him.' Flicking a crumb from her knee, Mary shook her head decisively. 'No, with Saoirse it's not about calf-love, or being tired or over-excited. She's got something weighing on her mind and, if you ask me, those parents of hers would do well to pay attention.'

CHAPTER TWENTY

Stephen put his head round the bookshop door. 'Hi. I'm your delivery man.' Catherine, who was behind the till, said, 'Oh, God, no. Fury's co-opting people again.' He came in and, leaning on the counter, told her about Fury's visit to the library. 'I was passing your door anyway, so I offered to bring the cards and the carousel.'

'That's amazing. Thank you. And so generous of Hanna. When Fury said he was going out to get things for tonight, I didn't know he'd be blagging from her again.'

'She wasn't worried. She said she wished she'd thought of it herself.'

They were setting up the carousel when Ann came hurrying down from the flat. Catherine, who'd been laughing, saw the phone in her hand and froze. 'Has something happened?'

'It's just that dippy Gaby again. She gave the wrong address so that special order for us has ended up at a second-hand bookshop in Carrick.'

'Well, it's her mistake and she's in a hotel in Carrick. Can't she bring them here, or put them in a taxi?'

'No, because she's already flown back to London.'

'Oh, thanks a billion, Gaby.'

'We're lucky the second-hand bookshop was decent enough to call us.' Ann went to the till. 'If I take over here, will you drive to Carrick?'

Stephen asked, 'Can I be helpful?'

Ann had been so focused on the latest crisis that she'd hardly registered his presence. Now, before Catherine could answer, she looked at him thoughtfully. 'Well, book boxes are heavy. You could go along and help Catherine with the lifting.'

'Mum! He's already driven this lot up from the library. I'm well able to lift book boxes. I don't need help.'

Stephen was looking from Ann to Catherine and, feeling she'd sounded like a stroppy teenager, Catherine said firmly that she couldn't trespass further on his time. He smiled. 'I've finished my day's session at the library. It'd be no trouble to whip into Carrick with you.'

Ann gave Catherine a nudge. 'Actually, you're standing here wasting his time. Why not say thank you, and go? The last thing we need is you putting your back out. Anyway, it'll be quicker if there's two of you.'

If looks could have killed, Ann would have been stretched dead by the till, but Stephen said, 'We'll take my car,' and, without quite knowing how, Catherine found herself with her coat on.

By the time they reached the main road she'd relaxed enough to admit that Ann had been right. 'It's nice to sit back and let someone else drive. Almost as nice having someone to talk to on the road.'

'A rep's job can be lonely. You think you make friends along the way but, mostly, they're just contacts.'

Poker-faced, Catherine asked, 'You mean George Lucas never calls you?'

'Not George. Not Brad. It's heartbreaking.'

'Not even Jessica Rabbit?'

'I'd definitely have avoided giving my number to Jessica Rabbit. Way too scary and sexy.'

Catherine laughed. 'I grew up with all the Disney videos. *Who Framed Roger Rabbit* was one of my favourites.'

'I was a nerdy kid when it came to animation. More into early Pixar than Disney. Then I got into blockbusters, and obscure things that won the Palme d'Or, and didn't look back.'

They'd reached Carrick and were just coming off the ring-road when Catherine had a text. Glancing across as he turned the wheel, Stephen asked, 'Trouble?'

'The second-hand bookshop's had to close for an hour. The owner's been called away and there's no one to cover.'

'Okay, so that's not the end of the world. Do you fancy a walk while we're waiting?'

The road into town ran alongside a broad river, and steps from a pull-in up ahead led to a path by the rushing water. Doubtfully, Catherine asked, 'Would we freeze?'

'Not if we keep moving.'

When they were by the river, she realised he'd been right. There was little warmth in the winter sun but the only sign of the previous night's snow was a white frill or two in sheltered places. Small birds were hopping under bushes by the path and, on the river, a pair of swans sailed past dipping their long necks. Taking a deep breath, Catherine said, 'I spend way too much time indoors.'

'I'd probably be the same if I didn't have the garden.'

'Is gardening your hobby?'

'In a very literal sense, you could call it a pastime.'

Remembering he'd said that his wife had had all sorts of plans for the garden at Bridge House, Catherine bit her lip. Afraid that she'd hit a raw nerve, she was considering how to reply when he said, 'There's a line about that in *Waiting for Godot*. One of the tramps talks about something helping to pass the time, and the other tells him it would have passed anyway.'

This could have sounded bitter but, when she looked at him, he was smiling at her. Still embarrassed, she answered at random: 'I was going to put pots in our backyard, but I haven't got round to it.'

'Well, as every gardener will tell you, there's always next year.'

Except when there isn't, thought Catherine. Your wife had a stroke out of nowhere. She was there one minute, gone the next, and all your plans came to nothing.

His matter-of-fact voice interrupted her train of thought. 'What will you plant?'

'Where? Oh, in the pots. I don't know. I thought I'd go online and order seeds or something.'

'"Seeds or something" covers a hell of a ballpark.'

'That's probably why I haven't got round to it.'

As they walked on, Catherine struggled to make sense of this exchange. At no stage had Stephen seemed troubled but, consistently, he'd thrown her off balance. Could it be that they'd edged too close to something he'd rather not talk about, and everything else, from *Godot* to pot plants, had been a sort of smokescreen? Thinking about it, this seemed to be the most likely explanation. And if that's the case, she scolded herself, who could blame him? It's bad enough to trespass on a comparative stranger's time without mentally trespassing on his private emotions.

When they arrived at the second-hand bookshop, it had reopened and the owner helped Stephen to carry the boxes and stow them in the car. Feeling redundant, Catherine went to the café next door and bought a couple of takeaway coffees. Then, back on the road with their mission accomplished, she and Stephen spent the next ten minutes arguing cheerfully about Samuel Beckett.

'Oh, come on, Catherine, his novels are just wordy.'

'You only say that because you think in pictures.'

'I do not think in pictures.'

'Says the guy who spent most of his life staring up at a cinema screen.'

'That's so pathetic it doesn't deserve the dignity of an answer.'

Laughing, Catherine asked, 'Do you still love films now, or does going to one just feel like going to work?'

'I'll always love films. Summoning the energy to go on one's own can be grim, though.' Suddenly it was as if they were back on the riverside path. This time he faced the unspoken full-on, and said, 'Sorry. That sounded maudlin.'

Immediately, Catherine was overcome by a sense of inadequacy. Intimate conversations weren't her thing, and the fact that she felt she'd said the wrong thing earlier made her uncomfortable. Simply to fill the silence, she said, 'I imagine it can't be easy being alone.' Then, with the implications of this remark hanging in the air, she found herself unable to stop talking. 'Well, I'm alone, obviously. I mean, I don't have a partner. Not at the moment. Well, never, really. I mean, I've never really gone in for long-term relationships. No, what I meant to say is it must be hard to be alone after years of being married.' She stopped abruptly, feeling foolish and wondering what he must think of her.

Stephen said, 'Sophie and I married in 1995, so we had a decent innings.'

Determined not to make bad worse, Catherine said nothing. It had started to rain and he'd switched on the windscreen wipers. She watched them sweep to and fro, thrusting aside the falling rain. Suddenly the road ahead seemed treacherous and she longed to be the one in the driving seat. After a moment, she said, 'Nothing in life is certain, is it?' and, without looking at her, he said, 'That's why it shouldn't be wasted.'

Silence fell again and, though Stephen didn't seem troubled by it, Catherine sat racking her brains for what to say next. Then her phone buzzed with a message and she grabbed it with relief instead of her usual knee-jerk twinge of dread. Opening the text, she read *Turn on Craic With Caitríona NOW*.

Stephen was keeping his eyes on the road. 'What is it?'

'It's from my mum. She wants us to tune in to Finfarran FM.'

'Any reason?'

'I've given up asking for reasons for anything these last few days.'

When he'd fiddled with the radio controls, the presenter's voice filled the car.

'... that was Councillor Joe McEnroe, listeners, calling in to talk about solstice customs in Finfarran. That's our phone-in subject today, so if you've any thoughts on it, give us a ring, and I'll be delighted to hear from you.' Apparently without taking a breath, the voice continued, 'So. Next up, we have Ann from Lissbeg Books there in Lissbeg. Hello, Ann, welcome along to the show, how're you doing?'

Catherine's jaw dropped as Ann's voice said, 'Hi, Caitríona. Thanks for having me on.'

'So, listen, you've got a great solstice evening ahead. Is that the story?'

'Preparations are under way as we speak.'

'And yesterday you had Adam Rashid's book launch.'

'That was the first of our Christmas events, Caitríona. Tonight is a celebration of the solstice. Tomorrow we have a visitor from the North Pole dropping in to say hi to all the kids who love books and reading. And on Christmas Eve we've a charity carol concert.'

'God, it's all go in Lissbeg! Tell us about your solstice celebration.'

'It's going to be a fantastic display, with late-night shopping.'

'And here's another great thing you've got going there at Lissbeg Books. You've got art installations, haven't you, Ann? A new one revealed each day. What's that all about?'

'Well, the bookshop's event programme is part of a wider community project. We've had contributions from an art group and the library. Oh, and individual businesses and artists.'

'And I hear the food at the Coolest Chef's book launch was catered by Lissbeg's own Garden Café. How cool is that?'

'In a way, what we're trying to do is embody the spirit of the solstice. Communities coming together to get through the darkest part of the year with lights and feasting and entertainment.'

'And plenty of signed copies of the Coolest Chef's new cookbook. Is that right, Ann?'

'Absolutely. And plenty of other books too. Lots of Christmas reading.'

'And lots of solstice fun. Thanks a million there, Ann.' There was a music sting after which the presenter came back, sounding even more bouncy. 'Up next on the phone-in, we've a lady who says Councillor Joe McEnroe has his dates wrong! Sounds like Finfarran fisticuffs. Stay tuned, listeners ...'

The moment Stephen turned off the radio, Catherine's phone rang. Ann's voice was breathless. 'Did you hear it? Was I okay?'

'You were amazing.'

'It was Fury. He made me do it. Just shoved his phone into my hand and said I was in a queue to talk to Caitríona. He'd phoned the programme and got me a slot. They line you up to talk to her, like planes coming in to land.'

Stephen said, 'Tell her I take my hat off to her. She was brilliant.'

'Stephen says you were brilliant.'

'I was terrified. Fury had keywords written out and I couldn't find my glasses, so I ended up squinting through his.'

'Well, it was amazing. And you flagged our other events as well.'

'He'd written that bit in huge capital letters.'

'We'll be back soon. We've got the books.'

'Okay, see you later.'

When they got back, the blackout was up and a sign on the door read 'JOIN US 7 – 10 p.m. FOR LATE-NIGHT SOLSTICE SHOPPING'. Leaving Stephen to park the car, Catherine tapped on the shop door. It was opened by Fury, who said, 'There you are. We thought we'd lost you.' He stepped back to let her in and, once again, Catherine's breath caught in her throat.

The scarlet and gold banners were gone and, right across the dust-sheet backdrop, a curtain of trailing holly and ivy hung from the beam to the floor. Dancing along just below the beam, a chain of animals was accompanied by a band of birds playing pipes and drums. Cats were dressed as fine ladies with long, streaming veils. There were hares in hoods and jerkins, with leather boots on their feet. A bear danced arm in arm with a fox, who was carrying a tray of pies, and a hound in a feathered cap was playing a trumpet. Birds' beaks and glittering eyes poked out between twigs. Flowers outlined with dots of gold leaf combined the four seasons of the year, wood anemones and marsh marigolds, mistletoe and rose hips weaving a pattern through the living foliage, along with the painted dancers. Coming out from behind the counter, Ann linked Catherine. 'Isn't it inspired? Just some of the cards Fury got us from Hanna, hooked over a string. I can't believe how effective it is.'

'It's stunning.'

Suspended dead centre, where yesterday Adam's framed posters had hung, a gold disc gleamed against the curtain of holly and ivy. It hung low, as if about to set, and, through the hanging tendrils, the splashes of colour on the backdrop showed like flowers in a meadow. Ann gave a shaky laugh. 'Fury cut the sun out of one of the flatpacks the kitchen cabinets came in. Then he demanded all our gold gift-wrap.'

The Divil's tree, newly decorated in gold and silver, now stood with its lower branches reaching into the window, as if embracing Catherine's book tree. Turning, Catherine saw Fury with a second gold sun in his hand. It was smaller than the other and surrounded by silver rays. 'I made it for your window display tonight, if you wanted it.'

'How did you do the rays?'

'Panel pins. I glued them between a couple of gold paper plates from the book launch.'

'I didn't know we had plates left over.'

'We didn't. Terry fished them out of the bin and The Divil cleaned off a couple of blobs of icing. Look, do you want this or don't you? We're running behind schedule.'

The little sun in his hand was the perfect size for Catherine's book tree. He held it out and she took it, saying, 'Of course I do. It's lovely.'

'Work away, then. Get it up on your tree. I won't interfere with somebody else's creation.'

Climbing into the window, Catherine replaced the star on top of the book tree with the sun. When Ann switched on the string of lights, it glittered to their pulsing rhythm. Enchanted, Catherine stood watching until Fury looked at his watch and said, 'Right, showtime in five. Where are these books you and Stephen picked up in Carrick?'

CHAPTER TWENTY-ONE

When Adam came into the hotel foyer, Lia was at the desk talking to the receptionist. He had reached the lift when she came to join him. 'Wayne's going to take my cookies down to the staff room. My surprise cake went down a treat there yesterday.' Flashing her eyebrows at Adam, she said, 'So, you and me. What about it?'

'Sorry?'

'You're taking me to dinner tonight, right?'

Having left so abruptly the previous evening, Adam had spent the day torn between hoping he hadn't offended her and thinking that, if he had, it was probably for the best. She had a boyfriend waiting for her in Dublin, and he was supposed to be focusing on his career. Now, faced with this dream come true, his response took an effort. 'Look, Lia, I really don't think this is appropriate.'

'You don't?'

'No, I don't.'

'If you say so. But, where I come from, guys are expected to pay their debts.'

'What? What are you talking about?'

'Dinner was my shout yesterday, right? So tonight should be on you.'

'But – but Seán …'

'What about him?'

'I don't know. Oh, okay, this is crap, but I'm going to say it. I don't want to take you out to dinner. Not if you're spoken for.' Having made himself say it, he met her eyes and saw blank astonishment.

'Hang on. You think Seán is my boyfriend?'

'Isn't he?'

'No. No, he's not. For feck's sake, Adam, what gave you that idea?'

'Well, the daily WhatsApp calls, and all the texts about your secret Christmas present, and the chocolates and the choice of wine.'

The receptionist was leaning on the desk, watching with interest, so Lia hustled Adam into an alcove by the lift. Hands on hips, she faced him and said, 'Okay, pin back your ears. Seán's a mate who's organising Christmas for a crowd of us. People I work with at the pub. He's super-picky, so everything has to be right and done his way, which makes him hell to be around, but ensures a fantastic meal.'

'But the texts …'

'We're doing Secret Santa, and he picked me out of the hat. But, being Seán, he's terrified he'll choose the wrong present, so he blew the secret bit in the first half-hour.'

'Oh.'

'And I WhatsApp Oz each day because I'm really close with my family, which I could have told you if you'd asked.'

Adam leaned against the wall. 'Oh. Okay. Sorry.'

'And "spoken for"? Who are you, Charles Dickens?'

'I said sorry.'

Relenting, Lia grinned. 'Okay, forget it. Are we having dinner or not?'

Every ounce of common sense Adam had was screaming, 'Don't do this,' but instead he said, 'Yeah. Sure. Why not?'

'Good. There's a list of local restaurants at Reception. Let's ask Wayne.'

'Absolutely not.'

'Eh?'

'I may be an idiot but I do know how to pick a restaurant. Give me time to change and book a table, and I'll meet you down here.'

Ten minutes later, towelling his hair at his bedroom mirror, Adam stared at his reflection and watched a blissful smile spread across his face. Since becoming the Coolest Chef, he'd had women queuing up to go out with him, yet here he was behaving as if he was fifteen again. Which was just what it felt like. A tingling, bubbling feeling of anticipation mixed with the fear that perhaps he was dreaming, and that when he went back downstairs Lia wouldn't be there. But beneath this was the knowledge that, if Dom knew, he'd disapprove. Dom viewed personal relationships as distraction. He preferred his clients unattached, and emotionally dependent on himself.

He stepped out of the lift on the dot of seven. Lia was sitting in Reception. She was wearing jeans, a green sweater and trainers; her coat, scarf and a bobble hat were on the sofa beside her. 'Hi. Where are we eating?'

'Would you mind if we drove back to Lissbeg? There's a place called Shepherds that's got a decent chef.'

'No worries.'

Adam helped her into her coat and they went out and down the front steps. Out of the corner of his eye, he'd seen a couple on their way to the hotel dining room, nudging each other and hovering in the hopes of saying hello. Aware that Lia had seen them too, he said, 'I'm really sorry. That's the result of the damn TV coverage. Lissbeg mightn't be much better, but Shepherds did seem to grasp that I wanted a quiet table.'

'You know, no one would give you a second look if you smarmed your hair down. It's the pricy signature cut that's the giveaway.'

'It's not a signature cut.'

'Oh, please! Don't tell me your guys didn't march you off to some hair guru. Here, hang on a minute.' They'd turned down an alley to the car park behind the hotel. Lia reached up to push his hair back. 'Shit, that's a helluva lot of product you use.'

Her touch had made Adam shy like a horse.

'Here, you can have my bobble hat as a disguise.'

'Don't be daft. Anyway, we're about to get in the car.'

'Fair point. Better to wait and wear it at the restaurant.'

'Oh, yeah, right. That'll be inconspicuous.'

When they got to Lissbeg, Adam parked on Broad Street. As they paused by the flower-filled horse trough on the traffic island, he dropped a coin into the box by the crib. Lia said, 'That's a cute nativity scene. It looks like each figure has been carved from a different kind of wood.'

'It's a good pitch for the charity box. Nobody likes to see people sleeping on the streets at Christmas.'

When they'd navigated the Broad Street traffic, they turned up Sheep Street. The air had a tang of frost and, as they passed the bookshop, they could see shoppers milling about inside. Lia stopped to admire the book tree topped with its radiant sun. 'I heard Ann talking about this on the radio. They're having a winter-solstice celebration.' Linking her arm in Adam's, she said, 'We have it in June in Oz. There's an awesome place in Wathaurong country where First Nation people laid out stone markers. Like, thousands of years ago, and the stones are still there.'

'What do they mark?'

'The positions of the setting sun at equinoxes and solstices.'

Half distracted by her nearness, Adam was trying to remember a name. 'There's a place like that here in Ireland.'

'I know. Newgrange. Older than the Pyramids. Older than Stonehenge. I went out to see it when I first arrived.'

'So, you're into astronomy?'

'Well, I do love a night sky but I'm no astronomer. I guess I'm just interested in stuff that people who run around chasing money don't think about.'

At the restaurant, they settled at a corner table, and the waitress brought bread and olives and went to fetch wine. Looking at Lia in the candlelight, Adam wondered if she always wore make-up at dinner, or if tonight it might be about looking good for him.

It was subtle, just a touch of eyeliner and a hint of colour on her cheekbones. Her long, curling lashes were naturally dark and her skin was great. Catching him looking at her, Lia laughed and asked if she passed muster.

'I was thinking you look great.'

Taking up a knife, she peered at her reflection in it. 'I never know why I bother with eyeliner.'

'You don't need it.'

'Nobody needs eyeliner. It's just a look.'

'Much like my signature haircut.'

'God, you're thin-skinned, you know that? Lighten up the hair's pretty good, actually.'

The menu came, and Lia said, 'This all looks great. Still, if it's Christmas and you're Australian, there's no choice. It's got to be prawns.'

'Have you been away from home long?'

'Nearly a year.'

'That's quite a stretch.'

'Yeah, but we WhatsApp all the time.' Lia grinned wickedly. 'And I'd be there now but I won a stupid competition.'

Struck again by the sheer luck of their paths happening to cross, Adam asked, 'Would you have gone home for Christmas otherwise?'

'Yeah, but I wasn't going to miss a freebie on the Wild Atlantic Way. I'll be home for New Year's, anyway. My nan's coming to my parents' for a big family get-together.'

'Your nan who glazes cakes with lemon myrtle leaves?'

'And fixes engines. Yep. She's Dad's mum. Mum and Dad wanted her to come to them for Christmas, but she's on a mission to straighten out Granddad's affairs. So they decided to party at New Year's instead.' Lia popped an olive into her mouth and said, 'Yum, that's delicious. Yeah, we WhatsApp all the time anyway, so hanging on here in Ireland for your course was no biggie.'

'That's a ringing endorsement.'

'Compliments are like crack cocaine to you celebrities, aren't they? I hear you get hooked on the dopamine.'

Pointedly ignoring this, Adam said, 'It's the prawns for you, then?'

Lia laughed. 'Actually, I'm loving the course. I think you're a great teacher.'

'Well, that's good to hear, given that teaching was never in the life-plan.'

Looking interested, she asked, 'So what was the life-plan?'

'Cook fresh food. Get paid for it.'

'That's it?'

'Pretty much.'

'But you teach so well. You're not snotty.'

'See, that's the kind of compliment that produces the dopamine rush.'

'You know what I mean. The way you're interested in Declan, and how you deal with Darina. You're good with people.'

With his eyes on the bread roll on which he was spreading butter, Adam said, 'Too many people think they can't transform their lives. Well, I'm living proof that that isn't true. Not because I won some dumb title, but because I know from experience that getting a grasp of growing and cooking is genuinely empowering. And one of the upsides of winning the dumb title is that it allows me to pass the experience on.'

'I like that.'

Instead of returning the warm smile she gave him, Adam suddenly groaned and said, 'Oh, shit. Here comes the downside.'

A man from a nearby table had pushed back his chair and was bearing down on them. 'Will you look at that! It's yourself, isn't it? Jamie? No. Marcus? No – don't tell me –Adam! Adam Rashid, the Coolest Chef, large as life and twice as natural!' All around, heads were turning. Lia saw Adam's face smooth into a mask of polite composure as the man leaned heavily on their table. 'Well, the wife won't believe me, I'm telling you that. She'll be raging now on her spa night below in West Cork. Ah, listen, I'll have to send her a photo. Sorry now, but I can't miss out on the opportunity. Here, will I buy us a drink? Waitress! Another bottle here. What're you drinking, Adam? Don't be reaching for money, now. I'm standing this.'

'I'm not drinking, thanks. I'm driving.'

'Well, crush in there now, and we'll take a selfie.'

Before the man could sit down, Lia stood up briskly. 'I'm really sorry, but we were just leaving.'

'But you've menus there and you haven't even ordered.'

She gave him a dazzling smile. 'We're going to be late if we don't get our skates on. Great to meet you. Bye.' Taking Adam's arm, she propelled him towards the door, where the waitress, who'd grasped what was happening, was standing with their coats. As she propelled him between tables, Lia leaned in and murmured in Adam's ear, 'You just can't take a steer, can you? If you'd worn the damn bobble hat, like I told you, I'd be sitting back there now, wolfing prawns.'

They paid for the wine, and left. Outside, frost had silvered the pavements. Across the street, at the bookshop, people were talking and laughing. Through its open door, Lia could glimpse the curtain of holly and ivy, with the dancing animals overhead and the gold disc of the sun. She hooked her arm into Adam's again. 'Let's go celebrate the solstice.'

'If I can find us a table somewhere else on a Saturday night. Look, I'm really sorry.'

'I don't mean a restaurant. We'll commune with the Atlantic. How about going to those cliffs we saw from the bus?'

'Lia, it's freezing, and you haven't eaten.'

'Oh, come on. Look at the stars, all hemmed in by houses. They'll be incredible seen from a cliff.'

'It'll be pitch dark. You won't see the ocean.'

'We'll hear it. We'll smell the salt. There'll be moonlight. Plus, I have chocolate. Honestly, what happened back there doesn't matter. Come on, Adam, let's go with the flow.'

They drove away from the town and down country roads that meandered towards the ocean. A fox crossing from ditch to ditch was caught in the car's headlights and, for a long moment, considered them through remote golden eyes. The further they went, the more the glimmer of starlight became apparent, and the wider the expanse of night sky. At a turn just past a field gate, a lane led onto a headland. Easing the car between ruts, and hearing briars scraping against its paintwork, Adam said, 'God knows what the hire company's going to charge me for this.'

'Should we back up?'

'Absolutely not.'

When they ran out of lane, they walked out to a headland and sat in the lee of a rock to look up at the stars. It was chilly but they were both warmly dressed and, around the curving bay, firelight flickered on high places and headlands like their own. Lia said, 'Gosh, some people here still light solstice bonfires.'

'Looks like it. You wouldn't get this up in Dublin.'

Breaking a bar of chocolate, she asked, 'How long did you spend in Finfarran when you were younger?'

'About six months.' Adam waited for another question but she just held out the chocolate. Taking a piece, he said, 'I've never really talked about it.' Then, when she still said nothing, he began to talk. 'I had a great childhood. Dad was a hospital pharmacist. Mum was a triage nurse.'

He stopped abruptly and, quietly, Lia asked, 'What happened?'

'He died. Got sick. Died. I was in bits. And somewhere in my head, I must have decided he'd abandoned us.' Adam stopped again, then went on with increasing fluency: 'That was daft, but kids come up with daft stuff, don't they? Especially if talking's not their thing.'

Holding her breath, Lia waited as he stripped the silver paper from the square of chocolate. He looked out at the solstice lights. 'Anyway, to begin with, we coped okay, me and Mum. She drank a bit, though, to help her keep going. She'd hardly have had a beer before Dad died. Then she got picked up by a boyfriend, a lazy fecker called Fergal, who moved in and sat around on his arse while she went out to work. He knew I couldn't stand him, and he wanted me out of the house. I was still at school, coming up to my Junior Cert. I'd been pretty good at schoolwork till then, but Fergal destroyed everything. He started knocking Mum around and I began bunking off. He was a racist bastard too. Went on about Dad being Egyptian, and used to call me a mongrel behind Mum's back.'

Still looking at the lights, he went on, as if speaking to himself, 'Anyway, things went from bad to worse and Mum stopped going to work. She was always hung-over or bruised or too depressed. Fergal controlled her and she lost all her self-confidence. Then, one day, when she was out, he started needling again and I went berserk. Scared the shit out of Fergal and trashed everything in sight. He got away before I could do him much damage, but I knew he'd call the guards, and when I saw what I'd done to the house, I couldn't stay there and face Mum. So I left. What I should've done was go to a teacher, or someone. But I was scared that, if I did, I'd be put into care. Anyway, I reckoned that, by then, the school would have given up on me. I suppose the bastard had sucked away all my self-confidence too.'

'What age were you then?'

'A couple of weeks shy of my seventeenth birthday. I knew social services couldn't touch me once I was eighteen. What I didn't know was that a year's a long time to last when you're sleeping rough.'

'So, how did you come to Finfarran?'

'Just by chance. The streets in Dublin were too much for me. I was shit-scared, and I thought things might be easier in the country. I met a guy who was making for Finfarran, so I tagged along.'

Lia could hear the sound of the ocean far below them, pounding against the cliffs and drawing back. Adam had gone silent again. She asked, 'Were things easier when you got away from the city?'

'Not a lot. But then I had flu, and was really sick, and when I left the hospital, I got lucky and was given a place in a halfway house in Carrick. It was run by a big slab of a priest called Martin. Hands like shovels, and a law unto himself. It's a vicious circle if you're a kid trying to escape the street. To get a job, you need a PPS number. To get a PPS number, you need to have an address. Martin found live-in jobs for people, to get the ball rolling. He got me one as a kitchen porter.'

'Where?'

'The Royal Victoria Hotel.'

'You're kidding.'

'Scrubbing floors, filling bins, and scraping burned pots.' With a strange look on his face, Adam turned and met Lia's eyes. 'You could sell that story if you liked. Find some tabloid journalist who'd be willing to give you the price of an upgrade on your flight home to your cosy family in Oz.'

SUNDAY

22 December

CHAPTER TWENTY-TWO

When Lia woke, she reached for the phone by her bed. Then she drew back her hand and rolled away restlessly. Too much and too little had been said on the headland the previous night, and she needed time to process how she felt. Lying on her back, she stared up at her bedroom ceiling, remembering the moon hanging above the ocean.

Adam's suggestion that she might betray his confidence had left her half outraged, half inclined to cry. But, having made it, he'd seemed more shaken than she was so, rather than pick a fight or demand comfort, she'd pointed at the sky. 'This phase of the moon is called gibbous waning. Getting smaller after having been full. It's associated with introspection and re-evaluation. And the winter-solstice moon has its own name. Did you know that?'

Adam had raised his head and looked at the pale, diminished sphere above them. At first Lia had wondered if he'd taken in what she'd said. Then, he'd started to speak again, in a voice so strained she could hardly hear it. 'There's a page in the nuns' book about what to plant when the moon is waning. Flowering bulbs, and vegetables that bear crops underground.' His face had looked grey in the moonlight, and his hands were clasped around his up-drawn knees. 'There's another page, about companion planting. Things that flourish beside each other. Like alliums planted round carrots deter root fly. When I worked at the Royal Vic, I used to come to Lissbeg on the bus, to volunteer in the nuns' garden.'

He seemed to have forgotten Lia was there and, briefly, it had seemed that he was going to shut down again, but he'd carried on talking, staring out at the fires that flared in the distance. 'There was a woman who came to the halfway house to help with what they called reintegration. She told me how to get qualifications and find out about training programmes. That kind of thing. When she found I'd always wanted to work in a restaurant, she said I ought to know how food is grown. She knew the nuns' garden was always on the lookout for volunteers, so she told me the way to Lissbeg and I went along. It literally turned my life around. Without her and Martin and the garden, I'd probably still be on the streets. Or dead, more likely, given the state I was in by the time I got taken to hospital.'

He'd seemed to run out of words after that so, not knowing what else to do, Lia had held out the chocolate bar again, but instead of accepting a piece, he'd gripped her hand fiercely. 'That was a rotten thing I said to you. I'm sorry. I'm so sorry, Lia. I'm not used to this. Another downside of winning the dumb title is that everybody's your friend and there isn't one of them you can trust.'

On the floor above Lia's, Adam had hardly slept and, when his wake-up call came through, he was lying in bed with his mind in turmoil. Why, when sitting with the girl he loved under a frosty sky, had he spouted crap he'd thought was long buried, and then been unforgivably offensive? She should have walked away and left him there. He would have deserved it. But she hadn't. She hadn't even sounded upset. Instead she'd started talking about the sky. The air had been full of the scents of salt and seaweed. Solstice fires had shimmered on distant headlands like fallen stars and, beyond his hurt and confusion, he'd been aware of the taste of dark honeycomb chocolate, and of grabbing her hand lest hissing waves should rise up and drag him down. And she hadn't walked away. She'd held onto his hand and they'd just sat there in silence for ages, listening to the ocean and looking up at the waning moon.

And now he had to psych himself up for the last day of his course not knowing if she'd be there or if, given how he'd behaved, she'd stay away. Sitting up wearily, he reached for his phone. The first thing he saw when he turned it on was a message sent by Dom the previous evening. *Things are looking good. Had an offer and Heads of Contract. They want you body and soul, so they'll have to up the fee, but I'm confident that won't be a deal-breaker. Thing is, Christmas is Wed. so I'll be out of office from tomorrow, Mon. Any chance of a call Sun. to discuss?*

Hitting Reply, Adam typed *Sure. Say 3.30?* and received an emoji thumbs-up.

In the bookshop, Catherine finished gift-wrapping the latest crime novel. Taking it, Hanna said, 'This has become a sacred tradition. I buy Brian a book for Christmas, and end up reading it myself before he gets round to it.'

'Where are you guys spending Christmas Day?'

'At home. Jazz is away this year, and my mother's coming to us for dinner. Whatever we cook will be wrong, of course, but that's traditional too. How's your kitchen going?'

'Done. Still wants painting, but it's a functioning kitchen. My mum will be doing dinner for us – she's the domesticated one.'

'In our house, I do bog-standard stuff, like the turkey. Brian goes wild with zabaglione, and things like sea-salt shortbread made with olive oil.'

'I bet they go down well with Mary!'

'Actually, where Mary's concerned, Brian can do no wrong.'

'She's a complex character.'

Hanna laughed. 'She's a roaring bitch on occasion. But, God love her, she's great fun too, and she's getting old. Mind you, she might outlive the lot of us. Garrybawn House has made a big difference. I think she was finding it hard living alone.'

'I suppose old age is ahead of us all. Assuming we live to see it.'

'Ah, now, Ann's only in her sixties. She won't be slowing down for a while.'

'I was thinking of myself, actually.'

'Would you pull yourself together! You're overworked, that's the problem. You'll have to put your feet up once you've got through Christmas Eve.'

'Listen, I'm just here, living from moment to moment, with no idea what's going to happen next.'

There was a crash beyond the dust sheets and Fury emerged from between them. 'C'mere to me, do you have any felt-tip markers? Big, solid ones you'd use for writing out a poster.'

'There should be some in the office.'

'I don't suppose you've got barricade tape?'

'What on earth is barricade tape?'

'It's got yellow and black zigzag lines and "KEEP OUT" printed along it.'

'Definitely don't have that.'

'Not a problem. Terry will pick it up when he goes looking for traffic cones. I'm doing a temporary poster to get us through the noise of this morning's work.'

He disappeared, and Catherine looked at Hanna. 'See what I meant? I haven't the faintest clue what he's on about.'

'And now I need to stay to find out.'

'Be my guest.'

Moments later, Fury reappeared with a large scroll, cut from a roll of lining-paper. Looking over his shoulder as he unfurled it on the counter, Catherine and Hanna saw what he'd written in huge, scarlet letters: 'BACK OFF. DANGER. BEWARE ELVES.'

When Adam arrived at the centre, Phil popped out of her office to say she'd arranged a farewell photo session to end the day.

'They'll all want individual shots and souvenir selfies, so we'll get them done first and then take a big group shot by the tree.' The thought of posing for a selfie with Lia surrounded by everyone looking on had freaked him, so he reached the kitchen door simultaneously longing to see her and fervently hoping she'd stayed away. But when he got in, she was there by her bench, putting on her apron and, though she didn't look up, she seemed perfectly calm.

Forcing himself into performance mode, Adam said, 'Welcome, everyone, to our final session. I'll be cooking for you today, and I may need assistance. Looking at you, Saoirse.' He turned, expecting to find her beside him, but Saoirse was standing at the back with her shoulders hunched.

Hearing her name, she jumped, said, 'Sure,' and received a sharp look from Mary.

Determined not to lose his own concentration, Adam explained they'd spend the morning making a Christmas buffet, to eat together as a farewell lunch. 'Festive food created around a simple centrepiece, using ingredients everyone's likely to have in the store cupboard or the fridge at Christmas time. I'll prep and cook a salmon, and show you how to come up with the easiest of last-minute puddings. You'll be creating accompaniments and blinis.'

Inevitably, Mary announced that blinis were only some class of a foreign scone. Karen said surely she meant a pancake. Mr Maguire said that, while the ingredients were not dissimilar, the methods produced very different results. 'A knowledge of the distinctive chemical processes involved is what divides the chefs from the cooks.'

Pleased to have provoked a challenge, Mary tied her apron strings in a double-knot. 'I know exactly what to do with flour, butter and eggs, thank you. I've been throwing them together since God was a boy.'

Yesterday, a spat like this would have led to a flash of amusement between Adam and Lia. Now, not daring to look at her, Adam kept going. 'Today's timing will have to be structured to bring everything together. To begin with, I'll show you the prep for the salmon. As soon as that's in the oven you'll swing into action. There'll be seven of you on blinis, each making a batch of twelve. It's a yeast-free recipe, so it doesn't need proving time, and there's a choice of ingredients for you to top them with. You'll need to plan your toppings first as a team, to make sure you don't double up on textures, flavours and appearance. Then you'll break out to your benches with your chosen ingredients. Meanwhile, the remaining two of you will be making soda bread and potato salad. Anyone want to volunteer for those?'

Mary said she'd rather throw together a few decent cakes of bread than fiddle about with fancy bits and pieces.

'Okay. So, it's Mary on soda bread. Who's up for the potato salad?'

Janice raised her hand. 'I could do some plain, and some with chives or pickled gherkins.'

'Perfect. The acidic gherkins make a lovely contrast with the mayo, and chives are a milder choice. And choice is what buffets are all about.'

Having gathered them round the table, he began to prep the salmon, telling himself he had only a few more hours of this to get through, and that, so far, he'd managed to keep his cool.

But to Lia his tension was evident, and the resolute way in which he was coping made her feel wretched. Having struggled to process what had happened the previous night on the headland, she'd concluded it would probably be best not to see him again. The leap from what she had taken to be an easy-going acquaintance had felt way too sudden and intense. Anyway, as she'd be leaving Finfarran tomorrow, she didn't see where they could possibly go next.

She'd gone down to breakfast inclined to give the group's final session a miss, but as she'd eaten her eggs she'd changed her mind. If she didn't turn up, the others would surely wonder what had happened to her, and it didn't seem fair to spoil their last day by stirring up speculation, or to expect Adam to handle it. So she'd decided the better option was to go in as usual, and behave as if last night hadn't happened. After all, it was only a matter of a few more hours' baking, and wasn't it likely that Adam, too, would be eager to lighten things up?

But the moment she'd seen him walk into the kitchen, she'd realised she'd been wrong: he was wound up like a spring and evidently her presence was making things worse. Watching him combine avocados and lime juice, the picture of efficiency in his immaculate chef's whites, Lia remembered how, the previous night as they'd driven back to Carrick, she'd asked if his mother was okay now, and he'd answered, without taking his eyes off the road, 'She's dead.'

'God, Adam, I'm sorry.'

'When Dad was alive, I used to watch cookery programmes on telly with Mum. That was what got me interested in becoming a chef.'

He'd shown no inclination to want to talk any more about it and, wishing she hadn't asked, Lia had said no more. Now she wished she hadn't teased him about being a celebrity. Blessed with a supportive family, and friends whose trustworthiness she'd never had reason to question, it hadn't occurred to her to wonder how hard a road he might have travelled to gain it, or that he might be facing the world alone.

It wasn't long before the table laid with ingredients for the blini toppings was looking like a rummage sale five minutes after the doors had been opened. Having put his salmon in the oven, Adam left Saoirse to clear up, and went round the benches to see how things were progressing. Except for Darina, who was struggling with frying, most of the team of seven already had blinis cooling, and were getting creative with smoked salmon, goats' cheese, beetroot, quail's eggs, figs or avocados. Janice was steadily peeling potatoes, and Mary was perched on a stool completing a small crochet doily. Looking up as Adam approached, she remarked that it took five minutes to knock up a few cakes of soda bread, which would need only twenty minutes in the oven. 'We'll want it hot or there's no decent eating in it, so I'm not going putting flour to a board at this hour of the morning.'

Adam moved on, checking benches and making encouraging noises. Sooner or later, he'd have to go and talk to Lia and, as the moment grew closer, he had no idea how he'd cope. Appalled by how he'd turned and snarled at her on the headland, he was still struggling to understand why it had happened. When he'd decided he wanted to come and give this course in Finfarran, he'd been certain that he'd moved on and left his past behind. He'd wanted to recall his days in the nuns' garden, go to the library to look at their book again, talk to Hanna, and feel that, by agreeing to come, he was giving something back to the place that had set him on his path to celebrity. The idea of staying at the Royal Victoria had been a bit of a joke, especially as no one on the present staff could recognise him from before. It had never occurred to him that it would drag other memories to the surface, or that he'd walk into the breakfast room and fall in love with a girl whose home was on the other side of the world.

Now, as he stood by Darina's bench, watching her burn blinis, he realised it wasn't surprising that yesterday, as he'd got ready to go out to dinner with Lia, he'd felt like a teenager dressing for a first date. Since becoming the Coolest Chef, he'd booked plenty of restaurant tables for two. But, mostly, those occasions had been photo-ops set up by Dom, with girls who had careers of their own to promote and were happy to play along. Often they'd had families and kids to go home to when he'd returned alone to his studio flat. Before that, in the years when he'd worked in hotels and restaurant kitchens, there'd never been time for anything but work and sleep. And before that again, he thought, I was a scared kid way out of my depth, hungry, cold and just trying to stay alive. The crazy truth is that last night was my first real date, the only one that's ever mattered, and I made a pig's ear of it.

He wished he'd had more chances to talk to his dad. They hadn't spent much time together, because of the long hours Dad worked at the hospital. But sometimes they'd go to the pool in Portmarnock, dive from the highest board and splash about like brown fishes while other kids and their freckly dads shivered and watched from the side.

His dad never talked about the past, he'd tell you it didn't matter. Life was for living now, and looking back was a waste of time. According to Adam's mum, immigrants often took that view. 'Walking away from all you've known takes courage, Adam. You have to hoard your strength and concentrate on the here and now.' His mum, who wasn't much of a talker either, had made a courageous choice too. She'd married despite unspoken disapproval from her family, which had crackled in the background throughout Adam's childhood. Sometimes he'd told himself that if he'd had her fair skin and red-gold hair, his Irish grandparents, who had lived no more than a couple of miles away, might have been there for him when Dad died. But after the funeral they'd seldom called and, knowing how they'd felt about her choice of husband, his mum hadn't reached out to them for help. Instead she'd lain around drinking and having rows with Fergal. Afterwards, Adam had been tormented by the thought that he should have held his ground and not allowed Fergal to push him onto the streets. Wrapped in a sleeping-bag, ashamed and lonely, he'd been angry with his mum for failing to cope.

Life on the streets had taught him that, as well as his looks, he'd inherited his dad's resilience. It had taken longer to discover that it wasn't his mum he'd been angry with at all. Instead he'd been furious with himself for not knowing how to protect her.

CHAPTER TWENTY-THREE

Mr Maguire's blinis were a sight to behold. Beautifully textured and perfectly uniform, both in shape and colour, they were expertly finished with the simplest, most elegant of toppings. With infinite care, he placed them on a slate platter to a chorus of praise from everyone at the surrounding workbenches. Then, adjusting his half-moon specs, he shook his head sadly. 'You're very kind but, of course, you're wrong. A traditional blini is made from buckwheat flour and raised with yeast. And, properly speaking, they want double-proving.' Adam had come to admire his bite-sized offerings, each crowned with rare beef, sour cream and dill, and positioned in perfect symmetry on the glossy black slate. 'Congratulations, those are really exceptional.'

Looking at him reproachfully, Mr Maguire said, 'Thank you. The *classic* topping would have been caviar.'

Janice had filled three large bowls with potato salad and was competently chopping parsley. Adam spoke to her briefly and, knowing he couldn't avoid speaking to Lia any longer, crossed to where she was spooning blueberry compôte onto her blinis. He opened his mouth with no idea what he was going to say and, before he could speak, was interrupted by Mary, who suddenly shot off her stool and shouted, 'Pat Fitz! What in the name of God are you doing here?' Startled, everyone turned and saw Pat's anxious face peering round the door.

Reprieved, Adam grasped the edge of Lia's workbench and, stepping into the room, Pat gave him a self-deprecatory smile. 'I know I'm the world's worst to be interrupting, but I just need to give Mary a little message. The thing is, Mary, we're having an extra carol rehearsal now, just down the hall.'

Mary set down her crochet doily. 'Is it in the gym?'

'It is. That was the only space Phil had empty.'

'And the one with the worst acoustic. God knows what the council was at when they put my Hanna's library into the school assembly hall. Hadn't the nuns a grand stage there, and great sound that came back at you from the oak panelling? And look at it now, ruined with that ridiculous glass wall and all the books.'

'Time moves on, though, Mary.'

'It does, and it seldom changes things for the better.'

'Isn't that what we all say at our age, girl? You wouldn't want to listen.'

'I wish you'd say what you came to say and let me get on with me bread.'

'Is it bread you're making?'

'It is, and I don't know why Jazz had to fork out a king's ransom for me to sit here waiting for hours before I'd throw it together. Thanks be to God I had my bit of work with me to pass the time.'

'Is it a doily?'

'The last of ten. They're a Christmas present for Jazz. The young seem to have nothing they need in their houses, these days. I'm giving her the freebie yokes they throw out to us here, as well. One of those chef's aprons, a whisk and a piping set.'

'Isn't that great altogether? Does she do much baking?'

'None at all.'

By this stage, everyone had suspended what they'd been doing. The ladies from Cork were fascinated but too polite to gape, but most of the others were watching open-mouthed, with the air of people wishing they had popcorn and a Coke. Suddenly aware of silence, Pat looked disconcerted. A tiny woman, she seemed engulfed in the bright yellow anorak she wore over an Aran jumper and a neat tweed skirt. Her hair was cropped in an urchin cut and, unlike Mary who favoured buckles and patent leather, her feet were encased in sensible shoes with Velcro straps. Peering around, she said, 'Ah, lookit, I've gone and cracked the zone. I'm so sorry. No, listen, Mary, it's only just that we've added a final Alleluia. It's Ursula Flood from the pharmacy that's composed it. Just a short roar for the end of the concert, to send us off with a bang.'

'And who the hell is Ursula Flood to be throwing in Alleluias with no notice?'

'It was only last night it came to her, when she was having a go at her mouth-organ variations. She says it was like an angel's voice whispering in her ear. No, and look, I won't keep you now. I just wanted to tell you. We'll be rehearsing in the gym, but, since you're not available, I can take you through it tomorrow at my place. Will you pop in?'

'I will in me hat. I've more to do with my time than mugging up stuff at the last minute. It's downright unprofessional, and I won't be put upon.'

'Ah, don't be that way. She's put a special line into it for you.'

About to return to her doily, Mary turned sharply. 'D'you tell me that?'

'And you can't go turning down a divine intervention. I mean, where would we all be now if Our Blessed Lady had slammed the door on the Angel Gabriel?'

'That's downright blasphemy, Pat Anastasia Fitzgerald.'

'You have to admit it's a fair point, though.'

Pursing her lips, Mary said she had a few bits and pieces to pick up in the town the next day. 'My bus home doesn't go till six. I'll step in to you before that.'

Pat beamed and said that'd be great altogether. 'I'm sorry now, everyone, I'll be off. I'll be gone now, I won't disturb you. And come here till I shake your hand, Rasher. I'd no chance at the book launch. You're very welcome back to Lissbeg. You know that, don't you? It's great to see you.' Beaming, she thrust out her hand and approached Adam, and, to Lia's surprise, his answering smile held none of the polished charm he used on fans. Instead, holding Pat's hand, he bent his head to greet her almost as if he was going to give her a kiss. She stood on tiptoe, touched his cheek for a moment and, when he took her to the door, gave him another sweet smile before she left. Then he came back to Lia's bench and, watching him approach, she saw his professional self take over again.

The interruption had seemed to relax him and, having sensed how wound up he'd been, Lia wondered why Pat's arrival should have released the spring. Then, irritated, she told herself it was none of her business to wonder. Other than being a bloke she'd happened to meet on the west coast of Ireland, he was nothing to her, since she didn't expect she'd ever meet him again.

Stephen had had a late breakfast and couldn't be bothered to think about lunch. Beyond the conservatory door, two robins were fighting for the crusts he'd put on the bird table. Despite the food left out, he seldom saw finches this time of year, as they tended to join larger feeding flocks and forage more widely in winter. He knew they'd come back, as they always did, but he missed their friendly presence.

He lit the fire in the living room, made more coffee, sat down and tried to decide what to do with the three copies of *Cakes To Come Home To* he'd bought at Catherine's book launch. Everyone he knew in Finfarran had probably got their own, and now it was too late to put these in the post to friends in Dublin. Eventually, he decided to discard the festive gift-wrap, and set them aside to use during the year as birthday presents. Unwrapping the first copy, he saw they'd been slipped with Catherine's bookmarks, reproductions of the shop's scarlet banners with the website address on the back. It was typical of her, he thought, to pay that kind of attention to detail, and make use of each possible chance to market her business.

Running his finger across the gilded lettering, he thought of what Catherine had said about her decision to come to Finfarran. She'd called it a dream come true but, almost in the next breath, had told him she felt she was living in a nightmare.

The apparent contradiction wasn't surprising: it took courage and vision to sell two homes and invest every penny you had in a risky business, particularly in a town where you had no connections. Which was why he'd made that lame crack about seeing the nightmare as a challenge.

Sitting back in his chair, Stephen looked out at his wintry garden wondering if there'd been more to the challenge than just a business venture. She'd told him she'd been tired of her job, but nothing about the roots she'd had to pull up to make her move. But why should she? He admired her, but he couldn't expect to become her confidant on the strength of a few days' acquaintance. Thinking of roots, he stood up and went to his fireside bookcase. He knew that somewhere on his shelves there was a book on container planting. Given that Catherine was a bookseller, she'd find it easy to source one herself but, from what she'd said on their riverside walk, she was planning to go online and buy things at random, which was a recipe for disaster.

Finding what he was looking for, Stephen sat back on his heels and turned the pages. If Catherine wanted pots in her yard, there was plenty of inspiration in the book's illustrations, and the text was well laid-out and informative. Perhaps, if she'd like to borrow it, he could advise her on seeds and germination, and even offer slips from his own garden. The cost of buying established plants could be eye-wateringly high, and he'd gathered that part of the nightmare this week was a fear of not making ends meet.

Pleased with his plan, Stephen went back to his armchair, settled down again with his coffee and started to read the book. He was looking at a half-section of a pot layered up with compost when, suddenly, he remembered the drive back from Carrick, how rain had slipped down his windscreen like tears, and the flustered way Catherine had talked about not going in for relationships. For a moment the memory seemed no more than an idle thought. Then, sitting upright in dismay, he felt his heart lurch. Why had she chosen to tell him that? And why had she seemed so awkward? Might it have been because he'd come across as a needy widower who kept turning up at her shop uninvited? And now he was proposing to push in again unasked, with offers of advice and suggestions for how she could save money.

Shocked, Stephen laid aside the book and stared again at the garden. When he'd got up this morning he'd planned an afternoon stroll down Sheep Street to look in on the bookshop event and offer to help if anything needed doing. Now, in imagination, he could see Catherine roll her eyes and murmur to Ann that he was becoming a bore. At the back of his mind, he knew that this was nonsense. That in the last few days, they'd been grateful for his help, and that what he'd been able to do for them had made a real difference. But now he could see that he wanted more than gratitude from Catherine, because what he'd grown to feel for her was more than admiration. Having found one perfect partner, he hadn't thought he could find another, which, he supposed, was how love had managed to creep up on him unnoticed. Yet that was what had happened. And now, having lost Sophie, it seemed he had no hope of winning Catherine.

Standing up, he closed the book and replaced it on the shelf, telling himself it was time to drop the nonsense and face reality. Catherine had said she wasn't into relationships. That was a fact. A fact he supposed he'd deliberately been suppressing. A fact that made it impossible for him to stroll down Sheep Street, and drop into her shop as if he just happened to be passing.

CHAPTER TWENTY-FOUR

As it was Sunday, the Garden Café was closed to customers, but Bríd had come in to make mince pies for the bookshop's carol concert. She was cutting pastry cases and bopping along to 'Driving Home For Christmas' when she heard a knock on the back door. Outside she found her cousin Aideen, with a small child in a padded snowsuit holding her hand, and a large, lumpy sack at her feet. 'Hi. Parsnips and onions for tomorrow's soup, as requested. There's a proper frost out the country today. We'll have snow on the wind tonight.'

'Come in, then. Don't freeze on the doorstep.'

Pulling off a beret, and shaking out her red hair, Aideen said, 'We're awfully excited about seeing Santy this afternoon.'

Bríd gave the little boy a kiss. 'Hello, Ronan. Will Santy have Rudolph with him, do you think?'

Ronan shook his head. 'Santy's going to be in a bookshop. You can't muck out a bookshop so they don't let reindeer in.'

Aideen grinned. 'He's been helping his dad with the cows, haven't you, pet? You've been farming.' Unzipping Ronan's snowsuit, which had a hood with bear's ears, she asked Bríd how the mince pies were going.

'Grand. I'm on the last batch. Hang on till I turn off the radio. This wall-to-wall Christmas stuff is totally doing my head in.'

'Stop trying to sound like Scrooge. I saw your moves through the window.'

Ronan repeated loudly that Santy was going to be in a bookshop.

'I know, love, and you'll see him soon. Mummy and Bríd are going to have a chat and a coffee first, and we'll get you your dinner while we're here. Would you like a banana sandwich?'

'Will Santy give me a book?'

'He might. Or maybe a sweet.'

'I want a book.'

Bríd laughed. 'Nothing like stating your objectives. Come on, we'll go through to the café and sit at a table.'

In the café, Ronan stopped dead at the sight of the Christmas tree strung with popcorn and cranberry chains. Aideen told Bríd it was really effective. 'And Fury's a dote the way he brings a tree round every year. Is it true he has art installations in the bookshop? I heard Ann say so on the radio, but it didn't sound right.'

'That's what they're calling them. In fact, they're camouflage. The entire back ceiling came down, and if Fury hadn't stepped in, they would've been closed for the week.'

'God, they'd have lost a fortune.'

'I talked to Catherine at Adam Rashid's launch and, God love her, she still looked shell-shocked. She said that, without their Christmas takings, they might have had to close the place for good.'

'Well, fair play to them for cracking on regardless.'

'Like Lia says, you go with the flow, don't you? When you're running your own business, there's no other choice.'

Aideen was slicing banana onto bread and butter for Ronan. 'Who's Lia?'

'That Australian girl who drove the cupcakes to the bookshop.'

'Did she really just offer to help you out of the blue?'

'Absolutely. Happened to be there, said she had the right licence, and Fury let her drive his van without so much as a murmur. I was gobsmacked.'

'Fury did? He must be losing his grip.'

'I think he just liked her.'

Holding out a sticky hand to be wiped, Ronan announced that he'd finished his sandwich. 'Will Santy have had his dinner? Will he be waiting?'

'You haven't finished at all. You've hardly started. And it's way too early for Santy. Look at the clock.'

Bríd asked, 'Can he tell the time now?'

'Of course not. That's just something the playschool calls positive reinforcement.'

'Positive reinforcement is something completely different.'

Spitting on a tissue, Aideen said, 'Look, I'm just a mother trying to get from A to B without fuss. And you know feck-all about kids, so don't question my methods.'

Ronan leaned over and jogged Bríd's elbow. 'I do so know the time. I know when it's time for the milking.'

Aideen grinned. 'See, there speaks a farmer's son. He knows stuff that actually matters.'

At the other side of the garden, in the Convent Centre's kitchen, Adam's salmon had just come out of the oven. He unwrapped the foil, releasing scents of fennel, lemon and peppercorns, and lifted an edge of silvery skin to reveal the pink flesh. 'Here we have it. Oven-poached in butter and white wine, and beautifully moist and tender. You can tell it's done by the way it flakes if you press it gently, see?'

Janice asked, 'Do you let it rest?'

'We'll have it with the blinis, bread and salads, so I'll let it cool right down and it'll be perfect. We'll leave it for now, and look at plating and presentation later.'

Mary said she hoped that by 'presentation' he didn't mean slapping it down on an old roof tile: what with that carry-on, and chips turning up in pretend tin buckets, you couldn't sit down these days and eat an ordinary dinner in comfort.

Rising to the bait, Mr Maguire asked if she was casting aspersions on his slate platter. 'Because, if so, it simply shows you've no idea of Cordon Bleu norms.'

After three days of this kind of spat, everyone had got used to ignoring them, so Adam set aside the salmon and talked about his pudding. 'It's a pie that's easy to do but looks like a million dollars and, at this time of year, you're likely to have the ingredients in your cupboard. A jar of mincemeat. Cranberries.

A block of ready-made marzipan, and another of shortcrust pastry. It's all about pulling something together quickly, say for unexpected guests.'

Mary said tartly that she thought he was all about local produce.

'I am, but I'm not a fanatic. Give me a break.'

Unexpectedly, Mary emitted a delighted snort. The response had reminded her of Jazz who, unlike Hanna, never tried to appease her. With a self-satisfied smirk, she said she'd known that, sooner or later, Adam would recognise the usefulness of Cassidy's supermarket.

One of the ladies from Cork asked if the pie should be served with cream or custard, and, with an air of daring, Darina said, 'Or crème fraîche. Or yoghurt.'

'Any of those. Or none. It's up to yourselves. The marzipan gives it a lovely, gooey, almond-flavoured layer, the fruit's moist and the pastry's buttery, so it doesn't really need anything extra.' Adam looked for Saoirse's help in setting the food on the table and saw that, yet again, she was sitting with one hand thrust into her pocket, apparently deep in her own thoughts. She looked as if she'd slept as badly as he had so, rather than call attention to her, he decided to do without assistance.

Once the pie was assembled, he wove a lattice lid out of pastry. As the others leaned in to watch, Darina groaned. 'You're making it look so easy and it's an absolute beast, I can tell.'

'You could just use a round of pastry and make a few slashes to let the steam out. Job done. Baking's about enjoying yourself, not feeling overwhelmed.'

Inspired, Darina said recklessly, 'I could prick the lid with a fork.'

'There you go. That would work. And you could use the fork to crimp the pastry round the edge.'

Lia had been watching from the sidelines. She was pretty sure that, ordinarily, Adam didn't give courses without professional assistance, and that he wouldn't have to work beset by moodiness like Saoirse's, Darina's demanding interruptions, or waywardness, like Mary's. Yet, he wasn't just coping: when dealing with them, his Coolest Chef persona seemed to vanish, as if he'd dropped a shield to reach out a helping hand. With an irrational sense that, without the shield, he'd made himself dangerously vulnerable, Lia felt an impulse to push past the others and hug him.

She was trying to get her head round this when the door swung open and Phil surged in, announcing she wanted them all to pose for photos. 'Everyone out in the corridor, and we'll take them under the tree! Year One in the Lissbeg Kitchen's Culinary Hall of Fame!'

They were lined up in front of the tree wearing their *Coolest Chef* aprons and waving their whisks and wooden spoons. Saoirse, who was placed next to Adam, held the complimentary copies of *Cakes To Come Home To* with her chin on the top of the pile, to make sure it didn't slip. Backing down the corridor to include everyone in the shot, Phil called, 'Say "cheesecake",' and they all obliged with smiles. It then became clear that she was aching to be in the photo herself, so Saoirse was given the camera and each of the others held a book.

After a good twenty minutes of smiles and selfies, Adam announced that they needed to get back to work. 'Mary and I still have to get our bakes into the oven and, if things are to be on the table in time, we've all got to crack on.' Enlarging a shot to make sure she was happy with her own appearance, Phil said she'd be along for the farewell lunch.

There was a stampede back to the kitchen, to get things finished, and Lia returned to her bench aware that, throughout the flurry of photos, Adam had taken immense pains to keep his distance from her.

On the dot of one, Mary broke four perfectly baked, crusty-topped loaves of soda bread into quarters, producing a glorious fragrance as they came apart. 'The point of cutting a cross in the dough is to break them like this before laying a hand to a knife.' Karen said she'd heard that was to let the fairies out. Mary gave her a withering look. 'Well, if you want to go in for whimsy, that's your own business, but when you get to my time of life and you've been liquidated, you tend to put away childish things.' She carried the bread to the table, demanded a crock of butter, and set them on either side of Janice's bowls of potato salad. Folding her hands on her flowery apron, she announced, 'Now, so. That's proper bread. Not a caraway seed nor a sundried tomato in sight.'

Crunchy with gherkins, flecked with chives, and creamy white under green chopped parsley, the three salad bowls flanked a long wooden board on which Adam had placed the whole salmon. He'd retained the head and tail and removed the skin from the body, which he'd decorated with cucumber ribbons and sprigs of watercress, and served with lemon wedges and a Hollandaise sauce. Mr Maguire said that, at last, this was classic Cordon Bleu presentation, and doubted he could have bettered it himself. Seeing a gleam in Declan's eye, Adam hastily asked them all to bring up their blinis. 'Work from the centrepiece, please, and lay them out however you like.'

The array of platters and plates supported a wealth of

creativity and varying levels of success. Everyone bravely had a go at Darina's burnt offerings, and Mr Maguire even accepted one of Declan's sweet blinis, on which single blueberries on crème fraîche were encased in little cages of spun sugar. Lunch was a mixture of laughter, swapped phone numbers, promises of reunion and exclamations about the food. The luscious pie was accompanied by a long speech from Phil, who presented Adam with a framed photo of herself.

After coffee, during which Adam inscribed the books, Mr Maguire shook hands and left, saying he had an important appointment for which he needed to go home and change. Phil gave Saoirse a hand clearing up, and loading the dishwashers. Most of the others hung about, wanting yet another selfie with Adam, and tending to get him in corners to tell him the story of their lives. Watching from the background, Lia noticed he'd hardly touched his food. When he saw her untying her apron, he came and said, 'I need to get back to Carrick by three. I've a call with my agent booked.'

'Oh? Okay.'

'I mean d'you want a lift?'

This was astonishing, given how carefully he'd avoided her earlier. Lia shook her head. 'I'm going to drop into the bookshop. They're open today, and I want to pick up a pressie.'

'Okay. But, Lia?'

'What?'

'You're leaving for Dublin tomorrow evening?'

'Yes.'

'Well, I thought … it just occurred to me … I mean, remember what Hanna said that day we were in the library? About Fury's forest?'

'That I ought to see it.'

'Actually, what she said was that I ought to take you there. And you said it was definitely on your bucket list. And, well, if you liked, we could drive there tomorrow, and you'll see it before you catch your train.'

To an onlooker, this would have seemed like no more than a friendly invitation but, after her troubled night and tense morning, Lia found her mind doing somersaults. Adam appeared as relaxed as she'd ever seen him, and the smile he gave her was nothing like the automatic charm he'd assumed for the cameras. It was as if she'd imagined all the angst she'd thought she'd been watching. Suddenly it occurred to her that she might have got things back to front. Having woken feeling freaked by what had happened the previous evening, had she simply projected her own feelings on Adam? Because, if so, what with Saoirse being moody and Darina being Darina, he might well have balked at dealing with more neurosis. But, if that was the case, what on earth had happened to her? Dammit, she was the least neurotic person in the world.

'Lia?'

Jerked away by his voice from what had felt like a yawning precipice, Lia blinked and said, 'Yes?'

'Are you up for it?'

'What?'

'A walk in the forest.'

'Yeah. Sure, Why not? I'd like that.'

'Okay, good.'

Leaning heavily on her workbench as Adam walked away, Lia assured herself that this proved beyond doubt that she wasn't neurotic. It was a friendly response to a relaxed invitation. It was lightening things up and going with the flow.

CHAPTER TWENTY-FIVE

Bríd and Aideen walked up Sheep Street. Frost had created a silver tracery between the flagstones and, swinging from their hands, Ronan was laughing at the sight of his own white breath in the air. Several of the shops they passed were open and doing good Sunday business, and a line of folded buggies stood outside Lissbeg Books. When they reached the bookshop, Bríd lifted Ronan to show him the book tree, but he wriggled and shouted, 'I can see Santy in there *now*.'

'For God's sake, Bríd, put him down before he kicks the window in.'

'I see your parenting doesn't include delayed gratification.'

'I'll get back to you on that one when you've got kids of your own.'

Inside, Aideen hitched Ronan onto her shoulders to give him a view over the adults' heads. Fury's backdrop was now crisscrossed with black and yellow barricade tape. In front of it stood a crimson armchair partially draped in green. On one side was a Lissbeg Books banner. On the other, as rotund as the figure that was sitting in the armchair, was The Divil's tree, hung with pine cones, cinnamon sticks and paper chains. Fury's temporary poster had been replaced by signs reading 'NO ENTRY, RESTRICTED ACCESS' and 'ELVES AT WORK', and a double row of traffic cones wreathed in gold garlands made a walkway around the shop to the chair. The furniture from the bookshop's children's corner was now among the rubbish in the yard, but in the alcove made by the banner there was a table with baskets of pine cones on it, and cinnamon sticks, coloured pencils in jam jars, tubes of glue and bundles of paper strips. Wide-eyed, Ronan asked what the signs said, and was told, 'We mustn't go back there. That's Santy's workshop.'

'Where his elves are?'

'They'll be working, so we have to keep out.'

Catherine, who was wearing a hairband sewn with bells and topped with reindeer's antlers, came over to say hi. 'We've got a bit of a backlog in the queue for Santa. Would you like to have a go at making a Christmas decoration?'

Nudging Bríd, Aideen said, 'This is one of the biggest deals about this particular Santa. Stuff to keep kids occupied, so their parents aren't driven insane.'

Catherine laughed. 'In fairness, it also means you stay longer and might buy more books!'

'We've got a picture-book fan here. He's mad for Dr Seuss.'

'Well, take your time, and ask if you've any questions. Classics on that side. Newly published Irish authors on the table. There's some great new books for his age-group out this year.'

At the table, kids and parents were creating paper chains, twisting threads to make hanging loops for pine cones, and tying ribbons around the cinnamon sticks. As Aideen took Ronan to join them, and Catherine went back to the counter, Lia came in, wriggled through the crowd, and reached Bríd. 'Well, this place is hopping. Am I allowed in without a kid?'

'I'm here on my honorary-aunt card, but you should be okay without one.'

'I want to pick up a book for my nan. Something with photos of Ireland.'

'Specifically Finfarran?'

'Or not. My family goes in for general nostalgia about the old country. Show us a picture of green fields, and we're happy.'

'Were your people Irish?'

'Generations ago. Granddad came and travelled along the west coast back in the day. I think he was looking for roots, but he never found them. Though, according to family legend, he did buy an actual green field from a man he met in a pub.'

'That's so cool.'

'Cool, but probably fantasy. Granddad was what's politely known as a larger-than-life character.' Checking out the shelves, Lia said, 'Look, *Emerald Ireland*. That's the kind of thing I need. Or how about *Irish Land and Seascapes*?'

'Aren't they both a bit big to put in your luggage?'

'Good point. Still, Nan's had a rotten year. I'd like to make her smile.'

Behind the counter, Ann, in an antler hairband, had taken over at the till. Gift-wrapping and chatting to people about their purchases, Catherine caught herself repeatedly glancing towards the door. As she slipped a bookmark into a copy of

The Snowman, she realised that, ever since opening the shop that morning, she'd constantly been on the lookout for Stephen. But why should he have any interest in a kids' event? There was no reason to expect him, and surely he must be sick of being pressed into service whenever he happened to stop by.

The previous day, having gone with her to pick up the books from Carrick, he'd stayed on to help transform the shop for the late-night shopping. Afterwards, when the solstice decorations were taken down, he'd shifted banners and held the ladder for Fury. So, more than likely, he'd want to get on with his own affairs today. Besides, thought Catherine, coming to what she'd deliberately been avoiding, he'd probably been freaked by that weird thing she'd said in the car yesterday. One minute they'd been arguing cheerfully about Samuel Beckett, and next minute she'd told him she didn't do long-term relationships. Stephen had seemed to ignore her announcement. Perhaps he hadn't really heard it. But that was too much to hope for. He'd probably just been baffled or too polite to respond.

Frowning, Catherine tried to remember what could have possessed her. He'd said that summoning energy to go out on one's own could be grim. Remembering he was a widower, she'd come out with a facile response. And then, out of nowhere, she'd declared that she had no partner, and doubled down with the bit about not doing long-term relationships. Which was perfectly true. She'd loved her life on the road while it lasted, and had never wanted to feel tied down. But how bizarre to blurt it out at that particular moment.

Cringing at the thought, she looked down at her hands and immediately was jerked back to the present. Why had she just Sellotaped the copy of *The Snowman* into totally inappropriate gift-wrap? Having been specifically asked for something that wasn't girly, she'd picked up a sheet of paper that was pink and covered in candy-coloured Love Hearts. Blushing to the roots of her hair, she said, 'I'm so sorry. I'll change this.'

The woman who'd bought the book shook her head. 'Don't bother.'

'No, I will. I must. I'm terribly sorry. I wasn't concentrating.'

'Ah, listen, it's Christmas week, aren't we all at sixes and sevens? Don't worry about the paper. I'll whip it onto one of the other kids' presents.'

'If you're sure.'

'Of course I am. Aren't you giving us a free visit to Santy, and everything?' Grasping the child beside her by the hood of his anorak, the woman took the book and said, 'We'll shoot over now. This fellow's dying to see him, and it looks like the crowd's clearing.'

On the other side of Santa's backdrop, Declan had arrived with a box of pie. Fury and Terry were up ladders, fixing a sheet of plasterboard. Angela was trying an antlered hairband on The Divil, who was complaining loudly about the pressure on his ears. She looked round when the back door opened and, forgetting his antlers, The Divil shot over and sat expectantly at Declan's feet. Fury squinted down and said, 'Something involving pastry?'

'It's half a pie Adam made us for lunch. He said I could bring it along to you if I wanted to.'

'It is any good?'

'Bloody fantastic.'

'Right, we'll have it with tea. We're due a break once this board's up. Stick the kettle on, and don't let yer man get his nose into that pie.'

Breathing heavily, Ronan looped scarlet string around a pine cone. His head turned sharply, and he nudged Aideen. 'The elves are taking a break.'

'What, love?'

'In Santy's workshop. They've stopped knocking in nails.'

'Well, they'll probably get on with things in a minute. Have you finished your decoration? Will we go and talk to Santy now?'

'Can I take my pine cone home with me?'

'You can, of course. Catherine said so.'

'It's hard to make them hang straight with string.'

'I think it's great. Come on, and we'll stand in the line to see Santy.'

'I can go by myself.'

This was a recent development for Ronan who, previously, had tended to be clingy. Happy to encourage it, Aideen said, 'You can, of course. I'll go and talk to Bríd. You can give me a big wave when you reach Santy.' Looking angelic with the pine cone dangling from his hand, Ronan trotted over to where an excited line was moving along the route to Santa's chair. Keeping the little figure in her eyeline, Aideen went to join Bríd, and was introduced to Lia.

Bríd had *Emerald Ireland* balanced on her knee. 'Lia's looking for a Christmas present for her nan. What d'you reckon? The photos in this are great, but the other has sea shots.'

'Does your nan live by the sea, Lia?'

'No. Which is why she might go for it. But my parents do, so when she moves to be near them she'll have ocean views.'

'Then maybe you ought to go for this one.'

In the queue at the other side of the shop, Ronan hesitated. Seeing Aideen's attention was on the choice of books, he moved sideways, flattening himself between the wall and the edge of Fury's dust sheets. Then, he slid unnoticed through the gap he'd created, and found himself on the other side.

With large pieces of pie in their hands, Declan, Angela, Fury and Terry were hunkered on buckets and paint tins, using the pile of plasterboard as a table. Around them the heavy plastic sheeting gleamed, as if they were seated in an ice cave. Crouched by the wall, Ronan stared with eyes as wide as saucers. An electric screwdriver lay on the floor, with a saw and boxes of nails and screws. Fury had a hammer sticking out of the pocket of his waxed jacket. Declan had a pencil behind his ear and, to Ronan's delight, Angela was wearing a short leather apron with wire-strippers and pliers stuck into its pouches. Hearing a stifled gasp, Terry swivelled on his seat and, enchanted by his protruding ears and red woolly hat, Ronan edged forward. Then his eyes widened further at the sight of The Divil's antlers and, grasping Fury's knee, he said, 'You've got Max!'

This made no sense to Fury, who wasn't well up in children's classics, but, having raised Declan and Angela, Terry nodded solemnly. 'The Grinch was so sorry for stealing Christmas, he sends Max round to give us a hand every year.'

'Does Max like pie?'

'He does. And you shouldn't be here. Go back out now, and we won't tell Santy on you.'

'Would he bring me no presents if he knew I'd come in here?'

'Well, he's a fair man, but I wouldn't say he'd be happy.'

Deciding the best response to this was deflection, Ronan held up his pine cone. 'I made this. It's for hanging on a tree.'

Fury unfolded his long length from his bucket and held out his hand. 'Give it here till I have a look.'

'It doesn't hang straight.'

'That's because you haven't centred it. Do you want to?'

'Do I want to what?'

'Do you want it straight, or do you like it the way it is?'

'Show me how to make it straight.' Fury untwisted the string, retied it and hooked the cone onto his bony finger. Considering it, Ronan said, 'I liked it the way I made it.'

'Right so. We'll put it back that way.'

'Show me again how you fixed it, though.'

'I didn't fix it. I just did it differently.' Hunkering down, Fury demonstrated what he'd done, before undoing it and repositioning the string. He handed it back to Ronan and said, 'Did you know it was Max chose that tree Santy's sitting beside?'

Ronan turned to look at The Divil, who had perched himself on the plasterboard and was stealthily eating Fury's piece of pie. 'Did he cut it down?'

'Don't be daft. He's a dog. He wouldn't know how to lift an axe. No, he chose it, I cut it down, and we gave it to the bookseller. Your pine cone came out of the same forest.'

'If you gave the tree to the bookseller, would I give my pine cone to the tree?'

'I'd say you might.'

In a lull at the counter, Ann and Catherine were leaning against the wall. Carefully casual, Ann said, 'No sign of Stephen today.'

'Why should there be?'

'I'm only saying.'

'Well, don't. And do me a favour, Mum. Don't go announcing to passing strangers that I need help lifting boxes.'

'When have I ever done that?'

'Yesterday, when you practically forced him to give me a lift to Carrick.'

'Don't be daft. All I said was you could do with a hand.'

'Well, I didn't need one. And I could've done without you sending me off to buy him lunch.'

'What? When?'

'Last week, when we went to the Garden Café to pick up the sandwiches.'

'Oh, come on! That was basic politeness. He'd spent the morning decorating our tree.'

Catherine tossed her head, making the bells on her antlers tinkle. 'Oh, bugger this wretched hairband!' Pulling it off, she sighed. 'Sorry, Mum. I'm tired. I didn't mean to have a go at you.'

Reaching out an arm, Ann hugged her. 'We're both tired, but take a moment and look at this lot. And remember it wouldn't be happening if it wasn't for people like Stephen giving a hand.'

Catherine looked at the crowded bookshop. Customers were browsing shelves, reading books in the queue for Santa, or catching up with news of family who'd come home for Christmas. Several fathers appeared to have taken over the craft table, where they were happily messing with glue and paper. Children were reciting lists of presents they hoped for, and the stack of fliers for the carol concert was steadily going down. 'I'm not saying I don't like Stephen.'

Looking away to hide a smile, Ann said, 'Good, because I like him too.'

'I just don't think one should expect too much of people.'

'Nor do I. I never have. But I do think we ought to be open to what life sends us. Some things just happen and it's best to embrace them. Think of how Fury descended on us like a whirlwind. Think of Phil, who'd drive you mad but brought us more publicity than we've ever achieved ourselves. Look at how boring, infuriating, dependable Mr Maguire turns up each year in full Santa costume and beard.'

Enthroned on the armchair in a scarlet suit and hood trimmed with ermine, a buckled belt and a ringleted white beard, Mr Maguire looked severely over his half-moon glasses at a child who'd just told him the Santys in Carrick gave out bags of retro sweets.

'I think you'll find they give out bags of synthetic confectionary, full of polyols, glucose syrup and highly processed proteins.'

'Better than giving out a load of old guff about flying reindeer.'

'I suggest you take yourself off and find a book on basic nutrition before you succumb to obesity in your teens.'

CHAPTER TWENTY-SIX

Saoirse's mind kept replaying the scene from the previous day, when she'd gone upstairs and opened her mum's knitting bag. Everything about it had felt uncomfortable. Her struggle to close the zip when it caught on the needles. The awkward conversation with her dad. His troubled voice as he'd hovered in the doorway, and how he'd said respect for people's private lives and spaces was important. It had sounded to Saoirse almost as if he'd been telling that to himself as well as her. And there was the exchange of glances at breakfast. And Mum being cross about the rasher sandwich. And the way Mum had laughed and told Hanna Dad wasn't sophisticated, as if she thought he was boring, which he absolutely was not.

With each new thought, Saoirse turned the worry dolls in her pocket, hoping that touching them would reassure her. Instead it reminded her of waking in darkness, wriggling down to the foot of her bed to grab her Christmas stocking and running barefoot into her parents' room. She told herself the memory ought to fill her with anticipation, but anxiety had taken over, and all she could feel was dread.

When the dishwashers were loaded, Phil said she could go. 'You've done a grand job throughout the course, and I hope you've had a great time.'

'It was good.'

'I know Adam was impressed. If you need a reference later on, I'm sure he'd be glad to vouch for you.'

Only a week ago, the thought that the Coolest Chef might vouch for her would have made Saoirse fizzle with excitement. Now the world seemed to have lost all colour, and Phil's voice reached her through a fog. She nodded, said thanks and, shoving her apron into her bag, huddled into her coat and left the kitchen. As she walked down the corridor, she could hear Christmas carols, and supposed it must be Mary's lot rehearsing for their concert. Back home, Garrybawn House residents would be sitting in the lounge, chatting about presents and their plans for Christmas Day. They'd all made arrangements to have dinner out with family or friends so Saoirse had looked forward to a day with no calls on her mum and dad's attention beyond the need to cut more cake or decide which film they'd sprawl on the sofa to watch. She'd imagined discussing their upcoming trip to London, planning what she and Mum would wear to the theatre, and deciding whether to pack the latest nightgown sent by her aunt. Now she didn't feel confident that they'd even get to the airport, and the thought of an awkward, edgy Christmas Day made her want to cry.

Suddenly, the corridor echoed with voices bellowing, '*Alleluia!*' Ambushed by a grin, Saoirse relaxed a little, and reminded herself that, when she'd been younger, there'd been all sorts of weirdness in the run-up to Christmas. Doors that were hastily closed, Mum and Dad whispering in corners, and

Christmas shopping bundled away if she happened to enter a room. But, as Dad had said when he found her with the knitting bag, she was far too old for them to be doing that kind of thing now.

She'd left the building and was crossing the nuns' garden when she stopped and frowned. Dad hadn't said that at all. He'd told her she was too old to go searching for hidden presents. Looking back, she could see why he would have thought that was what she'd been doing. And it certainly would have been mega-weird. So had it been her behaviour, not his, that had created the awkwardness? Actually, now that she thought about it, what did the jumper prove?

Reaching the fountain, she sat down to think. Had she been making something out of nothing? Mum was working flat-out to ensure that Garrybawn's residents had a happy Christmas. Might she be snappy simply because she was tired? Staring at the water rising from the fountain's stone flowers, Saoirse wondered if the excitement of Adam's course had upset her own sense of balance. Or maybe, she thought, everybody got way too hyped-up at Christmas, what with all the ads showing perfect, smiling families, with no one in a bad mood, or sulking, or being hit with a streaming cold that made them sneeze over their sprouts.

It was at this point that she remembered she'd intended to go into Carrick to spend some of the money she'd earned on the course. Glancing at her phone, she saw the bus was due so, grabbing her bag, she made a dash for it, feeling her spirits rise. She caught it with seconds to spare and, sinking into the front seat, assured herself she'd been making mountains out of molehills. For the first time in her life, she had plenty of money to spend on Christmas presents, so why not relax and enjoy it? She decided to hunt down a bottle of her mum's favourite perfume, find something for Dad, then drop into the coffee shop where she and her Carrick friends used to hang out. The chances were that some of them would be there, chatting and drinking mochas, and they could catch up on each other's news. They'd never lost touch, but she did miss their day-to-day companionship. Besides, she'd texted them all when she'd got the *Coolest Chef* gig, and she knew they'd be dying to hear what Adam was like in real life.

Her favourite department store had the perfume and, on the next floor, she found a pair of high-end ear buds for her dad. Swinging the carrier bags, Saoirse left the shop by the mall entrance and took the escalator to the coffee shop. As she'd hoped, a group of her friends were at a window table, chatting, texting and showing each other Christmas presents they'd bought. Swept into a group hug, Saoirse became the centre of attention.

There were shrieks, envious sighs and questions, and while they were talking and drinking marshmallow mochas, someone uploaded a TikTok video captioned *Coolest Chef Conference!!* Laughing, Saoirse leaned forward to look and, through the window, saw two figures on a bench across the mall. A cold hand seemed to grip her heart, and her throat seized up in horror. The voices around her seemed to recede and all she could hear were the questions banging about in her own head. What was Mum doing here in Carrick with one of the guys she'd been friendly with at the hospital? A tall, good-looking staff nurse, called James, who'd sometimes come round to their house at weekends, with bottles of wine and, occasionally, bunches of flowers. A guy about whom they used to laugh because Dad had always called him 'your mum's fancy man.'

In his hotel room, Adam picked up the phone. 'Hi, Dom.'

'How was your last morning in BallyGoBackwards?'

'Can we move on swiftly from what you think passes for humour?'

'My great-aunt came from BallyBeyond. I'm allowed to make Irish jokes.'

'You really aren't.'

'Talk about touchy!'

'What's the story?'

'Here's the story, Adam, and it's a good 'un. *The Coolest Chef* company's done a deal with Amazon, so there's an upfront budget for two series. And you won't just be the pretty face. I got you a producer's credit.'

'I hate to keep reminding you, Dom, but I'm not a pretty face. I'm a skilled and highly trained chef.'

'Whatever. Okay, bottom line. With the producer's credit your fee's more than doubled. They won't want you in meetings, so it's money for old rope. Plus I've written in first-class travel and five-star hotels.'

'Have we established what the series is going to be about?'

'Duh – food. You're a chef, remember?'

Adam took a deep breath. 'I know it's the Coolest Chef Does Something or Other. But what?'

'Can we concentrate on first things first?'

'Are we talking local cuisine? What country? Do I get to visit farmers? Entrepreneurs? What's it about?'

Dom's voice held a note of suppressed irritation. 'What it's about will be budget-dependent.'

'You said the budget's confirmed.'

'Okay, let me spell this out. They'll find places that look good onscreen and that want to boost their tourist trade. They'll establish how much the governments concerned will be willing to chuck at enhanced visibility. And the decision about location will be based on the most attractive option on offer.'

'I'm still not hearing what the series is going to be about.'

'You've got a producer credit, Adam. You'll have input.'

'Sure I will. In all those meetings I won't be at.'

'You don't want to be at them. They'll just be talking nitty-gritty.'

Adam found he'd been pacing. He sat on the bed, felt vulnerable, and moved to a leather chair. 'Your email said they want me body and soul for a couple of years.'

'Finally, you've caught up! Two series, Adam. Two solid years. Guaranteed money. Your feet under the Amazon table. Plus a percentage on the merchandise. Did I mention that? No, I didn't, because you keep interrupting when you should be down on your knees thanking God. You should also be thanking me but, hey, nobody thanks their agent. Don't bother to apologise. I'll be happy with my cut.'

'Thank you.'

'You're welcome. Oh, and, Adam?'

'Yes?'

'I need that beefed-up biog straight after Christmas. Make it up if you have to, but make it good.'

After the kids' event Lia, Aideen and Bríd walked down Sheep Street. Bouncing between them, Ronan announced that he'd given his pine cone to the bookshop's tree. 'I hung it on one of the branches. It's Max's tree, really. Max gave it to Santy. Well, the elf did, but Max chose it. The Grinch lets Max help the elves at Christmas. He eats pie.'

Aideen looked down at him fondly. 'Is that so? You'll have to tell Daddy all about it.'

Recognising adult indulgence, Ronan stood still and glared. 'Cranberry pie. Max was wearing two antlers, not one. Like the bookshop lady. You get them in the Euro Shop.' Torn between wanting to be believed and the knowledge that he'd gone where he shouldn't, his lower lip began to wobble. Scooping him up, Aideen said, 'He's tired, aren't you, pet? We'll go home, Bríd. Lovely meeting you, Lia.'

'You too.'

'Hope we'll see each other again.'

'That'd be good.'

As Ronan was carried off, Bríd looked at Lia. 'He really has an amazing imagination. If ever I have kids, I am *so* buying them books.'

They strolled on and reached Broad Street, where the nuns' garden was bright with twinkling lights. The stained-glass windows threw spears of colour across the herb beds in which bay, thyme and rosemary were still growing green. Lia said,

'I think I'll go over and wait for my bus on one of the garden benches.'

'The next Carrick bus isn't due for ages.'

'If it gets chilly I'll take myself for a drink.'

'It's practically freezing now. Why don't you and I go for a pizza? There's a place right by the bus stop.'

'You don't already have plans?'

'I don't even have much in my fridge. Aideen's got a husband and Ronan to feed. I always end up snacking on crackers at midnight. Come on. My treat. I never thanked you properly for being my delivery driver.'

Over a couple of glasses of wine and a sharing platter of pizza, Lia asked, 'Did you say Aideen's husband grows produce for your café?'

'Conor does the growing – it's his family's farm. Aideen does admin, and helps with the market gardening. They supply shops and businesses, and they're working towards making it fully organic. And Conor would never give up his dairy herd. His dad and granddad reared it, so the cows are practically family.'

'I think it's cool they can make a living from it.'

'You couldn't live off farming round here without diversification. Aideen and Conor do weekly veggie-box deliveries too. Time was, they weren't sure they'd manage to keep afloat, but it's worked so far.'

'So everything you guys sell is organic?'

'Not everything. We're on our way, though.' Bríd took a mouthful of pizza. 'God, this is good. I was starving. Sorry, have I been rabbiting? I really ought to have more subjects of conversation than work.'

'It's not just work, though, is it? I mean, it sounds like it's what makes you happy.'

Bríd grinned. 'It does. We sell local honey and goats' cheese too, and one of our suppliers harvests seaweed and sea-salt, incredibly healthy stuff, and it sells like hot cakes. They use biodegradable packaging. So do Conor and Aideen. And Conor's looking at selling yoghurt and milk in glass bottles.'

'This is the kind of thing Adam was talking about on the course.'

'Was it good?'

'Yeah. So's the area. I feel like I haven't seen half of what's here.'

'When're you off?'

'Tomorrow evening. I figured the trains to Dublin would be packed on Christmas Eve.'

Bríd picked an olive from her pizza. 'Actually, that's wrong. Half the people who work in Dublin have families in the country. So the trains going up there on Christmas Eve are empty. It's the ones coming down that are jam-packed.'

'Really?'

'Yep. You could stay an extra day and still travel back in comfort.'

MONDAY

23 DECEMBER

CHAPTER TWENTY-SEVEN

Snow had fallen overnight. High on Finfarran's mountains it lay two feet deep. In upland fields, sheep huddled against walls while tractors bringing fodder edged along the narrow roads. Down in Lissbeg, the winter sun had melted much of the fallen snow, but out on the cliffs a fierce wind raked the short grasses, and foam at the edges of waves on the beaches crackled underfoot. Between the peninsula's mountain spine and its southerly cliffs lay Fury's forest, where white flakes wreathed the conifers and clung to the windward side of horse-chestnut trees and oaks. But little snow had penetrated to the forest's floor. There, falling between laced branches, sunlight made patterns of brightness and darkness on pine needles, fallen leaves and friable earth.

With just two shopping days left before Christmas, the twinkling lights in Lissbeg seemed to shine even more brightly and the pace of everything was speeding up. At eleven o'clock the bus pulled in outside Fitzgerald's butcher's and Mary descended, clutching an oilcloth bag. The shop window was crammed with raised pies marked 'Pork', 'Game', 'Chicken and Apricot', and printed signs said 'Barley-fed Bacon' and 'Speciality Spiced Beef'. Elbowing past a queue that reached through the door and onto the pavement, Mary went in and asked, 'Is she above in the flat, Des?'

From behind the counter, Des shouted, 'She is, Mrs Casey. She said to tell you she'd be down in a minute.'

Turning, Mary collided with the Christmas tree, which stood at the foot of the stairs festooned in crêpe-paper garlands, with packets of sage and onion stuffing balanced between its branches. 'Dear God Almighty, Des, could you not find someplace better for this?'

'We had it on the other side, Mrs Casey, but a new line in mustards came in, and we needed the space. You should've seen the size of the first one Fury tried to give us. Poor Mrs Fitz would have been stuck upstairs till Twelfth Night.'

When Pat came down, she and Mary set out for the Garden Café, linking each other across the road. It was full of shoppers having morning coffee and, settling herself at a window table, Pat said she thought she'd treat herself to a latte. Mary's eyes widened in horror. 'Pat Fitz, are you out of your mind entirely? Caffeine shrivels your vocal folds and drains your blood.'

'Is that a fact? I'd better have tea, so.'

'Ah, for God's sake, tea's only leppin' with caffeine. Nothing but spring water should pass your lips till the concert's over.'

'I suppose I can't have a chocolate muffin either?'

'You're doing this on purpose, aren't you? You know full well that the weight of caffeine in chocolate is disastrous.'

Pat said mildly that she supposed she could ask if Bríd had a Marietta biscuit.

'Joan Sutherland never touched farinaceous food before singing. It was twelve straight hours of unsalted nuts before that woman would even open her beak.'

'Nuts? Well, that's you banjaxed.'

'I have a vocal technique that allows me to rise above my teeth.'

Pat smiled serenely at a hovering waitress. 'We'll have two lattes, please, and a plate of your mini chocolate muffins. But apparently caffeine drains the blood, so could you stand by to call us an ambulance?'

Round the back of Tintawn Terry's Hardware Stores, Declan was loading carpet tiles into Terry's van. Slamming the metal warehouse door, Terry came to join him, banging his hands together to bring feeling back to his fingers. 'Right. Let's get going. Fury's already picked up the plaster from Shamie's. They must be raking in money back there. Can hardly be bothered to open at all in Christmas week.'

'In fairness, Dad, Shamie's a builders' merchant, and there won't be many builders working today.'

'Ah, but, lookit, his decorations are down already. Fury says, by the time he went by for the plaster, the tree he'd brought them was fecked out by the bins. It's woeful, but that's the way people are nowadays.'

Thinking of the tree positioned outside the hardware shop, which was hung with everything Terry sold, from potato-peelers to mousetraps, Declan grinned. 'Not everyone, not by a long shot.'

'Well, Fury's done too much down the years for Finfarran to be treated with that kind of disrespect.'

Frowning, Declan asked, 'Would you say he's all right these days, Dad?'

'How d'you mean?'

'Well, I hadn't seen him for ages, and yesterday I thought he looked shook. Like he's had a blow, or his health's not great or something.'

'There's no stopping him up and down the ladders.'

'I don't mean that he's not up to working. I just thought maybe something had gone wrong.'

'He's said nothing to me.'

'It's probably just that he's getting older.'

'Ah, sure, we're all doing that, son. It'll even come to you, if you live long enough.'

Saoirse was huddled under her duvet, remembering the sight of her mum and fancy-man James. At the time, her friends' voices had seemed to recede into the distance, but now they came back to her, awestruck, sneering, envious and excited, as they passed around the photos on her phone.

'I mean, wow, the Coolest Chef himself, and she got to be there and work with him.'

'She got to wash up the dishes.'

'She got to stand beside him for a selfie. How cool is that?'

'Oh, right, and now he's her very best friend?'

'Could you *be* any more jealous?'

'I am not!'

'You so are. And she didn't just do the dishes. Look at the photos. She was hands-on.'

'And was he hands-on too?'

'Shut *up*, you're disgusting.'

'Oh, please. He's a celebrity. Everyone knows what they're like.'

Her mum and fancy-man James had been laughing. Not snogging, or even touching. Not lurking or looking guilty. They'd been sitting on a bench in broad daylight. But they'd been really relaxed together. Intimate. That had been it. Relaxed and intimate, not cross or edgy. Not like Mum and Dad had been for weeks. As she'd watched them, Saoirse had heard a shriek and seen her phone fly by, narrowly missing a marshmallowy mocha. Furiously, she'd grabbed it and, when she'd turned back, the figures on the bench had gone.

Now, sitting up with her chin on her knees, she stared at her bedroom wall. Could she possibly have imagined that relaxed, intimate couple? Had they really been there? For a minute, the idea was scary enough to make her wonder if she needed a doctor. Because going around hallucinating was genuinely weird. But, reaching under the pillow for her worry dolls, she told herself she knew what she'd seen. It wasn't hallucination. Mum had been in Carrick with fancy-man James. The question was why?

In the flat above the bookshop, Ann looked at Catherine. 'It's amazing to think that, by this evening, we'll have our shop again.'

'The skim will be up, but it can't be painted till after Christmas.'

'It'll look fine, though, and Declan's promised to come and do the painting. What I'm finding hard to grasp is the thought that the floor will be done in time for tomorrow's carol concert.'

Catherine laughed. 'I'm way past doubting Fury's promises.'

Ann stood up and said she supposed she ought to go and get dressed. 'The lads should be here any minute. Angela's got Christmas shopping to do this morning, but she'll come by this afternoon to sign off the lighting.'

'I asked Fury about payment. He said they'll invoice when the job's complete. D'you think a book for each of them, as a Christmas gift, would be good now, though?'

'Let's do it. Mind you, I'm not sure The Divil reads. He might go for a graphic novel.'

'You'll probably find he doesn't just read, he publishes under a pseudonym.'

'Romantic novels?'

'More likely to be time-management studies. I've always suspected he's the one who actually does Fury's schedules.'

Avoiding a crowded bus on its way to Carrick, Fury turned his van onto the road to Lissbeg. The Divil, who'd woken early and disposed of several mice, was dozing comfortably in the passenger seat. Up ahead, muffled in a scarf and wearing her bobble hat, Lia was striding along clapping her arms across her chest. Pulling up beside her, Fury leaned out and said, 'Cold morning.'

'Beautiful, though.'

'D'you want a lift?'

'No, I'm good, thanks, Fury. There's a way to the beach somewhere here, isn't there? I got the bus driver to drop me off.'

'A couple of field gates along to the right. There's a boreen will take you straight down to the beach.'

The Divil, who'd shot upright, scrambled across Fury's knees and thrust his nose out of the window. Tickling his whiskers, Lia asked Fury, 'How's the battery case?'

'It didn't occur to you, I suppose, that I might have liked that rattle. I hope you're not standing there expecting thanks.'

Lia gave a shout of laughter. 'Not for a moment. And I don't expect hell to freeze over either. I grew up with a granddad just like you.'

'An old curmudgeon?'

'The family called him a character. He liked playing up to the name.' Lia took off her glove to scratch behind The Divil's ears. 'At his funeral, my nan said he was a man who never stopped chasing rainbows.'

'That's not a bad thing to have them say when you're gone.'

'Like, every year he used to say he'd bring us all over to Ireland. Then he'd decide to go panning for gold or learn the piano instead.'

'Did he find any gold?'

'Of course not. He never learned to play the piano either.'

'So what did he do for a living?'

'Construction. He did okay. He was a grafter.' Lia smoothed the wiry hair between The Divil's eyes. 'I wish I could've told him about coming here. The town and the nuns' garden and the people. And the psalter, and the incredible scenery.'

'You've enjoyed yourself, so.'

She wriggled her fingers back into her glove. 'There's so much I haven't seen, though. The beach was on my bucket list. That's why I'm off there this morning. I'm going for a walk with Adam this afternoon.'

'Do you tell me that?' Cocking his head at her, Fury asked, 'So when are you leaving us?'

'I had a ticket for this evening's train to Dublin, but I've changed it for tomorrow.'

'Unfinished business?'

'I found I could, so I did, that's all.'

Fury took a cigarette from behind his ear and reached for a match. 'You'll want to keep to the paths in the forest. It's easy to lose your way. Mind you, it's often the case that, when you do, you find a better one.' Giving Lia a bland smile, he struck the match and held the flame to his cigarette.

'Okay, I'd better get on. See you, Divil. Good to know you, Fury.'

Dropping a kiss on The Divil's head, she strode off down the road ahead of them, stopping to wave as they drove past and disappeared round a bend.

Fury threw The Divil a sideways look through the wreath of smoke in the cab. 'I wouldn't make too much of that kiss, if you don't want your heart broken. She hasn't admitted it yet, but that girl's in love.'

Absent-mindedly taking a second chocolate muffin, Mary suggested they order another round of coffee. 'So, come here to me, are you spending Christmas with your lad Frankie again?'

'Ah, now, Mary, don't start that. You bring it up every year.'

'If I do, it's for your own good.' Crossly, Mary pushed the muffins towards her. 'All I'm saying is if I had a useless bully for a son, I wouldn't be eating my Christmas dinner with him.'

'He's my only family here at home, Mary.'

'And that's the point, isn't it? He made damn sure when his father died that your other two lads didn't come home from abroad to cramp his style.'

'It wasn't that simple. They have lives made for themselves over in Canada.'

'The truth is that Frankie bullied your poor husband into his grave. He's a bad lot. Look at him, swanking around with his big house and his big car. And look at yourself, still keeping the business running at your age.'

'Now that's not true.'

'Ah, don't be annoying me! Frankie's happy enough to pocket the takings, but it's you that's living up in the flat, minding the books and keeping the door open. Sure, Frankie never even comes by to see you. The fact of the matter is he's ashamed he came out of a butcher's shop.' Having gone further than she'd intended, Mary sat back and compressed her lips. 'There now! I'm sorry if I've upset you.'

'You say that every year too.'

'Well, if you had a titther of sense I wouldn't have to.'

After a strained silence, Pat changed the subject. 'You'll be having your dinner at Hanna's, I take it?'

'I will. It'll only be the three of us this year. Jazz is over in London.'

'Brian was in the other day, buying a round of spiced beef.'

'Ah, he wasn't, was he?'

'What's wrong with spiced beef?'

'No offence now, Pat, it isn't the beef. It's your recipe. I can't be doing with juniper, and you never use enough sugar.'

'Mary Casey, that recipe was my poor Ger's speciality!'

'Well, I hate to speak ill of the dead, but all I can say is the man had no judgement. Couldn't see that his eldest son was a whited sepulchre, and no notion of how to spice beef.'

CHAPTER TWENTY-EIGHT

Adam's first thought when he woke on Monday was that he must have been dreaming. It didn't seem possible that he'd simply walked up and asked Lia if she wanted to come for a walk in the forest. And yet he had and, despite the way he'd behaved beforehand, she'd said yes. So, if nothing else, they'd have the morning together, and surely that was another sign that Fate was on his side? Leaping out of bed, he showered, dressed and took the lift down to Reception, expecting to find her at breakfast, but she wasn't there.

Turning away, he saw Wayne, the receptionist, mouthing at him. 'Mr Rashid, I've a note for you.' With a sinking feeling, Adam went to the desk. Lia must have changed her mind, and who could blame her? After all, he'd spent a whole morning elaborately keeping his distance and, at the last moment, had appeared at her elbow suggesting they take a walk. She must have decided he was a total weirdo. She'd probably only said yes because she was desperate to get away. Taking the note, he nodded his thanks and retreated upstairs, not trusting himself to look at it till he was safely in his bedroom. He then had to read it twice before he could take in what it said.

Decided to stay on till tomorrow, so changed my train ticket. I've gone to Lissbeg this morning to commune with the wild Atlantic. Meet you by the horse trough at three for our walk?

Adam sat down on the side of his bed wondering what the response would be if he called room service and ordered a double brandy for breakfast. But since, if he did, the story was likely to end up on social media, he called and ordered croissants and coffee instead. When the tray arrived he was sitting with his laptop on his knees, killing time before setting out for Lissbeg by focusing on work.

Clicking through his alerts, he could see his book soaring in the charts, though no one appeared to be hailing it as a call to arms. That wasn't surprising, given the wording on the cover, but knowing how well his group in Lissbeg had responded to his vision, he wished he'd had more say in how the book had presented it. He checked his social media, which was flooded with rapturous praise from Darina. Then, gritting his teeth, he created a blank document and typed 'Biog'. He had to come up with something soon or all hell would break loose after Christmas when Dom got back to the office.

Half an hour and a whole pot of coffee later, he was still staring at a blank page. He knew what was needed. A rags-to-riches story, not too dark but suitably high on menace and preferably with an exotic twist for what Dom called 'instant brand identity'. The crazy thing was that the story he was withholding ticked every box on the list. The problem was that he also knew exactly what would happen if he told it.

Instinctively, once he'd got off the streets, he'd spoken to no one about what had happened after his dad died. The bottom line was that he hadn't wanted to think about it, but he'd also been wary of putting off employers. Later, when he'd won the *Coolest Chef* title, he'd thanked his lucky stars that he'd kept his mouth shut. Gossip columnists and morning TV shows liked every success story to come with a side of jeopardy so, had Dom known about his past, it would have been served up with a flourish. And now, with a global marketplace in prospect, the stakes were higher. Which was why Dom was ferreting for clickbait.

Groaning, Adam hit Delete and tried starting again. The task he'd been given appalled him, and knowing that what he wrote for Dom would be reworked by a marketing team made it worse. He also knew that beneath his jokey aggression Dom was genuinely ruthless, so clients who failed to come up with the goods were in danger of being dumped. And without Dom there was no hope of survival, only the certainty of sliding back down a greasy pole. Another hour passed and, with more coffee cooling at his elbow, Adam glowered at his umpteenth attempt to write five hundred words. Then, giving up, he hit Delete and pushed away his laptop. There were at least three days to go before Dom got back on his case. Today belonged to Lia and the forest. And first there were loose ends to tie up with Phil, and people to say goodbye to.

Adam arrived in Lissbeg shortly after Mary had bustled into the butcher's, and found Phil in her office, wearing striped candy-cane earrings.

'Adam, come here till I give you a hug! You have no idea how much you've raised our profile! Remember *Get Gardening and Get That Festive Flab Off*? Nailed it! A double-page spread in a Wellbeing insert in one of the most-read Sundays. Big colour shot of you in the nuns' garden, and a piece about dropping mountains of fat on a grapefruit diet.'

'Phil, I don't endorse dieting.'

'I know, and don't worry. It won't say you do.'

'It will, if they use my picture.'

'Oh, God, you're not going to make a big thing of this, are you, Adam? It's only an inconspicuous little article.'

'In one of the most-read Sundays.'

But he knew that trying to contain what appeared in the press was a waste of time so, returning her hug, he told her not to worry. 'It's fine. Like I said when you got in touch, I wanted to do what I could to help here.'

'Well, you've done that in spades. The council says I can go ahead and organise more courses.'

'That's great.'

'Come here to me, will we do another selfie?'

'Another?'

'Well, I can't keep putting the same ones up on my socials, can I? Hang on a minute, I've a box of crackers – we can wear paper hats.'

Having managed to escape, Adam walked to the arch that led into the library courtyard, running one hand along waist-high rosemary bushes as he went. In the library, Hanna was dealing with loans for a large family of children. Seeing she was occupied, Adam went to browse the shelves and noticed Saoirse sitting at a table, half concealed by the Christmas tree that stood at the reading-room door. Her head was down, her hands were deep in the pockets of her hoodie, and its hood was pulled forward almost concealing her face. Recognising this air of combined misery and tension, Adam walked down the room and sat opposite her. 'I didn't get to thank you properly yesterday. You shot off.'

'Yeah. It's okay. I didn't say thanks to you either.'

She hadn't looked up when she spoke, and what he could see of her face was pinched. 'There's something the matter, isn't there?'

'No.'

'Look, I've done my share of sitting in libraries because it was cold and I'd nowhere else to go.'

'That's not what I'm doing.'

'You know what makes it less obvious? Having a magazine or a book in front of you.'

'I'm thinking.'

'You're running away from something.' She didn't respond, and he bent forward. 'Saoirse, I don't know what's wrong, and it's not my business, but whatever it is you can't run for ever. You've got to face it. Have you talked to your mum and dad?' Seeing the effect of his question, he sat back. 'Okay, I get it. That's where the problem is.'

'I'm not going home.'

'So, where will you go when the library closes?'

Battling tears, Saoirse said, 'I don't know.'

'Listen to me. You're bright and able and sensible. You can handle this.'

'Is that the reference Phil told me you'd give me?'

'It'd be the gist.' Adam chose his next words carefully. 'Look, if it's something heavy at home, there are places you can go to for help.'

Saoirse gasped. 'God, no. It's nothing like that. Mum and Dad are brilliant.'

'Then you're luckier than a whole lot of kids who sit in libraries because they can't go home.'

She muttered that she supposed so, but her face remained pinched and Adam could see that her jaw was set. Pushing back his chair, he stood up. 'Anyway, thanks for what you did on the course. You really were a help.' He gave her a smile and walked away down the long, panelled room, where winter sunlight danced on the steel shelving.

Saoirse saw him stop to say goodbye to Hanna, looking exactly as he did when you saw him onscreen. She recalled reading something about him supporting a shelter for the homeless in Dublin. Presumably, that's why he knew about people slumped in public libraries because they had no place else to go. And he's right, she thought, I am lucky. Whatever happens, Mum and Dad will always want the best for me. So there's no point in sitting here fretting. I'd better go and talk to them.

Getting up and, keeping behind the central shelving, she made her way to the door. She was pretty sure Adam was aware of her as she passed, but he didn't look round, which was nice of him because she didn't feel up to more conversation. It was surreal to think he'd noticed something was wrong and had wanted to help. Actually, it was uber-cool, when you came to think of it. Not something you'd want to share on TikTok, but proof that the girls in Carrick were wrong, and he really was her friend.

Ten minutes later, crossing the nuns' garden, Adam noticed that someone must have waded across to the fountain to hook a holly wreath around the statue's neck. He sat down to admire the saint's raffish appearance, and realised this was the bench where he'd sat on his first day as a nervous volunteer. A plaque on it read 'In loving memory of Sister Michael, a worker in this garden'. He recalled that the person who'd shown him around had said Sister Michael had been a lay-sister. 'Nuns needed a dowry to be accepted into the order. If you had no money you entered the convent and worked.'

'So she grew food?'

'And cooked.'

They'd been sitting there in summer sunshine, talking about herbs, when a tiny woman in a large yellow anorak had stopped and said, 'Isn't this a grand day to be working in a garden? My husband Ger was a great outdoors man, but sure half his time was spent inside in the shop.' Beaming at Adam, she'd added, 'We have the butcher's over the road. You and I haven't met, have we? My name's Pat Fitzgerald.'

At that point, Adam's minder had gone off to find a spade, leaving him with someone he'd seen as a pushy aul one likely to pelt him with unwelcome questions. So, getting in first, he'd asked if the butcher's was still family-run. To his horror, her eyes had glistened. 'I've a manager in the shop now, and a son who'd have more interest in the business side. My other two sons are married abroad. I don't hear from them, these days.'

Wishing he hadn't started this, Adam had nodded uncomfortably, and she'd run a forefinger under one of her wrinkled eyes. 'I'd say they kind of blamed me for not making life better at home. Their dad would've favoured their brother a bit, so things weren't that easy. I'd say half the time I did the wrong thing but, sure, you do what you can.'

The gesture had reminded Adam of his own mum brushing away tears and, remembering he had a paper napkin in his pocket, he'd pulled it out and handed it to Pat. 'It's clean. I took a handful of them when I got a burger for the bus.'

'You're a good lad.'

'Just because your sons aren't here doesn't mean they're not thinking about you.'

'Ah, I know, and they do send me a card at Christmas. But it's not them thinking about me that matters. I want to know what they're doing, and hear their voices, and know they're all right.' Dabbing her eyes with the napkin, she'd given him a sweet smile. 'You're not from round here. Where were you born?'

'Dublin.'

'Do you tell me that? And is your family still there?'

'My dad's dead. I'd say my mum's still there, yeah.'

'But you're not sure?'

He'd opened his mouth, but before he could speak, she'd put her hand on his knee. 'God, you must think I'm a nosy old biddy! You keep your business to yourself, son, don't mind me.'

'No, it's okay ...'

'Look, if you're not in touch with your mother, you'll have your reasons. But would you do this for me, love? Would you give the poor woman a ring and tell her you're safe?'

That night, when he'd got back to the Royal Vic, he'd made the phone call. It hadn't been easy and nothing had really been dealt with but, at least, he and his mum had talked. Then the struggle to do what the halfway house had called 'reintegrate' had taken over, and because he'd been focused on the greasy pole he'd been struggling to climb, he'd never seen his mum alive again. Watching hungry sparrows peck at a scone someone had dropped by the fountain, Adam wished he'd made time to visit her. Still, he'd kept in touch and she'd known how he was doing, and by the time Fergal had cleared out her savings and left her, he'd been making enough to be able to send her money regularly. She hadn't lived to see him win the Coolest Chef title. But because of Pat Fitz she'd heard his voice again.

Aideen and Bríd were serving when Adam came into the Garden Café, which was crowded with frenzied shoppers taking a break. The last bûche de Noël had just sold to a couple in tweed caps, and, working at lightning speed, Bríd was boxing a Christmas pudding. A sign on the counter announced that the soup of the day was parsnip, ginger and orange, served with homemade brown bread. Stepping back to allow a woman to pass him with a cake box, Adam went and joined the queue. 'Lia and I are going for a walk. I've borrowed a flask from the hotel. Any chance of soup as a takeaway?'

Bríd reached for the ladle. 'No problem. Will you want the bread too? It's just out of the oven.'

'Perfect.'

Ladling the soup into the flask, she said, 'Meet my cousin Aideen. Ade, this is Adam.'

Aideen, whose red hair was covered by a checked scarf like Bríd's, said, 'Hi. Sorry I missed your book launch. My husband was dealing with some farming disaster.'

'Did he manage to avert it?'

'He always does. I had to stay in and mind our little boy, though. Still, I'm told I'm getting your book as a Christmas present, so that's okay.' Adam leaned in to appreciate the smell rising from the soup tureen, and Bríd said, 'Made this morning. Aideen brought the vegetables in yesterday. Are you really planning a picnic in this weather?'

'It's more of a precaution. I've a feeling we might need thawing out at some stage.'

'Well, this ought to do the job.'

When he left the café, the outside temperature had risen slightly, and the birds picking at the scone were hopping between sunlight and shadow. Carrying the flask of soup and the paper bag of warm soda bread, Adam made his way through the garden onto Broad Street. Waiting for a gap in the traffic, he saw Lia perched on the edge of the horse trough, head bent and eyes on her phone.

Beyond the further stream of cars, Mary emerged from the butcher's, a short, self-important figure carrying her oilcloth bag. Adam found himself watching her with amused affection. There was something courageous about her stalwart assertiveness, apparently the opposite of Pat's gentle stoicism but, actually, coming from the same place. They were both widows getting on with life after decades of focusing on their families and husbands and, if Mary didn't bring grace to the effort, at least she brought energy. Adam had raised his hand, about to wave and call goodbye, when Lia glanced left and right as if looking out for him, and all his attention was drawn to the turn of her dark head.

The sight of her made him catch his breath. She was wearing a silver-grey parka jacket and, seen through the moving traffic, seemed as much part of the granite trough of purple and yellow pansies as the stone saint in the fountain was part of the flowers carved at his feet. Impossible to believe it was only six days since Adam had first seen her, an unknown girl in the Royal Victoria's breakfast room, who'd met his eye and looked down at her poached egg. Only six days since they'd sat on the bus together, and she'd broken a bar of chocolate in two and held one half out to him. Six days since she'd told him she'd entered some random competition and had come to Finfarran to attend his course. And the day after that, he'd known he was in love. The odds against their meeting at all still made Adam giddy, and the thought that he might not see her again after today was dreadful.

The traffic slowed and, crossing between a car and a delivery van, he reached the island where Lia was sitting. She stood up and, as if they were friends who'd made a casual appointment, said, 'Hi. I was just texting Oz. You ready for the off?' Taking his cue from her tone, he said, 'Sure. The car's in the car park.'

'Okay, let's go. I hope you're wearing several woolly vests.'

CHAPTER TWENTY-NINE

Fitzgerald's was crowded when Stephen reached the front of the chattering queue. He asked for a game pie.

'No problem at all, Mr Gallagher. What size are you wanting?'

'Small, please, Des.'

'Right you be. Anything else for you there, now?'

'No. That's the lot, Des. Thanks.'

'And your free box of stuffing's there in your bag. Compliments of Mrs Fitz.'

'I'm not doing a turkey, actually. Hang on to it, Des.'

'Oh, right, so. I suppose you wouldn't, you'd never eat your way through it. Happy Christmas anyway, now, and enjoy your pie, Mr Gallagher. We'll see you again in the new year, please God.'

Stephen left with a grim feeling that everyone had been sorry for him, and that the whole queue would break into tutting and sighs as soon as he'd gone. Out on the pavement he swung the bag from which Des had removed the box of Paxo stuffing. It seemed to weigh nothing compared to the bulging bags all around him, carried by shoppers stocking up for gargantuan Christmas feasts.

The forest lay in a valley approached by a high pass through the mountains. In the car, Lia unzipped her jacket and loosened her warm scarf. She wondered what would happen if they met oncoming traffic, with frost edging the potholes and miles of winding road to cope with in reverse. As the car climbed between a sheer cliff face and a scarily low stone wall, she looked down and saw a river below them in full spate. 'This is all a bit off-grid.'

'It's the quickest way to where we're going, though.'

'How come you know these back roads?'

'I explored a bit when I was here before. You don't get a lot of time off as a kitchen porter, but I borrowed a bike from one of the guys who worked in the hotel.'

'And took off on your own?'

'Yeah. I was lonely when I lived on the streets, but never when I was back here. I loved it. I had wheels, and a roof over my head to go back to. And work and prospects. That's what Finfarran gave me. That, and a room with a door that locked.'

The conversation seemed to have taken them back into dangerous territory but, somehow, this time it seemed okay, so Lia asked, 'Was the lock a big deal?'

'Massive. When you sleep rough, you're always waiting for someone to kick your head in or steal your gear. And you've nowhere to keep anything, so what you've got you carry around. Or dump in an alley and hope to God it'll be there when you get back. Which it usually isn't.'

Looking at his profile as he concentrated on the road ahead, she tried to imagine him as a skinny teenager, struggling to keep alive on the streets. He'd told her that when the halfway house in Carrick had taken him in, he'd been more than a stone underweight and still weak from his bout of influenza.

'But you managed the kitchen porter's work? That must have been hard.'

'Believe me, I wasn't going to lose the job once I'd got it. Anyway, having a bed to sleep in made a difference. Plus three square meals a day.'

As the car breasted the top of the pass, she asked, 'Haven't any of the hotel staff recognised you from back then?'

'New management. Not surprising. The turnover in the industry is huge.' Adam grinned. 'Anyway, I'm a celebrity in a Superior Room now. No one was going to recognise me as Rasher.' Lia looked at him blankly. Then she remembered. 'That's what Mary's friend called you. The little woman who turned up talking about carol rehearsals.'

'Pat Fitz. I met her when I was volunteering in the garden. Rasher was what I called myself in those days. It was my nickname at school.'

Suddenly, Lia recalled how Pat had reached up to touch his cheek, and how he'd bent his head as if he'd been going to give her a kiss. 'That's why you came back, isn't it? Finfarran didn't just give you a door with a lock, and a job, and prospects. It gave you a community and people you could trust.'

In Garrybawn House, her heart in her mouth, Saoirse looked at her parents. Theresa and Rory looked back in disbelief.

'You thought *what?*'

'Saoirse, pet, are you serious? How long has this been going on?'

Sitting opposite them at the kitchen table, Saoirse said, 'So you're not breaking up?'

They answered simultaneously: 'Of course not.' 'What on earth gave you that idea?'

'Saoirse, seriously, have you been thinking this for long?'

'Not that long. Well, only the last week or so, really. But things have been weird for weeks, haven't they?' Saoirse looked at her mum. 'You're not going to say they haven't? You've been going out, and I know it's not been to knit-and-natter. And Dad's been shifty, and you're always tired.'

Theresa put her hands to her cheeks and said, 'Dear God, Rory.' Looking at Saoirse, she said, 'I was the one who thought we shouldn't tell you.'

'Tell me what?' Leaning across the table, her mum took her hand. 'We're not breaking up, and there's nothing wrong. I've just been going to the hospital.'

Saoirse's stomach clenched. So that was it. That was what the matter was. Mum was sick. Properly sick, if they hadn't wanted to tell her. That was why Dad had been so weird. Maybe it was why they'd got Phil to give her the job on Adam's course, to keep her out of the house and occupied. With her head whirling, she snatched her hand away, reached for her worry dolls and, in pulling them out of her pocket, dropped one.

Mum said, 'What's that?' and then, 'Oh, Rory, it's those wretched dolls I made her. Saoirse, you haven't started carrying them round again?'

Desolate, Saoirse said, 'You should have told me you were sick.'

'What?'

'I'm not a baby. If you're not well I can help.' Her eyes widened. 'Is that why we're going on this holiday? Because they've told you you've got something awful? Is that why Dad said we need family time together?'

'Saoirse, stop!' Mum had her hands to her mouth and, to Saoirse's amazement, seemed to be stifling a laugh. Unless she was crying, though it looked like both, which made no sense, unless things were so bad that she was hysterical.

Bewildered, Saoirse looked at her dad, who said, 'Dear God, I'm driven mad with the pair of you.'

Mum dropped her hands to the table and seemed to pull herself together. 'Saoirse, listen to me. Nobody's sick. Everything's fine. There's nothing to worry about. I've been going to the hospital because I took on some night shifts there this month. I wanted us to have a bit more money to splash out on things when we're in London.'

'Night shifts?'

'Some nights. Some lates. You know the hospital's always looking for cover.'

Taking a deep breath, Saoirse looked at her dad for corroboration. With his arm around Mum's shoulders, he said, 'Don't look at me. I wanted to tell you. She knows I'm a dreadful liar.'

'I thought you were breaking up. And then I saw Mum in Carrick with James.'

'When?'

'Yesterday afternoon. You were in the mall, laughing, and I'd just bought you and Dad presents.'

'Love, I was there doing shopping myself, and I just bumped into him.'

'Oh. You've been really snappy with Dad.'

'You try doing lates and nights and then getting up to deal with the likes of Mary Casey.'

In a small voice, Saoirse said, 'You told Mary and Hanna that Dad was unsophisticated. James is different.'

Her mum laughed helplessly. 'Honestly, Rory, this is what comes of calling the poor fellow my fancy-man!'

'So now it's my fault?'

'I didn't say that.'

'You did, near as dammit.'

'I did not. But it was a stupid joke to make. I said so at the time.'

'Oh, right, now I'm stupid.'

Their arguing voices sounded very different from the snappiness that had spooked Saoirse. Catching her eye, her dad winked, and Mum said, 'Now the secret's out I can tell you we've upgraded to a hotel with a spa. I thought you and I could hang out getting massages while your unsophisticated dad does lengths of the pool.'

'How d'you know Dad won't want a massage too?

'You've got to be joking. That's not going to happen on my watch. I'm not risking him running off with some gorgeous blonde masseuse.'

The kitchen felt warm and safe and smelt of Christmas. Stooping to reach under the table, Saoirse picked up the worry doll she'd dropped. One shortass, one with hair that looked like she never got time to comb it. And if Mum would knit another they'd have the portrait of Dad that she hadn't had time to make before.

Adam pulled into a lay-by next to a track that led into the forest and, getting out, Lia looked up at the trees. They towered bare-branched above the rutted track, oaks stretching to alders, and hazel reaching out to downy birch. Below them, holly and rowan showed bright berries and, underfoot, the earth was springy and slightly damp. Adam came round the car behind her, hooking a backpack over his shoulder. 'I brought soup.'

'Genius move. That's why it's always wise to go walking with chefs.' Lia set off, calling over her shoulder. 'Now, there's a title. *Walking With Chefs*. You should sell it to your TV guys. Make it *Walks With the Coolest Chef* and you'll have exclusive rights.' Catching up with her, he said, 'You don't know much about TV, do you?'

'Nothing at all. Why?'

'If you did, you'd know that the pretty face doesn't get that kind of clout.'

'You're not a pretty face.'

'Why, thank you.'

'I mean not just a pretty face.'

'That's better.'

Lia stopped dead. 'Seriously, is that how they treat you?'

'Kind of.'

'Well, that's crap. You're the one who actually knows how to make things.'

'They know how to make money, though.' He hooked his arm through hers. 'Don't. Let's not talk about them. This is a day off. And, gosh, look. Winter chanterelles.'

If he hadn't pointed them out, Lia wouldn't have noticed the patches of mushrooms spreading in all directions among the moss and fallen leaves. Their caps were a nondescript brown but when Adam picked one she saw that the stems were a bright golden yellow. 'That's beautiful.'

'And delicious. And, wow, look, hedgehogs!'

'Where?'

'There. Can't you see? Chefs call them Sweet Tooth.'

'Cute little Mrs Tiggywinkle hedgehogs?'

'No, eejit. It's a name for a mushroom.' He was kneeling down to inspect them. 'These guys sell for twenty-five euro a kilo. I never know why more people don't get out and forage food.'

'Maybe because most people think mushrooms that don't come in plastic boxes are poisonous.'

'Yet there's so much here that's delicious. Nuts, berries, crab apples, wild garlic. Think of wild carrot. You can eat the young roots, or roast, dry and grind them to make a drink, like coffee. The seeds give a fabulous flavour to stews. You can even eat the flower heads deep-fried in batter.'

'Seriously?'

'Totally. And the plant's a wonderful pollinator. Farmers use it for companion-planting.' He grinned. 'I can see people's point about mushrooms, though. I mean, there's one that grows in Irish woods that's known as a Death Angel. And some of the ones that aren't actually poisonous are hallucinogenic. Reindeer in the wild get high on them, and leap around like they're going to take off and fly.'

'So Santa's reindeer are actually off their heads on magic mushrooms?'

'Could be where the idea came from.' Adam looked up at her. 'I know the idea that Santa comes down chimneys is supposed to be linked to Siberian shamans.'

'How come?'

'Because in Siberia huts would get almost buried by the snow. The shamans were healers who'd bring medicinal herbs to sick people and, in winter, the only way to get into a house was through the smoke hole in the roof.'

'Have you been hanging out in my dentist's waiting room?'

'This is just basic stuff you pick up when you're a highly trained chef.'

They wandered on to where a fallen log lay by the wayside and, feeling chilly, sat down to have their soup. Lia asked, 'Did you come into the forest when you were here before?'

Adam shook his head. 'No. Never did. It's pretty awesome, isn't it? Hanna was right.'

'Was she a volunteer in the nuns' garden as well?'

'Hanna? No.'

'Then how come you know her?'

Adam's eyes fixed on a thrush that was hunting snails under leaves. To Lia's dismay, his face seemed masked again. Holding the comforting cup of soup, she prayed that she hadn't asked one question too many. The thrush gave a thin cheep and fluttered away. Taking a long breath, Adam said, 'That's the bit of the story I haven't told you.'

CHAPTER THIRTY

Carrying his game pie, and a carton of milk he'd bought in Cassidy's supermarket, Stephen turned off Broad Street and began to make his way home. As he walked up Sheep Street, Catherine came out of the bookshop and stood on the pavement to look at her window display. She was wearing trousers and a shirt under a long, jade-green cardigan, held wrapped around her, to keep out the cold.

On the opposite side of the street, Stephen slowed down and stepped into the entrance to an alleyway. He could see lights twinkling on the book tree in Catherine's window, and posters advertising the carol singing the following day. Keeping well back, for fear that she'd turn and see him, Stephen remembered picking up one of her fliers in the library, and thinking it would be pleasant to hear carols in a bookshop on Christmas Eve. But now, having convinced himself that he mustn't keep dropping by, he realised he'd be sitting at home instead.

On the other side of the street, Catherine pulled her cardigan more tightly around her and, moving briskly, went back into the shop. Feeling sad and slightly idiotic, Stephen stepped out of the alleyway where he'd been lurking, and continued his solitary walk home.

Adam's shoulders were hunched, as they'd been when he and Lia had sat on the headland. Now she sat beside him in silence, fearful, as then, of stopping his flow of reminiscence.

'Lots of people you meet when you're on the streets are decent enough. Passers-by who smile and give you the price of a cup of coffee. Other rough sleepers who'd have your back and tell you what to avoid. Plenty of people I met had been homeless half their lives. Especially once I got out of Dublin. Up there, they didn't last so long. Down in the country, it was different. Like, there was an old fella in Carrick, called Tommy Banjo, was always going round shaking your hand and thanking you when you hadn't done anything for him. The locals knew him, and they'd give him a wave and a couple of euros, and the rest of us on the street kept an eye on him. And there was Gracie, who shuffled around with dozens of carrier bags, and had a huge, hairy dog called Gussie. She never said much, except to ask you what age you thought she was. By the look of her, she was well past eighty.'

Adam stopped and took a gulp of soup. 'Gracie used to sit in the library in Carrick. And the woman who was supposed to be reintegrating me ...' He stopped again, and looked at Lia 'Did I tell you about her?'

'The one you got assigned to at the halfway house?'

'Yes. Well, she'd said I ought to get myself a library card, and find out how to fill in forms, and get grants, and do training courses. That's how it worked. Martin would find you a live-in job, and be there in the background if you needed him, but he banged on all the time about self-empowerment.'

'Tough love.'

'It didn't feel like love. More like Martin was fighting a private war against the system. Anyway, that was the deal. I was supposed to get on and pull myself up by my own bootstraps. Gracie spent hours in Carrick library in bad weather. Plenty of rough sleepers did, though most just dozed off at a table. I'd done it myself, for a warm or to get in out of the rain. But once I'd settled into my job, I went there between shifts and got stuck in at the computer. It was that or wash pots for ever …'

Adam's voice trailed off. Crumbling a piece of bread in his hand, he shook himself. 'So, one day I went along and there was Gussie. Tied up outside to the railings with a bit of frayed string. He was a big yoke, like a cross between an elephant and a spaniel, with long yellow legs, like a winter chanterelle. Gracie was in the reading room when I went to use a computer, and I saw a snooty-looking woman pointing at her and muttering to the librarian. Then I got lost trying to find something on the internet. Next thing I knew, the woman was waving her phone and calling Gracie a vagrant, and saying she'd rung the guards because Gussie was blocking a public entrance. The library staff were nice enough. They tried to get Gracie to leave, but she didn't understand what was happening. She started wailing, so I went over. I thought, since she knew me, she might shut up and listen. I reckoned it made sense to get her away before the guards came, but a couple of them turned up before we could move her. Gracie was flailing around, and the woman was calling her drunk and obstreperous, and, when the guards tried to clear the room, I lost it and shouted at them. So the whole focus swung to me, and things got nasty. I ended up in a cell. Which was bad. But the real bugger was that the arresting officer was Nugent.' Adam's hands clenched, and he looked apologetically at Lia. 'Look at me. Still shaking when I think about the bastard.'

'Who was he?'

'Just a random guard with a scunner for rough sleepers. Everyone tried to avoid him. He'd get you up against a wall and call you a lazy git living on handouts. I think he got off on scaring people, even Tommy Banjo. He couldn't stand Martin either. Called him a feckin' do-gooder. He used to go for me because I look like I wasn't born here, so when he found me shouting the odds in a library, he must have thought all his birthdays had come at once. I was looking pretty rough when he got me down to the station, so he said I'd struck him while resisting arrest.'

'But did you?'

'I didn't even get a chance to. His partner was a decent skin who'd been trying to calm me down, but Nugent came in at a run, and floored me with a rugby tackle. It was like being hit by a ton of concrete, and I thought I heard a rib go. But all I could think about was my afternoon shift at the hotel, and that, if I didn't get back in time for it, my job would be gone as well.' Taking another deep breath, Adam kept going. 'One of the guards at the station brought a cup of tea down to the cell. He said if I'd been hurt in the ruckus, I'd a right to a doctor. Then he went and left me there. I knew by then there was no chance of making my shift, so I sort of broke down in tears. And then the door opened again, and it was Nugent.'

Adam's voice cracked. In his mind, he could see the bulky figure in the doorway.

'Guard Sullivan says you hurt yourself when I was bringing you in.'

His eyes had measured the distance to the emergency button, a million miles away on the corridor wall. 'I didn't say I needed a doctor.'

'That's good. Because I wouldn't want you to have any reason to.'

Somewhere at the back of his mind, he'd heard his mum's voice after his dad's funeral, telling him things just happened. You couldn't expect life to be fair: you just had to take what came and roll with the punches. Nugent had closed the cell door with an ominous clang. Instinct had made Adam cover his head with his arms, and back into a corner, but nothing had happened for so long that eventually he'd looked up. Nugent's eyes had been like stones, and a little tic had pulsed in one of his cheeks. Cornered, Adam had given up, slid down the wall and crouched in a ball on the floor.

Then the door had opened a third time, and Martin had stormed in, wearing jeans and a grubby sweatshirt. His face was set and his hands looked as if he'd been interrupted clearing drains. Immediately Nugent had seemed much smaller, and, scrambling up, Adam had found his voice. 'Martin, I never touched a guard. Honest to God, I didn't. I wouldn't. I did let a roar at the oul bitch, but she was threatening Gracie. And they'll tell you at the library that Gracie hadn't done anything wrong.'

Martin had stared Nugent directly in the eye. 'And I've got a witness ready to stand up in court and say that, me fine bucko. So, will we drop this now, or do it by the book?'

Adam looked at Lia. 'And that was that. He got me out of there. Nugent just went white in the face, looked at the other guard, and went away. It was like a miracle. Martin just walked in and got me out of there.'

'But how did he know what had happened?'

'The librarian. Gracie had told her who I was, and they'd gone round to get Martin. He knew what Nugent was like, so he waded in. I heard Nugent got disciplined later. I know they moved him off the streets. Afterwards, the library service kind of closed ranks around me. That's how I met Hanna.'

'And you didn't lose your job at the Royal Vic.'

Adam gave an unsteady laugh. 'Martin was always scarily persuasive. I sat outside scared shitless while he went in and talked to the chef. I don't know how he managed it, but I was back scraping pots that night.'

Out of the corner of her eye, Catherine had seen Stephen step into the entrance to the alleyway, evidently hoping she wouldn't notice. She'd managed to hold her ground and appear to consider her window display before going back inside as if nothing had happened. Now she realised she was standing stiffly by the counter, clutching her cardigan tightly across her chest. Glancing up from the till, Ann said, 'You're looking peaky. Is it colder out there?'

Straightening her cardigan, Catherine shook her head. 'A bit. Well, no, not really. The poster for the carols is looking good.'

Ann shot her a sharp look. 'Anything the matter?'

'Nothing. It is pretty cold out there, now you mention it. Oh, sorry, that's my phone.' Catherine moved away, saw the caller was Hanna and, taking it, hoped her voice wouldn't betray her. 'Hanna, hi. Anything I can do for you?'

'No. I'm just in a state here. And, look, I'm sorry to call when you're up to your ears.'

'No, you're fine. Has something happened?'

'Not yet, but I'm probably going to strangle my wretched mother.'

This was so unlike Hanna that Catherine forgot her own trouble. 'Wait, I'm going into the office.'

'Honestly, Catherine, I didn't mean to disturb you. I just had to talk to someone or I was going to explode.'

'You haven't disturbed me. Just let me shut this door. Now, talk away.'

'I know I ought to be grateful that the blasted woman's still with us.'

'Okay, stop right there. Let's take it as read that you're glad she's overground.'

Hanna gave a reluctant laugh. 'You know she's coming to us for Christmas Day?'

'Yes, you said.'

'Well, Brian went out and bought a round of spiced beef from Fitzgerald's. It's a traditional thing around here, and Mam's bosom buddies with Pat, who's an absolute sweetie, so Brian thought it would go down well. And Mary came by, and he mentioned it, and she was so dismissive. Said it ought to be eaten on St Stephen's Day, not Christmas, and she'd never liked it anyway, and why hadn't he asked her first? Well, that's just Mam. I know she's like that. And it was the stupidest little thing, but I went and lost my cool.'

'In front of her?'

'No, afterwards. I was raging round like the Antichrist, and when Brian tried to calm me what did I do but turn on him?'

'Oh, Hanna, I'm sorry. Have you fallen out over it?'

'No, because Brian's a saint. But the thing is, why should he put up with my mother? I mean, he can't have bargained for it when he decided to take up with me. I wouldn't blame him if he walked out tomorrow and left me to her.'

In her mind's eye Catherine could still see Stephen in the alleyway, stepping back with a haunted look on his face.

Hanna seemed to sense her distraction. 'Oh, no, I *have* called you at a bad time.'

'No, you haven't. Calm down. Pour yourself a drink.'

'I'm in the library.'

'Well, sit down and listen to me. You're blowing things out of proportion.'

It took several minutes to convince Hanna that falling in love with her hadn't ruined Brian's life.

'It's the best thing that ever happened to him, and he knows it. And I'm sure you'll have a lovely day with Mary in the end.' Hanna gave a derisory snort and Catherine laughed. 'Sorry, but when you do that, you sound exactly like her.'

Sounding less stressed, Hanna said, 'Oh, don't! Think of my own poor daughter in thirty years' time, trying to cope with me.'

'You could live to be a hundred and you'd never turn into Mary.'

'I suppose the truth is that I'm missing Jazz. She's invaluable when Mam and I rub each other up the wrong way.'

'Well, you don't begrudge her a break from the role of mediator, do you?'

'Of course not. And, after all, Christmas is only one day. Thanks, Catherine.'

'I'm not sure what I've done.'

'You've averted a murder.'

'Well, you're welcome. Mind yourself.'

'You too.'

Back in the shop, a man was struggling to get a double buggy over the threshold. Catherine went to help and, before closing the door, stepped onto the pavement again. She knew it was daft to think Stephen might still be there at the opposite side of the street, yet the impulse to look was too powerful to resist. But the entrance to the alleyway was empty, and she went back into her shop feeling bereft.

At the top of Sheep Street, Stephen crossed the road to the bridge and leaned on the parapet. Below him, the river gurgled in the darkness under the arches and, beyond his garden wall, the leafless branches of Sophie's birch tree were stark against the winter sky. He remembered a conversation he'd had in Dublin after her funeral, before he'd made his decision to move to Finfarran. A former colleague had appeared unexpectedly on his doorstep insisting on dragging him out for a couple of pints. They'd sat in a pub round the corner from his old office, and the colleague, who'd also been a good friend, had cleared his throat. 'I'm sticking my oar in here uninvited, so feel free to tell me to feck off. The thing is, Stephen, I know you took early retirement so you and Sophie could set up house in the country.'

'That was the plan.'

'Well, retirement itself is a huge step. Life-changing. And then to lose your wife, well, that's massive.'

'I don't want to be rude, but is there a point to any of this?'

'God, yes, I'm not interfering for the hell of it. It's only, I just thought, if you were interested, I'd say you could easily pick up a project or two on a freelance basis. You won't want to be sitting around at your age. I mean, I know you had plans before, but now ... Well, anyway, I'm just saying, if you'd like me to put the word out, I'd be happy to. If you felt like easing back into work, there's plenty would bite your hand off. Take your time. Think about it. Give me the nod if ever it feels right.'

At the time, Stephen had half considered the suggestion but, since coming to Bridge House, he hadn't thought of it again. Now he reminded himself that he still had friends up in Dublin, and the chance of finding interesting work. Maybe he should pick up his phone after Christmas, make a few calls and see how the land lay up there. Because what kind of life was there here for him now in a place so small that, wherever he went, he was likely to bump into Catherine? Why risk endless repeats of the embarrassment he'd just been through? Why not put Bridge House on the market, cut his losses, and leave?

Lia had laid her hands over Adam's to stop them shaking. He could feel her hair brushing against his cheekbone, as it had when they'd looked at the psalter in the library. He knew that, despite his resolve, if he turned to look at her now, he was going to kiss her, but he couldn't tell how she might react. So they sat there as the light in the cold clearing began to fade.

Then, with no sense of having come to a decision, he found he'd turned to face her and that his hand was under her chin. She allowed him to draw her towards him and he saw her lashes flutter, as if she was about to lower them and accept his kiss. Then her grey eyes widened and focused somewhere beyond his shoulder. 'Oh, my God, Adam!'

'What?'

'Look!'

With startled notions of bears or axe-wielding killers, Adam swung round and looked. She was pointing to where the sun was sinking behind the trees, huge, golden and astonishingly circled by vivid concentric rings of colour. Against a sky made pale by semi-transparent clouds, they shaded from red, orange and yellow through green, to blue, indigo and violet.

'Astronomers call it a halo. Light reflected and refracted by ice crystals, not water droplets. Adam, don't you remember? Think of the psalter.'

Immediately, Adam was back in Hanna's library, looking at a wren perched on a painted ash tree, its wings rendered with brown and black brushstrokes, its head raised and its beak open in song. Behind it there'd been a gilded disc outlined by concentric circles, laid on in verdigris, ochre, azurite and vermilion. He'd thought when he'd seen it that the bird must stand for some saint, like St Francis in the fountain whose head was backed by a granite disc. Now he looked at Lia. 'A halo's an astronomical term, as well as a holy thing?'

'Yup.'

'So what was the psalter trying to show? I mean, was someone trying to paint a picture of holiness or of something they'd actually seen in the winter sky?'

'Could be they didn't think there was any difference between them.'

Holding hands, they sat watching the sun disappear below the treetops. Time passed. Venus appeared in a sky as soft as grey velvet, and Adam said, 'Look, we're star-crossed.'

'Actually, that's a planet, not a star.'

'Lia.'

'What?'

'You do know that I was about to kiss you?'

'Yeah. Sorry. We definitely ought to refocus and get back to that.'

CHRISTMAS EVE

CHAPTER THIRTY-ONE

Lia woke early. Adam lay beside her with one arm curled under his pillow and the other dangling to the floor. When she reached out to touch him he sighed but didn't wake. Today, she thought, I'm booked on a train to Dublin and he'll be off to a job that'll devour him. Yet here we are in his bed and, as soon as we left the forest, we both knew that this was where we'd end up.

The previous night she'd said, 'There's always a girl, isn't there? On your courses. There's always someone you go to bed with.'

Rolling away from her onto his back, he'd said nothing for a moment, then, 'No, not always. But yes, now and again.'

'This is something different.'

It was a statement, not a question, and he'd turned his head to look at her. 'Yes, it is. Lia, do you want us to stop?'

'Could you?'

'If I had to.'

'I couldn't.'

Lia had no regrets but now, looking down at his half-hidden face, she knew why they'd both hesitated. Adam's career was the sole focus of his life. In the car on the way back from the forest, he'd tried to explain. 'You can't imagine what it's like sleeping rough. People see you as worthless. They literally spit on you. Martin used to say it was fear – that they'd look and know they were only a couple of wage packets away from a freezing shop doorway themselves. I'll never understand the aggression, but now that I've made it, I know the fear. You're only as big as your last job and all the time there's others behind you, fighting their way up. If you don't focus and keep going, you could find yourself back at rock bottom.'

And to be at rock bottom again, thought Lia, would break him, because there'd be no one there to help him back up.

In the forest, when they'd come to a stream, he'd hunkered down and trailed his hand in the water. 'I didn't see much of my dad when I was a kid. He was always working. But at weekends he'd sometimes take me fishing in the Royal Canal. He told me once that, when he was a child, my granddad used to take him fishing in the Red Sea, in a boat that had brown canvas sails.'

'Was your granddad a fisherman?'

'I dunno. Dad never said. He talked about making ruz sayadeya, though. It's an Egyptian seafood dish. He said he and his father made it with fish they caught in nets trailed behind the boat. It was mullet. They'd heat the oil in a round iron pan, caramelise onions and spices, and eat it with amber-coloured rice, cooked over a fire on a golden beach.'

'What did you and your dad catch in the Royal Canal?'

'Nothing, mostly. But we used to buy smoked cod and chips at a takeaway afterwards, and eat them on the bus on the way home.'

Moving softly, so as not to wake him, Lia sat up and looked at the trail of discarded clothes leading across the carpet to the bed. Still deeply asleep, Adam stirred and turned on his back, throwing one arm across his chest. His hair, which had lost its signature slickness, was damp on his faintly lined forehead. Edging out of the bed, Lia crossed the room and lifted the sheer net that covered the window. Craning her neck, she could see a row of industrial-sized bins far below her, standing to the left of the kitchen door. Adam had told her the ground-floor room he'd had as a kitchen porter had had the same view. 'Which was surreal because, only weeks beforehand, I'd been sleeping in the space between those bins and the kitchen wall.'

Catherine's first thought on Christmas Eve was how badly she missed Stephen and how it appeared that he wasn't missing her. When she'd seen him in Sheep Street the previous day, she'd nearly called out and waved, so the way he'd stepped into the alley had made her feel ridiculous. Now, brushing her hair at her mirror, she looked herself in the eye. There was no point in denying it. She'd fallen for him, and the chances were that she'd driven him off by behaving like an eejit that day in the car. And why was that? she asked herself, leaning in to glower at the little crow's feet around her eyes. Because you were scared that he'd think you were needy. You're a woman in your forties with a shop, a home and a track record in business, yet instead of allowing a conversation to take you where it was going, you panicked and like a teenager this is the result.

Downstairs, the skim on the ceiling had dried overnight. Carpet-tiles were stacked along the corridor, and in the shop, Terry, Declan and Angela were stripping the damaged covering from the floor. When Catherine came to open up, Fury had returned The Divil's tree to its central position against the dust sheets, and was moving the Lissbeg Books banners to flank it again. 'Right, so. Final default state. Plain and simple like it was the first morning. No decorations on the tree. You'll have your festive favourites playing, to cover the last of the noise, and we'll have everything done and dusted by lunchtime, with the set-up for your carol-singers in place.'

The sight of the tree's bare branches made Catherine wince. It was as if the memory of Stephen's presence had been erased. It's wrong, she thought. He was with us on the rollercoaster. He ought to be here on the final day, to celebrate what's been achieved. But as Fury and the others were still there, working like Trojans, she forced a smile and said the final default state looked great. 'The Divil's tree really is the gift that keeps giving. Where's himself this morning? Have you left him in the van?'

'He'd have picked the lock and made his escape if I'd tried it. Nothing would hold him when he'd get the smell of a woman preparing a Christmas dinner. No, he's above in your flat making big googly eyes at your mother in the hopes that one of her pigs in blankets might fall.'

'I wouldn't give much for his chances. She's a very focused cook.'

'I wouldn't doubt her. My money's on The Divil, all the same.'

Adam looked at the note he'd found by his pillow. He'd read it three times and still didn't know what it said.

Had forgotten I've an Oz WhatsApp. Not sorry. Didn't want to disturb you. Hope you're not. Life's all about going with the flow. Xx

He knew Lia's family WhatsApp calls had to be organised around time zone differences so, presumably, she'd woken early, remembered she had one and rushed to her own room to log in. But *Not sorry*? Not sorry about what? And *Didn't want to disturb you*? Was she talking about waking him up or turning his life upside down? He reached for his phone and realised they hadn't exchanged mobile numbers. Ought he to call Reception and ask to be put through to her room? But for all he knew she might still be WhatsApping, in which case he'd be lurching into the midst of a family chat. Best to stay put, then, and hope she'd be back when the WhatsApp session was over, and not dwell on the thought that, if she wasn't, he had no way of contacting her himself.

Stymied, he got up and paced around the bedroom, trying and failing to get his head straight. Yesterday, when still trying to be casual, he'd offered to drive her to catch her train today. But that had been before they'd ended up in bed together. Would she still want him to take her to the station? Maybe leaving without a word was her way of saying she wouldn't. Except that she hadn't left without a word. She'd left him a message so enigmatic he couldn't work it out. Suddenly Adam stopped pacing and stared at the rumpled bed. Was that what the note was? A test? A joke, maybe? She'd teased him before, but he couldn't believe she would now. Or might it be that, having made love, she was now as confused as he was? He didn't doubt for a moment that she loved him, but life was more complicated than that. Had she woken in the cold light of day, looked at the complications, and decided it would be best for them both if she simply slipped away?

Having opened the shop, Catherine sat at the counter and called Ann. 'Hi, how's it going up there?'

Ann looked down at The Divil, who was sitting on the kitchen floor. He was motionless except for his nose, which was quivering like an ultra-sensitive compass, and his large, liquid eyes, which hadn't blinked since his head had appeared round the door. 'Fine, I've got a visitor.'

'The Divil? Is he being persuasive?'

'There's a chance this turkey won't get as far as the oven with both its legs.'

'It's way too large for the two of us, anyway.'

'Are you okay, love? You sound peaky.'

'I'm fine. Tired. I expect it's because the end is nigh.'

'Now you're sounding morbid.'

'Don't be daft. I mean it's because we're so close to getting our shop back.'

'And not just as it was. Better.'

'I know.' Aware that she was still sounding down, Catherine kept talking so Ann could ask no more questions. 'Listen, Mum,

I've had a text from Bríd. She'll bring the mince pies in the back way, and take them up to you. We'll need to reserve some for the choir, and put the rest on trays to pass around.'

'No problem. Tomorrow's dinner's under control, so I'll get on to them. Any customers in yet?'

'Last-minute panic buying, and lots of enquiries about the carols. I'd say we're going to have a big crowd and, according to Fury, we're on schedule. God knows what he's planning. He's just announced he's off to buy rings.'

'What kind of rings?'

'I dunno. Five gold ones? Maybe he's going to produce a 'Twelve Days Of Christmas' extravaganza. Anyway, we're barred from the back of the shop till the flooring's down and the concert set-up's done.'

When Adam had woken that morning he'd felt a sense of release so intense it was almost frightening, but the shock of finding himself alone had driven it from his mind. Now, stuck in his room with nothing to do but wait for Lia, he realised that telling her about Nugent and Martin had freed something he'd kept buried deep in his subconscious ever since the day his father had died. It was years since he'd dealt with the irrational anger he'd felt towards his mother. But what he hadn't recognised till now was his unspoken conviction that, without his father's powerful presence, he'd never be safe again.

The sense of release had returned, bringing absolute clarity. So that's what I've done, Adam thought. I've spent all this time finding replacements for Dad. It began here in Finfarran, and it's gone on ever since. Looking back, he could see himself on the streets, alone and frightened, when Martin, with his huge shovel hands and air of authority had scooped him up. Martin, who'd been waging personal war against a system that failed to contain bigotry and violence. Martin, who could open doors because he understood what went on behind them. Martin, who didn't talk much but got things done. After that, there'd been the increasingly powerful chefs he'd worked for, from volatile, bad-tempered Anton at the Royal Victoria, to the brawny Englishman in Dublin, who'd sent him over to London, and on to the Michelin-starred restaurateur, who'd made him try for the Coolest Chef title. And now, thought Adam, there's Dom. Someone else who opens doors I feel I've no right to walk through. Another powerful, commanding figure, who'll fight my battles for me.

Crossing to the window, Adam looked down at the row of bins. There was a vent from the kitchen in the wall behind them, which meant that the space where he'd curled up in his sleeping bag had been warm. He remembered going through the gate to the yard, fearful that someone would corner him and have him arrested for trespass. I did that on my own, he thought, when I was only a kid. I kept myself going for months before I got too ill to manage, and once I'd recovered, and had a job and a place to live, I found my feet. Dom's had his slice of my success. I owe him nothing at this stage. But I owe it to Mum and Dad not to let him make clickbait out of what happened to me when Dad died. And I owe it to myself not to sell my soul, and that's what this big Netflix deal comes down to. I could choose to believe a producer's credit will give me power, but I know it won't. To be fair to Dom, he never conceals the truth. Not really. He just offers you ways to obscure it and, in the end, the choice is yours.

CHAPTER THIRTY-TWO

On Christmas Eve the Convent Centre closed for the holidays so Pat had offered to host the choir's final rehearsal. They climbed the stairs from the butcher's shop, unwinding scarves and clapping gloved hands together, telling each other Finfarran was set for a white Christmas this year. Mary said darkly that, with the price of bottled gas and the electricity, there'd be stories of people frozen to death in their homes before winter was out.

'Ara, Mary Casey, you'd put a downer on anything.'

'I'm not in charge of the weather or the retail price index.'

'You're showing off because you're snug as a bug in Garrybawn House.'

The choir mistress, Miss Clarke, had taught most of its members at school. 'Can we get the chatter over with, please, and settle down? We'll run straight through the programme without interruption, then deal with any problems.'

Mary, who'd poured herself a cup of tea from the pot on Pat's range, announced that she'd said from the start she'd be needing a platform. 'With the way you've lined us up, nobody's going to see me at all, Miss Clarke. Not with the rest of them in front.'

A tenor from Ballyfin, who'd worked on a trawler, put up his hand and said he'd brought a fish box. 'We'll have it upside down for her in the back row, Miss, and as long as she keeps her weight on the rim she'll be sound.'

Before Mary could object, they were chivvied into their places. The trawlerman and a former clerk at the back, then Mary on the box, and a couple of farmers. A second row, consisting of Pat flanked by two musical ladies. And old Miss Cassidy from the supermarket in front, next to Ursula Flood from the pharmacy and her mouth-organ.

'Now then! Shoulders back, chests out, work from your diaphragms. And remember that carols come from the French "caroles", and used to be danced as well as sung. So what do we feel?'

A meek chorus replied, 'We feel the movement of the music, Miss.'

'Exactly. All together and watch my baton.'

The run-through began with a rousing opener and continued smoothly, except for when Brendan the trawlerman came in unexpectedly with the ladies' *Glorias*.

'A little concentration, Brendan, *please*. We've been doing this since September.'

'Sorry, Miss. I was worried about Mary's fish box.'

Mary bristled. 'I'll have you know I was feeling the movement of the music.'

'The fact is, I whipped the box out of a yard behind the marina, and your man that owns it won't want it broken.'

'And what made you think I'd break it? Many's the solo I've sung off a three-legged stool.'

'Ay, but the base of that box is only three-mil plastic. And I'd say now, Mary, to be fair, you're carrying a bit more weight now than you did in the past.'

The discussion became general when one of the farmers said he reckoned it was more like two-mil than three. 'They changed the regulations a while back.'

'No, your man has had that box a good twenty years.'

'It'll be brittle then. You're right. She'd want to be careful.'

To the tap of the baton, they launched back into the programme and reached Ursula's *Alleluia*. After several last-ditch attempts to make sense of its setting, one of the hefty farmers raised his hand. 'By the time we get to this, they'll be gagging for mince pies. Why don't we all just belt it out together, and leave it at that?' Even Mary, who'd been promised her own line, was in agreement, and Ursula looked so relieved that Miss Clarke barely kept her temper.

When they'd finished, Mary accepted a hand down from her fish box and joined Pat, who'd gone to fill the kettle. 'Well, either Ursula's deaf or her angel wasn't classically trained.' Glancing round the room, she asked, 'Ah, Pat, have you not even put up a sprig of holly?'

'Can't I see all the grand decorations down there in the street from my window?'

'That's not the point, is it?'

'Hand me the teabags and don't be getting at me.'

'The fact is you're depressed because you don't want to spend Christmas at Frankie's.'

'Leave it, Mary. Blood's thicker than water, and Frankie's my flesh and blood. You concentrate on staying up on your fish box. I'll be grand.'

As Catherine finished serving a customer, Hanna came into the bookshop. 'How's it all going?'

'They're on the final stretch. Fury's moving The Divil's tree back there once the new floor covering's down. He says the concert set-up's on schedule, and who am I to doubt him?'

'You must be over the moon to be getting your shop back.'

'And, look, I have a card carousel on order. We'll get yours back to you ASAP.'

Hanna shook her head. 'No hurry. I see the cards have sold well.'

'Like hot cakes. It's a no-brainer, really. I mean we sell books and the psalter's the literary heart of Lissbeg.'

'Most of our psalter cards aren't remotely Christmassy. Would you think of stocking some here all year round?'

'We've wondered about that. Could you send me a link to your supplier?'

'Sure.'

Catherine leaned against the counter. 'We've been thinking about other products too. Scented candles, say, or gorgeous cashmere socks, or even bath-oil. Relaxing things to surround yourself with when you sink into a book. Preferably locally made so we'd be showcasing Finfarran.'

'It makes sense. What about Edge of the World Essentials at the Convent Centre? They make organic bath-oils. Candles too.

They source wax from a guy who keeps bees over near Fury's forest.'

'That's exactly the vibe. Tea and honey on toast with your feet up in cashmere socks as you sit by the fire with our latest bestseller.'

'I think diversifying is a brilliant idea.'

'Actually, it was Stephen's. He pointed out it could be a double-whammy. Tourist sales but also tapping into the local gift market.' But at the mention of Stephen's name, Catherine's voice had gone from excited to woebegone. Carefully casual, Hanna said, 'I'm looking forward to your carol concert later. I know he is too.'

'Is he?'

'Well, he was full of enthusiasm about it a week ago.'

Catherine looked rueful. 'Ah. Things may have changed since then.'

'Why? Have you two fallen out?'

'No, it's just ... I don't know. It's kind of complicated.'

'Oh, okay. Look, I don't want to pry. I'm sorry, though. Stephen's a great guy.'

'I know. He's wonderful. I mean, he's solid, decent and nice. And great company.'

'Lonely, too, a lot of the time, I'd say.'

'You think so?'

'He's the sensitive sort that's always afraid of pushing in where he might not be wanted.' Feeling she'd said enough on the subject, Hanna looked at her watch. 'I'd better go. My mother sent me a text this morning. She hopes I have squirty cream for the trifle.'

'And have you?'

'We haven't even got trifle.'

'Good luck finding the makings of it in Lissbeg on Christmas Eve.'

'I know. I just tried Cassidy's for the cream and the woman laughed in my face. Oh, well, like I said on the phone, there's only one day to be got through, and I've promised myself I won't lose my cool with my wretched mother again. Look, I'll see you later. Is there anything I can pick up for you if I do have to go to Carrick?'

'No, we're fine. Mum's upstairs preparing a meal that'd feed a regiment.'

'Okay. See you soon.'

Catherine went back to her work feeling despondent. When she'd heard Hanna say Stephen was looking forward to the concert, her mind had started to spin. Maybe she'd imagined the look on his face when she'd seen him yesterday. Perhaps he hadn't noticed her on the opposite side of the street. It could be he'd stepped into the alleyway to tie his shoelace, or to pick up something he'd dropped that had rolled away. But her hopes had been dashed, and now the thought of implementing the plans for the shop without him was horrible. Ann was already talking about planning meetings in January, and saying how energising it was to have Stephen's input. 'We could ask him to take a look at what you and I come up with. Or even see if he'd help us to brainstorm ideas. What d'you think?'

So far, Catherine had managed to avoid answering the question but, obviously, that couldn't go on. Though they were close, she and Ann had never gone in for heart-to-hearts about their feelings, and now she was going to have to tell her that on top of spoiling her own happiness she'd also deprived them of Stephen's useful advice. She was sitting at the counter trying to decide how and when to go about it when her phone pinged. Taking it from her bag, she saw a text from Hanna and opened it, expecting the promised link to the card supplier. Instead, it read: *Here's Stephen's number. He really does get in a state if he thinks people see him as pushy. Xx*

Looking thoughtfully at the screen, Catherine felt a flicker of hope returning. She reread the text, then scrolled down to look at the row of digits. Stephen's number. All it would take to call him was a single tap on the screen.

Fury had given Miss Clarke instructions to bring the choir into the bookshop via the backyard. 'Down the side lane and in through the gate, you'll see my van parked outside. I've a big effect planned and I don't want them pensioners straggling in through the front of the shop, d'you hear me? I need them lined up out of sight in the refurbished space, ready to start singing when it comes to my final reveal.'

So, scarved and gloved again, the choir made its way along Sheep Street and, before reaching the bookshop, turned down the lane. It was colder than it had been and they filed through the back gate hastily, Miss Clarke in front and Mary at the rear. In a corner of the yard was the huge mound of debris that Terry, Fury and Angela had barrowed out from the shop. The jagged plaster, shattered laths and buckled metal were edged with dirty chunks of half-melted snow. Poking from the heap were torn Christmas cards and books. On top was the discarded floor covering, its rubberised black backing visible in places, where the damaged surface hadn't been uppermost when it was tipped out.

Sitting at the foot of the mound on an upturned bucket, Fury was smoking a roll-up with The Divil at his feet. As the rest of the choir crowded through the door, Mary dropped back and planted her hands on her hips. The Divil's head was on Fury's boot and Fury's head was down, his forearms resting on his thighs and his hands dangling between his bony knees. 'Dear God, Fury, it's freezing out here. Would you not go inside and keep warm?'

'Do you never stop telling people what to do, Mary Casey?'

'That's a fine question, coming from you. You've been telling us all what to do for years.'

Fury flicked ash off his cigarette, just missing The Divil's ear. 'It's been a long week, Mary. I'm having a break.'

Mary squinted at him sharply. 'You're not looking well in yourself. Do you know what I'm going to tell you? You shouldn't be living out there on your own by the forest. What if you had a fall and needed help?'

'I'm not in the habit of falling.'

'Ay, well, none of us are till we do. What you want is to be proactive, Fury. Get yourself liquidated, like I did, and get a new lease on life.' Uncharacteristically, Fury didn't quell her. His eyes were on the glowing tip of the roll-up. Mary's voice softened. 'I'm not saying it's easy. It isn't. No one knows that better than me. I had a little bureau at home, left to me by my mother. It wouldn't fit in the Garrybawn flat, so I had to let it go. And I'd a shed full of Tom's tools that I cried salt tears over, though after he died I hadn't a clue what the half of them was for. They went to Johnny next door, and I'm still convinced

Tom'll never forgive me. He always said Johnny was careless with tools.'

Tightening her coat across her bosom, Mary looked round for something to sit down on. Finding nothing suitable, she continued to stand over Fury, her usually smug face lined with concern. 'We're all the same in Garrybawn. We've all left plenty behind us. There's Maude McGonigle has the single unit next to mine. She had that four-bedroom house her husband built in Crossarra. She was rattling round that place on her own for years. Two replacement hips and the stair carpet in flitters. Accident waiting to happen but, of course, she wouldn't be told. In the heel of the hunt, her son-in-law had to go in and talk sense to her. And, come here to me, at the end of the day, what was she hanging on for, only the dog? A little black pug about the size of a rabbit. Well, it made no sense, did it?'

Fury still had his eyes on the cracked concrete between his boots. Easing the wrist of her glove away from her watch, Mary said that, anyway, she'd better join the others. 'I hear you've a big coup de théâtre planned for this afternoon.'

'And I want the choir in position, so get your skates on.' He looked her straight in the eye and, having known him since their schooldays, she shrugged and nodded. 'Right so. I'll see you inside for the off.'

As Mary disappeared through the back door, Fury looked down at The Divil. 'I'm sorry you had to hear that.' Sitting up on his haunches, The Divil looked long and deeply into Fury's watery blue eyes. His own large brown ones were fringed with white lashes. Fury made a face at him, and pinched out his cigarette. 'Ah, for feck's sake, drop the Captain Oates impression. I'm not having you walking into a blizzard, saying you may be a while.' With an offended snort, The Divil lay down again, and turned his back on him. Digging in the pocket of his waxed jacket, Fury took out his iPhone. 'Here, you might as well look at this. I wasn't going to show you but, knowing Liam Carmody, he'll have a sign stuck on a pole by the forest road in jig time.' Finding the auctioneer's website, he held out the phone to The Divil. 'He has it up for sale online already. Offers In The Region Of. While we've been flinging fairy-dust round the bookshop, he's been inside in his office, sealing our fate.'

Standing up and returning his phone to his pocket, he bent and scratched The Divil behind the ear. Then, sticking the toe of his boot under the little dog's belly, he lifted him to his feet. 'Come on, we're not going back in there for my final coup de théâtre. I've done enough. You and I are going home.' The Divil shook himself and fell into step beside him. In the lane, Fury opened the cab door and let him jump onto the passenger seat. Opening the door on his own side, he got in and fastened his seatbelt. 'I'd say if I wanted to liquidate myself, I could hang on now and watch the price of our house rising. But, I'm telling you this, no fecker's going to shift me out of it. I'll still be sitting there when they're building their bloody luxury flats around me, so you needn't fear you'll be going the way of Maude McGonigle's pug.'

CHAPTER THIRTY-THREE

Adam had no idea how long he'd been sitting in his bedroom when a knock on the door jerked him to his feet. He rushed to open it, thinking it was Lia, and found a chambermaid consulting a list.

'Sorry to disturb. You're checking out today, is that right?'

'What? Yes. I am. I should be.' He'd packed nothing, and his clothes from the previous night were still scattered across the floor. 'Look, can you come back later?'

'Yes, sir. Checkout is at noon.'

Adam looked at his watch and saw it was now after half past eleven. He made for the shower and, twenty minutes later, rushed down to Reception. Normally, seeking information about a fellow-guest's whereabouts would produce a polite, professional refusal but, to Adam's relief, the young man at the desk was Wayne.

'Lia? She's checked out. I have her luggage there in the lock-up.' Scarlet to the ears, he added, 'You're Adam Rashid, aren't you? … Could we possibly do a selfie? I'm, like, a really massive fan.'

Instantly, the manager emerged from the office behind him. 'What's this, Wayne? You know perfectly well that asking guests for photos is inappropriate.'

'Sorry.'

'I'll speak to you later. Get back to your work at once.' Having crushed Wayne, the manager flashed a benign smile at Adam. 'Mr Rashid, I hope you've enjoyed your stay with us. I understand you're checking out today?'

'Well, yes. I think so. That is, I haven't packed ...'

'No problem at all. The check-out time rule is purely advisory. Perhaps you'd care to stay another night? Our executive chef does a wonderful Christmas dinner.'

'Possibly. It's just ... I need to go out now.'

All Adam could think about was that Lia's train left at three thirty. He'd woken with the feeling that his life had become a million times more complicated and, since then, had reached a conclusion that might make matters worse. Only a few hours ago he'd been willing Lia to accept the idea of life with a celebrity. Now he was freaked about how she might feel when she knew that, without any sensible plan for the future, he'd decided to dump his agent and chuck his high-flying career. He desperately needed to tell her he'd made up his mind not to sign his new TV contract, but it wasn't something he could explain on a station platform. They had to sit down and talk, but he still had no way of calling her. She hadn't come back to his room, and she wasn't in the hotel. So where was she likely to spend the next few hours?

The manager's smooth voice interrupted his panic. 'Of course, if you'd prefer to eat in privacy, we have an extended festive room-service menu, personally prepared by Jerome, our executive chef.'

'What?'

'Should you wish to remain with us over Christmas.'

'Oh. Yes. I'm sorry. I'm not sure what my plans are yet.'

'Incidentally, Jerome had been very much hoping to meet you, and I've wondered if you'd allow us to take a quick photo of you with him. To hang in a frame at Reception. If you have time.'

In the background, Wayne's jaw had dropped and, bad as his own troubles were, Adam sympathised with his suppressed indignation. Pulling himself together, he assumed a distant manner and told the manager photo requests had to go through his agent.

'Absolutely. Of course. I do apologise. And do, please, consider staying on if you'd like to. We can guarantee you absolute privacy.'

She disappeared into her office and, waiting till the door closed behind her, Adam turned to Wayne. 'Fancy that selfie, then?'

'Seriously?'

'Make it quick, though.'

'Wow! Thank you.' Wayne shot out from behind the desk, eyes on stalks and sweaty fingers slipping on his phone. Adam put an arm around his shoulders and smiled while, back in overdrive, his mind tried to work out where Lia could have gone. If only he had a starting-point, some notion of how to begin his search. Then the phone camera clicked and, out of the corner of his mouth, Wayne muttered, 'That lady you were asking about? The one who checked out earlier? She wanted to know the Christmas Eve schedule for buses to Lissbeg.'

What followed felt like a nightmare in which Adam ran faster and faster as sand slipped relentlessly through an hour-glass. Having driven to Lissbeg, he sprinted from Broad Street to the Garden Café.

'Has Lia been here this morning?'

Bríd put her head round the kitchen door. 'I saw her in town earlier looking like she was on a mission.'

'You didn't talk to her?'

'No. Are you coming to the carol concert at the bookshop?'

'What? No. I'm supposed to be flying back to London tonight.'

'Well, you'd better calm down or you'll have a heart attack before you get there.'

Back in the car, he wondered if Lia might have gone to say goodbye to the ocean. But, halfway down the lane to the beach, with his tyres throwing sand up like spray, he remembered she'd done that already, the previous morning. Reversing, he got caught in a slough and needed to shove wave-polished stones under the rear wheels, to get purchase. Then, on the road again, clutching his head, he suddenly thought of the headland. It was miles away in the opposite direction but, with no other hope on offer, he pulled a U-turn like a boy racer's, pressed the accelerator and sped away.

At the bookshop, people had begun to gather for the carols. The Divil's tree and the banners were gone, leaving the multicoloured dust sheets unobscured. Plates of mince pies were lined up on the counter, and Catherine's book tree, twinkling in the window, cast shimmering reflections on the frosty pavement outside. A queue of last-minute shoppers was chatting while waiting to pay for books and, here and there, chairs accommodated older arrivals and parents with toddlers on their knees. Then, at a prearranged signal, a mouth-organ flourish sounded behind the dust sheets, making everyone turn and tell each other to hush. Silence fell before Pat's sweet, high voice rang out, followed by Mary's contralto profundo.

The holly and the ivy
WHEN THEY ARE BOTH FULL GROWN
Of all trees that are in the wood
THE HOLLY BEARS THE CROWN

To gasps of amazement from the audience, the dust sheets separated and swung back, like a theatre curtain at the start of a show. By threading ropes through a diagonal row of curtain rings, which he'd sewn across the back of each, Fury had devised the system that had lifted them into swags for his final reveal. Standing in rows on the bright blue newly carpeted floor, Miss Clarke's pensioners crashed into the chorus:

O, the rising of the sun
And the running of the deer
The playing of the merry organ
Sweet singing in the choir ...

Still clutching the ropes they'd just pulled, Declan and Angela punched the air triumphantly as the choir swept into the first verse.

The holly bears a berry
As red as any blood ...

It was the perfect toy-theatre Christmas card of Catherine's childhood. Pressing her hands to her face, she exchanged delighted looks with Ann. The back and front of the bookshop were now seamlessly matched. Downlighters in the smooth new ceiling showed up the spotless floor, and were trained on the polished shelving along the walls. On one side of the choir, The Divil's tree, crowned with a golden sun, bristled with crimson bells dotted with sequins, and ceramic cupcakes, gingerbread stars and beribboned pine cones. On the other side, a fretwork screen in the shape of an antlered stag re-established the children's corner, where brightly painted stools had been set around a little table. Her eyes filling with tears, Catherine reached out and gripped Ann's hand beneath the counter. And the choir swung into the chorus again.

At the top of the rutted lane to the headland Adam left his car and started to run. The freezing mud made him stumble and, completing the nightmare sensation, the briars seemed to reach out to hold him back. Seagulls swooped overhead, shrieking and gliding on currents of air. Panting, he reached windswept turf and staggered out to the place on the clifftop where he and Lia had sat and looked at the moon. Now, in daylight, he could see right across the bay to where bonfires had gleamed on the night of the solstice. Above him, the screams of the gulls seemed to tear the sky. Far below, waves crashed like thunder. Leaning against a foam-slicked rock, he strained his eyes for a dark-haired figure in a silver jacket. But Lia wasn't there.

The choir took a deep breath and launched into its next offering.

Angels we have heard on high
Sweetly singing o'er the plains
And the mountains in reply
Echoing their joyous strains ...

Ronan had been standing next to Aideen. He began to drift to where Terry was perched on the edge of the window display, his red woolly hat sticking out of his pocket precisely at Ronan's eye-level. After considering it for a moment, Ronan asked, in a loud whisper, 'Where's the other elf?'

Terry looked down at him. 'You're here again, are you?'

'Is the other elf with Santy? Have they taken Max back to the Grinch?'

'Don't ask me, son. We don't keep tabs on each other.'

'I want to show the elf my pine cone on the Christmas tree.'

'Don't you bother your head about that. I know he's seen it.'

Standing on her fish box in the centre of the back row, Mary locked her fingers and stuck out her elbows. With her eyes on

Miss Clarke's baton, she was ready for the moment when a plunge down repeated cascades of notes would bring the chorus to its definitive *Gloria in excelsis Deo!*

When the moment arrived, she came in strongly and, wincing, Ronan put his hands over his ears. 'Why is that lady too loud?'

Terry hushed him reprovingly. 'There's no such thing as singing a carol too loud on Christmas Eve.'

'But she *is*.'

'Mind your manners. What would Santy say if he could hear you?'

Ronan's voice rose to a wail that topped the rapturous applause at the end of the carol. 'Santy wouldn't say *anything* because he *couldn't* hear me. He couldn't because that lady sings TOO LOUD.'

High on the cliff, Adam turned, thinking he'd heard his name, but it was only a sheep calling a lamb. The last time he'd felt this cold he'd been sleeping in shop doorways. Hunkering down by the rock, he attempted to control his breathing. Having struggled with how he and Lia would cope with the pressures of his celebrity, he was now freaked by the thought that she might lose interest in him without it. But she'd never seemed to think it was important. And, whatever his fears and imaginings, he knew their love for each other was as certain as the fact of the earth's rotation from east to west. That was all that mattered. That was what he had to hang on to. Feeling calmer, he relaxed against the rock. Then, with a jolt, he saw the sun was sinking towards the horizon. Lia was booked on a train that left in less than an hour. He had to get back to Carrick and make for the station.

Having restrained themselves heroically during the quiet bits of 'Adeste Fideles', the pensioners were about to pounce on their next item like unleashed hounds. The audience was equally happy to move on from what Terry had whispered to Ronan was 'holy stuff'.

'Why holy?'

'Because it's in Latin.'

'Why in Latin?'

'Because it's holy. Shut up.'

Miss Clarke's baton went up, and the choir inhaled collectively.

We WISH you a merry Christmas
We wish you a merry Christmas
We wish you a merry CHRISTMAS and a happy new year.
Good tidings we bring ...

The shop door opened and, turning automatically, Catherine saw Stephen come in. Their eyes met and he smiled. Drifting away from the counter, much as Ronan had drifted towards Terry, Catherine edged towards him through the crowd.

'Hi.'

'Hello.'

'I'm glad you came.'

'You made a good case for not missing the grand finale.'

'It is amazing, isn't it?'

'Noisy, though. Shall we go and see how it looks from outside?'

Viewed through the bow window, with Catherine's book tree in the foreground, the backs of the heads of the audience and the spotlit choir framed by the swagged dust sheets looked even more like a Christmas card. Catherine turned to say so to Stephen but he spoke first. 'You do know that we've been getting things wrong in exactly the same way but from opposite directions.'

'I have no idea what that means.'

'That we've both behaved like total eejits. But, Catherine, let's not be hard on ourselves. It's Christmas. Why not start again?'

Catherine swallowed hard. 'Just so I know, what are we aiming for?'

'Right now? I fancy a nice mince pie.'

'Sounds like a sensible starting-point.'

'Here we go, then.'

Stephen opened the door and a wave of warmth poured out from the crowded bookshop. As he and Catherine went in, Ann exchanged grins with Hanna and, let off the leash, the choir ignored Miss Clarke's signal for a diminuendo.

... Oh, bring us some FIGGY PUDDING
And a cup of good cheer!

Adam pounded up the steps at the station. There was no staff member in sight and he couldn't find the information board.

Frantically, he spun on his heels and realised that, directly above him, a digital display was scrolling to its next setting. Somehow, he got past a barrier and, having done so, discovered he needed to cross a footbridge that seemed miles away. The Dublin train was still standing at the far side of the tracks. He'd made it across the bridge and was charging down to the platform when a whistle blew and the train began to move. He didn't know if he'd shouted aloud but, anyway, it made no difference. Clinging to the iron railing, he watched the last carriage disappear down the track.

Breaking ranks, the choir made for the mince pies. Ursula's *Alleluia* had gone as well as could be expected, and the carols had ended in wild applause. Though the poster had made no mention of tea, trays of mugs had appeared and Bríd and Aideen were helping to fill them. Several people had raided the tree and were eating the gingerbread stars. Towards the front of the shop, Mary was shaking her head over Pat's vibrato. 'Dear God, she's still the vocal equivalent of a jelly.' Cocking an eye at Hanna, she added, 'And that reminds me. I hope you got the squirty cream for your trifle.'

'Actually, Mum, there wasn't any. Not even in Carrick.'

'Ah, for the love of God, can you not even do Christmas right?'

Hanna flushed. 'That's a rotten thing to say. Anyway, Brian's made tiramisu.'

''Tis far from tiramisu I reared you.'

'Well, tough, Mam, because that's what you're going to be eating for pudding tomorrow.'

The air crackled with the real possibility of a proper full-blown family row that would echo on for Christmases to come. Hanna set her teeth and concentrated on not bursting into tears.

Then, with a mighty effort, Mary controlled herself, reached into the crowd and grasped Pat's arm. 'Come here to me, I've been meaning to pass on an invitation from Hanna. Would you fancy having Christmas dinner with us over at her place?'

A nanosecond passed before Pat smiled sweetly at Hanna. 'Now, that's very kind of you. It's a difficult time of year when you're on your own.'

Thrown both by her own loss of cool and the fact it was Mary, not she, who'd acted to save the situation, Hanna groped for words and came up with nothing better than 'Oh? Right. Well, you'll be very welcome. Brian will drive over and pick you up.'

'Well, if he would, I'd be very grateful. Look, there's Catherine with the tea tray. Whip over and get yourself a cup before they're all gone.'

Mary hooked her arm through Pat's and drew her away towards the mince pies. 'There now! That's your problem with Frankie fixed for you. There's no law says you have to spend Christmas with family. I tried to tell you before, but you wouldn't be told.'

'Don't pretend you did that for me just now. You're a bold-faced woman. I may have played along, but I'm no fool.'

'God forgive you, Pat Fitz, you were never one for gratitude.'

'Not when it's not deserved. Anyone could see that, without Jazz in the mix at Hanna's tomorrow, you were desperate for a friend to leaven the loaf.'

Numb with misery, Adam made his way to the hotel lift. He stood with his back to it, waiting for it to open, and turned when he heard the doors ping. Inside was Lia, wearing her silver-grey parka jacket, knitted scarf and woolly hat. For a moment they stared at one another, each with one foot on the threshold. Then Adam leaped forward and the doors closed behind him. Half aware that, around them, several phone cameras were flashing, they hung on to each other and spoke in chorus.

'Lia! There's something I've got to tell you!'

'Adam! There's something we have to tell Fury!'

CHRISTMAS DAY

CHAPTER THIRTY-FOUR

'Merry Christmas.'

'You said that at midnight.'

Turning her head on the pillow, Lia grinned. 'I wasn't sure you heard me. You were concentrated on something else at the time.' Adam pushed himself onto his elbow and looked at her so intently that she reached up and touched his cheek. 'What's wrong?'

'It feels crazy. Like a fairy-story ending.'

'I know. But it isn't.'

'Tell me again.'

'Okay. Once upon a time …' Lia shrieked and rolled away as he made a grab for her. 'No! Stop. We'll wake the whole hotel.' Propping his pillow against the bedhead, Adam sat up. 'Start from when you disappeared leaving that dumb note.'

'It wasn't dumb.'

'It wasn't coherent.'

'You're not the only one who's been finding life complicated, you know.'

'Fair point.'

'I left you the note and went off to talk to my family. On WhatsApp. Like the note said.'

'Incoherently.'

'You're like a dog with a bone, you know that?'

'And, out of the blue, your nan dropped the bombshell?'

'It wasn't a bombshell. At that point we were having an ordinary conversation. She'd had an offer for her house. Dad was chuffed, and asked if that meant Granddad's estate was wound up. And she said yes, except for the Finfarran land.'

'Which nobody in the family had ever mentioned before?'

'Everyone in the family talked about it all the time. The point is, that Granddad never called it the Finfarran land. It was always "my green field at the end of the rainbow" or "my little piece of the auld sod". Nan reckons he couldn't remember where he'd been when he'd bought it. She only found out because it was in the paperwork that came from the lawyer when Granddad died.'

'It's all too much of a coincidence. I mean, what are the odds?'

'Stop arguing, Adam. Embrace it. The stars have aligned. They do sometimes.'

'Stars don't align. That's planets.'

'You know something? I could totally change my mind about being in love with you.' She glared at him, he kissed her, and she looked into his eyes. 'Okay, that was a hollow threat. I couldn't.'

'And your granddad's piece of the auld sod really is Fury's forest? Are you sure?'

'Yes, because there's a map attached to the deeds my nan has. And then she said an auctioneer in Lissbeg was selling it off, and I went apeshit. Which is why I leaped into a bus and went there.'

'Because, obviously, an auctioneer would be open on Christmas Eve.'

'Oh, Adam! We've been through this. He wasn't open. He lives over the shop. And, yes, I could have waited till after the holiday, but he'd emailed Nan an offer from a global consortium, and developers like that don't take Christmas breaks.'

'This Carmody guy wouldn't have lifted his arse before New Year's Day.'

'Trust me, Nan would've hustled him. Now that her house has sold, she's itching to move up to my parents.'

'I freaked when I found you were gone.'

'Yeah, you mentioned that.'

'And then there you were in the lift. You've put years on me.'

'Nothing a champagne breakfast in bed on a Christmas morning won't cure. Go on, call room service. I'm always starving after a night of passion.'

'Lia, you really won't mind that I won't be cool any more?'

'I'm just relieved that you're going to lose the hair product.'

Adam picked up the phone. 'So, a full Irish with your Bollinger?'

'As long as the eggs are lightly poached.' Lia reached up and kissed him. 'Oh, and ask if they'd do Christmas dinner for four as a takeaway later. If you've really decided to dump

Dommie Dearest and take your life back, I reckon you and I should go see Fury and The Divil.'

Catherine came into Ann's room with tea on a tray. 'Happy Christmas. It's snowing again so I thought you'd like breakfast in bed.'

'Oh, this is nice. Thank you, love.'

'And here's to many more Christmases ahead.' Sitting down with her own teacup, Catherine yawned and stretched. 'Isn't it bliss knowing everything downstairs is done and dusted?'

'And that nothing up here is likely to flood or blow up.'

'I had a quick look at the figures last night. By a whopping margin, this has been our best week ever.'

'And all due to the gift of a Christmas tree.' Propping herself comfortably with her back against her pillow, Ann took a sip of tea. 'How did Terry and the others like the books we chose for them?'

'There was a generational difference. Declan and Angela instantly ripped off the gift-wrap, and loved them. Terry's a traditionalist. He kept his to unwrap under his own tree this morning. I don't know about Fury and The Divil. I'd left his in the cab of his van before he disappeared.'

'And Stephen?'

'Stop sounding arch. I hung on to Stephen's. I thought we could give it to him over Christmas lunch.' There was a pause in which Catherine decided she had something more to say. 'Thanks for inviting him, Mum.'

Ann laughed. 'You were the one who pointed out I'd prepared enough food for a regiment.'

'No, seriously. Thank you. And, look, I know I don't say that enough. You've always been there to make things happen for me.'

'Of course I have. I'm your mother.'

'It can't have been easy bringing me up on your own.'

'Ah, now, don't be dramatic. I had your granny to cover my back, remember?'

'I know. Still, thank you.'

'You're welcome.'

They drank tea in companionable silence until Catherine looked at the snowflakes whirling past the window and said, 'I made a terrible mess of things with Stephen till I got sense.'

'I did wonder. And I wondered if I ought to offer to help.'

'I doubt if I'd have responded well if you had.'

'I know. That's why I didn't. But maybe I should have.' Ann put down her teacup. 'You're right, love. It wasn't easy being a single mum. And we didn't talk much at home, did we? There were never enough hours in the day. Either I was working or you were reading, and your granny was always quoting that proverb "Least said, soonest mended", so I suppose I took my steer from her.'

She looked so troubled that Catherine reached for her hand. 'Mum, it was a perfectly sensible view to take, and I had a perfectly happy childhood.'

'Sometimes I think I should have talked to you about your father.'

'Why?'

'I don't even know if you missed him.'

'How could I? He just wasn't there.'

Ann took Catherine's outstretched hand. 'But you must have wondered about him when you were growing up. I suppose I thought you'd ask if you wanted to know, but that was silly. I ought to have talked to you about him myself.'

'Truly, Mum, I didn't miss him. I was fine.'

'There was no dark secret involved, you know. It was just that he and I weren't suited. We were young, and if I hadn't got pregnant we probably wouldn't have seen each other after our first few dates. And when I did find out I was pregnant, I didn't want him round and your granny said we'd be better off without him. He certainly didn't want to be a teenage father. I think he was glad to be let off the hook.'

'Did you regret it?'

'No. But I do worry about you and your short-term relationships. Sometimes I think you grew up believing that all men move on.'

'That's daft. I've never said so – I've never even thought it.'

'But you've taken care never to stay with a man long enough to find out.'

With a dawning sense of discovery, Catherine said, 'Fair point.'

'It's different with Stephen, isn't it?'

'I think it probably is.'

Ann pushed back her duvet. 'Good. I like him. Besides which, he has some great ideas for the shop.'

Snow continued to fall throughout the morning. In the yard behind the bookshop, it covered the mound of debris, turning it into a ramshackle Mont Blanc. Across the town, it lay inches thick on windowsills and doorsteps, and blurred the distinction between pavements and roads. Down in Broad Street, people hurrying home from churches trod gingerly, eager to get out of the cold but careful not to slip. The sparrows fluttering round the fountain in the nuns' garden were puffed out against the cold, little balls of feathers with eyes and beaks. Someone had filled the statue's hands with crumbs and seeds and, in ones and twos, the birds darted down to snatch them before whirling away towards the trees.

At the window of her flat above the butcher's, Pat stood waiting for Brian, wearing her yellow anorak. She was glad that, when she'd come in yesterday from the carols in the bookshop, she'd put a few sprigs of holly behind the plates above her range. Maybe, she thought, come the new year, she'd call the lads in Canada and suggest she might fly out and spend next Christmas with them over there. But for now, when she'd done her bit to keep Mary and Hanna from killing each other, it was going to be nice to come back to her own home.

In Garrybawn House, Saoirse turned from the window, where she'd been watching snow blanket the garden. Her mum and dad, in dressing-gowns and pyjamas, were laughing and arguing over which film they ought to watch after lunch. Among sheets of discarded tissue paper there was a nightgown sent from Boston by her aunt. It was satin, sleeveless, and perfect for a trip to a London hotel. Happily, Saoirse crunched a stained-glass gingerbread star and, flicking one of the worry dolls she'd hung on the tinsel tree, went to join her mum and dad on the sofa, in her oversized Rudolph T-shirt and Santa socks.

The roof of Fury's shed was an angled white plane against a dark line of conifers, and a fast-disappearing track of paw-prints led from it to the house. Outside in the forest, the snow fell like plucked feathers. Fury was sitting in his living room by a crackling log fire in a tiled fireplace. In front of it lay The Divil with his chin on a graphic novel and, though he seemed deeply asleep, he cocked an eye when Fury spoke.

'Mind you, it was good of them to think of us and, God knows, there'll be plenty of time to read as the world burns.'

The Divil snorted and edged his chin further across his book towards the flames.

'You might think they made a bad choice for you, but that's where you'd be mistaken. There's a rake of dogs in there. You're going to love them.' Turning the pages of his own gift, Fury rolled his eyes. 'Ah, would you look at this? Does nobody ever ask someone who knows stuff before they go writing books? I've been reading the same crap about Druids and mistletoe all my life.' He looked across at The Divil, who had rolled onto his back. 'C'mere to me. Would we swap? I'll have your *Late Night Writers Club* and you have my myths and legends of the forest.' The Divil didn't respond, and taking an empty glass to the table, Fury refilled it from a bottle of whiskey. 'I'm not going to steal your damn book. I'll give it back to you later. I'll even write your name in it, if you like.' Swaying, he held up the glass to the light, and looked from it to The Divil. 'How about it? No? Nothing to say for yourself? Not even happy

Christmas? Well, how about we give up the pretence and sit here and get blind drunk?'

He'd gone back to his chair and was nursing the glass when The Divil pricked his ears and got to his feet. Accustomed to living alone, Fury was instantly alerted and, groping for somewhere to set his glass, half stood up. The Divil, with his back to the fire and all four paws planted, was staring fixedly across the room. There was the sound of a car drawing up, the slamming of doors and the boot, and a scuffle on the doorstep. With a volley of high-pitched barks, The Divil made a rush for Fury, circling him repeatedly and urging him towards the door. Still swaying Fury went and unlocked it. Outside, Adam and Lia were holding a wicker picnic basket, a tablecloth and two bottles of champagne.

CHAPTER THIRTY-FIVE

'Give him a mini black-pudding pie and he'll be fine.' Lia was sitting cross-legged with The Divil's graphic novel while Adam attended to Fury. The Divil had subsided by the fire with his chin on Lia's foot. Hearing the mention of pies, he looked up, but couldn't bring himself to leave her. Adam pushed Fury's head down till it nearly reached his knees. 'He sobered up when you told him the news. This is just shock.'

'Well, he'll perk up when it sinks in, won't you, Fury?'

Fury knocked away Adam's hand and pushed himself unsteadily to his feet. 'Don't patronise me in my own house, girl.'

'That's a nice way of saying thank you.'

Swinging away from her and back again, Fury swore picturesquely. 'You're telling me that your dead granddad over in Australia was the fellow my brother Paudie met in a pub?'

'Well, the two stories seem to fit. One way or the other, it's my nan who owns the forest now.'

'And she's taking it off the market?'

'You can check Carmody's website. The listing's gone.'

Sitting down heavily, Fury said, 'So what happens next?'

'A partnership. You, me, Adam and The Divil. We turn the forest into a hub. Totally protected. Managed by you. We run it as an ecological holiday experience. Food foraging. Cooking. Forestry. Star-gazing weekends. A unique glamping site.' She beamed at Fury. 'You can build yurts.'

'I can build *what*?'

'Round tents. Canvas or skins on a wooden structure. People put hot tubs in them, and hang up drapes. No, listen, Fury, that's no language to use in front of a lady.' She went to help Adam unpack the basket. 'It's a no-brainer. We'll offer activity holidays. We'll link up with the network Bríd and Aideen already work with, plug into Phil's Lissbeg Kitchen at the Convent Centre and Bob's your uncle.'

'Are you out of your mind?'

'No. It's a brilliant idea. Nan's all for it. But it can't work without you and The Divil on board, so what d'you say?'

Fury turned to Adam who shrugged. 'Don't look at me. I'm sold.'

'That's because you're in love.'

'Well, yes, I am. Head over heels. But it is a brilliant idea.'

Lia was looking for plates in a cupboard. 'It's better than that. It's genius. I'll give astronomy talks.'

Adam laughed. 'You'll have to come up with more than bits from the back of *Reader's Digest*.'

'Well, there's a library in Lissbeg, isn't there?'

The Divil put his forepaws on the table and inspected dishes of turkey, ham and sausages in crispy bacon. Glaring at him, Fury said, 'This is a Christmas dinner they've brought. It won't be Christmas every day.' The Divil turned huge, liquid eyes to

Lia who handed him a mini black-pudding pie. Fury threw up his hand in exasperation. 'Ah, for feck's sake! You're in love too. There'll be no sense out of you. Fair enough, I know when I'm bet. Where's this champagne?'

They talked about clearing trails and building benches. How food could be foraged along the shoreline as well as in the forest. Whether Ballyfin's fishermen could help them with their planning. How they might liaise with Martin's halfway house and run an apprentice scheme for homeless people. Adam talked of the day he'd fallen off his borrowed bike and found himself in a ditch with a wild carrot plant. 'All I'd been smelling for a year was dirt and traffic fumes. All I'd eaten was stuff I'd scavenged, and crap from fast-food places. All I'd seen were legs walking past and people not wanting to see me. And then there were miles of mountain road and little stone walls and, suddenly, this plant so close I could see every tiny star-shaped flower in its big, umbelliferous cluster. Each one separate and distinct, but all part of the whole. And a single, inexplicable, purple star in the very centre. No one knows for sure why that occurs, but it's beautiful.'

Feeding ham to The Divil, Lia said, 'There's this thing in Norway they call "Friluftsliv". It means "free-air life". Everybody can get involved – rich, poor, people with disabilities, psychological challenges, it doesn't matter. Seventy-seven per cent of the population spends time in nature on a weekly basis. Twenty-five per cent on most days. Mostly they go to the forests.'

'Let me guess. You read this in the dentist's waiting room.'

'Shut up, Adam. Norway is one of the happiest countries on the planet, and this is why. People walk. They sleep under the stars. They pick cloudberries. There's an actual bread they make by wrapping dough round a stick and cooking it outdoors over a fire. Friluftsliv gets factored into employees' time off. You can even take a degree in it. And the point is that you, me and Fury could make Finfarran Ireland's only Friluftsliv centre.' Lia offered the gravy boat to The Divil. 'But I'm not sure I'm pronouncing it right. We'll have to invent our own word for it.'

Fury said, 'Call it Innarsan.'

'What does it mean?'

'It's an old Irish word. The crowd that made the psalter would have known it. It means "what is sufficient to sustain".'

Over huge plates of dinner, they sketched out budgets, argued, laughed, pulled crackers, and made The Divil model a series of paper hats. Later on, by the fire, over hazelnuts, Stilton and oranges, they discovered it was Fury who'd carved the crib figures in Lissbeg. 'It was just something to do here of an evening. Once I'd finished, I didn't want them hanging round in the shed.'

'They're wonderful. And, wow, Fury, here's a thought. You could give woodcarving courses.'

'I thought I was going to build yurts.'

Breaking a bar of chocolate, Lia held it out and grinned at him. 'Okay, so maybe not everything all at once. We can go with the flow.'

It was past sunset when Catherine stepped out into Sheep Street and turned to lock her scarlet-painted door. At the back of the shop, The Divil's tree's decorations picked up flashes of light from the book tree in the window. Strolling arm in arm, Catherine and Stephen walked down to Broad Street where, in the nuns' garden, rosemary, thyme and bay were still growing green. The end of Catherine's scarf had come loose and Stephen tucked it back under her collar. 'Remember our walk by the riverside in Carrick?'

'When you quoted Samuel Beckett?'

'And you talked about growing things in pots in your backyard.'

Catherine laughed. 'I never get round to that. Maybe I will this summer.'

'I told you that day that gardening's my pastime. But the thing is, Catherine, being alive is a gift, and every minute of time is precious. That's what I tried to say to you in the car on the way back.' Turning up his own collar, Stephen looked at the stars that were glimmering above them. 'When Sophie died and I decided to move here, I had this notion that I could live out our dream. I'd watch her silver birch tree grow, feed the finches that nest in it, and welcome them back each year, like she'd have done. We'd had all sorts of plans for making new friends and putting down roots in our dream home. But it turned out that I couldn't do any of it without her. So, really, ever since I came here, I've just been passing the time. That's not the life we planned, and I know what Sophie would say if she saw me leading it.'

'What would she say?'

'She'd tell me I need to find my own dream.' Stephen tightened his hold on Catherine's arm. 'The other day, before you called me, I thought of leaving. Uprooting myself and going back to Dublin.'

'But now you won't.'

'No, I don't think so.'

'I'm glad.'

Smiling at her, he said, 'Thank you for my Christmas present.'

'You didn't already have it? Gardeners are hard to choose for. They always have masses of gardening books.'

'It's perfect.'

'I don't suppose one about Spanish gardens is likely to be of much practical use. The pictures are lovely, though, and it's only just out, so I thought I'd chance it.'

'The truth is I'm not really a very practical gardener. I just dream of a book and a deckchair in summer, with bees buzzing, a glass of wine, and a friend dropping by.' They had stopped in the halo of a streetlight, their breath showing white in the frosty air. Releasing Catherine's arm, Stephen took both her hands in his. 'You know, if you do buy those pots, you won't have a clue what to put in them.'

'You could give me advice if I dropped by to see you. We could discuss books and gardens over a glass of wine. We might even plan a trip to visit Spanish gardens together.'

'Would you like to?'

'Yes, I would. You know I would. And, Stephen, let's start now. Let's not wait for summer. Let's not wait for anything. Dreams are for living. They shouldn't be postponed.'

FURY

The fire had burned low and the room was in shadow. The latchkey, carefully pushed through the letterbox, lay on the doormat where it had fallen after the door was locked. Fury woke in his chair and heard an indignant yelp from The Divil. Stiffly, he got to his feet. 'That's enough out of you. You're the one who slept right through the pudding.' He looked around the room, which was in perfect order. No scattered bones or paper hats. No dishes in the sink. Nothing on the table but a clean dish upended to cover a plate. Lifting it, Fury found cold ham with potato salad and a sliced hard-boiled egg. Then, following The Divil's pointing nose, he opened a cupboard and discovered an orange alongside a bar of 75 per cent organic, Fairtrade chocolate.

Everything about the plate of food, even the way the egg had been sliced, and the blob of bottled salad dressing, reminded him of Christmases in his childhood. Having stacked and washed the dinner dishes, he, his father and brother had always gone for a long walk in the forest, and come home to kick off their boots on the doorstep and sit down to tea by the fire. His mother had had plates of salad waiting under upturned dishes, and a pottery bowl of oranges had stood on the kitchen table beside a box of Black Magic chocolates.

Now, returning to his fireside, he saw the log basket had been replenished, a lamp was switched on, and the hearth had been neatly swept. 'I'll say this for them, they know how to leave a place decent. Chef salad cream out of a bottle there on the plate and all. I didn't know you could still get it. And a ham bone for you wrapped in a bit of newspaper.' He looked sharply at The Divil. 'Don't try to tell me all this is down to her nibs, because I know better. The lad's handy too. I spotted that when he got stuck into the set-up for his book launch.'

The snow had stopped falling. The sun had set. The darkening sky was steel-grey through a lattice outlined in silver, and each trunk and branch in the forest looked black. Striding and trotting, they passed through frosted beech mast that crunched loudly under foot and paw. As the light faded, their senses heightened. Birds were silent but the presence of folded wings was everywhere. The Divil's nose twitched at small creatures rustling in the bracken, and Fury stopped occasionally to curve his hand around growth, feeling the bark and sensing the pith within. They followed badger paths, more easily found by feet than eyes, thousand-year ways along which wolves had padded before them, and brown bears, wildcats, wild horses, and giant deer with antlers twice as wide as Fury was tall. And the earth, which was older than any of them, yielded gently underfoot and reasserted itself when they passed.

All around, symbiotic relationships flourished. At one point, they heard the sound of water, where a branch had fallen across a stream that was hardly more than a trickle. In his mind's eye, Fury could see a network of filaments formed by fungi, connecting the roots of his trees in a constant exchange of minerals and water. Hunkering down, he observed the fallen branch. Ice had crystallised on moss on its upper surfaces, which were exposed to the freezing air. Below, where the running water had raised the surrounding temperature, moisture dripped from melting crystals into the moving stream. Fury found the drops by touch, as he'd found the stream by listening, and had known the dead wood by its rich smell of decomposition. Dipping his hand into the stream, he held it out to The Divil. 'That's life. It's star-given. We're all made of stardust hurled into space by exploding super-novas. Everything, and every one of us, made of the same stardust. The crowd with the power to make things happen know that. They just refuse to understand what it means.' The Divil flicked his warm tongue over Fury's cold hand, tasted the water and sneezed.

Pulling himself upright with the help of a branch above him, Fury remembered the dancing painted animals in the psalter. Cats dressed as fine ladies with long, streaming veils. Hares wearing hoods and jerkins. A bear dancing arm in arm with a fox who carried a tray of pies, and a hound in a feathered cap playing a trumpet. Birds' beaks, glittering eyes peering between twigs, and flowers outlined with dots of gold leaf combining the four seasons. Marsh marigolds jostling with mistletoe and irises with rose hips, while the dancers wove their way through the living foliage he'd strung across his paint-spattered dust sheets.

With his feet planted on the earth, he raised his head to the night sky where, beyond interlaced branches, stars glittered with cold purpose. 'Did I ever tell you the brightest of them up there is called the Dog Star? Stars are supposed to sing, you know. Like angels. People can't hear them but that's not surprising. People have always been thick as two short planks.' The Divil sneezed again and pointed his nose homeward. Fury's eyes were on the stars. 'What you and me have to do now is just keep ourselves going. A few days ago we thought we were banjaxed, and now look at the pair of us. Ham salad under a dish, and God-knows-what ahead.' Standing foursquare, The Divil was still pointing towards the house, his ears cocked and his rump quivering. Looking down at him, Fury rolled his eyes. 'It's that feckin' ham bone, isn't it? You've not heard a word I've been saying.' With a volley of shrill barks, the little dog circled him twice, stopped, sat on his tail and looked up with his tongue lolling. Fury grinned. 'Credit where credit's due, is it? Fair enough, I won't argue. All this would've been lost if you hadn't made me cut that tree we gave to Catherine. So, we'll go home and you can have your ham bone while I put my feet up by the fire with your book.'

ACKNOWLEDGEMENTS

In the crablike way that creativity seems to work, the inspiration for this book came from signing tours for my standalone novel *The Keepsake Quilters*. It was a wet November, and my husband Wilf and I took to the road to visit eighty bookshops across eighteen Irish counties, crisscrossing the country north, south, east and west. Each of our three week-long tours was immensely energising, and along the way I met so many friendly, dynamic, entrepreneurial, dedicated booksellers that distances and bad weather became irrelevant. And, somewhere between Wexford and Cork, I realised that, although the Finfarran stories centre on a local library, I hadn't created a bookshop for Lissbeg. From there it was a short step to imagining Catherine and Ann, their backgrounds and relationship with each other and the town.

Then, months after our road trips were over – in the kind of happenstance that authors recognise as gold dust – the real world produced a turning-point for the plot of *The Bookseller's Gift*. In Derry, Wilf and I had met Jenni Doherty, owner of an independent bookshop called Little Acorns Bookstore. Jenni is typical of all the booksellers we'd encountered, an enthusiastic reader, a tireless worker, and someone whose shop is a place where people of all ages make friends as well as finding, talking about and buying books. Though we'd never met before, she welcomed us with hugs and smiles, a table stacked high with copies of my book for signing, and a tour of the towering shelves in her lovely shop. Before I left, she videoed me talking about *The Keepsake Quilters* and posted it to social media. After that, we shared each other's social-media posts, a cheerful exchange that continued until one day, to my horror, I saw her sending out frantic online messages about water gushing through her shop's ceiling onto the books below. Her real-life neighbours rushed to help and online friends like me looked on anxiously as a concerted community effort to move the books minimised the damage and, while the shop closed briefly to deal with the aftermath, readers and booksellers all across Ireland piled in with good wishes and shared links to Jenni's website for online sales. That real-life disaster was less dramatic than the plotline I wrote for Catherine in *The Bookseller's Gift*, but my inspiration for it came from Jenni, her neighbours in Derry, and the warmth and solidarity of all the booksellers I'd met.

As well as being crablike, creativity can be circular. I was the youngest of five so most of the books I read as a child were passed down from siblings but, at Christmas, my godfather and his wife always sent me extravagant pop-up books, which I treasured. Those books, and the excitement and anticipation of opening them, have found their way into *The Bookseller's Gift* nearly sixty years later, as have the toy-theatre Christmas cards I remember from my childhood.

Another book I read as a child was *The Swish of the Curtain*, bought second-hand by my father in the Dublin Bookshop on Batchelor's Walk. It was the first in a 1940s–50s series by the

English actress and writer Pamela Brown, about a group of kids who do plays in a derelict hall, go to a London drama school and end up as a professional theatre company in their home town. It sparked my love of the stage, led me to study at a London drama school, and was one of the books I dramatised for BBC radio. The title of *The Swish of the Curtain* comes from a turning-point in its plot when, with rings stitched diagonally across them, makeshift theatre curtains rise with a luxurious swish. So, in a Christmas novel that's partly a tribute to pantomime, it seemed right for Fury to adopt the same method for what Mary calls his big coup de théâtre.

What else? I'm grateful to the Irish cartoonist and author Annie West for Catherine and Ann's gift to The Divil, and all the love of books, dogs and libraries in her graphic novel *The Late Night Writers Club*. My thanks to Bookselling Ireland, the Irish booksellers' association, which is run, in addition to their day jobs, by booksellers whose support for authors is immense. Also to the Library Association of Ireland which supports library workers, high standards of librarianship and of library and information services, and secures co-operation between these safe, inclusive spaces that enrich and serve local communities. Particular thanks also go to the DLR Libraries librarian whose tweet about lost worry dolls led me to create Saoirse's storyline.

Every avid reader knows how random images from books can lodge unexpectedly in the unconscious. Some of these sink so deep that it's hard to recall where they were first encountered, and for writers their presence can form part of the creative process. I have many which can emerge unbidden in my writing, and sometimes I don't realise till a novel's completed that a strand or a moment was prompted by another author's work. As a teenager, I read Mary Renault's historical novels including

The King Must Die, her recreation of the Greek myth of Theseus of Athens, taken with a group of teenage companions to serve as bull-dancers in Crete. In the chapter that covers their sea voyage to Knossos, she evokes their displacement and loss with a single sentence marking the day on which they ate the last of their food brought from home. While editing *The Bookseller's Gift*, I realised her powerful image must have prompted Adam's father's homesick memory of eating ruz sayadeya caught from a boat with a brown canvas sail and cooked on a golden beach.

In creating the recipes for Adam's course, I reached back to comfort food made in my mother's kitchen, for Christmases, birthdays, or as treats to heal all ills. I still make her cakes, and use the tablespoon with which she measured flour for soda bread, and pleasure comes from those associations as well as from the enjoyment of baking and eating. Many of her recipes were handed down from her own mother and beyond, so this book owes a debt to generations of home bakers in my family as well as to Mary Renault and all the authors whose works have been the foundations of my own.

Finally, as it takes more than an author to bring a book to its readers, I owe huge gratitude to my editor Ciara Doorley, copy editor Hazel Orme, to Joanna Smyth, Stephen Riordan, Ruth Shern, Elaine Egan, and everyone else on Breda Purdue's team at Hachette Books Ireland, and to Mark Walsh at Plunkett PR.

And thanks to Wilf, to my neighbours in London and Corca Dhuibhne for friendship, support, cups of tea and biscuits, and, as ever, to my stellar agent Gaia Banks and her colleagues at Sheil Land Associates, UK.